"THERE ARE SO MANY WAYS I WANT TO LOVE YOU, SWEETHEART, SO MUCH I WANT TO TEACH YOU," JOHNNY SAID.

"You can teach me nothing!" she snapped. "You're forgetting I am an engaged woman and Malcolm—"

"He'll never make love to you the way I will. Never."

"That's revolting. You're revolting. Dare you—"

"Don't dare me, darlin'. You do and I won't wait. I'll take you right here, right now." His hands slid up to enclose her raised face. "And that's not the way I want it to be."

She tried to pull free but he wouldn't let her. He framed her face securely in his brown hands and wouldn't allow her to look away. He made her look straight into his hot dark eyes. "I don't want to take it from you, sweetheart. I want you to give it to me."

"Never!"

"Soon," he murmured, kissed her, and was gone.

"Nan Ryan is hot! She's an extraordinary storyteller at the top of her form in Silken Bondage, *her sexy, humorous, most stirring tale yet."*

—Romantic Times

Silken Bondage

Nan Ryan

A Dell Book

Published by
Dell Publishing
a division of
Bantam Doubleday Dell Publishing Group, Inc.
666 Fifth Avenue
New York, New York 10103

ISBN: 0-440-20464-X

Printed in the United States of America

Published simultaneously in Canada

November 1989

10 9 8 7 6 5 4 3 2 1

KRI

To
all my readers

Part One

1

"Johnny Roulette's back in town!"

"Johnny's here in Memphis? Lilly, are you sure?" asked the excited Julia LaBlanc, clutching the lapels of her blue dressing gown together over her ample bosom.

"Do you suppose he'll come to see the show tonight?" said red-haired, brown-eyed Belle Roberts, a heated curling iron poised in her right hand, a gleaming lock of copper hair in the other.

"My lord, you know he will! If Johnny's in town, he'll be aboard the *Moonlight Gambler* as soon as the sun sets," Betsy Clark Stevens assured with a smile as she reached for a pot of coral lip rouge, then she added, "Julia, can I please borrow your green satin gown . . . the one that matches my eyes? You know you can't get into it since you gained those five pounds."

"Damn you, Betsy," Julia snapped. "You and Lilly monopolized Johnny last time he was aboard the *Gambler*. It's my turn!"

"And mine." Belle's hands went to her hips and her usually soft voice lifted loudly.

"Who is Johnny Roulette?"

For a second there was near total silence in the cluttered below-decks dressing quarters of the floating gaming palace, *Moonlight Gambler*. Only the gentle slap of calm waters against the *Gambler*'s gleaming black hull and the shouts of men loading cargo on the many vessels lining the bustling Memphis levee could be heard.

The four seasoned showgirls—Lilly St. Clair, Julia LaBlanc, Belle Roberts, and Betsy Clark Stevens—stared in disbelief, then exclaimed in unison, "Who is Johnny Roulette!"

Nevada Marie Hamilton swallowed nervously and looked up at the women crowding around her, shaking their heads piteously as though she had just confessed she didn't know who was President of the United States of America. "Should I know this Johnny Roulette?"

The women went into peals of laughter at such a question. Platinum-haired Lilly St. Clair, the tallest and oldest of the group, finally wiped the tears from her eyes, stuck a satin-slippered toe around the leg of a straight-back chair, drew it up beside Nevada, and sat down. "Honey, you've got to be joking."

Not particularly pleased with being an object of ridicule among these women whom she had met only hours earlier, Nevada proudly lifted her chin, turned from the mirror, and met Lilly's eyes squarely. "No, Miss St. Clair. I am not joking. I have no idea who Johnny Roulette is. Is there some reason I should?"

Lilly, crossing her long legs and signaling the others to stop laughing, reached for Nevada's hand. Holding it in her own, Lilly said, "Don't mind us none, Nevada. You just came aboard the *Gambler* today; no reason you'd know Johnny. You're just a kid and you've spent all your life on your daddy's flatboat. Forgive our manners. We've all known Johnny so long, we forget there could be anybody up and down the Mississippi who hasn't met him." She smiled kindly at Nevada.

"Well, what's so special about Johnny Roulette?" Nevada asked.

Lilly squeezed Nevada's small hand, released it, and leaned back in her chair. A wistful expression came into her violet eyes and she repeated Nevada's words. "What's so special about Johnny Roulette?" Lilly sighed. "Honey, just wait until you meet him."

And Nevada listened, as did the others, while the sophisticated Lilly St. Clair spoke of the elusive man they all adored, the half French, devil-may-care, darkly handsome gambler, Johnny Roulette.

"There's a cloud of mystery that surrounds Johnny Roulette," said Lilly. "Nobody seems to know exactly where he's from or if he has any family or if he ever had a profession, other than gambling. Johnny never talks about himself or his past. And anybody that's ever asked got no answer other than a shrug of his shoulders and a shake of his head." She smiled then and added, "But nobody really cares, least not here on the Mississippi. He's so damned good-looking, he hurts your eyes. Johnny's one of the biggest men I've ever met—stands well over six foot three—and not one ounce of fat on him. His hair is dark and wavy, his eyes are black as midnight, and he has a smile that can melt the coldest of hearts."

Nodding, Nevada listened with interest as Lilly continued to describe the imposing gentleman she obviously thought was a man among men. The others joined in, speaking dreamily of Johnny Roulette's muscular physique and his sleek mustache and his quick wit and his deft gambler's hands. They told how it felt to be chosen, after the show, to stand at Johnny's side while he gambled—to blow on the dice, to bring him luck, to be the envy, however briefly, of every other female on board. Johnny was more fun than anybody, they said; he made them laugh and he himself always wore an irresistible smile.

The white silk robe Lilly had loaned her falling off her slender shoulders and her long raven hair spilling down her back, Nevada Marie Hamilton listened attentively, her blue eyes wide with interest, her soft red lips pursed. Still, she was skeptical.

Surely no man could be quite so handsome and charming as this tall, dark, always smiling Johnny Roulette.

Johnny Roulette had a toothache. A mean, nasty toothache. Scowling, Johnny followed a uniformed steward into a huge, richly carpeted suite of the elegant Plantation House, the finest hotel in Memphis, Tennessee. Clutching his throbbing right jaw with a big hand, Johnny jerked at his tight, choking tie while the steward rushed forth to throw the tall French doors open to the balcony.

Turning then, the slender little man said, "Our most luxurious suite, as always, Mr. Roulette. You'll get the nice breeze off the river and I'll bring up ice water immediately. Will there be anything else, sir?"

"Yes," said the suffering Johnny Roulette. "Whiskey."

"Whiskey, Mr. Roulette?" The steward's pale eyebrows lifted. He'd never known Johnny Roulette to drink hard liquor, not in all the years he'd been staying at the Plantation House. Nor anything stronger than an occasional after-dinner brandy. Thinking he had surely misunderstood, he repeated questioningly, "Whiskey?"

"The best Kentucky bourbon you've got," Johnny Roulette answered, shrugging impatiently out of his custom gray linen suit jacket. He smiled weakly then and added, "I do so enjoy a glass of good bourbon in the afternoon."

"Y-yes, sir, right away," murmured the dumbfounded steward, bowing and backing away.

In minutes the little man returned with a tray bearing a large silver pitcher of ice water, a tall cut-crystal tumbler, a heavy lead shot glass, and a bottle of fine Kentucky bourbon.

Johnny, barechested now, nodded his thanks and immediately uncorked the whiskey. Ignoring the glasses, he turned the bottle up to his lips and took a long pull.

"God Almighty, that tastes awful," he said, making a face and gratefully accepting the glass of ice water the steward hastily poured and handed to him. "Thanks," he managed, still feeling the fire from the bourbon burn its way down into his chest and race into his long muscular arms.

"Mr. Roulette, I do not mean to intrude, but my employer and your good friend Mr. Robin mentioned while I was downstairs that you are suffering from a toothache. I happen to know a skilled dentist whose office is not two blocks from the Plantation House. He would be—"

"No dentists," said Johnny, shaking his dark head decisively. "Ben Robin should mind his own affairs. Tell him I said so. I don't need a dentist."

"But if you've a toothache, I'm sure—"

"Just a slight one," said Johnny. "Nothing that bothers me that much. All I need is a little nap." He grinned then to show he was really feeling fit.

"Very well," said the mannerly steward, smiling back at the big towering man. "I've turned down your bed. You'll be wanting your evening clothes pressed, I assume." Johnny nodded. "Mr. Robin says the dice have been rolling hot on the *Gambler,* of late." The steward reached the door. "Get some rest, sir."

"That I'll do," promised Johnny Roulette, smiling easily but frowning again as soon as the door closed.

"Owwww!" Johnny groaned as he headed for the whiskey bottle. And Johnny Roulette—a big strapping man who had looked down the barrel of a gun on more than one occasion and who had fought in the War between the States when he was still in his teens—hoped no one would suspect that he was so deathly afraid of the dentist, he couldn't have been dragged there by a team of wild horses.

And so it was that Johnny Roulette, in agony, terrified of dentists, sat alone in his river-view hotel suite on that humid June afternoon in the summer of 1876 and got pleasantly and profoundly drunk.

Soon he was so delightfully tipsy that his throbbing tooth stopped throbbing, his aching jaw stopped aching, and his pain-dimmed black eyes began to sparkle with their usual devilish light. By the time the sun was westering across the placid river, Johnny Roulette, grinning between pulls on a long thin cigar, thought to himself that he had been such a fool. All these years he had eschewed the delicious taste of good Kentucky bourbon. What a mistake!

He held a half-full tumbler of the whiskey up before his face and admired its pale amber hue, deeply inhaling its unique bouquet. Crushing out his cigar, he took a drink of the smooth, warm bourbon and, sighing with contentment, decided he would skip dinner.

At dusk Johnny Roulette, loudly singing a bawdy song he'd learned years before from a bearded riverboat pilot, splashed about in his bath, cigar in one hand, bourbon in the other, while in the outer room the hotel steward laid out a suit of freshly pressed black evening clothes along with a starched white shirt, gleaming gold studs, and polished black leather shoes.

Shortly after nine o'clock that evening, an impeccably groomed Johnny Roulette, smiling broadly, weaving slightly, descended the wide marble staircase into the opulent lobby of the Plantation House. When his old friend Ben Robin, the hotel's rich young owner, who was engaged in conversation with a pair of downriver planters, looked up and saw Johnny, he knew immediately that he was drunk. Excusing himself from the guests, Ben Robin crossed the spacious lobby.

"John," Ben said, placing a companionable hand on Johnny's left shoulder, "how about the two of us having dinner in my suite this evening? The dining room is very crowded tonight."

Wearing a foolish grin, Johnny blinked down at his friend. "Thanks for the invitation, Ben, but I'm not hungry. I'll allow you to buy me a drink though."

"Johnny, you don't drink."

Johnny frowned. "I don't?"

"No. Never."

"In that case, I'll be on my way."

"Where to? It might be best if—"

Smiling once more, Johnny Roulette interrupted. "Think I'll stroll on down to the levee and check the action on the *Moonlight Gambler.*"

2

A stranger looked back at Nevada from the mirror. She didn't know herself, couldn't believe that the pretty young woman with heavily lashed blue eyes and ruby-red lips and shimmering black curls could actually be her. She stared with frank admiration and astonishment at the unfamiliar reflection, her cheeks hot with excitement.

The gown she wore, a vivid blue satin with a tight bodice and low, revealing neckline and flounced skirts, was the most exquisite garment she'd ever laid eyes on. Exactly the kind of dress she'd dreamed of wearing all those nights when she'd stood in the pale moonlight aboard her papa's keelboat and sung her heart out while the crew clapped and whistled and shouted their approval.

Old Willie and Luke and Big Edgar. Slim and Teddy and "Black Jack" Jones. They'd all applauded and encouraged and assured her that she truly "sang like a nightingale." And of them all, her papa had been her most loyal admirer, the one who spun golden dreams of the future triumphs that awaited her.

Nevada Marie Hamilton never knew the small raven-haired woman who was her mother, nor the wild untamed land for which she had been named. Newton Hamilton, a restless young Southerner who in the autumn of 1857 drifted to the silver mines of the West, had stayed less than a year in Virginia City, Nevada.

A big sandy-haired man with a bass voice and twinkling green eyes, Hamilton had fallen in love with Beth Davis the first time he saw her. She was attempting to cross a busy street in boisterous Virginia City. She'd looked so young and fragile and helpless as she carefully picked her way along a wooden plank that bridged a loblolly of deep gummy mud.

Enchanted, Newt Hamilton hurried to her, reaching the small startled beauty in three long strides. Ignoring her cries of indignation, he plucked her up into his strong arms and carried her across the muddy street. By the time they reached the other side he was in love. In less than a month so was Beth.

They married in the judge's chambers and spent their one-night honeymoon in a second-floor room of the Silverado Hotel, right in the heart of loud, rollicking Virginia City. Beth Hamilton, the happiest of brides, never noticed the sounds of rinky-dink piano or the clatter of dice or the shouts and laughter coming from downstairs. Swept away by newfound passion, she gloried in the ecstasy of that long snowy November night spent in a soft featherbed with her amorous new husband.

And exactly nine months later, on a hot August evening when the thin mountain air was oppressive and not a hint of a breeze stirred the lace curtains in the stuffy little bedroom of her home, Beth went into painful labor that was to last throughout the night. Finally when the first streak of gray lightened the summer sky behind the towering Sierras, Beth, totally exhausted, her blue eyes dull and sunken, gave birth to a perfect baby girl with silky raven hair and a cute button nose and curved rosebud lips.

"You'll have to name her, Newt," whispered Beth, "I'm

just too tired." Those were her last words. She died before the sun came up.

A month later a brokenhearted Newt Hamilton closed the door to the cabin where he'd lived with and loved his Beth, leaving everything just as it was. He took only the squalling tiny infant he called Nevada; and together they left forever the state for which she was named.

Nevada's earliest memories were of the constant easy roll and pitch of the creaking old keelboat beneath her feet as she glided endlessly up and down the swirling waters of the Mississippi. And of the big, smiling, sandy-haired man who, more times than not, smelled of whiskey when he kissed her good night.

Nevada loved both with all her heart.

The treacherous, eddying, muddy Mississippi. And the big, heavily muscled, indulgent man who guided them safely down it. Save for those four awful years when Newt had left her, crying and screaming, in a fancy girls' boarding school in New Orleans while he went off to fight in the war, she had not been away from her papa. Or from the Mississippi.

Except for those lonely years when she'd been taught by stern-faced teachers to read and write and do her sums, her home had been the keelboat her father owned and operated. The necessary comforts were contained in their quarters—a boxlike dwelling with two small bedrooms, dining room, pantry, and a big room in front for the crew with a fireplace where old Willie did the cooking.

The top of the boat was flat and had seats and an awning under which she could sit protected from the fierce sun glinting off the river. From there she could watch her papa skillfully pilot the boat from one port to another, transporting tons of commodities. Bacon, flour, corn, lard, oats, butter. Barrels of cider and whiskey. Hemp and yarn and lumber and shoe leather. Apples and dried fruit and beans and tobacco. And sometimes even horses—spirited, beautiful Thoroughbreds sent from upriver to the racetracks of the South.

It was a life any adventurous little girl would have loved. Nevada was sure the children she waved to on the crowded levees envied her the lazy days of floating downstream with the current, trailing her bare toes in the muddy water, making elaborate plans for the future.

What she most wanted, she decided when she was ten years old, was to be a singer on one of the grand showboats plying the waters of the Mississippi. An entertainer like the beautiful ladies her papa told her about while she listened, awestruck.

"The fine ladies," Newt Hamilton said, the slight slurring of his words unnoticed by his rapt audience of one, "are very glamorous and talented, Nevada. And the gentlemen who court them are cultured and handsome. Rich planters and steamboat captains and moneyed scions of old southern families."

"Papa," said Nevada, her big blue eyes sparkling with anticipation, "when I grow up I want to be a singer on one of the big floating palaces. I want to meet one of those handsome gentlemen who'll fall madly in love with me!"

Newt Hamilton, the storyteller who most times was anxious to finish the story so he could go ashore and drink whiskey and visit the "fine ladies" he spoke of, always said "And you will, child. Nobody has a sweeter voice than you. Now say your prayers and go to bed. I won't be gone long. Old Willie and the boys will look after you until I get back." And he'd kiss his only child and Nevada would deeply inhale the unique scent that was her papa's—sun-warmed skin and strong soap and whiskey. Always whiskey.

Sure that, as she grew up, his daughter's foolish yearnings for a singing career on the river would be replaced with more worthy ambitions, the big man who needed lots of whiskey and lots of women never discouraged Nevada's harmless daydreaming.

As the years passed and she grew into a stunningly pretty young woman, the crew, like family to Newt and Nevada, warned the permissive Hamilton that it was high time he pointed the rapidly blossoming girl in another, more respectable direction. He would, he assured them, when the time came. But went right on as before, never discouraging her, instead telling her that she would have to wait until she turned twenty-one.

There was, he reasoned, plenty of time to worry about that far-distant day. But time itself was running out for Newt Hamilton and, with a strange kind of women's intuition, his young daughter sensed it. Her father's fading green eyes did not sparkle as they once had, not even when he was drinking whiskey. Slowly the big lovable man was disintegrating, wearing out, winding down. The old confidence was fading, his zest for life waning, the ever-present gaiety disappearing.

So Nevada was heartbroken but not shocked when her father, ever more combative and out of sorts, got into a fight one night in an Ashport, Tennessee, bordello. Newt Hamilton never saw the knife or even felt the pain as the gleaming blade, wielded by a big, ugly Arkansas farm boy, slashed open his stomach. He was too drunk to know he was dying.

Grief-stricken, Nevada decided to sell the keelboat to the crew and was shocked and horrified to learn that her father had long ago sold it to them, retaining for himself only a ten-percent interest. She sold them the remaining ten percent and said it was time she pursued her dream of becoming a singer on a big showboat. And she wondered why, to a man, they all shook their heads and did their best to dissuade her. Strong-willed, she refused to listen. She was, after all, eighteen years old. A full-grown woman. She would wait no longer!

Nevada put on her best Sunday dress, a frilly pink-and-white gingham with lace-trimmed sleeves and bodice, brushed her long ebony hair, packed her cardboard valise, wrapped her money in one of her father's linen handkerchiefs, put the handkerchief inside her bodice next to her heart, and marched out on deck.

All the crew hugged her and when old Willie embraced her she saw tears glistening in the sad devoted eyes. Swallowing back the lump in her own throat, she patted his bony shoulder and said, "Stop your frettin', Willie. By tonight I'll be entertaining on one of those fancy showboats."

"Dat's what I is afraid of," said the aging black man.

Undaunted, Nevada stepped onto the busy Memphis levee, turned about, and looked down at the six frowning men. Luke and Big Edgar and Slim. Teddy and "Black Jack" Jones and old Willie.

Bravely she smiled and said, "When you're back in Memphis, I'll come down to visit you."

Then, afraid she would cry just like old Willie, Nevada hurried away. The June sun was hot on her bare head and the suitcase was heavy, but she didn't have far to go. She'd known all along where she was heading. She'd seen the dazzling lights of the glittering floating palace, *Moonlight Gambler,* from the window of her keelboat bedroom.

She stood before the imposing steamer, looking with hopeful eyes up at the glass-enclosed pilothouse and the high texas deck and the gingerbread-fringed hurricane deck. The huge white sternwheeler looked sleepy and deserted in the middle of the quiet afternoon, but Nevada knew that come dusk the big pleasure palace would come alive with gambling and gaiety.

Hurrying anxiously up the long companionway, Nevada had her way barred by a huge barrel-chested man who stood, arms crossed, at the top of the gangway.

Miss," he said in a deep, authoritative voice, "the *Gambler* is not open to customers or guests at the moment."

"And I am not a guest, sir," she informed him. "I am a singer. I wish to speak at once with the person in charge of entertainment."

The muscular giant grinned and his big arms came unfolded. "That would be Pops McCullough. Is he expecting you?"

Nevada fibbed. "Yes, he is. This sun is fierce. If you'll kindly show me to Mr. McCullough's cabin . . ."

Like many gigantic men, the burly *Moonlight Gambler*'s fearless bouncer was easily bullied by women. Especially pretty young women.

"Right this way, miss," said the giant, his voice now friendly; and taking Nevada's suitcase, he escorted her to a closed door below decks. With calloused knuckles he rapped and announced to the man inside, "Pops, you have a visitor."

Pops McCullough looked exactly like a real live Santa. His hair, mustache, and full wavy beard were snowy white. His cheeks were ruddy, his eyes a light blue. Pops was dozing in his chair, hands folded atop a fat belly, his pink lips open just enough to make a high whistling sound as he snored.

Pops awoke with a start and his blue eyes opened wide when he saw, standing directly before his mahogany desk in the dim cabin, a tiny dark-haired girl who was so pretty and sweet-looking, he was sure she'd stepped out of his dreams. When he heard what she'd come for, Pops McCullough told her she was in the wrong place.

"Child," said Pops, "you look like an angel. You ought to try a convent." He closed his eyes and added, "Pull the door shut when you leave."

Nevada said, "I am not leaving."

He opened his eyes. "Yes, you are. This is a gambling boat, missy. The women who work for me are singers and dancers and . . . and"—he cleared his throat—"they . . . ah, entertain and charm men, if you know what I'm saying."

"Of course I know what you're saying," Nevada replied evenly, having no idea that she wasn't comprehending what he was trying to tell her. That the ladies who entertained on the stage of the *Moonlight Gambler* were sometimes called upon to entertain in one of its silk-walled bedrooms as well.

"You do?" Pops's white eyebrows shot up.

"Yes. Just give me a chance. You'll see, I can sing like a nightingale and dance like a dream and I've spent my entire life charming men." Nevada then favored the skeptical white-haired man with a dazzling smile.

Pops sighed and shook his head. "Very well. I was planning to hire another girl here in Memphis." He rose. "Come on, I'll introduce you to Leroy, the piano player, and then to the other girls. Tell Lilly I said for her to fix you up with a costume and to do something about that hair."

"Oh, thank you, Mr. McCullough. You won't regret it, I promise." Nevada couldn't hide her excitement.

"Pops. Call me Pops. And I just hope you won't."

"Won't what?"

"Regret it."

3

⟡⟡⟡⟡⟡⟡

For a man who was losing at cards, Johnny Roulette was in exceptionally high spirits. Johnny grinned confidently at the four gentlemen around the green baize poker table, took one more quick look at his cards, and said, "See your hundred and raise you two."

He continued to grin as he stacked up four blue chips, then four more, and pushed them to the center of the table. All eyes were on him. Johnny leaned back in his chair, reached for the glass of whiskey at his elbow, tilted it up and drank.

"I'm out," said the graying thin-faced banker next to Johnny.

"By me too," the off-duty riverboat captain echoed, and threw in his cards.

"Same here," said a disgruntled merchant.

"Call," said the slim Virginian who had begun this round of betting. He laid down his cards faceup. "It's full, Roulette. Queens over fives. What have you got?"

Johnny looked down at the full house staring him in the face. His wide grin remained well in place when he showed his own cards and said, "Not enough." He laid down a hand on which he should never have bet, much less raised on. "A pair of jacks and deuces."

It had been that way for the past hour. The distinguished Virginian had buttonholed Johnny the minute he stepped aboard the *Gambler* and directed him straight to one of the small salons off the main gaming hall where the others were waiting. Johnny, in a magnanimous mood, had put up no resistance.

"I warn you," he said, his words slurring slightly, "this is going to be my night." He ordered straight whiskey and took his place at the table.

And promptly started losing.

Johnny's luck at cards and dice had been consistently bad for more than six months. It had been so long since he had won at anything, he had almost forgotten what it felt like. The thick roll of bills he always carried was much thinner than usual, and the accounts in various banks up and down the river were getting dangerously low as he withdrew great sums of cash to cover his gambling debts.

Still, he was smiling as he sat losing and never noticed that the gentlemen at the table were staring at him and shaking their heads and wondering what had gotten into the big dark-haired man who was usually such a cool, unreadable card player.

Anteing up, Johnny remarked, "Lilly's onstage. I'd know that whiskey voice anywhere," and fanning his cards out before his face, he hummed along in a deep baritone, blithely ignoring the looks of annoyance he drew from his dead-serious companions.

"Now, you're going to be fine," Belle Roberts said to a very nervous Nevada Marie Hamilton.

The pair stood in the wings just offstage, watching Lilly wind up her rousing rendition of "When Johnny Comes Marching Home Again." The tall blond Lilly, attired in virginal white, had lifted one edge of the gossamer gown and was marching across the stage, her right hand raised in a salute to Old Glory as a dozen flags unfurled from the ceiling. Exposing glimpses of her long stockinged legs and flashing a naughty smile, Lilly was bringing down the house.

Watching the popular performer, Nevada wondered how she could possibly follow such an impressive act.

"Belle, after seeing Lilly, those gentlemen will boo me off the stage," she said, her heart pounding with fear.

"Not bloody likely," said Belle, laughing at Nevada's foolish doubts. "Honey, they are going to think you're an angel come down out of heaven." She affectionately tucked one of the small blue satin bows back in place amid Nevada's upswept raven curls, and added, "You'll see. Trust old Belle. I know most of these boys."

Too frightened to speak, Nevada clung to the hand Belle offered and did her best to draw long reviving breaths while she peeked out at the cavernous hall beyond the foot-lit stage.

It was a long, rectangular room filled with tables crowded with gamblers, tables for all kinds of games Nevada had never seen before. There were tables for roulette, for blackjack, for faro. And big, heavy tables at the room's far end around which men stood playing dice.

Along one side of the smoke-filled room was a long, polished mahogany bar where men stood laughing and drinking. Opposite the bar, on the other side of the room, were doors leading into small private salons meant for poker and red dog.

Around the whole of the big, noisy room, ran a wide balcony where heavy mahogany doors led into plush salons where Nevada assumed leisurely midnight suppers were served in private. Most of the doors stood open at this early hour.

Nevada's eyes returned to the area right down front,

below the stage. There, at white-clothed tables meant only for dining and enjoying the show, sat gentlemen who had come aboard the *Gambler* solely to watch the entertainers.

Nevada looked from face to face and felt her heart sink a little. Almost all were middle-aged men, many overweight and balding. Nowhere in the loudly applauding, whistling crowd did she see the kind of "refined handsome gentlemen" her papa had told her about.

All at once the applause grew thunderous and Nevada realized that Lilly's well-received act had come to a close. The tall blonde was bowing and blowing kisses as she inched her way steadily off the stage. Out of breath, perspiring, Lilly joined Nevada and Belle in the wings, the brilliant smile immediately evaporating.

"He's not here." she said, obviously disappointed. "I looked at every male face in the whole damned room! Johnny hasn't shown up."

"Relax. Johnny Roulette will be here," said Belle. Then turning to Nevada, "Honey, you're on. LeRoy's playing your intro."

Frozen, Nevada stood rooted to the spot. "I—I can't."

Lilly, wiping her shiny face on a linen towel, put her disappointment aside temporarily and smiled. "Sure you can. The only problem you'll have is getting them to quiet down long enough for you to sing." Nevada turned big, questioning eyes on the tall blonde. Lilly lowered the towel and impulsively hugged the tiny, terrified girl. "I mean because you're so pretty, Nevada.". She gave the trembling beginner a motherly squeeze, turned her about, and pointed her toward the stage. "Get out there and give them what they came for."

"Good luck, Nevada," offered Belle, giving her a pat on her shiny blue derriere.

Nevada, knowing it was now or never, shook off all

traces of doubt, squared her slender shoulders, and walked confidently onstage while LeRoy, seated at a black walnut piano, winked at her and gave her a wide, reassuring grin.

Lilly had been right. The throng of ringside gentlemen took one look at Nevada and went wild. They shouted, they whistled, they stamped their feet, and one excited admirer tried to rush the stage. He was quickly and soundly discouraged by the *Gambler*'s giant bouncer, Stryker. Stryker was at the drunken man's side in the blink of an eye and, grabbing him up by the scruff of the neck, calmly deposited him back in his chair with a warning from his raised eyebrows.

Stryker's sudden appearance had a calming effect on the crowd and LeRoy, recognizing the opportunity, snapped his fingers, nodded to Nevada, and said in a loud, warm voice, "Now, child. Sing it!"

She did.

With the aplomb and poise of a seasoned veteran, Nevada went immediately into a song well-suited to the leering all-male crowd. A song that was brand-new, one she'd learned only that afternoon. One that the talented piano man LeRoy had taught her.

Hands going to her hips, Nevada bent one knee slightly —just as Lilly had showed her—and belted out the show-stopping lyrics:

> Frankie and Johnnie were sweethearts,
> Oh, Lordy, how they could love . . .

In the small salon where he was losing at poker, Johnny Roulette, picking up the cards that were being dealt him, abruptly turned his dark head to listen. Above the din he heard an unfamiliar female voice singing an unfamiliar song.

"Pops hire a new girl?" he asked, looked at his hand. Discarding, he added, "Give me three, Cap'n Henley."

"So I hear. Pops says he found a real little beauty, a young girl that looks like an angel," said the riverboat pilot as he shot Johnny three new cards.

Johnny laughed, as did the others. The *Gambler* girls were hardly angels, but then angels were not what a man was looking for when he stayed the night on board. It was unspoken knowledge that for a handsome price any one of the friendly beautiful women would, after entertaining on-stage, willingly entertain an amorous gentleman in one of the fancy upstairs suites.

Johnny looked at his three new cards, shoved all five together, and tossed them in. Rising, he said, "Looks like I can't beat you gentlemen this evening. Give me a chance to get my money back tomorrow night."

Nodding good night, he made his way out into the big gaming hall and looked at the girl onstage. From his vantage point at the far back of the room, he could see little save the fact that she was tiny and dark-haired.

Intrigued, Johnny Roulette, carefully balancing a nearly full glass of bourbon in his big right hand, unsteadily weaved among the crowded tables, making his way toward the stage. He didn't stop until, happily ignoring shouts of "down in front," he stood directly below the stage, not ten feet from Nevada.

Johnny was drunk but not too drunk to appreciate Nevada's youthful beauty. Blinking to clear his liquor-clouded vision, he studied the little girl with the big voice and decided then and there that he wanted her.

Gleaming hair, the color of his own, was artfully arranged in shiny curls atop her head. In a delicate oval face with high dramatic cheekbones were the bluest pair of eyes and the cutest turned-up nose and the reddest, softest lips he'd ever seen.

Swallowing a drink of the bourbon, Johnny allowed his eyes to move with lazy appreciation from the bare ivory shoulders and the pale tempting bosom to the waist so small he knew he'd have little trouble spanning it with his big hands.

The ice-blue satin of her evening gown was molded tightly over a flat stomach and flaring feminine hips that made his throat go dry. He turned up the whiskey again as his gaze climbed reluctantly back to her beautiful face. Nevada's heavily painted eyes, cheeks, and lips, coupled with the fact that Johnny was uncharacteristically inebriated, caused him to badly misjudge her age.

He surmised she was somewhere on the green side of twenty-five, young enough to still be blessed with a ripe lush beauty, old enough to know how to use her charms.

Feeling the first pleasant stirrings of physical desire, Johnny unbuttoned his black evening jacket, pushed back one side, shoved a big hand down into his pants pocket, and stood there, feet apart, looking up at Nevada, allowing his black eyes to caress her. Lazily looking forward to when his hands would.

Nevada had momentarily lost her place, forgotten the words to the new song, when she saw the tall, broad-shouldered, dark-complexioned man making his sure, purposeful way toward the stage. He'd emerged from the smoke and noise like a mysterious masculine apparition emerging from the mists of her girlish dreams.

Stumbling over the words, repeating one entire line of the lyrics, Nevada felt her breath catch in her throat when she saw the approaching man stop directly before the stage, unbutton his jacket, thrust a hand down into his trouser pocket, and lift his glass in salute.

His presence was so overpowering, Nevada couldn't take her eyes off him. Soon she stopped trying. She wanted, she thought fleetingly with the part of her brain that was still functioning, to memorize everything about this magnificent man.

A man she recognized at once to be the handsome, infamous Johnny Roulette. No wonder the girls were excited that he was back in town!

Nevada was far too young and naive ever to have had sexual fantasies. Until tonight. With a jolt of shock and shame, she looked at Johnny Roulette and imagined what it would be like to be held and loved by him.

His thick wavy hair gleamed in the illumination of the stage's footlights and his eyes, almost as dark as his hair, flashed with heat and mischief. His nose was straight and pleasingly prominent, his cheekbones high and chiseled. His mouth was wide and full, and as he smiled—he hadn't stopped smiling from the first moment she saw him—his even teeth shone starkly white in his dark, handsome face. Most appealing of all was a sleek, well-trimmed mustache above those heavy male lips.

Nevada forced her eyes from that marvelous mouth and down over his strong brown throat. An ebony European-cut evening jacket strained across a pair of broad shoulders, while fashionably long matching trousers fell to a perfect break atop shiny black leather shoes that were apart in a distinctly arrogant stance. His starched snow-white shirt contrasted dramatically with the darkness of his smooth olive skin and, going down the shirt's carefully pleated front, gold studs glittered in the footlights.

Most disturbing of all was the fact that with only the slightest movements of his big lean body, the dark handsome man was expressing emotion and sensuality with an extraordinary potency. So powerful was the language of his body, Nevada was weak and awed and ready to follow him anywhere, though they'd not yet spoken a word.

She had, she knew beyond any doubt, met her rich handsome gentleman her very first night onstage. Now all she had to do was make Johnny Roulette realize that he was meant only for her. Maybe he could see it too. He was looking at her as though she was special, as if she were already his sweetheart. And she would be, if he wanted her, because she sure wanted him to be her man.

Excitement and hope building, Nevada, looking straight into Johnny Roulette's flashing dark eyes, sang the closing line of her song, never suspecting that the sad, mournful words might prove prophetic:

He was her man, but he done her wrong.

4

The song had ended. The heavy red velvet curtains were slowly descending. The crowd of captivated men whistled and clapped and shouted for more!

All, that is, but one.

The darkly handsome Johnny Roulette neither whistled nor clapped nor shouted for another song. Instead the tall, smiling man casually turned and walked away as the curtain came down.

The billowing curtain was immediately raised so Nevada could give the enthralled crowd a few extra bows. But she gave no bows or kisses; she was too preoccupied with looking for the tall, deeply tanned man with the coal-black hair.

But Johnny Roulette was gone.

Nevada's hopes came crashing down with the second lowering of the red curtains. What should have been a moment of glory and triumph was instead one of disappointment and confusion.

Heartsick, she made her way to the dressing quarters and managed to smile bravely when Lilly and Belle and Julia and Betsy all crowded around to offer their sincere congratulations. Guiding Nevada into the cramped quarters, the women were all talking at once but Nevada, distracted, caught only a word here and there. She did hear enough to know they were all keenly aware that Johnny Roulette was aboard the *Gambler.*

A loud knock didn't silence the excitedly chattering women, but when Lilly opened the door to admit Stryker, the enormous bouncer lifted a hand for quiet. He looked over Lilly's head at Nevada and stated calmly, "Miss Hamilton, Mr. Johnny Roulette has requested your company for supper."

Nevada's heart was beating alarmingly fast. She clung to Stryker's arm as he guided her through the crowd and when she spotted Johnny Roulette at a dice table, his back was to her. Stryker abruptly stopped, turned to Nevada, leaned down and said into her ear, "You're safe as long as you're on board the *Gambler,* Nevada. I'm always around, even when you're not aware of my presence, so there's nothing to be afraid of."

"I'm not afraid," said Nevada, wondering what this big fierce-looking man was going on about.

The giant Stryker smiled at her. "I know. All the same, I'll keep an eye on you."

Before she had time to respond he was again guiding her through the crowd of gamblers and in seconds she stood directly behind the tall, dark-haired Johnny Roulette.

Stryker spoke his name. Johnny slowly turned around and Nevada stopped breathing. Close up, he was even more handsome than she had realized.

"Miss Nevada Hamilton," Stryker said, "meet John Roulette."

"Nevada, do you like dice?" Johnny Roulette asked with a grin, reaching for her hand, and Nevada felt her cold fingers being firmly gripped by his warm ones.

Looking up into his dark, flashing eyes, she said honestly, "I'm not sure, Mr. Roulette. I've never shot dice."

Gently pulling her closer, Johnny said, "Then, sweetheart, it's high time you gave it a try." Putting a long arm around her narrow waist, Johnny shook hands with Stryker and said, "Thanks, Stryker. I'll take good care of her."

"You do or you'll answer to me," said Stryker. Then he turned and walked away.

"You'll protect me from Stryker, won't you, Nevada?" Johnny teased, leaning down so close his warm breath ruffled a curl near her right ear. He smelled of whiskey, but Nevada didn't find it offensive. Quite the opposite; it was a pleasantly familiar scent she associated with another big, smiling man who used to kiss her good night and make her feel safe and loved.

"The point," Johnny Roulette was saying as he lifted her hand, turned it over, and deposited two black-dotted ivory dice in her soft palm, "is to throw a seven for me. Think you can do that, sweetheart?"

"I'll sure try," said Nevada.

"That's good enough for me," he said, leaning over and placing a tall stack of red chips on the green felt of the table's front pass line. He grinned at Nevada, picked up his bourbon glass, and said, "We're all waiting, darlin'. Just fling those dice to the other end of the table."

Nevada didn't hesitate. If Johnny Roulette wanted a seven, she'd do her damnedest to give him one. Her tiny hand flew right out and she let go of the dice. The twin cubes struck the table's wooden frame, clattered, spun dizzily, and finally rolled to a stop. One showed a three, the other a four. Nevada had thrown the seven.

While the croupier paid off the bettors, Johnny, his grin wider than ever, said to Nevada, "That's good, darlin'. Now, how about an eleven?"

"Whatever you say, Johnny," she answered confidently

and wasted no time throwing one. Then she repeated. Then threw another seven. Then got six for a point and bucked it, tossing a six right back. And all the while her heart was drumming with excitement as the unsmiling croupier kept pushing chips across the table and Johnny Roulette, his hand possessively riding her waist, kept laughing and praising her and drinking his whiskey.

A half hour later when Nevada finally sevened-out, Johnny Roulette threw back his dark head and laughed loudly as she exclaimed, "Damnation! Johnny, I'm sorry."

Enchanted, he hugged her to him and said, "Honey, you just made me ten thousand dollars." He kissed the top of her dark head and added, "You're my Lady Luck. I'll never let you out of my sight."

Johnny's careless statement thrilled and pleased the smitten Nevada. She never wanted to be out of his sight, nor to have him out of hers. So she didn't question him when, telling the croupier to collect his winnings and hold them, Johnny turned her away from the table and, guiding her across the crowded hall, said from over her head, "Let's order us some French champagne and oysters and get better acquainted."

She wanted nothing more than to get better acquainted with this dark, compelling man. And she suddenly realized she was quite hungry. She'd had nothing to eat since boarding the *Gambler*.

In minutes Nevada found herself on the upstairs balcony, preceding Johnny through one of the heavy carved mahogany doors. Inside, she gasped at the opulence that greeted her. She stood in a stateroom where a sparkling chandelier cast honeyed light on a sofa and chairs upholstered in plush navy velvet and a deep carpet of the same hue. The walls were covered with a shimmering beige silk and one entire side was accordion doors that were open and folded back to allow a spectacular view of the lights along the river.

In the center of the room a round table, draped in beige damask, was set for two. The fragile china and heavy sterling and sparkling crystal were finer than anything Nevada had ever seen. A heavy carved silver candelabra graced the table's center along with freshly cut white roses.

After knocking on the door, a white-coated steward entered bearing champagne in a silver ice bucket, and by the time Nevada was seated across from Johnny at the table, the waiter had returned with dishes of steaming bouillabaisse, a heaping platter of oysters and shrimp, a basket of hot breads, and an assortment of cooked vegetables and fresh fruits.

"Johnny," said Nevada, looking up at the smiling man who was watching her from across the table, "there's so much food! How will we ever eat it all?"

He gave her a slow, lazy grin and his black eyes took on an appealingly drowsy expression. "Darlin'," he murmured, his voice deep and low, "we can always finish it at breakfast." His sleepy-eyed look disappeared and his black eyes gleamed devilishly, but Nevada missed his meaning.

Deftly, Johnny popped the champagne cork and poured. Handing Nevada a glass, he stopped her when she started to drink. "Hold on, sweetheart. I want to propose a toast to you." He raised his glass and said, "To my beautiful Lady Luck." He touched her glass with his and they drank, Johnny downing his quickly, Nevada sipping hers cautiously.

Watching the tiny dark-haired beauty behave as though she'd never before tasted champagne, Johnny was quietly amused. Apparently she'd chosen, this evening, to play the role of the innocent. Perhaps she thought that's what he found appealing. And still in a warm haze of bourbon, he did find the mixture of make-believe innocence and blatant voluptuousness to be powerfully seductive. Remarkably there was a freshness about this painted miniature doll that seemed almost genuine.

But smilingly watching her sip the bubbly wine as if for the first time, Johnny was glad her seeming vulnerability, her air of chastity, was nothing more than a well-acted role. What the hell, he'd be glad to play along, treat her as though she were a refined young lady allowing her only lover to take her to bed. There was no denying she was a tempting sensual beauty and he had no objection to taking his time. They had the entire night. He would go along with her little game.

It suited him just fine.

Rising, Johnny asked Nevada's permission to remove his jacket. Smiling happily, she said, "Certainly, Johnny." She watched, fascinated, while he shrugged out of it, drawing her attention once again to the impressive width of his shoulders and chest. When he tugged at his black silk tie, slid it from under the stiff white collar, and tossed it atop a navy velvet chair, she simply sighed and took another sip of champagne.

Returning to the table, Johnny struck a sulphur match, set the candles aflame, then turned out the gaslight chandelier overhead, casting the intimate room into soft romantic candlelight.

"Better?" he inquired softly, looking down at her.

"Perfect," Nevada replied.

Dropping back into his chair, Johnny corrected her. "Not quite perfect."

"It's not?"

"No. You're too far away." He pushed his chair back from the table. "Come here, darlin'."

Nevada felt her pulse speed. Quickly she took a big gulp

of champagne, rose, and circled the table. When she stood directly before him Johnny smiled up at her, slowly put his hands to her small waist, and felt his fingers overlap in back, his thumbs touch in front. Grinning, he languidly slid one thumb down until it rested atop the small indentation of her naval.

"God, you're a tiny little thing," he said, his black eyes warming with desire.

"God, you're a great big thing," Nevada retorted saucily, her naturally impudent spirit enhanced by the champagne she'd consumed.

Johnny Roulette loved it. Laughing heartily, he pulled her between his spread knees, wrapped his arms tightly around her, and pressed his face into the softness of her satin-draped bosom.

Deeply inhaling her sweet fragrance, he said into the softness beneath his cheek, "That I am, sweetheart." He lifted his head, boldly kissed the bare swell of her breast above the shimmering blue satin bodice, and Nevada trembled. His warm lips against the bare flesh, he said, "I don't know . . ." He inclined his dark head toward a closed interior door. "What I have in mind may be impossible for us."

Weak and dizzy from the wine and the man and shocked at the frightening heat his lips were spreading through her entire body, Nevada had no idea what he was talking about. But she was certain that nothing was impossible for Johnny Roulette and her. So she said breathlessly, looking with wonder down upon the dark head bent to her, "We can do anything we set our minds to."

That brought more liquored laughter from Johnny. Giving her bare bosom one last kiss, he lifted his head, gently urged her down to sit on his left knee, and laced his long fingers around her waist. "Baby, it's our bodies I'm talking about. I'm twice your size."

"What difference does that make?" asked Nevada, totally baffled.

"None. You're right, it makes no difference," said Johnny. "I've never objected to a female assuming the superior position." And he promptly envisioned this tiny raven-haired charmer in bed, gloriously naked and seated astride him. "Matter of fact, it might be fun for you to be the dominant one right from the beginning." Grinning, he reached up, plucked a tiny blue satin bow from Nevada's dark curls, looked at it intently for a minute, and dropped it on the table. "Kiss me, Nevada."

Nevada stared at him. *Superior? Dominant?* What in blazes was he talking about? He was not making a great deal of sense but his full sensual lips beneath that sleek black mustache certainly were tempting. She had wanted to kiss this big handsome man since the first moment she saw him.

And after all, it wasn't as though she had never been kissed before. Why, only last winter she had been kissed by Jimmy Bradford, the young hand her daddy had hired temporarily, and before that she had been kissed by a planter's son, Harry Douglas, when she and her papa had delivered racehorses to the Douglas plantation below Baton Rouge.

But they had both kissed her.

Was Johnny Roulette bashful? Was that why he was asking her to kiss him? He seemed so confident, so sure of himself. Could it possibly be that this big handsome man did not know how to kiss?

Touched, Nevada swallowed hard, put her fingers into the thick wavy hair at the sides of Johnny's head, and lowered her tightly closed lips to his.

5

———∞∞∞∞∞———

Johnny Roulette *did* know how to kiss.

Nevada found out that he knew quite well, knew far more about kissing than Jimmy Bradford or Harry Douglas. Or her. After only a few seconds of allowing her to press her firmly closed lips to his, Johnny took slow, sure command.

His warm full mouth opened beneath hers and his arms tightened around her, urging her closer. His well-trimmed mustache tickled her pleasantly, just as she had imagined. For a fleeting second her nose twitched and Nevada felt she might burst out laughing. But not for long. Not when his sensual lips began to play with hers, teasing her, thrilling her, surprising her so completely that her eyes flew open and she made a weak sound of protest, signaling it was time for him to stop.

But Johnny didn't stop. He was only getting started. Turning a deaf ear to her muffled outcry, he slid a big hand caressingly up from her waist over the slender curve of her back, even as the wet tip of his tongue slid aggressively, tantalizingly along the seam of her closed lips. Lips that naturally parted under such powerfully pleasant persuasion.

With the parting of her lips, Johnny Roulette ended that first sweet stirring kiss and slowly pulled back. Smiling easily, he winked at Nevada, lifted a hand, and proceeded to pluck the remaining tiny blue satin bows from her upswept hair. When all half dozen bows lay upon the beige damask tablecloth, he found the pins holding her hair in place. He languidly slid them from the inky curls and watched, entranced, as the long black tresses tumbled down around her lovely face and bare shoulders.

Nevada didn't make a sound. She sat there on Johnny's knee, spellbound, not quite sure what he might do next, but quite, quite sure she would like what he did next.

Johnny ran long tanned fingers through Nevada's unbound dark hair, sighing contentedly and smiling as though the simple act gave him great pleasure. Carefully he drew a large portion of the shining hair to his face, inhaled its perfumed fragrance, and sighed more deeply. Then he opened his hand, released the raven locks, and watched them fall and settle alluringly upon the bare swell of Nevada's ivory bosom.

She held her breath when he laid his big spread hand almost reverently atop the flared hair and the naked flesh beneath. Suddenly it was so quiet and close in the warm stateroom she could hear her heart drumming in her ears. It was beating much faster than usual and she wondered if Johnny could feel its furious pounding beneath his hand.

He must have, because the easy smile left his handsome face and she saw a muscle flex in his smooth olive jaw. His hooded black eyes gleamed in the candlelight as his face moved closer to her own. And his hand slipped beneath the curtain of her hair and moved with slow deliberation over her breast and back down to her waist.

"Now," he said, his deep, low voice tenderly commanding, "really kiss me, Nevada."

Then his lips were on hers, warm and open, and Nevada realized she just thought he had kissed her before. Johnny

Roulette's masterful mouth did new, strange, and wonderful things to the inside of hers in a slow, burning caress that caused her to sigh and squirm and run her nervous hands over his muscular shoulders and up to the back of his head.

Anxiously she grabbed handfuls of the black wavy hair that grazed the top of his white collar. She gripped the thick dark locks frantically when she felt Johnny's teeth—those white even teeth that made his smile so spectacular—gently nip at her trembling bottom lip before he sucked it into his mouth.

Johnny's provocative kiss caused her mouth to open wide and at once his tongue, like silky fire, thrust inside to stroke, to ignite, to set her ablaze. Dazed with wonder, Nevada's eyes fluttered open to see that Johnny's were tightly closed, the sweeping black eyelashes fanned flat against his dramatic cheekbones.

As though he sensed her every move, those sweeping eyelashes lifted and he was looking directly into her shocked eyes. The effect was devastating. Both sighed and deepened the already flaming-hot kiss.

While the flickering candlelight bathed the pair in its pale illumination, the long, ardent kiss continued between the big dark man seated on the tall-back velvet chair and the tiny fair-skinned woman sitting on his knee. Nevada, her long gleaming hair spilling down to her waist, was completely swept away by her first *real* kiss.

If not swept away, Johnny Roulette was nonetheless enjoying the smoldering kiss. He had kissed dozens of women just the way he was kissing Nevada. And he knew already, could tell from her strangely pure yet passionate kisses, that Nevada was going to be one sweet fiery lover in bed.

At long last their heated lips separated and Nevada, wrung out, trembling with emotion, feeling as though she were literally afire from head to toe, weakly nodded yes when Johnny said, "Darlin', I think we'd better have supper." He brushed a kiss to her cheek and added, his lips remaining on the flushed dewy skin, "You'll need your strength, because we're going to have a grand time tonight."

And they did have a grand time.

When Nevada made a move to return to her own chair across the table, Johnny refused to let her go Hugging her tightly to him, he said, "No, baby, you just stay right here. I'll feed you."

He didn't have to say it twice. Flattered and thrilled, Nevada smiled sweetly at him, content to sit upon his knee for as long as he wanted. While she laughed and shook her head and clung to his neck, Johnny, with one hand, filled a china plate with food; his other arm stayed possessively around Nevada's waist.

There was much laughing and teasing and carrying on during the late-night meal. Johnny would lift a forkful of food to Nevada's waiting open mouth, then, not giving her a chance to chew and swallow, he would kiss her again. She found eating very difficult and kept shaking her head no to more food.

Johnny didn't eat. He drank instead and enjoyed to the fullest watching the lovely glowing girl on his knee happily sample the tempting dishes. She possessed an endearing childlike quality; she acted as though everything was brand-new and exciting for her. Her enchanting manner brought to the bought-and-paid-for tryst an illusion of sweet romance. It seemed almost as though it was the first time she had ever sat on a man's lap in this silk-walled stateroom. As if this playful prelude to passion was actually a genuine delight for her.

While she giggled girlishly, adventurously sampling the

varied foods, Nevada rolled her eyes and lifted her bare shoulders appreciatively. And unwittingly offered Johnny Roulette glimpses of her breasts, bare and beautiful inside the low-riding satin bodice of her gown. When she moved, the satin pulled and slid and revealed, more than once, a flash of a soft pink nipple topping the creamy flesh.

Grinding his teeth, Johnny continued to feed the lovely laughing girl until finally Nevada pushed the poised fork away, patted her flat stomach, and said, "No more, Johnny. My dress is getting so tight I'm afraid I'll split the seams."

"Just one more strawberry," said Johnny, laying the fork aside, choosing a fresh ripe berry and dipping it into the silver sugar bowl. He lifted it, and his heavy eyebrows, questioningly.

And laughed loudly when Nevada nodded happily, leaned up, and closed her lips quickly around the sugared berry, murmuring, "Mm, delicious."

But his laughter subsided when, reaching for a linen napkin to clean the sugary residue from his fingers, Nevada stopped him. "Let me, Johnny," she said, and taking his hand in both of hers, lifted it to her mouth. The muscles in his lower belly tightened and he drew a labored breath when, her eyes shining like a naughty imp's, Nevada sucked on his fingers, one by one, until all the sugar was gone.

"How's that?" she asked, licking her lips.

"How's this?" was his reply as he pulled her to him, buried his mouth in the curve of her neck and shoulder and sucked playfully, making her dissolve into happy laughter.

They continued to play. And to enjoy themselves immensely. Johnny Roulette liked this laughing dark-haired beauty on his lap. Not only was she extraordinarily pretty, she was also sweet-tempered, uncomplicated, and fun-loving. She was no more interested in his past than he was in hers. She had not asked a single probing question, a fact he found both refreshing and surprising. Most women, the moment they met him, wanted to know all there was to know about him. He regarded their inquiries as tiresome intrusions. Apparently this one was a true professional who knew exactly why she was in this opulent stateroom with him.

To give him pleasure for the money he was paying for her time and services.

She had done just that from the moment downstairs when he handed her the dice to toss. Yes, Johnny mused contentedly, his appreciative gaze resting on her satin-draped breasts, he had finally gotten lucky tonight. He had won for the first time in months. Won big. Won money that he badly needed after the long dry spell. And he would wager his favorite gold studs that his gorgeous little Lady Luck was just as good in bed as she was at the tables.

Could any man ask for more?

Pleased with his run of good fortune, Johnny kept kissing his living, breathing good-luck charm hotly between drinks of champagne from a shared glass. Nevada's appetite for food had been sated but she continued to be thirsty, so she gratefully took long cooling sips of the chilled wine. And had no idea that she was growing increasingly tipsy.

For that matter, Johnny Roulette had no idea she was either. He was far too inebriated himself to recognize the condition of his captivating companion. The only thing he was completely sure of was that he wanted to feel this doll-like creature's small soft hands on him without further delay.

Drunk though he most certainly was, Johnny deftly removed all the gleaming gold studs from his pleated shirtfront. When they lay in the palm of his hand, he placed them atop the table. The movement caused the open white shirt to part and Nevada's eyes were drawn to his dark muscular chest. She swallowed hard when Johnny encircled her wrist in his fingers, raised it to his lips, kissed its pulse, then drew her hand inside his opened shirt.

"Touch me, sweetheart," said Johnny, releasing her hand.

"Johnny," she breathed, amazed by the heat and strength beneath her fingertips. "Johnny, Johnny," she softly murmured, her wide eyes slowly lowering to look at the bare brown flesh he had exposed. Tentatively she allowed her fingers to glide over the thick crisp hair covering his broad chest. Like a child with a fascinating new toy, she stared and stroked, pushing his shirt farther apart, her bottom lip sucked behind her teeth in awed concentration.

Johnny Roulette was astonished by the pleasurable torment her small hand was causing him. His heartbeat promptly quickened and he reached out, captured her chin, and urged her mouth to his.

It was a fiery lingering kiss, and during it, Nevada, anxiously molding her parted lips to his, moved her hand down from the hard flat muscles of Johnny's chest to the smooth bare flesh of his abdomen. And softly winced with wonder when she realized that her flattened palm lay directly atop a strong pulse point in his stomach. She pressed her eager fingers more closely to that rhythmic beating and sighed with joy when the fierce throbbing surged right through her fingertips and she was no longer certain whose heartbeat she was feeling. His? Hers? Theirs. Two heartbeats becoming one.

Two hearts becoming one.

Nevada sighed softly with rising ecstasy. The chilled wine, the warm night, the heated kisses had worked their subtle seductive magic on the young, inexperienced girl longing for love. She was deep in a beautiful dream. Dwelling in a glorious loveland. A floating Eden where she wanted to drift for all the rest of her days, wrapped in the strong protective arms of the awesomely masculine, ruggedly handsome Johnny Roulette.

She was so lost in that romantic dream, it seemed the most natural thing in the world when Johnny, holding her in his arms, rose from his chair and crossed the room. Pausing before a white interior door, Johnny lowered his dark head and kissed her deeply, then said, "Love me, baby."

"Forever, Johnny. Forever."

6

Smiling at her, Johnny turned around, nudged the door open with his shoulder, and carried her into a dimly lit, luxuriant beige boudoir, again kissing her.

Nevada's glorious love dream continued as Johnny kissed her with exquisite tenderness and slowly lowered her to her feet. Then for a long, tension-filled minute they stood there, not touching, looking only at each other.

When finally Nevada's eyes lowered from Johnny's, she was alarmed to find they were standing directly before an oversized bed where sheets of shimmering beige silk had already been turned invitingly down. Her nervous gaze immediately returned to Johnny's dark face, her large blue eyes questioning, the color high in her cheeks. Johnny, grinning drunkenly down at her, experienced an unfamiliar surge of regard and concern for this bought beauty.

At once he was annoyed with himself. He was allowing her fragile looks to affect him. Her wee size made her appear vulnerable and sweet. That was it; there was nothing more to it. She was, in truth, as jaded and world-wise as he. Matter of fact, this woman who was so small she had to tip her head back to look up at him could probably show him a thing or two.

That happy notion chased away any lingering apprehension and Johnny, grinning drunkenly once more, impatiently jerked the long tails of his white shirt up out of his tight black trousers.

Staring helplessly at the perfect symmetry of his bare sculpted shoulders, his deep muscular chest and long bronzed arms, Nevada gasped when he reached out, wrapped warm fingers around the back of her neck, and gently, commandingly urged her up on tiptoe as he bent to her.

Her hands quite naturally gripped his corded ribs and she found herself pressed to his naked torso. The heat he radiated was almost frightening, as were the hard, ungiving contours of his big lean body. She stood on her toes, clinging to him, turning a deaf ear to the tiny warning bells jangling in her tipsy brain. Instinctively she pressed her satin-covered breasts to his bare chest, marveling at the strange texture and tickle of the crisp chest hair against her sensitive flesh.

But when, in the middle of the smoldering kiss, Johnny reached between their melded bodies and freed her right breast, Nevada drew in a quick, strangled breath. Then gasped into his covering mouth when Johnny pressed her so close her naked breast flattened against him.

She made an attempt to pull away, but Johnny's arms were like steel around her and his hard, hot chest with its thick crisp hair was delightfully abrasive to her bare breast. The contact was so excitingly pleasing, Nevada instinctively began rubbing her bare, aching breast against him, having no idea what she was doing to Johnny.

He felt his blood pulsing and no longer bothered with trying to slow down the hardening of his groin. The touch of Nevada's bare breast against his chest gave birth to the kind of raging passion that his body could not deny. The tautened nipple moving in seductive little circles just below his pounding heart made him want to rip the blue satin dress from her tempting curves, swiftly bury himself in her, and attain his release.

He didn't do it.

Johnny pulled back a little and set Nevada from him. Shaking with emotion, she looked anxiously up at him and frantically pulled at the bodice of her dress. Johnny grinned, caught her hand, drew it to his lips, kissed it, and placed it on his chest. Then pushing the bodice back down, he gently cupped her bare right breast in his hand and rubbed his rough thumb over its aching tip.

Her throat dry, her eyes round, Nevada, blushing, murmured, "Johnny, no."

"You're very sweet and beautiful," he murmured, as his thumb continued to play with her breast.

"Y-you are too, but—"

"May I?" he said, and not waiting for an answer, languidly peeled down the other side of her satin bodice. "What's this, darlin'?" he asked, seeing and promptly lifting a neatly folded man's handkerchief that was pressed to the undercurve of her breast.

Blushing more deeply, Nevada reached for it. "My money," she said. "All the money I have in the world."

"Well, darlin', you'll have more after tonight." He grinned knowingly.

"I—I . . . will?" She gave him a puzzled look and holding the handkerchief tightly in one hand, attempted to cover her naked breasts with the other.

Johnny gently took the folded handkerchief from her, tossed it onto the night table, and pulled her back to him. "God, you're adorable," he said, drunkenly discerning that she was bent on continuing to play the game, to pretend that this riverboat rendezvous was actually *l'amour.* She was, he slowly decided, as smart as she was desirable. Eight to five said that her "helpless little girl" routine generally gleaned her more money in one night than the rest of the *Gambler*'s girls made in a season. "So sweet," he said, urging her up against him, his hands locking behind her. "So desirable."

He kissed her tenderly, then said against her lips, "I want to undress you. I want to hold you naked in my arms. Will you allow me that pleasure, sweetheart?"

"Johnny Roulette!" She gasped, her small body going rigid. "Certainly not!" Then she began to struggle, trying to free herself from his imprisoning arms. "We should go into the other room. Or back downstairs to the tables. Let's gamble some more."

"We'll gamble later," he said, his voice heavy with desire. "You know what I want, sweet. Give it to me." He slid his hand down over her bottom, lifted her a little, and pressed her close. And he kissed her again.

Nevada vainly struggled against the intoxication of his kiss and was left so weak and dazed by his masterful mouth, she could only shake her head helplessly when his heated lips finally released hers. Johnny turned her about so that she was facing away from him. His hands shook a little as he went to work on the tiny hooks going down the back of the blue evening gown. When Nevada caught her breath and realized exactly what he was doing, she knew she had to put an end to this madness at once.

There would be plenty of lovely passion-filled nights once they were man and wife. They could wait.

"Johnny, we really should wait until . . ." She said it softly, sure he would understand.

She tried to step away and found she was caught up in a battle she had no chance of winning. Johnny pulled her back against him so swiftly, she felt all the air leave her body.

"I have waited, baby." His voice was still low and calm,

but his hands were determined as he pushed the sleeves down her arms and soon the gown's bodice lay in shimmering folds at her waist.

Nevada trembled, flustered and afraid.

"Ah, baby, don't," said Johnny, gently drawing her back against him, putting his arms around her, silently applauding her acting ability. If she was intent on continuing the game, he would allow it. At least for a few more minutes. His chin resting lightly atop her dark head, he said, "It's all right. All right. I won't rush you."

The back of her head resting on his broad, bare chest, Nevada, misunderstanding, closed her eyes and laid her small hands atop his. "Thank you, darling." She sighed, relieved. Dreamily she added, "After all, we have the rest of our lives."

"Mm. At least the rest of the night," said Johnny, kissing her raven hair. He moved his hands from beneath hers and urged her trembling body more fully to his, letting her become thoroughly aware of his physical condition. His voice was hoarse, whispering into her ear, "Feel what you've done to me, darlin'."

"Johnny!" Growing panicky now, Nevada twisted wildly, desperate to be free.

Pressed against him as she was, her urgent squirming only served to further arouse him.

"Let me, baby," he murmured and bent to press kisses to the curve of her neck and shoulder while one big hand cupped her breast and the other slid down over her flat belly to cup the satin-covered V between her thighs.

"Johnnnnny!" She gasped again, shocked at what his hands were doing and frightened by the heat exploding throughout her body. Catching Johnny totally by surprise, Nevada abruptly threw off his bold hands and made a terrified dash for the door. She was at the open portal when he caught her.

Grabbing her, Johnny wrapped long fingers tightly around her upper arm, pulled her back inside, slammed the door closed, spun her swiftly about, and pushed her up against it.

"Don't you think this has gone just about far enough?" he said, a slight edge creeping into his voice.

He gripped the doorframe on either side of her, trapping Nevada inside. He loomed tall and menacing before her, his bare broad chest, only inches from her face, rising and falling rapidly. His handsome features had hardened and a dangerous light now glinted in his black eyes. Nevada swallowed hard, her bare back pressed to the door's intricately carved surface. Nodding anxiously, she said quickly, "Yes, yes, I do."

"Good," he said.

Expecting him to step away and let her go, she stared openmouthed as his hard lips, cruel and punishing, descended to hers. She gave a brief moan of protest before his tongue swept the warm wet recesses of her mouth. In a futile attempt to resist, Nevada stiffened and pushed on his massive chest.

It didn't work. He was immovable.

The hot, insistent mouth holding hers prisoner was again spreading that all-encompassing heat, and Nevada began to fight herself as well as Johnny. She moved her head from side to side, trying to escape that hot, brazen mouth, and she continued to resist with all her strength until, rankled, Johnny lifted his dark head, grabbed her pummeling hands, and pushed them up over her head.

Pinning them there with one of his, he let his heated gaze slide down to touch her bare, lifted breasts. Speechless, Nevada stared at him, her blue eyes pleading with him to let her go. He didn't. He bent his dark head and captured a quivering nipple, drawing it into his hot wet mouth.

Nevada shuddered violently and frantically tried to pull her hands free of his. It was impossible. Easily he held her fragile wrists high above her head and continued to feast on her breasts, running his tongue around the stiff little peaks, sucking gently, setting her afire.

Still she struggled, torn between desire and shame. While her flushed body demanded more of the unbelievable pleasure his mouth was causing, her brain told her she must stop this forbidden bliss and flee at once. So Nevada strained against his imprisoning hands and his questing mouth and finally Johnny lifted his head.

"I have," he said, growing increasingly annoyed, "had just about enough of this charade."

Uncharacteristically drunk and achingly aroused, Johnny wanted what he was paying for. And he wanted it now. So he curled his long dark fingers into the fabric of the blue satin gown at her waist and forcefully yanked it down, turning a deaf ear to Nevada's shrieks of outrage. When it lay in a shimmering heap at her feet and Nevada stood there wearing nothing but her lace-trimmed drawers, Johnny leaned down and kissed her mouth.

At first she refused to respond, tried valiantly to turn her head away, but it was hopeless. Then, at last, she thought for sure he had given up when his lips left hers. Baffled, she watched Johnny put his lean forefinger into his mouth and wet it. Immediately his lips were back on hers and, while he kissed her, Johnny's hand went beneath her lace-trimmed underpants. It swept down over her quivering belly, moved through the raven curls between her thighs, and sought the feminine sweetness that he yearned for and had to have.

With the first touch of his skilled, wet finger on that ultrasensitive flesh, Nevada's total surrender began. An incredible warmth engulfed her and the will to resist was melted in the intense heat.

She had no idea how long they stood there against that door, her hands above her head while Johnny kissed her, caressed her, and guided her along the seductive path toward total fulfillment. She never knew when Johnny released her hands. Didn't realize when they fell limply to her sides, then crept up to grasp his rock-hard biceps.

She only knew that she no longer wanted to leave this room, this man, this splendor. While his plundering lips and tongue turned her gasps and moans of objection into gentle sighs of pleasure, and his magical fingers caused a wild new kind of joy to suffuse her entire body, Nevada felt the last traces of logical reasoning slipping away. Her mouth and body and heart were open to this magnificent man in whose arms she would become a complete woman. So while Johnny continued to arouse Nevada with such leisurely devastating expertise, her concern for right and wrong began to seem terribly foolish, as though life's rules did not apply to the two of them. She loved him. What did it matter if their honeymoon came before the wedding?

Johnny lips finally left hers.

"That's right, sweet," he murmured thickly against her throat, his eyes a hot, liquid black. "Don't fight it."

He had her totally snared and he knew it. She would give him no more trouble. He kissed her breasts until they were pink and tingling and he deftly finished undressing her. And he told her, in a deep masculine voice, all the forbidden things they were going to do together.

". . . keep you naked always, baby . . . kiss you all over, sweetheart . . . make love until we're both exhausted, love . . ."

Nevada loved every arousing caress of his skilled hands, thrilled to every shocking act he proposed, savored every glorious second of her well-handled sexual awakening.

Immersed in erotic pleasure, she stood there against that door and undulated and sighed and memorized everything about the luxurious showboat bedroom where her heart and her virginity were being offered to the only man who would ever be given either.

The beige silk walls shimmered handsomely in the subdued light from a lone golden wall sconce located directly above the wide bed. A pair of navy velvet chaise lounges sat at right angles to a round table of shiny gold-streaked beige marble. High above the table were two small portholes open to the night. Slatted doors directly opposite the bed led to a spacious bathroom where a beige marble tub with gold fixtures rested atop a pedestal in the center of the room. Carpeted steps led up to the massive tub and around it, on three sides of the room, were tall mirrors in gilt frames.

Johnny Roulette felt his heart kick painfully against his bare ribs when he looked at the tiny dark-haired beauty, naked save for her sheer black stockings, blue satin garters, and blue satin slippers. Of all the women he'd had, of all the ones he'd seen nude, the one standing before him now was by far the most beautiful. Taking a step back, he shook his head, unbelieving.

"Jesus, darlin', you're pretty." She started toward him. He held up both hands, palms out. "Stay there just as you are for a minute. Let me look at you, sweetheart."

Shyly, Nevada stood before him, an erotic nymphet from his fondest sexual dreams. Her dark hair cascaded down around her shoulders; a long shimmering lock curled appealingly around one breast. Her skin was a luminous alabaster that brought to mind fine cultured pearls. Her breasts, high and full, were tipped with the palest shade of rose. Her delicate ribs showed beneath the pale skin; her waist, as he'd already learned, was incredibly small. Her stomach was so flat as to be concave, but her hips flared voluptuously. Her legs were not long, but they were perfectly shaped, her knees dimpled beneath the black stockings. Between her ivory thighs a perfect triangle of dense curls was as black as the seductive stockings hugging her legs.

Staring at her with hot appreciative eyes, Johnny Roulette was again struck by the highly seductive blend of babyish innocence and earthy provocativeness. She was every man's fantasy of sweet and naughty sexiness.

Swallowing hard, Johnny Roulette smiled, took a step toward her, put his hands into her hair at the sides of her head, and tilted her face up to his. Brushing his open lips to hers, he said into her mouth, "Let me love you."

It was all a sweet blur for Nevada after that. There were hot, hot kisses and Johnny, on his knees before her, taking her shoes off, peeling her black stockings down her legs, and impulsively kissing her naked toes while she clung to his wide bare shoulders to keep from falling.

Then she was lying on her back in the very middle of that soft, cool bed and Johnny was leaning over her, murmuring endearments, pressing kisses to her eyes, her ears, her cheeks, her throat.

When he rose from the bed and began unbuttoning his tight black trousers, Nevada turned her head and watched shamelessly. Her eyes swept over his broad, powerful chest and heavily corded arms, his long muscular legs as he removed his trousers. When he sent his white linen underwear to the thick carpet below, allowing his thrusting masculinity to spring free, Nevada experienced a twinge of fear. She had never seen a man naked, and while in a way she was horrified, she couldn't take her eyes off that frighteningly huge shaft of engorged flesh surrounded by thick black curls. Her throat grew tight and dry. Something Johnny had said earlier came rushing back to her, and now it held new meaning; *What I have in mind may be impossible for us.* Staring at the awesomely big, naked man, Nevada knew exactly what he had meant and her apprehension escalated.

But then Johnny was back on the bed, kissing her, his hand cupping her face tenderly, his tongue on hers, and her fear evaporated.

She settled into the softness of the satin-sheeted bed and sighed with pleasure when Johnny nuzzled his sure, slow way down to her breasts. And when she felt his warm wet lips enclose a throbbing nipple, she said his name and put her hands into his hair. She held him to her while he gently sucked, his tickling mustache adding to her bliss.

For a long, lovely time Johnny did nothing more than kiss her mouth and her breasts. When finally she was writhing against him, her little body burning, Johnny laid a hand on her flat, trembling stomach. A muscle jumped in his jaw when he realized that this beautiful naked woman was so small his big square hand practically covered her entire belly.

Nevada noticed too. Her passion-glazed eyes lowered to the hand resting lightly atop her stomach. It looked larger than ever and darker, lying there on the whiteness of her stomach. It was a square, powerful hand. The gambler's fingers were long and tapered, nails blunt cut and clean. A hand strong enough to choke the very life from a man.

But it was a slow, gentle hand on a woman.

Nevada watched that big brown hand move caressingly down over her stomach. She held her breath when it nudged her thighs apart and Johnny, turning his hand over, let his knuckles glide down the sensitive insides of her thighs. And she found out just how gentle that brown hand was when, carefully, slowly raking through the curls concealing that most feminine part of her, Johnny again caressed her with one well-placed dark finger.

Nevada's back arched and her head bore into the satin-cased pillow as the tip of Johnny's middle finger touched her with a tenderness and skill that made all the air rush from her lungs.

"Johnny!" she exclaimed, her eyes flying up to his handsome face. His gaze met hers and she saw a hot light shining in the depths of his black eyes.

"I know, sweetheart," he whispered. "Feels good, doesn't it?"

Nodding frantically, Nevada became aware of other things that felt good as well: the crisp hair of his groin, the hot hardness of his erection pulsing against her bare thigh. His need was physically evident.

But desire, she would soon learn, is often a greedy, selfish emotion, and being healthy and quite human, Nevada was most aware of his slipping, sliding fingertip spreading heat and pleasure with its slow, gentle touch.

Johnny, brushing kisses to Nevada's open mouth, continued to caress her until he had her silkily wet and completely ready. Carried away, blazing hot, Nevada simply sighed and nodded her agreement when he murmured, "Darlin', you can take me easiest if you get on top."

Johnny swiftly stretched out on his back, put his hands to Nevada's waist, and lifted her astride him. With one strong hand remaining at her waist, he urged her up into a kneeling position, then slowly, carefully brought her back down on his straining erection. Nevada was so blazing hot and so much in love, she didn't cry out from the piercing agony of his penetration. Her small body quivering with shock and pain, she gripped Johnny's ribs, pushed down and settled herself on his engorged flesh, and made not a sound.

But Johnny Roulette did.

His black eyes widening with drunken dismay at what he had done, he swore loudly, "Dear God in heaven!"

7

Johnny Roulette awoke the next morning with a toothache, a headache—and a heartache.

Bright summer sunlight streamed through the open
portholes of the luxurious *Moonlight Gambler* stateroom
and into his closed eyes. Slowly his heavy lids lifted and
Johnny reluctantly roused from a deep liquor- and loving-
induced slumber. Everything about him hurt. His jaw was
throbbing, his head pounding, his stomach afire, his heart
squeezing painfully in his naked chest.

Cautiously, hoping against hope he was alone in the
tumbled bed, Johnny slowly turned his aching head. And
saw on a beige satin pillow beside him, the pale angelic-
looking face of Nevada Marie Hamilton. Turned toward
him, she was sleeping as peacefully as a newborn babe in
her crib. Long dark eyelashes made spiky crescents on her
ivory cheeks and her mouth—that soft sweet mouth—was
slightly parted.

Frowning, Johnny let his eyes slide down only as far as
her bare lovely breasts before turning away, impulsively
gritting his teeth and paying dearly for it. The stabbing
pain in his aching wisdom tooth increased dramatically
from the thoughtlessly applied pressure.

Johnny's eyes closed with agony, physical and mental,
as it all came flooding back. The onset of the miserable

toothache. Drinking hard liquor in his Plantation House suite. Boarding the *Gambler* at dusk.

Nevada onstage, singing "Frankie and Johnnie." Nevada tossing the dice and winning. Nevada sitting on his lap at supper. Nevada standing before him wearing nothing but black silk stockings and blue satin shoes. Nevada, naked and beautiful, willingly climbing astride him and . . . and . . .

Johnny's pain-clouded black eyes came open to stare unseeingly up at the ceiling. *Damn my hide! Damn me to eternal perdition! It wasn't bad enough that in my drunken stupor I took the girl's virginity. I didn't stop there!*

Johnny's eyes squeezed tightly shut once more as the memory of the remainder of the long night came back.

"Dear God in heaven!" he had sworn loudly when he felt the tearing of tender female flesh and saw the agonized look come over Nevada's pretty face.

At once he'd gone completely still beneath her and, putting his hands to her upper arms, he'd meant to ease her up and off him as painlessly as possible.

But Nevada had willfully shaken her head no, settled more closely down on him, and squeezed him with her tight sweet body until he'd found it impossible to stop. And after that he'd managed, in his whiskey-and-champagne haze, to shove any demand for adult, responsible behavior aside. He'd lain beneath the bucking beautiful girl, mesmerized by the bounce of her bare breasts, her grinding hips, the close warmth sheathing him, squeezing him, driving all logical thought and good intention right out of his head.

Afterward he had carried her straight to the opulent bath, climbed the carpeted stairs to the marble tub, and stepped into it holding her in his arms. He bathed her, and himself, and climbed out, telling her, Stay right where you are. Trailing water and soapsuds across the deep, rich carpet, he soon returned carrying chilled champagne and two sparkling glasses.

They sat in the tub and drank until at about three in the morning Nevada yawned and said, "Johnny, I'm getting sleepy."

"I know. Let's get some rest, sweet," he said.

But when she stood in the tub and stretched unself-consciously, her small slender body gleaming with beads of water, he wanted her again.

"Wait, darlin'," he said, continuing to recline in the tub below her.

"What is it?" she asked sleepily, soapy bubbles sliding down her pink-tipped breasts and shapely thighs and slim legs, her naked glory reflected in the tall gilt mirrors surrounding them.

Reaching for her hand, Johnny laced her slender fingers through his, rose to kneel on one knee, and pulled her to him. Burying his face against her slippery belly, he pressed hot kisses to the clean smooth flesh, unbothered by the taste of soap on his tongue.

"Johnny," she weakly protested, and reluctantly lifting his head, Johnny grinned, puckered his lips, forcefully blew away a cluster of thick bubbles clinging alluringly to the raven curls between her thighs. Nevada giggled, but when his dark face made a move toward her, she gripped the hair of his head and jerked his head back. "Johnny!"

Smiling, he lithely rose before her, took her in his arms, and kissed her. When his lips left hers, he cradled the back of her head in his hand and pressed her face to his gleaming chest. He looked over her head at their images in the mirrors behind her. While he leisurely admired the slender curve of her bare back and narrow waist and firm rounded little bottom, Nevada began to press warm openmouthed kisses to his wet chest.

They stood in the marble tub, embracing amid the glistening bubbles, becoming more and more aroused with each breathless kiss, each intimate touch, each glimpse of their bare entwined bodies reflected in the mirrors.

Desire dictating, they climbed out of the marble tub but did not return to the bed. Wet, slippery, and passionate, they mated wildly there on the deep blue carpet before the tall gilt mirrors, relishing the sweet joy and recording forever in their respective brains, the erotic sight of themselves making love.

It happened all over again once they were back in their soft bed. Meaning only to go to sleep, they lazily kissed each other good night. When those kisses strayed to other places, to other parts of the body besides their mouths, a slow sure fire began to burn, a fire that was finally extinguished by a pleasingly lethargic kind of loving. They took their slow indolent time about it and when, long after the act had begun, they attained fulfillment together, it was by far the sweetest, deepest climax of them all.

"I love you, Johnny Roulette," Nevada said happily, while she lay draped atop him, her cheek resting on his chest, his body still a part of hers.

Those words rang in Johnny's ears as he lay naked in the harsh morning sunlight. Sober, guilty, and sorry, he had taken the virginity of a foolishly naive girl who, with her face washed clean of paint and powder, looked to be about fifteen years old.

Wanting nothing more than to get dressed and be gone, Johnny, carefully easing Nevada's arm from his chest, moved to the bed's edge, swung his long legs over, and stood up. His eyes never leaving the sleeping woman, he circled the big bed and began collecting his discarded clothes and hurried into the other room.

He was dressed and peeling off some bills to leave her, when she spoke his name. Johnny jumped as though he had been shot and turned to face her. She stood in the open doorway, a sheet wrapped around her, a puzzled expression on her face. He laid the bills on the table. "Why didn't you wake me, Johnny?"

"I . . . there was no need. . . ." He shrugged wide shoulders.

"You're leaving?" She lifted a hand to push the sleep-tumbled hair from her face.

"Yes, Nevada, I am."

Barefoot, she padded into the room, holding the sheet together with one hand, shaking her head as if to clear it. "But why? I thought . . . Johnny, don't leave me. Please don't leave me. I—I love you." She reached him, touched his forearm.

Johnny drew a deep breath. "No, Nevada, you don't love me, you think—"

"I do. I love you and I'll always love you!"

Johnny's big hand covered the small one now gripping his sleeve. "I'm sorry, sweetheart. In me you've picked a very bad prospect."

"That's not true, you must love me too . . . you . . . you held me and—"

"Listen to me, Nevada. I was very drunk and you're very beautiful and I desired you. It was nothing more. Nothing. I don't love any woman. I never have, never will."

Bright tears stinging her eyes, Nevada, refusing to believe what she couldn't bear hearing, anxiously reached up and gripped his lapels with both hands. Her covering satin sheet fell away and slipped to the floor.

"Oh, Jesus," groaned Johnny. Quickly grabbing both her wrists and holding them in one hand, he bent, picked up the sheet, and whirled it around her naked body. Clutching it together atop her left breast, he looked into her tear-bright eyes and said, "I'm not like you, Nevada. I don't know what it is like to love somebody. That part of my makeup was left out altogether."

Nevada's dormant pride began to surface, despite her breaking heart. She nodded bravely, blinking back her tears, and said, "I want you to go now, Johnny Roulette." Her jaw hardened ever so slightly and she lifted her chin defiantly.

"All right, sweetheart," said Johnny, releasing her hands. As soon as she took hold of the covering sheet, he took a step back. "You . . . you take care of yourself, you hear?"

Her small raised chin quivered, but she said, "I'll do that. You do the same. And, Johnny . . ."

"Yes, Nevada?"

Tucking the sheet's edge in securely over her breasts, she walked to the table, picked the bills he had placed there, and held them out to him. "You're forgetting your money."

"It's yours, sweetheart." He flashed her a boyish smile. "I left it there for you."

"Why?" There was a cold, sad look in her blue eyes.

The timbre of his voice was low, kind. "Well, darlin', for all the happiness you gave me last night."

The tears she'd tried so hard to hold back surged and spilled over, washing down her pale cheeks. But her voice was level and firm. "I did not come to this stateroom with you for money." She walked directly up to him, reached out, grabbed the waistband of his trousers. Stuffing the bills

down into his pants, she added, "Now, get out of here, you
arrogant, insulting bastard."

"Ah, honey, don't—"

"Out!"

8

Nevada stood staring at the carved door long after it had quietly closed behind Johnny's departing back. Moving not one muscle, she held her breath, waiting. Waiting for the heavy door to fly open. To see Johnny standing there, grinning at her, his arms open wide, apologizing, telling her he couldn't live without her.

A loud knock on the door made her heart race with happiness. She flew across the room, laughing and crying at once, and called out teasingly, "Yes? Who is it?"

The *Gambler*'s burly bouncer, Stryker, answered in a low, gravelly voice, "Miss Nevada, you okay? Did Roulette do anything out of line?"

"No, no," she called out, heartsick and disappointed, "I-I'm fine, Stryker."

"You sure?"

Hand going to her mouth to hold back the sobs threatening to erupt from her aching throat, Nevada shook her dark head yes.

"Nevada?" he said again.

"I-I'm . . . sure," she managed, jerking the hem of her covering sheet loose and shoving it into her mouth to stifle her weeping as the hot, stinging tears poured down her cheeks.

"All right, then," said the big bouncer. "You get some sleep before afternoon rehearsals." He turned and left.

Nevada, hearing his heavy footsteps falling away, sighed with relief and pulled the choking sheet out of her mouth. Trembling like a leaf in the wind, she turned about and leaned back against the door for support. Still, her weak legs would not support her. Slowly she sagged to the carpeted floor, sat flat down, and cried until there were no tears left.

Then wearily she rose, crossed to the bedroom, and stretched out on the rumpled bed. Flat on her back, every muscle in her body aching, Nevada slowly turned to look at the empty place beside her. Her red, swollen eyes fell on the pillow where Johnny's dark head had left a deep indentation. Reaching out, she clutched a corner of the satin-cased pillow, drew it slowly to her, and placed it directly atop her bare breasts. Her arms came around it and she hugged the pillow tightly to her, inhaling deeply the unique masculine scent that clung to it.

Nevada lay there hugging Johnny's pillow, feeling as though she were somebody else, not herself, not Nevada Marie Hamilton. And indeed she was a new person. The starry-eyed, innocent girl who had preceded the roguish, heavily intoxicated Johnny Roulette into this lavish floating playroom for grownups was gone forever.

In her place was a sad young woman with swollen lips, an unfamiliar tenderness between her legs, and a painfully aching heart, who clung tenaciously to all she had left of her handsome, heartless lover.

Exactly one hour after Johnny had gone, Nevada—face washed, hair brushed, broken heart bravely concealed— exited the scene of her loving and loss. With a tight smile she stepped out onto the wide inside balcony and, almost at once, Stryker materialized out of nowhere. His frowning florid face wore a look of inquiry as his keen eyes swept slowly over Nevada. He looked at her as though he was checking all her parts to see that they were still intact.

"How are you this morning, Stryker?" Nevada asked, smiling, making her voice sound cheerful.

"It's afternoon and I'm always okay." He blocked her path; his eyes met hers. "I knew it," he said through clenched teeth.

"Knew what?" Nevada asked nervously.

"You're in love with him."

"I'm sure I don't know what you're . . . I most certainly . . ." She was faltering badly, but pressed on. "I'm far too sophisticated to . . . to . . . I . . ."

Stryker shook his sandy head and his arms opened wide. Nevada fell gratefully into them. "There, child," he crooned, patting her back awkwardly with a big, gentle hand. "I knew what would happen when Roulette took you upstairs."

Nevada found herself swallowed up in Stryker's gargantuan arms, her face pressed to the rough cotton shirt stretching across his broad chest. To this big strong man she said, "Stryker, don't tell the other girls I was fool enough to fall for Johnny. Promise me."

"Say anything you please to the others and I'll back you up," assured the tenderhearted bouncer.

So that's exactly what Nevada did. Smiling as though she were guarding a delicious secret, Nevada swept confidently into the dressing quarters where Lilly and Belle and Julia and Betsy were relaxing before afternoon rehearsals.

They looked up and saw her. Their squeals and shouts were loud enough to be heard all the way downriver to New Orleans. They crowded excitedly around Nevada, all firing questions at once, dying to know everything that had happened between her and Johnny Roulette.

It was Lilly, her arm around Nevada's slender shoulders, who said truthfully, "We are all green with envy, Nevada. My God, I've been trying to get Johnny in my bed since the first night I saw the handsome devil some four, five years ago."

The others concurred, all in awed agreement that she, Nevada Marie Hamilton, was to the best of their knowledge the only *Gambler* gal who had ever spent a night with Johnny Roulette.

"Was he as good as he looks?" Belle asked.

"Is he highly passionate?" quizzed Julia.

"Is he as pretty without his clothes as he is in them?" Betsy asked, then went into peals of laughter.

Nevada's only replies to their embarrassingly candid questions were knowing smiles and the lowering of her dark lashes, until Lilly asked the one question that demanded an answer. "Will Johnny be coming back to see you?"

Desperately needing to retain some small trace of her bruised pride, Nevada did the only thing she could do. She lied to Lilly.

"Johnny Roulette is mad about me," Nevada heard herself saying with cool assurance. "Of course he's coming back. I'm expecting him tonight."

They didn't believe her for a minute.

His dark face set in rigid lines of pain and self-loathing, Johnny squinted angrily in the glaring afternoon sunshine. Stone-cold sober now, he walked hurriedly from the levee, his destination firmly in mind.

Hands shoved deep into the pockets of his black trousers, he walked briskly, though every time his heels struck the wooden wharf, pain exploded behind his hooded eyes. With his soiled white shirt open at the throat and his disheveled dark hair falling onto his furrowed forehead and his face badly in need of a shave, Johnny looked sullen and dangerous.

Dock workers scattered to get out of his way, sensing that the big gambler who was generally so friendly and good-natured was in no mood to be messed with. Everyone gave him a wide berth.

Back on the city sidewalks, Johnny intended to go at once to see a dentist. If he had done so yesterday, he reflected miserably, he wouldn't be the world's biggest heel today.

Far too stubborn to return to the Plantation House to ask the steward for his dentist's name, Johnny walked the streets for several blocks until he saw, painted in gold letters on a wide window of frosted glass: J. T. McClanahan, Dentist. Painless and affordable.

Johnny stood before the dentist's closed door. The old pervasive fear returned and the shiny perspiration on his face quickly dried. He felt like a scared little boy and considered turning to leave. Then he reminded himself that little boys didn't do what he had done last night.

Johnny barged in the door, startling the dozing dentist. The small man sputtered and blinked and jumped up out of the patient's chair.

"Yes? Is there something I can do for you, sir?" he asked, unconsciously backing away from the big, fierce-looking man backlit by the sun.

Johnny stuck a forefinger into his mouth, pointed out the throbbing wisdom tooth, and said, "Pull it!"

"Well, yes, certainly, ah . . . sit right down and I'll have a look," said the dentist. Johnny slid into the chair while the dentist washed his hands. Then the little man, who smelled of peppermint, poked, probed, shook his balding head, and finally told Johnny, "You're right, son. That tooth's got to come out. I'll just bring down a bottle of whiskey so . . ."

"No liquor, doc," said Johnny, shaking his head.

"But it will hurt like the devil," protested the dentist.

"I deserve it" was Johnny's reply.

Pale and shaken, Johnny stumbled back out onto the street a few minutes later, the offending tooth having been extracted.

After a bath and a shave in his Plantation House suite, he was beginning to feel better. And to quit blaming himself for Nevada Hamilton.

Dressing in the afternoon dimness of his heavily draped hotel bedroom, Johnny pulled on a cool summer suit jacket of tan linen, reasoning that what had happened was as much Nevada's fault as his. Didn't she know that the girls entertaining on the *Gambler* made most of their money in the bedrooms, not onstage? Sure, she did! The hell with her. She'd gone into it with her eyes wide open. He just happened to be the unlucky cuss who was her first.

Pushing her out of his thoughts, Johnny went in search of a game. The Silver Slipper, a small, classy joint built on stilts at the river's edge, was one of his favorite places for afternoon action. The Slipper was filled to capacity with well-heeled gentlemen who, like himself, enjoyed wagering on the turn of a card, the throw of the dice.

Johnny, grinning, relaxing at last, sat down at a faro table. He was not lucky. He dropped two thousand before leaving the Slipper. It was the same story at the Four Queens. Johnny couldn't win at cards, couldn't win at craps.

His luck was lousy. He had the superstitious hunch that if tiny dark-haired Nevada Hamilton was at his elbow, luck would turn his way. He continued to buck the tables. And to lose. And although he had shaken off the foolish

idea several times throughout the losing afternoon, when
night fell Johnny found himself standing on the levee before the party boat, *Moonlight Gambler.*

He climbed the long companionway, headed at once for
the gaming room, and was stopped by the swarthy slender
maitre d' at the door.

"Mr. Roulette, you can't go in. You're not dressed for
evening and . . ."

Johnny, hearing an unmistakably sweet feminine voice
coming from inside, replied, "Sorry, Franco, I left something inside last night. I've come back to claim it. Won't
take but a minute." And he breezed right past and into the
smoke-filled gaming palace.

There she was. Onstage, singing about "Johnny doing
her wrong" and looking like she was forty years old.
Johnny Roulette swallowed hard and raked a brown long-
fingered hand through his hair. God, she had aged! It was
the eyes, those deep blue eyes that had flashed so excitedly
only last night. Now they looked sad, hurt. Old. Maybe
she was dreading what was before her, after she left the
stage.

Johnny started moving toward the stage. At the same
time he let his black eyes do a slow, deliberate sweep
around the room at the patrons. Whose bed would she
warm tonight? Tables of drooling, excited red-faced men
were looking up at the pale fragile girl as though she were
something good to eat and they could hardly wait for their
first greedy taste.

Heroes, her good luck had sent her!

Johnny swore under his breath, "Well, she's my Lady
Luck and they can't have her!"

And not waiting until her number was finished, he
strode determinedly down to the stage and plucked the

shocked Nevada from it in midsong. Before he could turn around, Stryker was upon them like a charging bull.

Stryker's powerful arms enclosed both Johnny and Nevada and he shouted above the pandemonium that had broken out, "Put her down, Roulette, or I'll squeeze the life out of you where you stand."

"No!" Nevada screamed to be heard. "Stryker, please don't hurt Johnny!"

Never loosening his hold, Stryker said to Johnny, "You're not taking this girl back upstairs, Roulette."

Johnny said, "No, I'm not. I'm taking her out of here for good. Off the *Gambler*. Tell Pops she's my good-luck charm and she's coming with me." Stryker's bulging arms relaxed their punishing death grip. Johnny turned to face the overly protective bouncer. "You tell me, Stryker. Is she better off here?" He inclined his dark head, indicating the loud, hungered throng surrounding them. "Or with me?"

Stryker said, "Take her, Roulette. She's got no business on this tub. But you treat her right or I'll kill you. Now, go."

While dozens of puzzled, disappointed men shouted and booed and whistled, Johnny quickly picked Nevada up and tossed her over his shoulder.

"You're coming with me whether you like it or not," he told her as he carried her through the angry, shouting crowd.

Overjoyed, wanting nothing more in the whole wide world than to go anywhere with Johnny Roulette, Nevada said happily, "Oh, Johnny, you came back for me! You do love me, Johnny, you do!"

9

~~~~~~~

"No, Nevada," Johnny told her firmly when he had carried her from the smoke-filled gaming room, outside onto the *Moonlight Gambler*'s deck, and down the companionway to the wooden wharf. Setting her on her feet, he stood looking down into her expectant, upturned face. "I don't love you. I'm never going to love you. Get that through your head right now." She started to interrupt. He stopped her. "But you're my lucky charm—I need you. And it's evident you need me as well."

Nevada blinked at him in confusion when he took her arm and guided her across the levee, lecturing her sternly. "You have no business entertaining on the *Gambler*, Nevada. It's time you aspired to something higher and I am going to help you."

Almost running to keep up with his long, sure strides, Nevada clutched at her skirts, looking up at his dark, handsome face with questioning eyes. "How? What?"

They had reached the levee's edge. Johnny handed Nevada in front of him up onto the steep wooden steps that led to the Memphis city streets. He said, "I'll make you into a genteel, cultured lady so that you can one day meet and marry a fine gentleman."

Nevada stopped abruptly, whirled about, almost bumping into him. He stood on the steps just below. Hands going to her hips, she said, "Hellfire, I don't want no fine gentleman. I just want you!"

"Nevada, you can't have me, so stop talking nonsense. And stop cursing. And get on up the steps, we're going over to the Silver Slipper."

She frowned at him. "You'll teach me to be a lady at the Silver Slipper?"

Johnny frowned back at her. "No. I'll find out if you're really my lucky charm. You'll learn to be a lady in London."

"You're taking me to London with you?" Her eyes began to sparkle and she smiled again.

"That's up to you," Johnny said, turning her around again and pushing her up the steps. "Bring me luck, I'll take you to London."

"I'll bring you luck, Johnny Roulette," Nevada assured him over her shoulder, thinking that nothing could be more wonderful than a romantic ocean voyage. Just the two of them. Johnny Roulette and her. Alone together on the high seas. Making love in an opulent stateroom as they had on the *Gambler*. By the time they reached England, Johnny would realize he loved her as much as she loved him.

Those pleasant thoughts were running through Nevada's head when Johnny ushered her along the cobblestones of the steeply sloping Memphis waterfront and into the plush gambling casino called the Silver Slipper on Front Street. Perched on tall, sturdy pilings at the river's edge, the Silver Slipper, Nevada noted with breathless curiosity, had silver-painted walls and ceilings and a small stage where silver curtains were parted to reveal a silver stage upon which a tall beauty with silver hair and a shimmering silver dress and high-heeled silver slippers stood beside a gilt piano singing "Silver Threads Among the Gold."

Nevada was all eyes.

Johnny Roulette was not. He hurriedly guided the gaping Nevada across the crowded silver-walled hall to a pair of double doors at the back of the big room. Holding her by the arm, Johnny lifted a hand and knocked.

One of the doors opened and a pallid-faced man in evening clothes smiled in recognition.

"Johnny, come in," he said, and nodding to Nevada, "Miss."

"Tell Crook I need five thousand. I'll sign a marker," said Johnny.

"At once," replied the club's manager. He turned and went immediately to speak in private with the Slipper's owner, Blair Crook. In moments Crook himself, a dapper little man with drawing-room manners and river cunning, appeared.

He looked from Johnny to Nevada, then back to Johnny. Smiling, he said, "I'd love to oblige you, Johnny" —his gaze kept straying to Nevada—"but it's really not possible. Perhaps you've forgotten the two thousand on your tab from this afternoon's losses."

"I've forgotten nothing," Johnny said.

"Really?" said Crook. "In that case you must surely understand why I can't . . ." He lifted his shoulders in a shrug. Then reaching out, he took Nevada's free hand, raised it to his lips, and brushing a kiss to it, added, "unless you can offer, in return for the five thousand, some . . . ah . . . collateral." His small gray eyes lighted as he lifted his head and looked up at Nevada.

Johnny Roulette protectively freed Nevada's hand from Crook's, put an arm around her, and drew her close. "Don't even think it," he told the small, crafty club owner. And then, one-handed, just as he had done in the silk-walled boudoir of the *Moonlight Gambler,* Johnny slipped the gleaming gold studs from his shirt front. "Here's your collateral," he said, holding the heavy studs out to Crook.

Crook chuckled softly. "Not exactly what I had in mind, Roulette." He pocketed the studs. "Five hundred on the jewelry, just as always." Then, addressing Nevada, he said, "I've had these studs in my wall safe almost as often as Johnny has worn them."

Johnny was unbothered by the insult, but the young unsophisticated girl looked the smiling club owner in the eye and told him, "Well, this will be the last occasion that you'll get them."

Charmed by her quick defense of a man he was certain didn't deserve such fierce loyalty, Crook said, "And why is that, my dear?"

"Because now Johnny Roulette has me as his lucky charm." She lifted her chin. "He'll have the studs back within the hour. And the five thousand you refused him as well."

"Indeed?" Crook glanced up at Johnny. "The lady seems quite certain. A side bet, Roulette?"

"Sure! Why not?" said Nevada before Johnny had time to reply.

"Forget it, Crook," Johnny said, wrapping his long brown fingers around the back of Nevada's neck. He turned her about and escorted her toward a dice table. "Don't," he cautioned her, "ever do that again."

"Do what?"

"Speak for me about anything. Do you know what kind of side bet Crook was speaking of?"

"I suppose he wants—"

"You."

"Me?"

"You. And I don't mean he wants you to sing on the Slipper's stage."

"He thinks that I would . . ." Her words trailed away.

"Jesus, you've got a lot to learn," said Johnny, shaking his head in annoyance. He commandingly guided her up to the table. A croupier handed him the dice and Johnny's mood sweetened immediately. Smiling down at Nevada, he maneuvered her into position, saying, "I want you to stand at my right side, sweetheart."

"Johnny, you're superstitious," she accused.

"No I'm not," he said, grinning. "It's bad luck to be superstitious."

She laughed and so did he. Then he said, "Sweetheart, you just do the same thing you did for me last night, all right?"

Nevada took the dice from Johnny's upturned palm, nodded, and said, "I will, Johnny. You know I will."

And she did.

Nevada rolled a seven. Then an eleven. Then another seven. And Johnny, confident she'd bring him luck, let the five hundred Crook had advanced on the gold studs ride on the pass line. His stack of chips grew taller and taller as Nevada made point after point. Totally relaxed and impervious to the looks of disdain his beige linen daytime suit and the open white shirt were drawing from the evening-clad patrons, Johnny complimented and encouraged and laughed and gave Nevada's small waist affectionate squeezes.

And when exactly forty-eight minutes after she had picked up the dice, Nevada finally sevened out, Johnny Roulette, tens of thousands of dollars up, impulsively wrapped his little Lady Luck in his long arms, kissed the top of her head, and said, "Sweetheart, you're the greatest. Let's get my gold studs out of hock and go to the Plantation House."

Her flushed face pressed against Johnny's open shirt

front. Beneath her hot cheek, Nevada felt smooth warm flesh and crisp hair and a steady rhythmic heartbeat. And she remembered exactly how it felt to have that broad hot chest pressed to her bare breasts.

"Yes. Let's go to the hotel," she murmured.

In moments the pair walked into the lobby of the Plantation House and Johnny Roulette smiled broadly when his old friend Ben Robin, the hotel's owner, approached them from the back dining room.

"Ben," said Johnny, "meet Miss Nevada Hamilton, my personal lucky charm."

Ben Robin looked at Nevada with a mixture of curiosity and disbelief. Ben knew Johnny well. And never had he known his friend and fellow gambler to bring a woman of Nevada's kind back to his hotel suite. He thought her pretty in a tawdry way, but the satin gown she wore and the painted face proclaimed what she was, even before she spoke.

"Miss Hamilton," said Ben, bowing, "welcome to the Plantation House." He glanced at Johnny, then directed his attention back to her. "You wish to dine?" His smile was warm. "We've a splendid menu and the chef's—"

"We'll have something sent up if Nevada has an appetite," Johnny interrupted. "She's a little tired and so am I."

"Oh," Ben said, understanding written clearly in his eyes. "Yes, yes, of course. May you rest well, then, Miss Hamilton."

"Thank you, I will," said Nevada, knowing she and Johnny would rest little, but uncaring.

"Good night, John." Ben looked at him.

Johnny threw back his dark head and laughed. He knew exactly what his old friend was thinking. Well, let him think it.

"Meet us for breakfast, Ben. Around eleven," Johnny

added carelessly, then took Nevada's hand and led her across the deeply carpeted lobby.

Ben Robin shook his blond head, turned, and went toward his office wondering what Johnny's river doll would look like without all that paint.

"Wait," said Johnny when Nevada lifted her blue satin skirts to climb the stairs. "I need to reserve you a suite."

She gave him a questioning look. "Why?"

He ignored the question and Nevada assumed that he felt he had to engage an adjoining room for appearance's sake. When he spoke with the tall hotel clerk briefly, then returned to inform her he had taken quarters that connected with his suite, she smiled knowingly.

When they got upstairs and Johnny ushered her into his sitting room, Nevada sighed happily and turned to face him, expecting him to take her in his arms at once.

"Are you hungry?" he asked.

"No. Not a bit," she said, wanting only to be held by him.

He stepped past her, pointed to a closed door across the dimly lit suite. "That's your room. I'm sorry you have no night clothes. You'll have to sleep in your . . ."—he gestured with one lean brown hand—"in whatever you're wearing under that dress. Tomorrow we'll go shopping." Yawning, he shrugged out of the beige linen suit jacket.

She stared at him. "Johnny?"

"Hm?"

She stepped closer, put her hands on his shirtfront. "Aren't we going to sleep in the same room?"

"Most assuredly not." Johnny moved back a step and began again slipping the gold studs out of the buttonholes of his white shirt.

That done, she watched him jerk the long shirttails free

of his tight beige trousers. She said, "Let's make love in your bed and then—"

His hands stilled. "Dammit, girl, we are not going to make love. Not now. Not ever."

"But why ever not? Last night we—"

"I told you, last night I was drunk. That was a mistake. It won't happen again."

"But, Johnny—"

"Go to bed, Nevada. Get some rest. We leave Memphis tomorrow."

She sighed but nodded. "Will you please help me with the hooks, I can't . . ." She reached behind her.

"Sure," said Johnny and stepped around her. Nevada was struck by the deftness with which his gambler's nimble fingers made quick work of the tiny hooks holding her dress in place. As for Johnny, he was struck—once again —by the beauty of her slender curving back, totally bare beneath the evening gown.

"Don't you wear underthings?" he said, a hard edge to his voice.

"Just underpants," she told him, turning her head to look back over her shoulder. "I couldn't wear anything else with this dress—it's too damned low."

"Yes, well, go on to bed. We'll buy new clothes for you. Decent clothes."

Nevada turned to face him, holding the opened gown up. "I thought you liked this dress. It's the same one I wore last night when you said—"

"Forget the things I said last night, will you!" He sounded angry but his dark, dark eyes lowered to the bare swell of her bosom as the loosened gown's bodice slipped dangerously low. For a split second a heated expression came into his eyes. It was gone at once and he said irritably, "And now good night, Nevada."

"Good night, Johnny," she said, and backed away from him.

In the big ivory bedroom that was hers, Nevada wriggled out of the borrowed blue satin gown, took off her shoes and stockings, and climbed onto the double bed. She turned out the gaslight lamp on the night table and stretched out on her back, raising her arms above her head.

The tall windows were thrown open to the Tennessee summer night. A steamer's whistle sounded in the distance. A cooling breeze off the river ruffled the gauzy curtains and lifted wisps of her dark hair around her face.

Nevada lay there in the moonlight, wishing, hoping, praying that Johnny Roulette would quietly open the door, silently cross the room, strip away her satin drawers, and make sweet, hot love to her while the river breezes tickled and teased their bare bodies.

Nevada never knew how close she came to getting her wish.

In his own bedroom across the sitting room from hers, Johnny Roulette, his lean brown body totally naked, lay stretched out in the moonlight, smoking a cigar. And considering going back on his word.

Despite the pleasant, cooling breezes from the river, the blood in his veins was hot. His body, responding to the remembered sight and smell and feel of the naked Nevada when he'd made love to her last night, grew rigid with desire.

He ached to experience again the sweet satisfaction she had given him and would willingly give him again.

Johnny Roulette stubbed out his smoked-down cigar, then swung his long legs over the edge of the bed.

Why the hell not? What was he trying for? Sainthood, for chrissakes? After all, he was going to be paying for her keep, so he might as well get something for his money.

What difference would it make if he slept with her now and then? He'd enjoy it and so would she.

Johnny left his bedroom. Tense and naked he crossed the darkened sitting room, anticipation growing with his arousal. He stood before her closed door, lifted a hand, and knocked softly. "Nevada, honey?"

"Yes, Johnny?" came that sweet girlish voice and he knew he couldn't do it.

Johnny ground his teeth. " 'Night, sweetheart," he said through the closed door. "Sleep well."

"You too, Johnny."

"I will," he said, and turned away muttering oaths under his breath.

10

━━━━━━━━━━━━━━◊◊◊◊◊◊◊━━━━━━━━━━━━━━

So tall, so dark, so handsome, his beautiful white teeth flashing beneath his rakish mustache, Johnny Roulette stood at the railing of the river steamer *Memphis Maiden*. Bright noonday sunlight glinted in his midnight-black hair, warmed his smiling olive face, and reflected in his dark flashing eyes.

Nevada, having just stepped from her cabin and onto the *Memphis Maiden*'s polished decks, caught her breath and stared at him. Merely looking at Johnny caused a sweet longing to stir inside her, and Nevada fleetingly wondered at the wisdom of an Almighty who had seen fit to bring such a compelling man into her life but had not made him love her.

Well, she would simply have to manage where God had failed. No one, not even Johnny, could convince her that a man could make love to her the way he had aboard the *Gambler* and not care a little. Not want her again. All she had to do was make him realize it.

Her gaze still fastened on the big broad-shouldered man attired in a crisp summer suit of dove-gray, Nevada felt a shiver of excitement race up her spine. Here she was, Nevada Marie Hamilton, wearing a beautiful new yellow organdy dress that Johnny had bought for her. She was trav-

eling downriver with him. And soon she would be crossing
the ocean with him. Seeing the sights of London with him.

Nevada drew a deep, slow breath and smiled, recalling
the way her day had begun. When the warm summer sun
had streamed into her Plantation House windows and
shone right through her closed eyelids to waken her, she
had heard a firm knock on the door. Unsure where she
was, she had turned her head slowly and then Johnny's
deep voice had called to her.

"Nevada, I've ordered our breakfast. I'm handing one of
my shirts in for you to wear. Come get it."

The door opened a crack and a brown hand holding a
snowy white shirt was thrust inside.

"Coming, Johnny," Nevada said, and bounded from the
bed. Wearing only her satin drawers, she hurriedly crossed
the room, took the offered shirt, and slid her arms into the
long sleeves. She lifted her hands to button the shirt. And
realized there were no buttons. Shrugging narrow shoulders, she pushed her sleep-tumbled hair back off her face,
clutched the shirt together over her breasts, and went into
the sitting room to join Johnny.

His back to her, he was shirtless. He stood at a linen-
draped table pouring coffee from a silver pot into two
china cups. Sleek muscles pulled and bunched beneath the
smooth dark skin as he lifted his muscular right arm, and
Nevada had the almost overpowering urge to walk up behind him, open the borrowed white shirt she wore, and
press her bare breasts against that long, beautiful, deeply
clefted olive back.

"Johnny," she said softly.

"Good morning," he said, and smiling easily, turned to
face her, a cup of coffee in his hand.

"Your shirt has no buttons," she said.

Johnny's smile slipped slightly when he saw her standing there in the morning sunshine holding his shirt together. She looked like a helpless child, with her mane of dark hair all tangled and falling into her face and his white shirt reaching almost to her knees and her tiny feet bare. And those big blue eyes looking at him, awaiting direction.

He had the uneasy feeling that she was going to be more trouble to him than if she were a child. It wasn't too late. Maybe he should split the money they had won at the Silver Slipper and send her on her way. He didn't need the aggravation.

Johnny blinked when, as though she had read his mind, Nevada said, "Where shall we gamble tonight, Johnny? I know we can win more money."

A dark eyebrow lifted and Johnny grinned. Setting the cup back on the table, he said, "On board the *Memphis Maiden*. We'll leave this afternoon for Baton Rouge." He crossed to the tall mahogany chest of drawers and picked up a couple of his gold studs. "Come here, Nevada."

She came to him at once and when he told her to release her hold on the shirt, she automatically obeyed. And was certain she noted a brief flare of fire in his dark eyes when the shirt fell partially open over her bare breasts. Her own eyes flared when Johnny's brown hands pulled the shirt back together and he went about pushing his gold studs through the buttonholes. His fingers barely grazed her flesh, but she felt their warmth all the way to her bare, curling toes.

Too soon the pair of gold studs were in place and Johnny was turning back toward the table.

"Let's eat before our breakfast gets cold. Then we'll go down to Monaco's and see about some clothes for you." He held out a tall-backed chair of rich green brocade.

"You're taking me to Monaco's?" Nevada asked, sliding

into the chair he held for her. "That's the most elegant ladies' shop in Memphis."

"So they tell me," Johnny said, as he circled the table and took his own chair. Taking a drink of black coffee, he added, "I want you to look your best when we get to Baton Rouge."

"Why are we going down there?"

"Never mind that now. We have to hurry." He picked up a heavy sterling fork and knife.

Nevada followed suit. She ladled two spoonfuls of sugar into her coffee, then poured in enough thick rich cream to turn the brew a light blond color. Jerking up her fork, she lifted a heaping forkful of scrambled eggs to her mouth, chewed eagerly, and took another bite. With her fingers she lifted a piece of crisp bacon and bit it in half. She reached for a hot biscuit, tore it in two, dunked it in her coffee and lifted it, dripping, up to her open mouth.

Sighing with satisfaction, she thoughtlessly drew her bare legs up and repositioned herself so that she was seated cross-legged on the armless green chair. So engrossed was she with the meal, she didn't realize that Johnny was not eating. He was watching her. Staring at her. Frowning.

Finally, her mouth full, Nevada lifted her eyes to his and saw that he was scowling at her. She chewed hurriedly and swallowed.

"What's wrong, Johnny?"

He didn't mince words. "Nevada, I've known field hands with better table manners than you."

Taken aback, Nevada, staring at him, said, "You have?"

He shook his head. "Put your feet on the floor where they belong. Take bites half the size you've been taking. Keep your biscuit out of your coffee. And stop picking up your bacon with your fingers." He paused, then added, "That is, if you ever have any hopes of resembling a lady."

At first Nevada was stunned. She sat there for a long minute, silent, badly stung by his insensitive reprimand. Her feelings hurt, she felt as if she might cry. Nobody had ever talked to her like that in her entire life. Nobody. Worst of all, Johnny didn't even care that he had hurt her feelings. He was continuing to eat his breakfast, unconcerned. Nevada felt her temper rising.

As Johnny poured his second cup of coffee from the silver pot, Nevada abruptly threw her fork down. She stood up, hands going to her hips, and said, "Just who do you think you are that you can talk to me like that?" Her blue eyes flashed fire at him.

Calmly, Johnny said, "I'm your guardian, your friend." He gestured, pointing to her chair. "Now, sit back down and finish your breakfast."

"Oh, I'll finish my breakfast all right," she said, and before he could stop her Nevada reached out, grabbed the white table cloth, and snatched it right off the table. The food, china, and cutlery went flying. Johnny Roulette shot to his feet, a look of astonishment on his face, bits of scrambled egg clinging to his chest hair.

Nevada hiked up the shirt and sat down cross-legged on the floor amid the scattered mess. From a broken china plate she grabbed a large bite of ham and looked about until she spotted half a blueberry muffin. She reached for it, then shoved both the ham and the muffin into her mouth at the same time. Her cheeks puffing out, she chewed, swallowed, and glared at Johnny, unfazed by the mean expression in his black eyes.

"This is the way field hands eat!" she informed him. "Only usually it's right off the ground and out in the hot sun. But then you wouldn't know about things like that, because you've never done an honest day's work in your life!"

Johnny started toward her and Nevada had to steel herself to keep from flinching. She dropped the ham and muffin and rose to meet him. Violently kicking the scattered dishes aside, Johnny reached her. Nevada blinked but fearlessly met his narrowed gaze.

Johnny's hand shot out like a striking serpent. He took hold of her wrist and jerked her to him with such sudden brute force, her head rocked on her shoulders.

He said coldly, "If you ever do a thing like that again, I'll blister your butt until you can't sit down."

She laughed in his angry face. "You think I'm afraid of you?"

"No, you haven't enough sense to be afraid."

Her jaw jutting, she clawed at the punishing fingers encircling her wrist. "Let me go!" she ordered.

"Not quite yet. You've not finished your breakfast."

Nevada eyed him warily. "If you think you're going to make me eat that mess on the floor, you're mighty wrong."

"Why, no," Johnny said, his full lips beneath his mustache beginning to stretch into a hint of a smile. "That's not what I had in mind at all."

"What then?"

His black eyes softened, then gleamed mischievously. "You've had your ham and your muffin." He jerked her closer to him. "Time now for your scrambled eggs."

Her face on the level with his broad, bare chest, she saw the bits of cold egg matted in his crisp chest hair and made a sour face. Her eyes lifted back to his. "You don't actually expect me to . . ."

"I should. But I won't."

Nevada sighed with relief.

"But you have exactly one minute to clean it off me. The method you choose is of no interest to me. Pluck it off.

Wash it off." His fingers tightened threatening. "Or lick it off."

Nevada started to protest but immediately changed her mind and smiled sweetly. "Why, sure, Johnny. I'll be happy to." And she lifted her free hand, grabbed a bit of egg, all tangled up in curly black hair, and yanked as hard as she could.

"Owwwww," Johnny yelped in pain and automatically released her wrist to raise his hand to his smarting chest.

Nevada whirled away from him, dashed madly for her room, and when she was safely on the other side of the door, she shouted through it, "My daddy might not have been no fine gentleman, but he never came to the table shirtless!"

"Yes? Well, you won't be coming to the table at all after that little show of defiance!" came his heated reply. "You'll have nothing to wear."

"Oh, damn," Nevada muttered to herself. She'd completely forgotten that Johnny had promised to take her shopping this morning. Now he wouldn't.

Hellfire, would she never learn to keep her big mouth shut?

"Nevada, you must learn to express yourself occasionally," Johnny teased later that morning as he sat on a plum-hued velvet *causeuse* in a private salon at Monaco's, the most exclusive ladies' shop in Memphis. By nature an easy-going man, Johnny had already forgiven Nevada for misbehaving at breakfast. She was, he reminded himself, a child of the river who'd not had the proper advantages.

So he smiled indulgently as Nevada tried on gown after expensive gown behind a dressing screen of peach-and-gold. She was so excited, she couldn't keep quiet.

The shop itself was something to see with its sixteenth-century Isfahan carpet covering floors of ivory Carrara marble. Gold-framed paintings lined the peach walls. Gleaming furniture from France graced the spacious downstairs entry.

A graying, matronly lady who introduced herself as Madame Nicole Jousset led Johnny and Nevada up a grand staircase, down a wide corridor, and into the private salon with the velvet couch and dressing screen and a tall gilt-framed upright mirror.

Nevada saw no clothes anywhere. She gave Johnny a questioning look. He grinned and sat down on the sofa, plucking at the sharp creases in his gray trousers and stretching his long legs out before him. Not knowing what else to do, Nevada quickly sat beside him. At once the matronly Nicole Jousset told her to stand up. She did. Madame Jousset walked around and around her, critically appraising her small slender form, and making suggestions concerning the choices of afternoon dresses and ball gowns and intimate apparel.

When the knowledgeable couturiere had decided on several possibilities and smilingly turned to leave them, Nevada made a move to get up and follow. With a hand on her arm, Johnny stopped her.

"Wait here," he said, and seemed not the least bit surprised when a white-coated porter came quietly into the salon bearing a silver tray with refreshments. Placing the tray on a polished Chippendale side table at Johnny's elbow, he was gone by the time Madame, followed by two cheerful female assistants, returned carrying a half dozen of the most beautiful afternoon dresses Nevada had ever seen.

"Monsieur?" questioned Madame, holding up a French-made garment of soft, flouncy yellow organdy.

"Yes," said Johnny. "Let's see what it looks like on."

Beaming, Madame Jousset turned her attention to Nevada. "Mademoiselle, if you please?"

Nevada looked at Johnny. He said, "Try it on."

"Where?"

He grinned. "Behind the screen."

At first Nevada couldn't believe that Johnny actually intended to remain in the small salon while she tried on the new frock, but he did stay and she found it strangely exciting to undress behind the screen while he continued to lounge comfortably on the sofa, not twenty feet from her.

The screen, of course, shielded her body from his sight, but it reached only to her shoulders. He could look right at her and she at him as she changed. While the industrious assistants brought forth armloads of dresses and nightgowns and lace-trimmed underthings, Nevada stood behind the screen, her face flushing, talking to Johnny.

When the new yellow gown fell into place and was fastened, she swept from behind the screen to model for him, turning around and around, liking the look of approval in his eyes.

It was wonderful fun and Nevada decided then and there that being a fine lady wasn't so bad, after all. And the thought made her want to laugh. Who would have believed that fine ladies dressed and undressed right in the room with a man! It seemed to her like a naughty game.

She was glad that they did. She liked it. It was a new experience that filled her with an unfamiliar exhilaration, made her feel warm and lightheaded and vitally alive. And daringly risqué.

Nevada tried on dresses and evening gowns and robes and underwear, liking the feel of luxurious textures next to her bare flesh, which had begun to tingle pleasantly. That tingling increased dramatically when she found herself, moments later, left totally naked. Madame and her helpers were out of the room. They had gone in search of more garments, leaving her there with Johnny. And no clothes. Not even any of the lacy, silky underthings they had shown them.

She didn't know exactly how it had happened. All she knew was they had left nothing behind the screen for her to slip on. Even her trusty old blue satin gown was missing. But then she wouldn't have reached for it, had it been there.

Awakened to her innate sexuality by Johnny's experienced lovemaking, Nevada trembled and instinctively moved her bare feet apart. She drew in a shallow, excited breath and smiled seductively at the darkly handsome man looking at her.

"Johnny," she said, her voice like warm honey.

Johnny Roulette felt heat rise to his dark face. Without being told, he knew that Nevada was naked. That behind the screen, which reached barely to the tops of her shoulders, she was gloriously, provocatively, temptingly nude.

The look in her blue eyes was boldly inviting. For one so young and basically still an innocent, she was incredibly erotic. She exuded a potent, steamy sexuality that was almost palpable. And she didn't even realize it.

Or did she?

Johnny came to his feet. "Stop it, Nevada."

"Stop what?"

"Making love to me."

She blinked. "Are you crazy? How could I possibly be making love to you when you're there and I'm here."

"It's easy." He walked away. At the door he paused and looked back at her. "I don't want you ever to be naked and alone in a room with me again, Nevada."

"How can you be sure I'm naked?"

Johnny Roulette just shook his dark head and left her.

Looking at him now, standing at the white railing of the *Memphis Maiden* as the steamer made its slow, sure way downriver, Nevada wondered again how he had known that she was wearing no clothes behind that dressing screen.

And she wondered how he thought two people could make love without touching. Impossible. She didn't believe it for a minute. He was teasing her, making fun. People had to get into bed to make love; everyone knew that.

Lifting the skirts of her new yellow organdy afternoon dress, Nevada went forward to join Johnny. She wanted to find out why they would be stopping off in Baton Rouge, Louisiana.

11

She didn't like it one bit. Johnny's answer.

When Nevada had stepped up beside Johnny at the steamer's railing, she touched his forearm, smiled sunnily up at him, and asked, "Why are we stopping in Baton Rouge?"

His slow, sure answer was, "To call on Miss Annabelle Delaney and see if we can't persuade her to accompany us abroad."

"I don't like it! I don't like it one damned bit!" Nevada quickly objected, as the first twinge of jealousy she'd ever experienced in her life shot through her. "You don't need other women, Johnny. I'm woman enough for you. I am. I know I am."

Johnny roughly took hold of her arm and escorted her away from a trio of sugar planters who had turned to stare as Nevada's voice rose loudly with passion, breaking the deep stillness of the Mississippi.

Forcefully guiding her across the steamer's polished deck and up a steep flight of steps to the deserted texas deck, Johnny drew her to the ship's bow.

There he released her arm, and glaring at him, she rubbed it, letting him know he had hurt her. He was unmoved.

Gripping her slender shoulders in his big hands, Johnny

said, "I will try one more time to explain things to you and I want you to pay close attention, because I'm running short of patience. You are not my woman, Nevada. You are Lady Luck. Fortune's lodestone. And I, I'm your guardian, your mentor, your friend. I'll take care of you, watch out for you. Like an older brother would."

"How can that be? Brothers don't make love to their—"

"Holy Christ, will you stop it! Put that night behind you once and for all."

"I can't."

"You have to, dammit." Gently he shook her. "You've a wonderful life ahead of you if you'll do as I say. You're very sweet when you set your mind to it. And very beautiful. And when some of the rough edges have been polished away, you'll be sought after by any number of rich young gentlemen." His hands relaxed on her tensed shoulders, the olive thumbs lightly rubbing, coaxing, as Johnny began to smile, hoping to convince her that everything was going to be fine. "You will adore Miss Annabelle Delaney. She's a kind, gentle middle-aged spinster with impeccable manners. A true aristocrat of the Old South. Miss Annabelle will be the perfect chaperon to travel with us. A patient teacher for you."

Nevada shrugged his hands away and turned to lean on the ship's forward railing. She felt a little better, knowing that Annabelle Delaney was not in competition with her for Johnny's affections. Still, she resented the intrusion. She would have liked to have had him all to herself, but she was clever enough to realize she must change her tactics if she was to have him at all. Apparently he could love only a refined lady, so she would have to become one whether she wanted to or not.

"I'm most eager to meet Miss Delaney." She flashed him

a wide smile. "I'll be ever so grateful if she'll agree to become my teacher."

Johnny's wide shoulders relaxed visibly. "Between the two of us, I'm positive we can convince her." He slowly turned about, leaned back against the ship's railing, and said kindly, "You've told me so little about yourself, Nevada. Is there family somewhere who would—"

"No," she interrupted, her gaze sweeping out over the eddying waters to the unbroken flatness of the riverbanks. There luxuriant palmettos and towering live oaks and silvery weeping willows rose from a dense profusion of tangled undergrowth. Partridgeberry vines and grounded wild iris and jewelweed sprang from the rich soggy soil.

"Papa was all the family I had, and now he's gone."

"Your mother?" Johnny prompted.

"Died having me." Her lids slid low over cool blue eyes. "Papa brought me from Nevada when I was still a baby." Her attention was suddenly caught by the sudden flight of a snowy egret flapping its wings loudly, its long bill catching the sunlight. "I've been on this river since then. It's the only life I know. It's my home, Johnny. I love it." She paused, "I loved my papa."

Touched, Johnny said, "Sounds like you had a wonderful childhood."

"I most certainly did," she murmured, and looking back into her past, she regaled Johnny with her happy, adventurous days on the Mississippi. She talked and talked, telling him of her papa's keelboat, of the crew, of the nights she sang for them under the stars. Of her early but brief schooling in New Orleans. Of her papa's fondness for liquor and women, of the night he was knifed to death.

Johnny listened quietly, and with each childlike admission, each poignant revelation, felt his sense of protectiveness grow toward the raven-haired girl. That she was the neglected daughter of a drunken riverman was evident. That she was not responsible for her fate was just as apparent. That she had no idea anyone would pity her was appealing.

That she most definitely needed someone to watch over her was glaringly obvious.

Finally Nevada stopped speaking, and for a time they stood there quietly, each lost in thought. It was Nevada who broke the silence.

"Now," she said, tilting her head, smiling up at him, "you know all there is to know about me. It's your turn, Johnny. Tell me about your home and family."

His only reply was a negative shake of his handsome head and a fleeting expression that passed over his dark eyes and was gone. Then he smiled engagingly, and straightening, shoved his hands deep into the pockets of his custom-cut trousers and said, "Enough reminiscing. Hurry down to your cabin and start dressing for dinner. Wear that apricot silk with all those fancy flounces."

"Yes!" she said excitedly and promptly lifted her skirts and whirled about. "Will you help me with my hair?"

A faint smile played around the corners of his mouth. He took her elbow. "Don't be absurd."

"Papa used to brush my hair and help me pin it up."

Johnny sighed heavily. "All right, I'll try it this one time, since there's no one else to do it."

And so it was that a half hour later, Johnny, dressed in black evening clothes and white ruffled shirt, sat astride a blue velvet vanity bench in Nevada's cabin. And she, in her fancy apricot silk gown, sat on the plush carpet before him. Running the silver-backed brush slowly, gently through her long dark hair, he allowed his big left hand to follow the brush's path over the crown of her well-shaped head and down her back, where the thick tresses fell just short of her waist.

Her head thrown back, her eyes closed, Nevada said, "You're even better at this than Papa was."

"Ah, now, I doubt that," Johnny replied and kept to himself the fact he'd probably had more practice than her papa.

Johnny had known lots of women, had made love to dozens, and had lived for short periods of time with a number of them over the years. He was no stranger to a woman's bath and dressing room and he had on more than one occasion obliged a breathless lover with her bath and shampoo. His gambler's hands were every bit as dexterous with a bar of perfumed soap and a firm-bristled hairbrush as they were with a deck of glassines.

Too soon to suit Nevada, Johnny had brushed away all the tangles and had expertly pinned the heavy locks into shiny curls atop her head. She had wanted the pleasant intimacy to continue. She so enjoyed sitting curled on the richly carpeted floor between Johnny's parted knees while he pulled the brush gently, slowly through her hair and followed its descent with his warm hand.

It was a lovely simple pleasure that caused her heart to sing within the tight bodice of her new apricot gown, and she smiled dreamily as Johnny spoke of inconsequential things, his voice deep, low.

The summer sun was setting behind the tall pines on the river's eastern edge and the light streaming in the open portholes was a warm, suffused copper. The harsh croaking voices of the roseate spoonbills had already begun as night fell on the river.

All heads turned when the handsome pair entered the *Memphis Maiden*'s gaslit dining room moments later. Nevada, naive though she was, didn't miss the fact that a half-dozen women were looking at Johnny with interest. She gave a willowy blonde in a daring white dress a scathing look, tightened her hold on Johnny's bent arm, and hoped to high heaven he hadn't noticed the forward woman.

He had.

After they had been seated at a table for two against the satinwood paneling beneath a flickering wall sconce of burnished brass, Johnny let his dark eyes move around the room, then allowed them to settle on the woman in the white gown. Stroking his mustache, he smiled almost imperceptibly and nodded his dark head in silent acknowledgment. And Nevada almost choked on the crawfish bisque when, midway through the meal, Johnny, effortlessly catching the attention of a waiter, said quietly into the uniformed man's ear as he bent close, "Send a bottle of your finest Lafite to the lady whose table is beside the far potted palm. And give her this message." Johnny whispered something behind his hand that Nevada couldn't hear.

The waiter looked in the blonde's direction. "Ah, the lovely Mrs. Harrison. Right away, sir."

"Why on earth are you sending champagne to a married woman?" Nevada hotly demanded. "What will her husband think?"

Smiling lazily at the blonde, Johnny reluctantly turned his attention back to the girl across from him. "Eat your dinner, Nevada. I'm eager to get to the card parlor."

"Will I go with you to the card parlor?"

He grinned, wiped his full mouth on a damask napkin, and reached for a cigar. "Certainly. You're my Lady Luck."

She brightened. And pointedly turned her head and gave the blond Mrs. Harrison a smug, triumphant smile.

In the smoky card salon on the steamer's hurricane deck, Nevada promptly noticed that she was the only female. So did the gentlemen gamblers. Some sports cast admiring looks at her, others were openly annoyed. Johnny didn't seem to care, so Nevada didn't either.

Before Johnny took a seat at a table with four serious players ready for high-stakes poker, he pulled a chair up for her, just to the right of his, and sat her down. And Nevada felt heady with power when, settling himself on her left, he leaned to her, took one of her hands, kissed its palm, and placed it atop his right shoulder.

He whispered close to her ear, "Sweetheart, be a good girl and sit here quietly beside me. Keep your hand on my shoulder for luck, and I'll win us some money."

She did and he did.

When they left the card parlor three and a half hours later, Johnny had seven thousand five hundred dollars in cash and banknotes stuffed into the inside breast pocket of his black evening jacket, and Nevada was gloriously proud because he credited her with his win.

The moon had risen over the river and the humid, heavy air had cooled. It was a lovely romantic night and Nevada, after hours of sitting at Johnny's side, looked forward to a leisurely stroll around the ship's decks.

But Johnny took a gold-cased watch from his pocket, flipped it open, and said, "Bedtime, Nevada."

"No! It couldn't be. What time is it?"

"Almost eleven."

"That's early! Good Lord, I haven't gone to bed before midnight since I was ten years old." She smiled and took his arm. "Let's walk in the moonlight and listen to the sounds of the river."

"Not tonight," he said. And he took her straight to her

cabin and left her there, barely taking the time to say good night.

Inside her quarters, Nevada frowned with displeasure. And noted that when Johnny left he didn't enter his own cabin next door to hers. He walked off in the other direction. Curious, Nevada went at once to the porthole and peered out. She was still there when almost an hour later she heard Johnny's unmistakable laughter. Squinting out into the night, she saw him.

He stepped up to the railing thirty yards from where she stood at the porthole, the moonlight glittering on his jet-black hair and shadowing half of his dark face. And he was not alone.

A tall, slender woman with silvery hair and a white shimmering dress draping slender curves was with him. She came to stand before him, looking up into his eyes. She put her hands on his white shirtfront and her tinkling laughter carried on the quiet night air.

Nevada's mouth fell open with shock and anger and envy when one of Johnny's arms slid around Mrs. Harrison's slim waist and he pulled her to him. He lifted her chin with his thumb and forefinger and bent to her.

Johnny kissed Mrs. Harrison and she molded herself to him, wrapping her bare arms around his neck to pull his dark head down. It was a long, slow, smoldering kiss that left the jealous observer trembling with emotion.

Eyes riveted on the embracing pair, Nevada thought she might be ill when one of Johnny's lean dark hands slowly slid up from Mrs. Harrison's slim waist to the undercurve of her breast. His long fingers cupped and caressed the woman's satin-draped bosom, and Nevada's own breasts ached and her nipples tingled with sensation as though Johnny's hand were touching her.

The couple left the railing and, to Nevada's horror, they

headed in her direction. Not daring to breathe, she moved away from the porthole as they passed within a foot of where she was standing, her back pressed to the wall. And her pounding heart froze in her chest when she heard the cabin door next to her own open.

Johnny's cabin.

They went inside together. The door to Johnny's stateroom closed behind them. Nevada strained to hear. She quietly stole across her darkened cabin to the satinwood door that connected the two staterooms. Angry, confused, jealous, she slowly, carefully put her hand over the silver doorknob, gripping it with shaking fingers. It wouldn't turn.

The door that had been open all afternoon was now firmly locked.

No! Nevada's tortured brain screamed. *No, no, no!*

Then she heard Johnny's voice murmuring words that she couldn't quite make out, followed by high feminine laughter that filled her with loathing. It was a tinkling sound of undiluted joy, as though Johnny had said—or done—something that thoroughly delighted the sophisticated Mrs. Harrison.

Johnny's deep male murmurings continued. So did Mrs. Harrison's delighted feminine laughter. So did Nevada's almost unbearable agony at hearing the pair. She felt as if she would surely scream at the top of her lungs if that damnable giddy laughter didn't stop at once!

And found when the laughter finally stopped that she wished with all her heart it would start again. Far, far worse than the sound of Mrs. Harrison's laughter was the rustle of clothing, the gentle sighs, the breathless voice murmuring, "Johnny, Johnny."

12

─────────── ⌇⌇⌇⌇⌇⌇ ───────────

Her home for the past twelve years had been a small, sparsely furnished gatehouse. The drafty dwelling was at the front edge of a large river plantation below Baton Rouge, Louisiana, where she had been born on a frosty morning in the winter of 1826.

When alone inside the once-deserted gatehouse Miss Annabelle Delaney managed to preserve for herself the world of her southern upbringing. Genteel, placid, romantic, sentimental.

While whistles of river steamers sounded on the waterway below and robins nested in the lower bowers of the ancient oaks surrounding the steep-roofed house, Miss Annabelle rose each morning before dawn. She went about watering the iris in the window boxes and polishing the scarred cherrywood table that had once graced the main house. And very gingerly dusting the matching pair of English porcelain vases that had been brought back from her father and mother's London honeymoon.

If there were any possessions on this earth that meant everything to their nostalgic owner, they were those delicate, expensive, irreplaceable vases. Simply to touch their smooth perfection caused Miss Annabelle's thin mouth to lift in a smile of pleasure.

While she worked each early morning Miss Annabelle

hummed softly to herself, as though she had no more cares than when she'd been a happy young girl and lived in splendid ease in the big white mansion on the bluffs.

The mansion had been owned for more than a decade now by the Morgans, a large family of wealthy northern carpetbaggers who had bought the vast estate for a fraction of its worth shortly after the war. But the palatial white structure had been built by Annabelle's grandfather upon his arrival from South Carolina in 1794, a wedding present to his fifteen-year-old bride.

One of the first of many such plantations to line the lower river, it was, and would always remain, one of the most magnificent.

Annabelle's father, Winston, had been born in the master bedroom of the mansion. Thirty years later her older brother, Thomas, was born in the same tall fourposter and two years later, so was she. The last of the Delaneys to open his eyes on his first light of day on the plantation had been her adored nephew, the fair, blond baby, Samuel Winston Delaney.

When Sam's mother had succumbed to the fever in the hot, damp summer of '51, Miss Annabelle had stepped quite naturally into the role of mother to the adorable six-year-old boy. And she had loved Sam as though she had given birth to him.

The ten years that followed were the happiest, most contented of Miss Annabelle's entire life. With fierce pride she watched Sam grow tall and strong and handsomer with each passing year. He was a pretty, slender sixteen-year-old when the War between the States broke out. Sam's father, Thomas, enlisted immediately and Sam had wanted to go with him.

Thomas ordered him to remain at home, assuring Sam and Miss Annabelle that the war wouldn't last but a few

weeks at most. Sam was to stay behind, be the man of the
house, and watch over Miss Annabelle. Sam obeyed. But
when two years had passed and Thomas Delaney had been
killed at Gettysburg and still the war raged on, Sam kissed
his aunt good-bye and bravely marched off to fight for the
Cause.

Miss Annabelle, dry-eyed and stoic, had stood on the
broad gallery and waved a lace handkerchief while her last
living relative hurried off down the oak-shaded drive, his
handsome face still beardless.

From that moment on, every visitor to ride up the drive
for a neighborly visit disappointed the woman who looked
longingly down that road for hours on end, hoping that the
next sound of horse hooves, the next clatter of carriage
wheels, the next footfalls on the mansion's wooden steps
would mean that her nephew Sam had returned.

It happened when she least expected it. It was a cold,
dreary Monday afternoon in November of '63. The rain
had started before daybreak and continued to fall into the
dark, dismal afternoon. Miss Annabelle heard voices
through a front window thrown open to the wide, protective gallery.

She turned her head and listened for only a second before leaving her upholstered chair that was pulled up close
to the fire. She hurried to throw open the heavy front door,
waving away Lucas as he came shuffling in from the back
of the big silent house. Squinting out into the rain, she saw
two bedraggled soldiers coming up the drive on foot.

Both were bareheaded. One was dark, tall, with jet-black
hair. The other, slightly shorter and thinner, was blond.
Very blond. Miss Annabelle's heart began to pound as the
pair drew nearer. Her eyes clinging solely to the slender
blond man, she began to smile as her pulse quickened with

elation. She'd know that distinctive Delaney walk anywhere.

"Sam. My Sam," she gasped, and pushing the screen
door open, she ran out onto the porch, down the steps, and
across the soggy yard. "Sam!" she shouted jubilantly.

Sam hurried to meet her, sweeping her off her feet and
whirling her around while she laughed and clung to his
neck and thought she might surely burst with happiness.
And when finally her nephew put her down, Miss Annabelle turned at once to the tall dark boy and said, "Forgive
my rudeness, Lieutenant, but I've not seen my nephew for
months. I'm Annabelle Delaney."

The soldier took her wet hand. "Ma'am, John Roulette.
I'm very pleased to meet you." Then gallantly he swept
from his wide shoulders the gray caped cloak and swirled
it around her slender frame.

Johnny laughed when Sam again swept his aunt up into
his arms and dashed madly for the house, with Miss Annabelle calling over his shoulder, "Come along, Lieutenant
Roulette! Get inside, out of this rain."

The boys—and they were boys, Sam not quite eighteen,
Johnny Roulette a tender sixteen—spent three lazy pleasant days at the Delaney mansion with Miss Annabelle, and
by the time they left she'd grown almost as fond of Johnny
Roulette as she was of her beloved nephew. Johnny came
home with Sam a couple more times during the war and
was wonderfully entertaining company, although not once
did he speak of his own home and family, and Miss Annabelle astutely surmised that the dark young man was a
stranger to love. Still, he corresponded with Miss Annabelle from the front. And when Sam was killed in the war's
waning days outside Shreveport, the last capital of the
Confederacy, it was Johnny Roulette who wrote her the
sad news.

When the war ended, Johnny immediately came down-river to call on Miss Annabelle. Thin and haggard, the tall dark man held Miss Annabelle's frail hands in his big ones and smiled down at her when she said, "Why, it's Cap'n Roulette now, is it?" And tears glistened in her eyes.

Johnny answered all Miss Annabelle's anguished questions about her lost nephew with the candor he knew she appreciated. When it was time for him to leave her, he offered her money, all that he had. She declined. She was, she reminded him, a Delaney. A Louisiana Delaney could not accept charity, not even from him.

"But please, Cap'n Roulette, keep in touch," she had requested when he reluctantly left her there alone with only a handful of faithful old servants.

"Count on it, Miss Annabelle," he said, and meant it.

Johnny had kept his word. Although it was months between his much-read letters, Miss Annabelle knew he had never forgotten her. On a half-dozen occasions through the years he had come to see her. She looked forward to his letters and occasional visits and that kept her going.

It was enough.

Enough to make her feel as though she was not entirely abandoned in a world that no longer resembled the one in which she had been reared.

Loud laughter and shouting pulled Miss Annabelle from her reveries and instinctively she shuddered slightly. The distracting cacophony meant it was nearing eight o'clock and that the Morgan children—all eight of them—would be invading her private domain for the next five hours.

Miss Annabelle was allowed to live in the gatehouse and earn her keep by tutoring Carl and Betsy Morgan's off-spring. The bargain had been struck when the big burly ex-logger and his flamboyantly dressed wife had bought the Delaney mansion directly after the war and moved in.

There had been only three Morgan children at that time. Six-year-old Frank, five-year-old Cal, and three-year-old Mary. Now there were eight, ranging in age from four-year-old Patsy to Frank, now eighteen. And not a scholar in the bunch.

Carl and Betsy Morgan insisted that their children receive an education but refused to allow Miss Annabelle to discipline the unruly bunch, so teaching them anything was next to impossible. It did no good for Miss Annabelle to try and talk with their parents about the problem. Carl Morgan, more afternoons than not, could be found sound asleep on the veranda wearing nothing but his underwear. A coarse, loud man, Carl's main interest was the bottle. He enjoyed drinking the mornings away, then sleeping through the long, still afternoons, rousing around supper-time to start drinking again.

Happy in the way only those can be who don't waste one minute pondering life and its meaning, Betsy filled her time with the supreme pleasure of shopping for, buying, and wearing new clothes. She loved bright colors and flounces and ribbons and ruffles and laces. She choose youthful, fussy frocks with low, daring bodices and skirts skintight down to her dimpled knees. Every garment she picked emphasized her enormous bosom and broad bottom, but Betsy thought she looked voluptuous, because her drunken husband told her she did. The fact that his vision was usually whiskey-clouded never entered Betsy's happy head.

No, Miss Annabelle couldn't go to either parent with her problems regarding the children. She could only do her best to instruct and instill in the youngsters the values she felt were important.

Standing at the door where she waited for the children, Miss Annabelle saw Frank and Cal nearing the cottage and she drew a long, calming breath. The boys were already as tall as their father. And like their father they were surly, rude, and vulgar.

She had ordered them to wear shirts when they came down for their lessons, but they had paid her no mind. Again this morning they were naked to the waist. As they stepped past her into the gatehouse Frank gave her a sneering smile and pointedly scratched at his hairy belly, daring her to say something.

She didn't.

In truth, Frank frightened her. So did Cal. They were headed for trouble and there was no mistake about it. She would, she mentally noted, again tell Betsy Morgan that in her opinion the two oldest boys had had enough schooling.

Johnny had no idea why Nevada was so quiet at breakfast the next morning. Or why she refused to eat. He asked if she was sick.

She shook her head.

He asked if she was angry about something.

Again she shook her head.

He asked if she had changed her mind and didn't want to go with him to Baton Rouge and then on to London.

She finally answered.

"I want to go with you, Johnny, but not if . . . if . . ."

"If what?"

Nevada's delicate jaw hardened. "Just what went on in your cabin last night with Mrs. Harrison? Answer me that!" Her blue eyes flashed fire at him. "Don't try denying it. I saw you take a man's wife into your stateroom and I think it's downright disgusting and if I were you I'd be ashamed and just what have you got to say for yourself, Mr. Johnny Roulette?"

Calmly, slowly, Johnny chewed his food, swallowed, picked up his cup, took a drink of black coffee, then patted his mouth with a napkin. Leaning forward, placing a fore-arm on the table's edge, he said, "That's it. I've had enough. Get your things together."

Fear instantly gripped Nevada's heart. "Get my . . . why . . . where are we going?"

"Not *we. You.* You're the one who's going. Back to Memphis. Back to the *Gambler,* if you like."

"No! I want to stay with you."

"That's your hard luck." His dark eyes were cold.

"I'm your good-luck charm, Johnny Roulette. You won't win without me. You'll be broke."

"Yes, well, I'd rather be broke than have to account for my every move."

"I won't do it anymore."

"You can't help yourself, Nevada."

"I can. I don't care whose wife you take to . . . I mean . . ." She caught herself; her words trailed off.

Johnny lifted his hand to idly stroke the left side of his mustache. "Mrs. Harrison is a widow. But even if she were not, I would have taken her to my stateroom if she wished to go. I've told you, Nevada, I'm not the kind of man a lady should love. I'm no gentleman."

"And I'm no lady. You said so yourself. So I am going to love you."

He said, "No, I won't allow it." He added, "Besides, we are going to make you into a fine lady and then I won't be good enough for you." Johnny pushed back his chair. "So what's it going to be? On to Baton Rouge with me and no more inquisitions? Or back to Memphis alone?"

"Baton Rouge with you."

"Fine. We should touch there by noon."

It was nearing noon and the end of another session of school at Miss Annabelle's gatehouse on the river. The

Morgan children had been more unmanageable than usual and Miss Annabelle had developed a frightful headache.

"Alex, stop that!" She dodged a spitball. "Benny, William, you boys sit back down!"

"Ma said we don't have to mind you," William shouted.

"William's right," said Frank, propping his feet on the cherrywood table and lacing his hands behind his head. "You're too bossy for a woman. No wonder you never could get a man." He laughed and Cal, seated beside him, laughed too.

Then Cal, rising, reached a big dirty hand out to the mantel where Miss Annabelle's matched porcelain vases rested. He chuckled evilly when he saw her face turn white and she drew in her breath.

"What's wrong, old maid? You afraid I might drop your fancy vase?" Cal picked the vase up and Miss Annabelle's eyes closed when he said, "Hey, kids, catch!" He tossed the vase in the general direction of ten-year-old Alex, who had started toward the front door. Alex put out his hands but missed. The vase struck the floor and shattered on the worn carpet.

"Dear me, no!" Miss Annabelle said, and hurried forward, falling to her knees to gather up the shards of china.

Frank motioned to Cal to hand him the broken vase's mate. Cal, sure his brother meant to break it, nodded eagerly and placed the vase in Frank's big hand. Frank swung his long legs down from the table and stood up. He crossed the room to where the distraught Miss Annabelle was on her hands and knees.

He stopped right in front of her. His shadow fell across her face. Slowly she lifted her head to look up at him. He stood, his feet apart, grinning down at her, the vase gripped in his right hand.

"No," she said softly, shaking her graying head, her eyes imploring him not to do it.

"No, what, teacher?"

"Don't break it. Please, Frank."

"Break it? Why, I wouldn't do that to your precious vase," he said. "No, sireee, I wouldn't do that. Know what I *am* going to do with it, Miz Annabelle, ma'am?"

"N-no," she said, looking up at him.

All the children grew deathly quiet. Frank's free hand went to the buttons of his pants. He flipped the top one open, then the second. "I'm gonna piss right into your fine . . ."

The sentence was never finished. An expression of shock and fear came into Frank Morgan's eyes as a strong, choking arm clamped around his neck and a brown hand reached out and helped Miss Annabelle to her feet and a deep, sure voice said, "Carefully hand the vase to Miss Annabelle. Then apologize for your crudeness." The imprisoning arm slackened slightly.

"I—I . . . apologize for my crudeness, Miss Annabelle," said Frank, handing her the vase and wondering who the big man standing behind him was.

"School's dismissed," said Johnny Roulette, his expression daring any of them to make a peep.

13

Smiling, Miss Annabelle watched Johnny admiringly. He was bigger, handsomer than she had remembered, and so overwhelmingly masculine. His tanned face, with its high cheekbones and strong, finely sculptured jaw and coal-black mustache, had lost its youthful innocence. His broad-shouldered lean frame was sleek and powerful. All traces of the boyish Johnny she had known during the war were gone.

He was a mature man.

Miss Annabelle's eyes left Johnny and settled on the lovely young girl beside him. Extraordinarily beautiful, she had the blackest hair and the bluest eyes Miss Annabelle had ever seen. Dressed tastefully, her small, slender form revealed gentle feminine curves, but she was clearly still just a girl. Without the poise, the calm self-assurance, of a worldly woman.

An inexperienced girl.

As soon as the last Morgan child trooped past Johnny, his face softened and his firm mouth stretched into a wide, winning grin and he stepped forward, extending his big right hand. "Miss Annabelle, how are you, dear lady?"

Clutching the vase tightly to her breasts, she laid her trembling hand in his and felt the strong fingers close around her own.

"Wonderful, now that you are here, Cap'n Roulette."
And she closed her eyes and blushed like a young girl
when he bent and kissed her pale cheek, his thick silky
mustache tickling her pleasantly.

Wrapping a long arm around her shoulders, Johnny
pulled her close and said to the slender woman whose pale
blond hair was beginning to turn gray, "Miss Annabelle,
I've brought a friend with me." He introduced the two,
noted their immediate unspoken acceptance of each other,
and thanked the fates for small favors.

Within half an hour of their arrival Johnny was leaning
far back in his chair, his long body stretched out, smilingly
watching while the excited Miss Annabelle rushed about,
packing her meager belongings with Nevada's help.

Johnny was amazed by the rapidity with which she had
agreed to his proposal to accompany them to England as
chaperon and tutor to Nevada. When he brought up the
subject he had been quick to tell her he'd give her some
time to make up her mind.

"Miss Annabelle, you don't have to say yes this minute," he had told her. "Take a couple of days to consider
it. Right, Nevada?"

"I need no time to think it over" had been Miss Annabelle's quick response. She turned at once to Nevada,
"Dear, if you'll help me with the packing, we might be able
to catch the four-o'clock steamer to New Orleans."

"I'll help, Miss Annabelle," answered Nevada. "Just tell
me what to do." And the two women went eagerly to
work, Miss Annabelle pointing out the few things she
wanted to take.

At a quarter to four the trio stepped out into the afternoon sunshine, Johnny loaded down with Miss Annabelle's valises, one of which contained, carefully wrapped

in tissue paper, the prized porcelain vase Johnny had saved from ruin.

Earlier in the afternoon Johnny had gone alone up to the mansion to inform the Morgans that Miss Annabelle was resigning her position and leaving the estate. A sleepy, drunken, underwear-clad Carl Morgan had blinked and coughed and snorted and, finally, scratching his head, had snarled, "So that's the thanks I get for taking her in and giving her a home. Well, to hell with her. I never did like her noway with her snooty stuck-up ways and all." He picked up a half-full bottle of whiskey, took a long pull, and suddenly he was grinning, Miss Annabelle completely forgotten. He said, "Wanna join me in a little drink, son?"

The steamer's whistle gave two loud blasts as it neared the private levee and Miss Annabelle, clutching the crown of her straw hat with a gloved hand as she preceded Nevada and Johnny down the sloping riverbanks, felt the blasts go right through her heart.

Pausing, she turned about to look wistfully up at the huge old mansion high on the bluffs, gleaming white in the broiling sunshine. She trembled, feeling strangely cold despite the heat of the June day. And was amazed by the depth of understanding displayed by one so young when Nevada took her cold hand, squeezed it tightly, and said, "I know how it feels, Miss Annabelle. It hurts your heart to leave your home."

Miss Annabelle simply nodded and allowed Nevada to lead her on down to the landing. And as soon as they had boarded the *Orleans Belle* for the trip downriver, she began to feel good once more. She, Annabelle Darcy Delaney, was going abroad, something she had dreamed of doing all of her life. And she was going with two handsome young people who were gay and fun-loving and entertaining.

It would be, Miss Annabelle felt certain, a glorious trip with plenty of adventure and excitement. And she was right. When they reached New Orleans and debarked, Johnny said they would stay a while in the Crescent City until he could book passage for them on a New York–bound steamer. He took rooms at the elegant St. Louis Hotel, located right in the heart of the Vieux Carré, and when evening came they dined on steamed pompano and chilled champagne in the hotel's grand dining hall.

It was nearing ten o'clock when the sumptuous meal was finished and Miss Annabelle, worn out from travel and excitement, expressed her desire to retire.

Smiling at her across the candlelit table, Johnny said, "We'll see you up to your room. You rest well and tomorrow night we'll go to the opera, *La Traviata.*"

Nevada, not one bit tired or sleepy, was relieved to learn that Johnny had no intention of going to bed. Or of forcing her to go to bed. When Miss Annabelle was safely inside her room, Johnny, smiling and taking Nevada's bare arm, guided her outside into the sultry southern night, hailed a taxi, and instructed the black driver to take them to Pradat's.

The Canal Street gambling house was crowded with men of wealth and prominence who, Johnny told her, thought nothing of pouring a hundred thousand dollars a year across the green baize gaming tables. Johnny led Nevada through the closely pressing throng to a roulette table near the back of the opulent room.

"Have a seat, sweetheart," he said, indicating a padded tall-backed chair of supple black velvet.

Nevada eagerly took the chair between two gray-haired distinguished-looking gentlemen and giggled happily when the croupier, a thin brown-haired man with expressionless gray eyes, placed a stack of bright red checks directly in front of her.

"Johnny?" She wasn't quite sure what she was to do.

A brown hand on the back of her chair, Johnny leaned down and said near her right ear, "Nothing to it, Nevada. Just pick the number on the layout that you feel will come up on the wheel when he spins. Choose and place some chips on the number."

"How many chips?"

"As many as you like."

Nodding, Nevada looked at the thirty-six black and red numbers and the one green zero and quickly calculated that there was only one chance in thirty-seven of picking the correct number. If she placed a lot of chips on a number that did not come up, she would lose money for Johnny. On the other hand if she placed only one chip on a number and it came up, she would lose money for Johnny.

She wouldn't lose.

How could she, when she was playing roulette—a game obviously named for Johnny. Looking up over her shoulder at him, she asked him, "How old are you?"

"Twenty-eight," he said. And added evenly, "The wheel's turning, Nevada. Place a bet before it stops."

Confidently Nevada shoved every red chip before her onto the number twenty-eight, sat back, and smiled at the two graying gentlemen gamblers who turned to stare at her. Johnny, admiring her true gambling spirit, threw back his dark head and laughed.

The little white ball flew around the varnished wheel so rapidly Nevada couldn't keep up with it. She held her breath as the wheel began to slow and clapped her hands excitedly when the white ball finally clattered into the stop on number twenty-eight.

"Johnny, I won, I won!" she shouted.

"You sure did, darlin'," said the tall, laughing man standing possessively behind her. "Now show me you're really a gambler after my own heart."

"How?"

"Let it all ride."

She snapped her head around to look at him. "Damnation, that's a lot of money!" She wasn't sure how much, but there was an abundance of shiny red chips.

"Exactly nine hundred dollars," said Johnny calmly. "Let it ride."

She did and she won.

The lucky, laughing girl began to draw stern looks from the club's manager, who was nervously pacing nearby, his worried glance returning again and again to the stack of red chips growing taller and taller before her. Finally Johnny put his hand on Nevada's bare shoulder, squeezed gently, and said, "It's time to cash in." He tossed some checks to the dealers.

Thousands ahead, they left Pradat's.

"Are we done?" Nevada's eyes glittered with exhilaration as they stood outside on the banquette.

"Not on your life, my little Lady Luck," assured Johnny, and impulsively hugged her close. He hailed a cab and took her on a breathless round of all the fancy gaming halls. Elkin's and Charton's on Canal Street. Hawlett's and Toussaint's and St. Cyr's on Chartres Street.

And finally to McGrath's on Carondelet Street, a gambling palace where the richness of appointment and elegance and variety of services outshone all the others. A sumptuous buffet supper served free each evening to the well-heeled patrons was the talk of the town. Upon seeing the mounds of Russian caviar and Gulf shrimp and crawfish gumbo, Nevada told Johnny she was starving. Johnny gallantly fixed her a plate and took her into a small intimate alcove, but he could hardly wait for her to finish so he could get her back to the tables.

It was almost three in the morning when the pair stepped out of McGrath's. In the carriage on the way back to the St. Louis Hotel, Johnny was in a magnanimous mood, so he didn't object when Nevada sleepily leaned her head against his shoulder.

Instead he smiled, lifted his arm, brought it around her and gripped her shoulder with his big hand. Nevada sighed and gratefully laid her cheek on his chest. His slow, steady heartbeat beneath her ear, the touch of his warm hand on her bare shoulder, his clean, unique scent made her gloriously happy.

Johnny Roulette, his firm chin resting lightly atop Nevada's dark head, was happy too. Happy because his tired little good-luck charm had won him more than thirty-three thousand dollars at the tables. Delightfully content yet still aglow from the thrill of gambling, Johnny felt as he often felt after a long, profitable interlude of winning. Calm yet strangely tense. Amorous. Warm. In the mood for love-making.

Nevada stirred, instinctively cuddling closer, pressing her soft breasts against his chest, gripping his ribs with her hand. Johnny felt his blood begin to heat. It had nothing to do with Nevada Hamilton—she just happened to be the warm sweet female draped across him.

At the St. Louis, Johnny hurried Nevada upstairs and to the door of her suite. "You were wonderful, sweetheart," he said, anxious to be gone. "Good night." He started to walk away.

She caught his arm. "I won you lots of money, didn't I?"

"You sure did."

"Then I deserve a good night kiss."

In a hurry, in no mood to argue, Johnny took Nevada's face in his hand and bent to brush his lips hurriedly against hers. But when his mouth met hers Nevada threw her arms around his neck and kissed him with all the love and passion she felt for him, her warm lips opening beneath his, her tongue seeking his.

His response was instinctive and immediate. Groaning, Johnny deepened the kiss, his lips opening wide, his tongue sliding deep into her mouth. His hands clasped her narrow rib cage to lift and press her closer to his hard body as he gave himself up to the hot sweetness of her kiss.

When at last Johnny tore his burning lips from Nevada's, they were both breathless, trembling, and Johnny fleetingly considered taking her into his darkened hotel room, stripping the pink silk dress from her tempting curves, and feasting on them just as he had feasted on her lips.

Nevada sensed the war going on inside him and prayed his passionate side would win. Anxiously she pressed an open-lipped kiss to his brown throat just above his stiff white collar and said, "Yes, Johnny. Yes."

"No!" He firmly set her back. "No! Goddammit, no!"

He released her shoulders, turned, and stalked off down the carpeted corridor, down the stairs, and out into the sweltering humid night.

Sighing, Nevada went inside, quietly undressed in the room she shared with Miss Annabelle, and lay awake for a long time, burning for the big dark man whose lips she could still feel on hers.

Johnny, burning too, headed straight for the most expensive, luxurious brothel in all New Orleans. He climbed the steps of the lighted brick mansion and, within minutes, was upstairs in a spacious bedroom with a gorgeous red-haired young woman in a black satin evening dress. She called herself Belinda. She called him her dark lover. And when she kissed him with wet red lips, Belinda let her hand slide between their pressing bodies to expertly unbutton his tight black trousers and slip her hand inside to examine his impressive erection.

"Oooooh, my dark lover!" she exclaimed. "Is that really for me?"

"Who else?" said Johnny Roulette.

14

The sound of music, the clatter of chips. Each evening, every night. Opulent gaming halls with scarlet moiré walls and marble floors and gold-framed mirrors. Gentlemen in dark evening clothes and lushly gowned ladies in diamonds and pearls.

The world of Johnny Roulette.

A gambler's glamorous life. Thousands bet on the turn of a card, a toss of the dice, a spin of the wheel. Unreadable faces, cool exteriors, negligent postures. Heartbeats quickening, throats tightening, breaths cut short.

Fortune. Chance. Destiny. Fate. Break. Godsend. Windfall. Fluke. Words often on the lips of every gambler, from the nervous young novice shooting craps in an alley to the imperturbable seasoned veteran playing cards in a lavish club.

Whether in an darkened alley or chandeliered hall, the thrill of gambling was much the same. A kind of exquisite torture, a feeling of being vitally alive, of standing on the threshold of untold riches. At the same time, the sense of being in peril, of purposely courting danger and destruction. Only a true gambler could appreciate the anguish and the ecstasy.

Johnny Roulette was one of those. He made his living by gambling, but it meant much, much more than simple livelihood. At the gaming tables he had found his place. His calling. His home. While some gamblers suffered from bouts of guilt and despair and vowed they would give up the cards, the dice, the horses, Johnny was perfectly satisfied with his chosen lot. He was, he would tell anyone who asked, a gambler. It's what he did, who he was, how he planned to spend the rest of his days. He had no one to account to but himself, and anyone who did not approve of his profession would do well to stay away from him.

And it was gambling that took him to London each season. A highest-stakes game that attracted sports from around the world. The winner-take-all game was played each autumn within a stone's throw of the Queen's palace. Johnny, like so many of the other players, liked to arrive several weeks early so that by the day of the big game he was well rested from the ocean crossing and adjusted to Britain's damp, drizzly climate.

This year he would have to adjust as well to having Nevada and Miss Annabelle with him in London.

Dressing for the opera on their second night in New Orleans, Johnny placed the gold studs in his shirt. His thoughts were on the upcoming London game when Nevada called to him through his closed bedroom door.

"Johnny, Miss Annabelle and I are ready. When are we leaving?"

Johnny scowled at himself in the mirror. What had he gotten himself into? Saddled with two women. One so young and foolish she thought she was in love with him. The other so kind and intelligent he felt obliged to take her to the opera when what he really wanted was to get to the tables.

"Be right there, Nevada," he called. He took his black suit jacket from the mahogany valet, slid his long arms into the sleeves, cocked his wrists so that just the right amount of French cuffs showed, and went forth to meet the ladies.

Miss Annabelle, seated primly on a blue winged sofa, looked almost pretty, Johnny thought, as she smiled at him. Her dress of beige faille was new, chosen only this afternoon from a small expensive shop a block off Jackson Square. Johnny had insisted she and Nevada buy new gowns for the opera. It was the first new dress Miss Annabelle had bought in years, and she had proudly shown it to him when they returned from the shopping spree. Nevada had refused to show hers, saying she wanted to surprise him.

Crossing to the stately pale-haired woman whose eyes were sparkling with excitement, Johnny said, "You look lovely, Miss Annabelle."

"Thank you, Cap'n," she answered. Her smile slipped a bit and she said, "Wait until you see Nevada." Her thin eyebrows lifted and Johnny caught a flash of stern censure in her eyes.

"Where is she? I thought she was ready to go."

"I am, Johnny," Nevada said, slinking seductively into the sitting room, feeling more grown-up and pretty than she had ever felt in her life.

Johnny turned, looked at her, and almost had a heart attack.

She wore a gown of scarlet satin that looked like something the *Moonlight Gambler* gals had discarded as too daring. With the aid of a tight corset her waist was nipped in and her breasts pushed up and almost spilling from the gown's scandalously low-cut bodice. Shimmering scarlet satin pulled so indecently tight over her hips and bottom and down to her knees, she could hardly walk.

Her face was painted. Her Cupid's bow mouth was flaming scarlet, a black beauty mark beside it. Another was on her left breast just above the plunging bodice. Her black hair was piled high atop her head and adorned with cheap rhinestones.

"What do you think, Johnny?" she said, slowly turning about. He saw that the naughty scarlet dress was slashed all the way to her nipped-in waist in back. Not totally certain whether he wanted to paddle her little scarlet-covered bottom or bare it and caress it, Johnny waited a heartbeat or two to speak. Nevada turned back to face him, smiling, pleased with herself and his stunned reaction.

He said, "Nevada, sweetheart, I'm afraid you've overdone it."

"Overdone it? Whatever do you mean?"

Johnny glanced to Miss Annabelle for help. She lowered her eyes, her lips were compressed, she was not going to comment.

"Your gown, Nevada. It looks cheap. *You* look cheap." Johnny frowned.

"Cheap?" Her hands went to her hips. Hurt, disappointed, she said angrily, "I'll have you know this dress is the latest style and I think it's beautiful and I don't care what you think!"

Johnny was struggling to control his temper. This foolish young girl seemed to make him lose it quicker than anyone he had ever known. He took his gold-cased pocket watch from inside his white vest pocket, flipped it open, glanced at it.

"The curtain goes up in half an hour." He returned the watch to his pocket. "That dress will not do. You can't wear it to the opera. Please change clothes immediately."

"Change clothes? I'm not about to change clothes. I picked this dress. I like this dress. I'm damned well wearing this dress to the opera!"

That did it. Johnny Roulette got angry.

A muscle working furiously in his tanned jaw, he advanced on Nevada. "You're not going to the opera in that dress."

"Oh, yes, I am!" She looked past him to the nervous lady seated on the blue couch. "Are you ready, Miss Annabelle?" Nevada started for the door.

"Excuse us, please, Miss Annabelle," said Johnny, and crossed the room in half a dozen long strides. He took hold of Nevada's bare arm and spun her around.

She jerked her arm free, causing the low, slippery bodice of her scarlet dress to slide even lower. "Stay away from me! You can't tell me what I'll—"

"You're wrong," said Johnny, cornering her. "I can and I will." He picked her up and carried her, cursing and screaming, into the large bedroom she and Miss Annabelle shared. He kicked the door closed behind him and Miss Annabelle jumped as though she'd heard a pistol shot.

Inside the bedroom Johnny went straight to the tall armoire where a profusion of colorful dresses hung. He lowered Nevada to her feet but clung to her waist with one strong hand. With the other he riffled through the dresses, choosing a girlish summery white silk with puffed sleeves and ruffles around the neck.

He said, "Either you put this on or *I'll* put it on you."

Glaring at him, Nevada replied forcefully, "I'm not putting that dress on, Mr. Johnny 'God Almighty' Roulette!"

"Suit yourself." He jerked her about and began unhooking the scarlet satin gown. The battle of wills quickly turned physical and became a strenuous wrestling match on the plushly carpeted floor. Unmerciful in his quest, Johnny roughly stripped the scarlet gown from Nevada's body. Her fancy hair came tumbling down, rhinestones scattered, and tears of anger caused tracks of black from her painted eyes to drip down her flaming-hot cheeks.

Amazed by the strength of a girl so tiny, Johnny, breathing heavily, pinned her to the floor with a long leg over her knees so he could rest for a minute. One of her hands gripped firmly by his was shoved high above her head, but the other was inside Johnny's white shirt, clawing and scratching.

"Owwww!" yelled Johnny. "You're hurting me."

"I'm hurting you?" She choked, anger clogging her throat. "What do you think you're doing to me, you big ape."

Johnny moved his leg at once and loosened his grip on her fragile wrist. "I'm sorry, Nevada. I forget my own strength at times. You all right? Have I hurt you badly?"

"I don't mean physically!" She closed her eyes and tears washed down her cheeks. "You've hurt my feelings, Johnny Roulette."

Johnny ground his teeth. "I'm sorry."

Her eyes fluttered open, wet lashes clinging together. "I just wanted to be beautiful."

He looked down at the half-naked, crying girl and felt like the biggest heel in the world. "You are beautiful, Nevada. You're always beautiful."

And she was, he thought, as his dark eyes traveled down from the perfect face, marred by make-up and tears, to the ivory bosom rising and falling rapidly with emotion. He felt his stomach tighten. In pushing her arm up over her head he'd caused a barely covered breast to pull free of the low, lace-trimmed chemise. A shy pink nipple, as smooth and supple as satin, was visible.

His eyes darkened.

Tempted to bend his head and kiss the soft nipple until it blossomed and hardened in his mouth, Johnny forced his attention back up to her face.

"I apologize for hurting your feelings. I was insensitive

and mean and I'm sorry. If you want to be beautiful, please wear the white dress to the opera." A brown thumb went to the black smudge beside her mouth. "You don't need beauty marks or lip rouge."

"I don't?"

He smiled at her. "That's for older ladies who want to look young. You are young. And pretty, very pretty." His voice was soft and deep and persuasive. "Wear the white dress for me."

Warmed by his voice, his gentle hands, his coaxing black eyes, Nevada sighed and nodded. "Will you help me so we won't be late for the opera?"

"At your service, madam," said Johnny, and levering himself from the floor, reached out to her.

Miss Annabelle, having heard the scuffling and shouting and crying coming from behind the closed door, was relieved when the pair came breezing back into the parlor, laughing and acting as if they had never had a cross word.

Nevada, she noted, was wearing a lovely frothy white dress and all the vulgar paint had been scrubbed away. Her dark hair had been brushed and was held back off her unblemished face with a pair of oyster-shell combs. She looked young and fresh and happy.

"Shall we go, ladies?" said Johnny, drawing on a pair of white kid gloves.

Nevada was awed by the magnificence of the Théâtre d'Orléans. And by the glittering crowd in attendance. She noticed that Johnny was not the only gentleman wearing white kid gloves, and she asked him about it. He told her it was expected, just as it was expected that the ladies attending the opera be dressed tastefully. And he raised a dark brow and grinned at her.

Miss Annabelle was breathlessly happy. She was where

she belonged and in all her glory. She loved the opera and the crowds and the way of life it represented. She had been reared on visits to New Orleans and the opera, and as she sat now in the coveted dress circle she waved and blew kisses, acknowledging old friends, reclaiming her place among the Old Guard. She was, despite the fact that she was penniless, still a Louisiana Delaney, a respected member of the elite, a lady of impeccable background who had not relinquished her position in high society along with her deed to the lost Delaney mansion.

She still had the name.

The opera began and Miss Annabelle lifted the mother-of-pearl opera glasses purchased just that afternoon. Nevada lifted hers as well but soon lowered them and looked up at Johnny. His jet hair and black eyes gleaming in the muted light, he turned his head to look at her and his lips beneath the suave mustache lifted into a grin. He winked at her. She was relieved. He didn't care for the opera either. He was just as bored as she.

When finally *La Traviata* mercifully ended, Miss Annabelle, her face aglow, turned to them, clasping her hands together as though in prayer and said, "Cap'n Roulette, Nevada, have you ever heard such glissandos and arpeggios in your life?"

Johnny looked at Nevada, his expression asking, You want to answer that one?

"I never have, Miss Annabelle," Nevada said, then whispered to Johnny as Miss Annabelle turned to acknowledge an old acquaintance, "And I hope to high heaven I never do again."

He whispered back, "Well brought up young ladies are supposed to enjoy the opera."

"I was raised on a keelboat, and opera bores the pants off me. Let's go gamble."

15

~~~~~~~~

"She has no regard for convention," said the prim Miss Annabelle Delaney.

"That's very true," admitted Johnny, "so I appreciate your task will not be an easy one."

The two were having breakfast alone in a sunny sidewalk café, while the topic of their conversation slept the morning away in the St. Louis suite. It was the first chance they had had to discuss Nevada.

Johnny recounted Nevada's background to Miss Annabelle, relating all that he knew, up to and including her brief stint as an entertainer on board the *Moonlight Gambler*, where he had found her. He did not include the fact that they had shared a night of passion.

Miss Annabelle listened intently, nodding, shaking her graying head and murmuring, "The poor child. That poor sweet girl."

"You can understand, then, why I felt obliged to take her off the *Gambler*," said Johnny, spreading sweet creamery butter atop a hot French roll.

Miss Annabelle took a sip of her café au lait, then set her cup down. "You could have done no less. I hate to think what might have happened to the girl had you not come along, Cap'n Roulette." Her eyes narrowing, she spoke exactly what was on her mind. "Why, some despicable amorous rogue might well have . . . have . . . taken advantage of the innocent child!"

Johnny wondered miserably if he looked as guilty as he felt. Purposely keeping his voice level, he said, "Yes, that was entirely possible," and quickly changed the subject. "Nevada's safe with us now, Miss Annabelle, and I'm depending on you to teach her all the things she needs to know."

"It will be my pleasure, but I will need your cooperation."

"You have it, of course."

Miss Annabelle's expression became one of mild accusation. "In the future I will be the one to help Nevada with her wardrobe."

Johnny's mind flashed immediately to last evening's altercation over Nevada's choice of evening gowns. Grinning sheepishly, he said, "Absolutely. I won't interfere again. You have my word on that." He shook his head then and added, "You'll find, however, that Nevada is very strong-willed. Her father indulged her and apparently he spun unrealistic dreams of romance."

"Cap'n, I'm glad you brought up the subject of romance." Miss Annabelle colored slightly, patted her thin mouth with her napkin, and continued. "While I'm no expert on affairs of the heart, my instincts tell me that Nevada cares far too much for you."

Johnny's collar suddenly felt too snug. He said, "She thinks she does. A childish whim, nothing more."

"Still, you must stop calling her sweetheart, Cap'n," Miss Annabelle gently scolded. "Or any other endearment that could be misconstrued. She's young and impressionable and you must not allow her to think that you feel anything for her other than proper adult concern for her welfare."

"Yes, ma'am," replied the chastened Johnny.

"Exactly what are your plans for Nevada, Cap'n?"

Johnny shrugged wide shoulders. "To provide her with advantages, to see her educated and transformed into a lady like yourself, Miss Annabelle. To make it possible for her to meet a respectable young gentleman and make a good marriage for herself." He smiled engagingly. "To help her realize her girlish dreams."

Miss Annabelle smiled back at the dark man whose own dreams, if indeed he had any, he had never shared with her. Or with anyone else, she suspected.

She said, "You've a good heart, Cap'n Roulette. As soon as we're settled in London I shall begin Nevada's lessons. She's quite intelligent, so I'm sure she'll learn rapidly."

He nodded his agreement.

"One more thing"—she paused, nervously touched the cameo pinned to her high lace collar—"you must stop taking Nevada to those gambling dens." Her hand dropped away and she looked him squarely in the eye.

"That I can't do, Miss Annabelle," said Johnny, without apology. "Nevada brings me luck."

The trio arrived in New York City on a sticky, hot day in late June. Miss Annabelle, once again a product of her pampered upbringing, felt weak and faint after the long carriage ride across Manhattan, as any grand lady would, and so went straight to her bed upon reaching the St. Nicholas Hotel.

Nevada, on the other hand, felt fine. Curious. Wonderful. Excited. The carriage ride itself had been a thrilling adventure as it rolled along broad avenues lined with the tallest buildings she had ever seen. She had turned and twisted and craned her neck and pointed and grabbed Johnny's arm and asked a million questions.

They stayed a full week in the teeming city and Johnny, who had enjoyed New York's varied delights numerous times, was surprised to learn he found new pleasure in the familiar as he squired the two awed women around town.

Morning strolls through the New York Gallery of Fine Arts, ferry trips to Staten Island, lunches at a vine-covered sidewalk café in front the Thalia Theater, afternoon shopping at Lord & Taylor's with its steam elevators and Tiffany chandeliers. Twilight rides through Central Park, dinner at Delmonico's, and evenings at Broadway's glittering theaters.

And of course, late-night visits to Morrissey's, the Twenty-fourth Street casino famous the world over for its magnificently furnished gaming rooms and splendid buffet suppers.

"Please, Johnny, can't we stay just one more week?" Nevada begged on their last evening in New York, knowing that the country's continuing Centennial celebration would climax on Independence Day. "Hellfire, don't you realize that in just four days it will be July 4, 1876, the one hundredth anniversary of our nation's independence!"

Johnny, seated in an easy chair by the spacious suite's tall front windows, leisurely lowered his newspaper. "I am aware, Nevada, but I've booked passage for tomorrow."

"Well, unbook it! Miss Annabelle says there'll be parades and picnics and bands playing and fireworks and dances and crowds, and I want to be here."

But Johnny would not be swayed or bullied. He had business in the United Kingdom. "We leave tomorrow," he said, and turned his attention back to the *New York Herald*.

Nevada sat sulkily between Miss Annabelle and Johnny in the roomy hired carriage headed toward the Hudson

River on that warm Saturday morning, July 1st. Annoyed with Johnny for being so selfish, longing to remain in the city for the glorious July 4th celebrations, she ignored his attempts at polite conversation and resented his long arm stretched out behind her on the leather seat.

Refusing to even glance at landmarks he was pointing out, Nevada looked only at her gloved hands folded in her lap.

But as the carriage neared Pier 51 and she caught the scent of the water and heard the shrill cry of circling gulls, she couldn't keep from lifting her eyes. She saw it at once: the towering SS *Starlight* anchored in the harbor, its sixty-foot white hull gleaming in the hazy New York sunshine. And she forgot her disappointment.

Excitement filled the air as barouches and victorias crowded the wooden docks and drivers in full livery assisted rich, well-dressed ladies and gentlemen from the fancy conveyances. Dollies stacked high with steamer trunks dotted the wooden wharf and flower and fruit vendors pushed their carts through the crowds.

Nevada couldn't keep from smiling at Johnny when, after first assisting Miss Annabelle, he put his hands to her waist and, lifting her from the carriage, said, "If I buy you some violets for your dress, will you forgive me?"

Suddenly happy and optimistic, she wanted to hug his handsome neck and shout, Of course, you fool! I love you to distraction, I'd forgive you anything, but she did not. Although she certainly did love him to distraction and meant to make him her own, come hell or high water, she was clever enough to know she must start keeping her desires to herself. For now.

She said coyly, "Buy the violets, then I'll decide."

Grinning, he bought the flowers, tipping the happy vendor handsomely. Miss Annabelle preferred to carry her corsage, but Nevada wanted to wear hers and enlisted Johnny's help. He obliged and when he deftly pinned the fragrant purple blossoms to the bodice of her pale blue traveling suit, Nevada's heart skipped a beat beneath his dark fingers.

He said, "What's the verdict, Miss Hamilton? Have the violets put me back in your good graces?"

Before she could answer, a quartet of eager travelers unintentionally jostled her so that she felt herself losing her balance but was powerless to do anything about it. Only Johnny's quick reflexive action saved her from a fall and she found herself encircled in his arms, her cheek pressed to the linen lapel of his cream-colored suit jacket.

"Thunderation!" she said into his chest. "They almost knocked me flat on my—"

"Let's go aboard where it's less crowded," said Johnny hastily, and keeping a protective arm around her, guided her and Miss Annabelle up the long gangway and onto the polished deck of the Cunard Line's most modern and luxurious ocean-going vessel.

First-class passengers milled about the twenty-thousand-ton luxury liner, locating their regal staterooms, calling to friends, drifting in and out of the main salon now crowded with children, valets, maids, trunks. Others leaned over the promenade railing, waving wildly to those on the levee while champagne corks popped and laughter filled the air.

Nevada quickly realized that they were traveling top cabin and gloried in the revelation. While a mannerly uniformed steward of slender build and carefully combed brown hair beneath his billed cap ushered them to their staterooms, he spoke proudly of the SS *Starlight*'s accommodations.

"She boasts a half dozen saloons, all of them aglitter with gold and crystal and mirrors. There's more than eight hundred cabins. The staterooms you've engaged are the largest available on the *Starlight* and have bathtubs and hot and cold running water, so you should be quite comfortable during your crossing." His eyes twinkled as he said, "No finer vessel can be found than this pride of the Atlantic, the SS *Starlight*." Then he added, "Naturally you'll find the finest cuisine prepared by a small army of French chefs and a menu so extravagant it will be unnecessary to dine on the same food twice during the entire nine days of your crossing."

He continued with his studied monologue, informing his interested passengers that everything was readily available for their comfort and convenience. That the full SS *Starlight*'s capable staff was on call twenty-four hours a day.

Leading them down a wide paneled hallway, he unlocked a door, extended his arm, and allowed them to pass before him into a large airy stateroom where a huge bouquet of cut flowers and a basket of fresh fruit and a magnum of chilled champagne awaited.

"This is the ladies' suite," said the steward, crossing the deeply carpeted stateroom to throw open the curtains over the portholes. "The gentleman"—he glanced up at Johnny —"will be right next door."

After assuring them that all their luggage would be brought up shortly and a maid would be sent up to help with the unpacking, the steward showed Johnny to his stateroom. After Johnny had given him a generous gratuity, he left, saying, "We should be departing in half an hour, sir."

Johnny, relaxing, waited exactly twenty-eight minutes, then knocked on the door of Nevada and Miss Annabelle's stateroom. Nevada answered it to see Johnny, a muscular shoulder leaning against the doorframe, grinning down at her.

"I thought I'd go out on deck for the departure. Anyone care to join me?"

Her eyes grew as large as saucers. "Is it time already?" Not waiting for an answer, she spun around. "Dear Lord in heaven, where did I put my blasted suit jacket? Miss Annabelle, I can't find—"

"Forget your jacket, child, and go along with him," said Miss Annabelle."

"Aren't you coming?" Johnny asked.

Preoccupied with overseeing the unpacking, Miss Annabelle declined. She smiled and shook her head when Nevada, beside herself with excitement, tugged on Johnny's hand, saying, "Come on! If we miss the launching I'll never forgive myself!"

Out on deck the pair stood at the crowded railing, waving and laughing, and Nevada's heart began to pound when the huge steamship began backing away from the Hudson River landing. The captain and two expert steam tugs smartly maneuvered the huge liner out of its berth through the tideway, and toward the open sea. Cheers and whistles went up from the gay passengers and Nevada cheered and whistled loudest of all.

And as the merry mayhem continued around them she tugged on Johnny's lapel. Smiling, he lowered his dark head. Nevada stood on tiptoe, put her hand to his tanned jaw and her lips against his ear. She said, "To hell with New York! This is a damn sight more fun than any old Centennial celebration!"

16

~~~~~~~~

First aboard the *Moonlight Gambler*. Then down in New Orleans. Up in New York City. And now here, out on the high seas. It was the same wherever they were.

Women looking at, flirting with, throwing themselves at Johnny Roulette! Nevada was sick of it. She wanted to run at them, to scream and shout and flap her arms; to drive them away as if they were a revolting pack of hovering vultures, intent on swooping down to strip the juicy flesh from Johnny's bones. Which, in Nevada's eyes, they were.

Simmering, Nevada returned with Miss Annabelle to their stateroom on the first full morning at sea. Breakfast in the main dining hall had been disastrous, despite the fact the food had been delicious. She had hardly tasted the fluffy buckwheat cakes, the sugar-cured ham, the poached eggs, or the fig preserves.

Seated at a table nearby a pair of attractive, expensively gowned ladies had spent the entire meal smiling and looking at Johnny as though he were far more appetizing than the berries and rich cream before them. Worse, Johnny smiled back at the simpering pair, and when the meal was ended he excused himself, deserting Nevada and Miss Annabelle, and joined the enemy.

Sighing miserably, Nevada followed Miss Annabelle into their sunny stateroom and flung herself facedown on the bed. Her jaw aching from gritting her teeth, she squeezed her eyes tightly shut and pounded her fists on the mattress.

"My dear child, what is it?" said Miss Annabelle, laying aside the long-stemmed rose that had graced their breakfast table.

"Damn them both to burning hell!" sputtered Nevada, flopping over onto her back and bolting upright. "And Johnny Roulette with them."

"Nevada! You mustn't say such—"

"Yes, I must!" Her face was red with emotion, her blue eyes shining with unshed tears. "Johnny's out there right this minute promenading around the decks with those two brazen hussies on his arms after flatly turning me down when I suggested a stroll earlier this morning."

"You suggested . . ."—Miss Annabelle's slender fingers went to the cameo at her throat—"earlier? I don't understand. I was with you when we met Cap'n Roulette for—"

Waving a dismissive hand before her angry face, Nevada said, "Not then. I woke up early, before the sun. You were still sleeping when I went next door to Johnny's and asked him to go for a walk with me."

Her intelligent forehead wrinkled, thin eyebrows drawn together, Miss Annabelle said, "Johnny was up and dressed before dawn?"

Nevada shot her a look that said Don't be ridiculous, then told her, "No, of course not. You know Johnny—he's the soundest of sleepers and never rises before eight in the morning." Her face softened a little. "He was asleep, all right." A foolish grin began to play at her lips. "God, he's so beautiful when he's asleep. His hair was all mussed and he doesn't wear pajamas and his bare chest was—"

"Nevada Marie Hamilton!" Miss Annabelle's tone caused Nevada to blink.

"Yes, Miss Annabelle?" Nevada swallowed nervously.

Miss Annabelle drew several long, deep breaths, the lace-trimmed blouse covering her thin torso quivering with her efforts. She was slowly, deliberately calming herself, regaining her usual control. At last she came to Nevada, pushed an errant lock of jet-black hair behind her ear, and sat down beside her.

She said, "It's fortunate we have some time alone this morning. I've been meaning to speak with you." She smiled and took Nevada's hand. "You are aware that Cap'n Roulette is—"

"Why do you keep calling Johnny *Cap'n*?" Nevada interrupted.

"He attained the rank of captain during the war and is entitled to it for the rest of his life. I address him as *Cap'n* out of respect, much the same as he addresses me as *Miss Annabelle.*"

"Hm. Well, I don't respect him all that much, so I'll just—"

"Let's not get off the subject. As I was saying, you are well aware that the cap'n employed me to be your chaperon and tutor. So far, I have been lax in my duties. We thought it best to wait until we're settled in London to begin—"

"I agree with you on that!"

"Dear, don't interrupt me again. It's rude to interrupt."

"You should tell that to Johnny. He's forever interrupting me."

Miss Annabelle softly sighed. "Never mind that. About the cap'n, Nevada, you must *never* again go into his stateroom alone, especially when he is in bed."

"Oh, it's all right. He was angry at first, when I woke him up, but when he saw I had brought him a cup of coffee he stopped grumbling." She grinned, remembering.

"That isn't what I . . . now hear me carefully, Nevada.

Young ladies do not go into a gentleman's bedroom." Her face grew pink. "Why, reputations have been forever spoiled over less."

"I suppose. But I don't give a flip about my reputation. I know who and what I am."

Miss Annabelle cleared her throat needlessly. "Dear, I'm concerned with more than your reputation. I've a idea you are too . . . um . . . too . . . fond of Cap'n Roulette and—"

"Fond of him?" Nevada again interrupted, "Hellfire, I'm in love with Johnny." Nevada snatched her hand from Miss Annabelle's and crossed her arms over her chest.

"Possibly you think that you are, but I suspect it's simply a matter of hero worship."

"Hero worship? Johnny's no hero, far as I can tell. He's just a gambler, but I love him."

Miss Annabelle tried once again. "Let's just say that you are naturally very grateful to the cap'n for offering you help and guidance."

Nevada shook her head negatively. "Johnny's not the only man who ever helped and guided me, Miss Annabelle." Her blue eyes turned almost wistful. "The men on my papa's keelboat all helped and guided me. Luke and Big Edgar and Slim. Teddy and 'Black Jack' Jones and especially old Willie. Then when I went on the *Moonlight Gambler* there was Pops McCullough and Stryker. Stryker told Johnny he'd personally kill him if he ever mistreated me. Stryker's the *Gambler*'s bouncer and he's even bigger than Johnny. A giant."

Miss Annabelle felt rattled, as though she might be losing her train of thought. "Yes, well, no danger of that. What I'm trying to say, Nevada, is that you are mistaking Johnny's kind concern for your welfare as being something more . . . different . . . from what it is."

"Really? What would you say if I told you that Johnny and me . . ." Nevada caught herself and fell silent. What she and Johnny had done that night on the *Moonlight Gambler* was something beautiful and special and secret, not to be shared with anyone.

"The cap'n is your friend, Nevada. And nothing more." Miss Annabelle rose from the bed and crossed the state-room. She paused at the open porthole, inhaled deeply of the damp salt air, turned and said, "Possibly the best friend you'll ever have. I know him. He would never mislead you. Never. He simply is not that kind of man. He does care for you but only as a benefactor cares for his ward. Or, perhaps, as an older brother toward a younger sister."

"But I want him to—"

Miss Annabelle raised her hand for silence. "Dear, I'm afraid you're a trifle spoiled. *I want* is a phrase that passes your lips far too often. You must learn that you cannot have something merely because you want it. Nor can you command a man to love you. Life just doesn't work that way."

Nevada lowered her head. Miss Annabelle hastily crossed to her. Reaching out, she lifted Nevada's chin. "Don't fret so. While there will always be things you can't have, there are just as many you can have. You're quite beautiful and I predict there'll be more than one handsome young gentleman who'll fall in love with you once you've learned to be a lady." She smiled kindly and said, "Lesson one: Ladies never swear. You must stop swearing, dear." She sat down, put an arm around Nevada's shoulders, and hugged her. "One day you'll make us proud, the cap'n and I. We've great plans for you, child."

For a time they sat in silence. Then Nevada's chin lifted. She looked the older woman in the eye and announced,

"You and Johnny may have plans for me, but I have plans for Johnny."

Undaunted, Miss Annabelle continued trying to reason with Nevada, failing to realize just how much in love and how stubborn her young charge was. Nevada was respectful enough to listen, and some of the things Miss Annabelle said did get through to her. While the wise older woman went on and on about the importance of behavior and manners and the like, Nevada concluded that if she could manage to become a lady, then surely Johnny would love her.

But by early afternoon Nevada had completely forgotten her desire to become a lady. In truth, she was fit to be tied. She'd not seen Johnny since breakfast. He had been absent at lunch and she suspected his absence had something to do with women, as opposed to poker.

Nevada wanted desperately to be with him. To have him all to herself. To hear that deep drawling voice speaking her name. To see that full sensual mouth stretch into a devilish grin beneath his sleek mustache. To have those dark eyes looking only at her.

She came up with a rather ingenious idea. She would pretend to be ill, too ill to spend the afternoon alone. Someone would have to stay with her and since Miss Annabelle had mentioned she was eagerly looking forward to a bridge game in the ladies' salon, Johnny would have to be the one to stay with her.

"*Ooooh!*" Nevada suddenly moaned, clutching her stomach.

Miss Annabelle swiftly laid her book aside. "What is it, child?" she asked anxiously. At the same time there was a knock on the door. "Yes, come in," she called impatiently.

"I'm not feeling well," said Nevada, making a face and then biting her lip to keep from smiling when Johnny, his beige suit jacket hooked on a thumb and slung over his right shoulder, walked in. "I'm sick," she said for emphasis, and watched through lowered lids as Johnny tossed his jacket over a lyre-backed chair and came to the bed.

"Dear me!" said Miss Annabelle. "Should I ring for the ship's doctor?"

Not answering, Johnny sat down on the bed facing Nevada. He pressed a brown hand to her forehead. "No fever," he said. Then, "Where does it hurt, Nevada?"

"Here," she said, pointing. "My stomach."

"Think it's a touch of seasickness?"

"Yes," Nevada was quick to reply. "I'm seasick. I feel miserable."

"I'll dampen a cloth for your forehead," Miss Annabelle offered, and rushed to the bathroom.

Johnny laid a spread hand on Nevada's flat stomach. "Tummy churning?"

She didn't have to lie. Her stomach began fluttering like crazy the instant his big warm hand touched her. "Yes," she said, "it is. I feel weak too."

Miss Annabelle, returning with the cool cloth for Nevada's head, said, "Thank goodness she wasn't alone. I was just about to leave for my bridge game. Ten more minutes and I would have been gone."

Johnny, moving his hand from Nevada's stomach, rose from the bed. "Miss Annabelle, I've no plans for this afternoon. Go on to your bridge game. I'll stay here with Nevada."

"Why, Cap'n, I wouldn't hear of it," said Miss Annabelle.

"Well, why not?" said the patient, raising herself up on one elbow. "I—I mean, you shouldn't miss your game, Miss Annabelle. Johnny can look after me."

But Miss Annabelle was adamant. It would not be

proper for a gentlemen to sit alone with a sick young lady. She shooed Johnny right out the door and took up her post at Nevada's bedside.

Foiled, Nevada came clean with the truth. "I feel fine, Miss Annabelle, truly I do. Go on and play bridge."

"Child, why would you feign *mal de mer.* . . . Was it nothing more than a trick to be with the cap'n?"

"I'm sorry."

"I'll not lecture you, but I will say that should I return from my bridge game to find you and the cap'n alone in either his or our cabin, I shall not let you out of my sight for the remainder of the crossing."

"Yes, ma'am. May I please take a walk?"

Miss Annabelle thought it over. "Only because a degree of fresh air and sunshine are necessary to insure good health." She smiled then and added, "Do *not* leave our deck and don't be speaking to strangers."

"Thank you, Miss Annabelle," said Nevada, and impulsively hugged the taller older woman.

His hair was as silvery as the precious metal upon which his vast fortune was built. His face was as smooth as a baby's and as pink. His eyes, wide set and as deep blue as the Atlantic, shone with a mischievous light. A well-trimmed silver goatee covered his chin and a full silver mustache almost hid his red smiling lips.

His gray suit was custom-cut to fit his tall slender frame, his shirt had a stiff boiled collar, his cravat was black-and-silver striped. In his lapel was a vivid lilac orchid and in his right hand was a varnished malacca walking stick.

Nevada, lazily reclining in a deck chair, shaded her eyes against the northern sun and watched as the tall silver-haired man strolling past paused when a steward rushed up to him. Holding out a silver salver, the steward waited respectfully silent while the tall dapper man read the missive.

"Will there be a reply, King?" the uniformed steward asked.

"Yes," said the silver-haired man, and his voice, strong and melodious, carried on the breeze. "When I damned well feel like it."

"Sir? That is your message?"

"It is," said he and walked away, the silver head of his malacca cane glittering in the sun.

Her mouth agape, Nevada leapt from her deck chair and hurried to intercept the steward. "Excuse me," she said, tapping him on the shoulder. "Is that gentlemen actually royalty?"

"Beg pardon, miss?"

"That silver-haired man. You called him a king."

The steward smiled. "The gentleman is Mr. Theodore Cassidy of Nevada. His fortune was made in silver. He's the silver king and he's come to be known as King Cassidy."

"And why is King Cassidy going to London?" asked Nevada.

The smile left the steward's face. "Miss, I do not trespass into the motives of my passengers." He glanced warily about, then added, "There are rumors of a late autumn poker game in London." He turned and walked away and Nevada went back to her deck chair.

Moments later the tall silver-haired man returned, and Nevada blinked when he came straight toward her. Standing between her and the sun, he leaned on his cane, smiled, and said, "What say we strike a bargain, miss?"

"Sir?"

"A bargain. You shall have the chair from noon until three o'clock. I'll claim it from three until six. Sound fair?"

"Sure," said Nevada. "This your favorite deck chair, then?"

Grinning, he said, "Something like that. Allow me to introduce myself. I'm—"

"I know who you are," said Nevada, jumping up to face him. "You're King Cassidy from Nevada." She stuck out her hand. "My name's Nevada. I was born there and my papa named me after the state."

King shook her hand warmly. "Why, we might be kinfolk, Nevada, and I'm certain we're going to be friends."

Liking him instantly, she replied, "King, my papa was Newt Hamilton and my mama was . . ." She took his arm and they strolled away, Nevada telling him her life's story, King listening with interest. In minutes the silverhaired silver king had learned that Nevada was the daughter of the only woman to whom he had given his heart.

A heart which she had refused.

The young beautiful Beth Davis had rejected him. At thirty-six he was too old for her, she had told him and had, within a week of turning down his proposal, married a young handsome southerner new to Virginia City.

Now, all these years later, he was looking into the eyes of the enchanting product of that union.

17

∾∾∾∾∾∾

"She's a girl of extremes," said Johnny, drawing a thin brown cigar from his inside coat pocket. "The way she has developed, there's a quality about her that is . . . ah . . . this incredible sensuality that a woman-child has, a true woman-child. Her voice is a child's, her attitudes, the way she walks and moves her hands about, childlike." He struck a match and drew on his cigar. "But she's a woman, with a woman's ripe body. The mixture is explosive."

The deep blue eyes of the silver-haired man across the table from Johnny snapped with righteous indignation, then quickly softened with understanding. Johnny's description of Nevada was all too close to the mark and the fifty-five-year-old silver king had, within hours of meeting her, become extremely protective of the tiny porcelain-skinned girl with the jet-black hair and large blue eyes who fancied herself madly in love with the dark-haired young sport now facing him.

Ignoring Miss Annabelle's stern admonition to stay away from Johnny's cabin, Nevada had gone there as soon as her thrilling shipboard afternoon with King Cassidy had ended. Pounding on Johnny's stateroom door, she rushed in out of breath as soon as it opened. Distracted at once by the sight of him naked to the waist, with shaving soap covering his lower face, a white towel draped around his neck, she swallowed and began telling him her exciting news.

"You'll never in a million years guess who I met this afternoon!"

Johnny, slowly closing the door after her, absently toweled foamy white lather from his face. "Jesus, Nevada, you're not supposed to be out meeting—"

"Will you stop it! You sound like Miss Annabelle." She came to him, picked up a corner of the white towel, and smiling foolishly patted at a dab of lather clinging to the left corner of his mustache.

And she momentarily forgot her news. Standing so close to Johnny, with his broad, bare chest mere inches from her upturned face, it was hard to think, hard to breathe.

He loomed over her, so tall and powerful and appealing. Overwhelmed by his potent masculinity, she inhaled and swayed helplessly to him.

Johnny swiftly took her shoulders, set her back. "Don't! You'll get us both in trouble." He released her and took a step backward.

Entranced, attracted, Nevada eagerly followed. "No one need ever know, Johnny." She lifted a shaking hand to his chest and sighed as her fingers made contact with hard warm flesh and crisp dark hair. The pleasure was fleeting.

Johnny's long fingers encircled her wrist and he swiftly pulled her hand away. His dark face set in harsh lines of annoyance, he clung tightly to her wrist, drew her across the room to a brocade-covered chair, and deposited her there.

"Don't move from that chair," he ordered, shaking a finger in her face.

She frowned but stayed put, her eyes following him as he showed her his back. Taking a fresh shirt from the mahogany chest, he put it on and turned to face her, buttoning it up to his throat.

"Now," he said, rolling up the shirtsleeves over dark forearms, "what's this about you meeting someone?"

Nevada's eyes again flashed with excitement. She told Johnny of her newfound friendship with the silver king and about how they had become acquainted. King Cassidy had, for some reason, chosen the very same deck chair that she had chosen.

"What is it?" she asked, when Johnny, rolling his eyes heavenward, began to laugh. "What's so all-fired funny?"

Charmed by her genuine enthusiasm and marvelous ignorance, Johnny came to her, crouched down on his heels before her. Putting a hand on either arm of her chair, he said, "Ah, darlin' . . . darlin' . . ." He caught himself using the endearment, and thinking that Miss Annabelle would rightfully have his head for backsliding, quickly amended it. "Nevada, Mr. Cassidy preferred the deck chair you occupied, because it belongs to him."

"The deck chair's his?" She laid her pale hands atop the brown ones resting on the chair arms. "Johnny, this can't be."

He grinned and said, "He doesn't actually own it, but the deck chairs are chosen and engaged for the duration of the crossing. Paid for. You were obviously sitting in Mr. Cassidy's chair."

"Jesus, Mary, and Moses!" Nevada exclaimed, twisting at the dark hairs on the back of Johnny's hands. "King must think I'm a real dunce."

Johnny laughed. "I believe that's Jesus, Mary, and *Joseph*." He rose to his feet, bringing her up with him. "It's my fault, I failed to tell you where our deck chairs are located. Tomorrow I'll show you, so you won't be taking someone else's." He was guiding her toward the door.

"I'm not ready to leave yet," she said.

"You are leaving now, before Miss Annabelle catches you in here."

She balked like a mule. "But I've not told you everything about King Cassidy. He's very rich, owns silver mines all over Nevada, and . . ."—she paused for effect—"he gambles!" She gave Johnny a smug look.

"No?" he teased. "Imagine that."

"Guess what else?"

"I give up."

"He's waiting in the gentlemen's smoker to meet you this very minute!"

Johnny cocked his head, his interest piqued. "Are you telling me King Cassidy wants a game?"

"Hellfire, I can't do everything. You have to help a little. Isn't it enough that I've told him about you and set up this appointment between you?" She sighed as though explaining something to one who was dim-witted. "I didn't tell him you're a gambler, I was afraid of scaring him off."

"Good thinking," Johnny admitted.

"I just told him that you're my . . . I told him we're traveling to London together and that I'd like him to meet you." Nevada kept it to herself she had confided to King that she was in love with Johnny. Her eyes sparkling, she added, "He has invited us all to dine at his table this evening. Isn't that great?"

Skeptical, wondering just what this silver baron wanted, and suspicious that it might be the tempting little Nevada, Johnny said, "I'll meet the gentleman, but don't count too heavily on dining with him tonight."

"Why not? He's a fine man and I like him a lot and I know Miss Annabelle will too and I promised him that—"

"We'll see," said Johnny. "Now, go. And don't tell Miss

Annabelle you've been roaming the decks collecting strangers."

Now Johnny, seated across from the silver-haired gentleman, felt that he was the one on trial. Where he had once been dubious of the silver king's intentions toward Nevada, he had quickly learned that the middle-aged gentleman had his own suspicions.

King Cassidy's dark blue eyes were steely when he slammed a fist down on the marble-topped table and said, "All this talk of sensuality and such. Why, Nevada is a child, goddammit!"

"Sir, tell me you don't see—"

"I do, I do," King reluctantly agreed. "It's the God's truth that she is . . . what did you call her, a woman-child?" He tossed off his glass of slivovitz, made a face. "It's all the more up to us to keep her out of peril." His dark blue eyes narrowed as he fixed them on Johnny. "Nothing personal, son, but when I was your age—"

"We've a chaperon traveling with us, King." Johnny kept his voice level, but felt that now-familiar twinge of irritation and guilt.

"Mighty fine! And that's as it should be." King pushed back his chair, signaling the end of the interview. Rising, he said, "Did Nevada relay my dinner invitation?"

Johnny rose, pulled some bills from his pocket, dropped a couple on the table. "She did and we'll be honored to join you. Shall we say nine?"

King Cassidy grinned and stroked his silver goatee. "Why don't we make it earlier?" He paused, looked Johnny dead in the eye, and added, "I guess Nevada failed to mention the fact that I enjoy cards."

Johnny grinned too. "She might have said something to that effect, sir."

King Cassidy roared with laughter. "You better watch that child, Johnny." His blue eyes atwinkle, he added, "And you better watch *me,* son. Eight to five says I'll beat you tonight."

Johnny watched King Cassidy walk away, the silver-headed malacca cane hooked over his bent arm, his silver hair gleaming under the skylight. Slowly Johnny sat back down, a pleased smile curving his full lips beneath the black mustache.

King Cassidy.

The King Cassidy.

Johnny Roulette had known that Cassidy would be aboard the SS *Starlight.* He had been tipped off about the silver baron's booking on his first night in New York. And had wasted no time in making certain he too would be on the Cunard liner when it departed for England.

King Cassidy's wealth was legendary. So was his penchant for any and every game of chance and it was said that he won and lost with the same good grace, with equanimity.

Johnny's smile broadened.

Thanks to Nevada's ignorance of shipside protocol, it would not be necessary to bribe some passenger to exchange deck chairs. Johnny had been prepared to pay handsomely for the privilege of "just happening to be" in the deck chair next to King Cassidy. Striking up an amiable conversation with the rich Nevadan. Choosing as his opening subject the falling stock market or Presidential politics or silver prices or beautiful women.

Anything but gambling.

Now none of that was necessary. He'd be dining with King Cassidy this very evening, and afterward they would join a game or play heads-up poker.

Johnny's smile broadened.

Nevada really was his lucky charm.

At half past seven, in the vast chandelier-lit dining hall, with its walls of hammered glass and cast-glass panels and two-story-high ceiling with arabesqued marble arches, Nevada Marie Hamilton, radiant in an exquisite gown of pale pink satin, sat across the damask-draped table from the silver king.

On her right, Johnny, debonair in black evening clothes, was ordering dinner for them at King Cassidy's request, the French rolling off his tongue without effort or accent.

Directly across from Johnny, Miss Annabelle, a shawl of Irish lace draped around her thin shoulders, was smiling shyly at their silver-haired host.

Famished as usual, Nevada dug into her broiled quail on toast with such gusto that Miss Annabelle cleared her throat in censure.

Chewing a huge mouthful, Nevada apologized with her eyes and caught King grinning indulgently. Waiting until Miss Annabelle's attention returned to her filet of halibut, Nevada winked and lifted her slender shoulders in a shrug.

It was a lovely evening for them all and Nevada noticed that Miss Annabelle was more animated than usual. She smiled a lot and there were spots of high color in her cheeks when King Cassidy, addressing her, looked straight into her eyes.

Over the caramel custard Nevada innocently suggested that they all go dancing after dinner. And openly pouted when King Cassidy said, "Not tonight, child. Perhaps another evening."

"We should be getting back to our stateroom," said Miss Annabelle, both relieved and disappointed.

"We'll see you ladies safely there," offered King Cassidy, rising to pull out Miss Annabelle's chair.

The moon had risen. It glinted silver on the dark Atlantic waters. A strong breeze was blowing out of the north, swirling locks of Nevada's loose hair about her face. Soft music wafted from the open portholes of the main ballroom. It was a breathtakingly beautiful night.

Nevada, clinging to Johnny's arm, strolled dreamily along the slightly rolling decks in the moonlight, pretending they were lovers on their way to the privacy of their stateroom. A few yards in front of them, Miss Annabelle and King Cassidy walked together, talking quietly, the sound of Miss Annabelle's gentle laughter rising on the winds.

Nevada whispered to Johnny, "I believe Miss Annabelle likes King, don't you?"

"She seems to," he replied casually.

Nevada stopped abruptly.

Johnny slowed, turned back. "What is it?"

"Do you like me, Johnny? Do you care at all about me?"

Johnny sighed.

She grabbed his arm and urged him to pause at the ship's railing. "Well, do you?" She leaned back against railing. A thick lock of glossy hair blew directly over her mouth.

Johnny brushed the hair back off her face and gently cupped her cheek in his hand. "Yes," he said. "I care."

"Then kiss me. Kiss me just this one time and I'll never, ever ask you again as long as I live, I swear it." Meaning only to placate her, Johnny didn't hesitate. He bent his dark head and brushed his lips softly to her cheek.

But Nevada quickly turned her head, sliding her mouth around to meet his. She grabbed his satin lapels and kissed him hungrily, hotly, her lips open, her tongue sliding along his closed white teeth, anxiously seeking entrance.

Abruptly pulling free of her embrace, Johnny wrapped his hands around the varnished railing on either side of her, enclosing her inside his arms. His dark eyes black with anger and desire, he said, "When in God's name are you going to give up?"

Breathless, trembling, she replied, "When are you?"

18

~~~~~~~~~~

"I have wanted," he said in a drowsy drawl, "to do this all evening."

His long dark fingers skimmed along the top edge of her snug satin bodice, lightly brushing her skin.

She trembled.

Nevada didn't remember coming here, couldn't recall slipping down the dim wood-paneled passageway, but here she was. With Johnny. Alone with him inside his shadowed stateroom, the rustle of satin and the pounding of her heart the only sounds in the warm silence.

Her back was pressed against the carved wood of the closed cabin door and Johnny, his black eyes smoldering beneath thickly lashed lids, towered over her, his wide, black-jacketed shoulders blocking out the suffused light from a lone lamp burning behind him by the bed.

She felt the slick satin slowly sliding over the swell of her breasts and she was delighted that Johnny was such a slow, deliberate lover. At the same time, she wanted to scream at him to hurry. Please, darling, hurry.

"We've all night, sweetheart," Johnny murmured softly as if reading her mind. He lowered his head to brush a kiss to her open lips. His mouth was warm and pliable. He tasted of wine and tobacco, and the skill of that delicious mouth left Nevada hungering for more as he straightened and whispered again, "all night."

The enticing dark fingers that were toying with the shimmering pink satin were almost indifferent, decidedly lazy in their endeavor. Squirming, on fire, Nevada could wait no longer to be naked, to have Johnny's hands on her. She couldn't help herself—the attraction was too strong, the desire he enkindled too compelling.

"Johnny"—she was breathless—"I don't want to wait all night. I want you to touch me now. Now."

He smiled then, a slow, sexual smile. And he said, the rich timbre of his voice a caress in itself, "Whatever you desire, sweetheart."

And as if he held a magic wand in his dark hand, he touched her and the pink satin gown fairly melted away and all at once she was totally naked, right down to her bare toes.

A soft gasp of pleasure passed her parted lips and her throat constricted as Johnny's mouth closed over hers and he pulled her into his arms. His hands moved with seductive knowledge over her bare shoulders and down her back, lingered for a second at her waist before sliding over the flare of her hips.

He kissed her and kissed her again, covered her throat with kisses. The clean masculine scent of him assailed her senses as he drew her close. She could feel against her bare breasts the slick satin of his lapels, the silkiness of the pleated white shirt, and his muscular chest beneath it. Through the fabric of his trousers, the hard, powerful muscles of his thighs pressed against her bare, trembling legs as he kissed her with a kind of dangerous unchained passion that both excited and frightened her.

It was a strange, glorious sensation, standing there naked against her fully clothed lover, the tightened nipples of her swelling breasts and the tingling flesh of her bare belly brushing against teasingly abrasive cloth instead of a warm naked body. Nevada inhaled deeply and threw her head back as Johnny's hot lips moved down the bare column of her throat.

It seemed that a part of her was standing apart, watching them, an invited voyeur. It was thrilling. She enjoyed it. She was seeing Johnny, big and dark and handsome as a stage actor in his black evening clothes, holding in his strong masterful arms a shamelessly naked her. She appeared excessively white and exceptionally small against his massive dark strength, and from out of her memory walked a pleasant but warning recollection. Her wide, interested gaze clinging unashamedly to the passionately kissing pair, she remembered Johnny's original concern regarding the vast differences in their sizes. Recalled vividly the solution he had come up with in the consummation of their lovemaking aboard the *Moonlight Gambler*.

The voyeur and the participant merged as Nevada, her lips an inch from Johnny's ear, whispered breathlessly, "Darling, you haven't forgotten that—"

"That I weigh twice as much as you?" His lips traveled along her delicate jawline and up to her temple. "No, sweetheart, I haven't."

"Then undress and get on the bed first and I'll—"

He grinned, a slow, teasing grin, and said, "I've an even better idea." His hand gently cupped her left breast, his thumb brushing back and forth over the pebble-hard nipple.

"You have?" Her heart thundered in her chest.

"Mm. Why don't we make love in the chair?"

Kissing her into silence when she started to object, Johnny picked Nevada up, carried her across the room, and gently lowered her into the blue brocade easy chair.

She felt suddenly very shy and foolish, seated there, naked, in the chair. Instinctively she frowned, crossed her legs primly, and clasped her hands together in her lap.

Johnny shrugged out of his evening jacket, slipped his black silk tie from under the stiff white collar, and removing the gold studs from his shirtfront, said, "Sweetheart, you once told me you'd always trust me."

"I do, but—"

"If you don't enjoy making love in the chair, darling, we can always move to the bed. Just give it a chance."

Her eyes on the thick thatch of black chest hair he was uncovering, she nodded and replied, "I guess it wouldn't hurt to give it a try."

After that Nevada didn't speak. She couldn't. Johnny was casually removing his clothes, allowing them to fall on the carpet, revealing a dark powerful chest, corded ribs, strong muscular arms, and long sturdy legs.

And when the last garment, snowy white underwear, fell away from his tall brown body, Nevada gasped. The awesome tumescence she had felt pressing her through his clothing sprang proudly free. Her astonished gaze riveted to that splendid symbol of virile masculinity, she unconsciously licked her parted lips and gripped the chair arms tightly, nervously.

He stood there with his bare brown feet apart, a living, breathing statue of flesh-and-blood perfection. A magnificent Adonis, sculpted by the Almighty's masterful hands. A beautiful God of Love possessed of the power to give her glorious ecstasy.

"No," she said when he made a move toward her, "let me look at you a moment more."

Nevada's legs came uncrossed. The texture of the chair's silky brocade was pleasing to her bare skin and she writhed and stretched and never took her eyes off Johnny.

He came to her, his dark eyes aglow with passion and with love. Very slowly he eased her legs apart and Nevada felt a sweet expectation build with the languid movement. He knelt between Nevada's legs, and lifting his hands to her face, gently drew her forward and kissed her, a long, deep kiss that left her shaken and breathless.

"Johnny," she murmured, her hands gripping his broad, bare shoulders.

"My only love," he answered, and bent to kiss her right breast. His shiny black curls tickling her, his mouth enclosed the nipple warmly, sucking so gently Nevada arched her back in a silent eager plea. But his lips released their treasure and he raised his dark head to look into her eyes.

He knelt there between her parted legs, touching her gently, caressing her with his long, skilled fingers and his heated black eyes. Allowing the anticipation to build, permitting the dazzled girl to grow so totally aroused there would be no discomfort when he took her.

Johnny knew exactly when the instant arrived, and murmuring soft endearments, he drew her legs around his waist, then guided the tip of his pulsing phallus into her. For long, sweet moments they stayed like that, Johnny, barely inside her, remaining purposely still.

Waiting.

Nevada, deeply in love, on fire for him, gripped Johnny's smooth shoulders and began to move, slowly at first, cautiously, inching farther off the chair, sliding more fully onto Johnny, settling herself warily on that rigid, thrusting masculinity.

Johnny, exercising extraordinary control, continued to remain perfectly fixed there in place, kneeling before her, his hands resting lightly at her waist, while she sank deliciously down onto him.

When at last Nevada had carefully but fully impaled

herself upon him, Johnny's hands moved down to her bare bottom. His pulse beating visibly in his tanned throat, he gripped her firm buttocks tightly in his splayed fingers and urged her off the chair. He bent his knees and spread them apart, then sat back on his heels, bringing her with him.

There on the deeply piled rug before the brocade chair, Johnny made love to Nevada, his hands guiding her hips, his pelvis rising rhythmically to meet hers. Nevada, her pale thighs draped over his hard brown ones, looped her hands behind Johnny's dark head, stiffened her arms, and leaned way back.

Looking into his blazing eyes, she abandoned all prudent precaution and anxiously, eagerly ground her hot, pliant body to his. Recklessly she pushed down on him, tightly she squeezed him, gloriously she felt him filling her, stretching her.

And all the while she was looking at him, thrilling to the sight of his dark face hardened with passion and his wide, powerful shoulders and arms gleaming with perspiration, the biceps bulging and pulling.

The pleasure was growing so intense Nevada felt herself slipping dangerously close to the edge. Her mouth open, she panted. Her gaze locked with Johnny's.

"I love you, sweetheart," he said.

"Oh, Johnny, I . . . I'm—"

"I know, darling. Let it come. You're so beautiful. So beautiful."

Her nails cutting into the flesh of his bare shoulders, Nevada's dazed eyes slid down to Johnny's chest where the thick crisp hair was beaded with moisture. One diamond drop poised on a flat male nipple. Nevada impulsively leaned forward to kiss the tiny droplet away as her climax began.

Her lips were pressed to his chest, her tongue was eagerly licking and savoring the salty taste when the deep, wrenching pinnacle of passion overcame her.

"Johnny, Johnny!" Her mouth went up to his slick shoulder and she bit him punishingly in her wild, searing joy.

"Ahhhh, darlin'," groaned Johnny, her deep fulfillment becoming his own. "I love you, baby. I love you."

When their breaths returned and their heartbeats slowed, they tumbled over onto the soft carpet and Johnny, gathering Nevada close, leaned over her, kissing her hair, her eyes, her lips, and punctuating each kiss with words of love and devotion.

"Oh, Johnny," she whispered happily, "I knew you loved me, I knew it."

"I do, sweetheart," he said. "I love you, I want to marry you."

"Yes! We'll be married and Papa will be there. I'm so happy. So very happy. We'll tell Papa, and he'll like you too. And . . . Johnny . . . Johnny . . . no, Johnny . . . don't go . . . don't leave me . . . Johnny . . . Johnny . . ."

Nevada's eyes fluttered open and her searching hand swept the empty space beside her, patting frantically, futilely feeling for the warmth that was not there.

"Johnny!" she murmured despairingly in the darkness. "Come back . . . Johnny . . ."

Her hand encountered only the cool silkiness of the sheet stretched tightly over the soft mattress of her bed. Truth dawning, Nevada sat up and looked anxiously about. And saw, in the bed across from hers, Miss Annabelle sleeping soundly.

"Johnny . . ." Nevada foolishly whispered his name again. The dream had been so real, so vivid, she couldn't believe he was not with her.

But Johnny was not there. Had never been there. She was in her stateroom with Miss Annabelle and Johnny was . . . A crushing sadness weighed down on Nevada.

Only a dream. Nothing had changed. Her papa was dead. Johnny didn't love her. Johnny would never love her. Johnny didn't want her love.

Nevada lay back down. She shut her eyes tightly and tried very hard to relive the beautiful fantasy. Johnny undressing her. Johnny carrying her to the blue brocade chair. Johnny removing his own clothes and kneeling before her. Johnny kissing and touching her. Johnny saying he loved her as together they ascended to paradise.

Sadly she could not recapture the magic and within seconds the entire episode was growing cloudy, extremely vague. In minutes she could not even recall any of it. It had vanished completely, an illusion gone forever. Her love dreams had ended.

For a long time Nevada lay awake in the darkness, restless and disturbed. It was after four in the morning when finally, to the rhythmic roll and pitch of the vast ocean liner, she fell back into a dreamless sleep.

19

〰〰〰〰〰

Up with the rising of the sun, Nevada recalled nothing of her erotic dream.

She remembered only that Johnny had not invited her to sit in on last night's poker game with King Cassidy, a fact that had greatly disappointed her. If Johnny was the big winner, he might no longer need his lucky charm.

She couldn't wait to find out what had happened and yet she supposed she would have to. Johnny, she knew, would not come out of his stateroom before noon.

Frowning, the idea suddenly struck her that King Cassidy would be an early riser. He would be at that very minute enjoying breakfast in the ship's main dining hall.

Glancing at Miss Annabelle still sleeping peacefully, Nevada's frown turned to a smile. If she was quick about it, she could be dressed and out of the cabin before Miss Annabelle stirred.

In minutes Nevada had slipped quietly out of her stateroom and was standing in the arched doorway of the ship's vast dining hall. The enormous room was almost deserted at that hour. Only a handful of early birds were seated at scattered tables, all of them gentlemen.

The rich aroma of freshly brewed coffee was strong in the air and stewards carrying large silver trays passed among the sparse crowd, serving the first-class passengers from a varied breakfast menu.

Ignoring the looks of inquiry she drew, Nevada smiled when she spotted the gleaming silver head almost hidden behind a tall potted palm.

"Were you to meet one of the gentlemen for breakfast?" Nevada looked up to see a tall thin uniformed man smiling down at her.

"Why, yes," she answered without hesitation, "I'm to join King Cassidy."

"Right this way, miss," said the impressed head waiter and led her straight to King's table.

King Cassidy sat alone at a square table against the east wall, studying a gold-tasseled red leather menu. He looked up as Nevada approached him.

"My dear, what a pleasant surprise," he said, rising and smiling warmly at her. "I had no idea you'd be up this early."

"'Morning, King," she said, and slipped quickly into the chair held out for her. As soon as King Cassidy had reclaimed his chair, Nevada eagerly leaned forward. "Well?"

He looked puzzled. "I'm afraid I don't know—"

Nevada sighed impatiently. "Last night's poker game! Who won?" She held her breath.

King smiled at her. "Certainly I would not want to sound like a braggart, but—"

"Will you kindly get on with it! Who won? You or Johnny?"

"I did," he said firmly. "Now, what can I order for you? The flapjacks are light and delicious."

Nevada sounded casual when she said, "Ah . . . did you win a lot?" She picked up the red leather menu.

King stroked his silver goatee. "Nevada, it's bad form

for a gambler to disclose the amount he takes from an opponent."

"That makes sense." She said, then smiled and added, "I'll bet you're a good gambler, King."

"I've gambled a lot and it's a great life," said King, pausing to grin impishly before adding, "when you're winning."

She laughed easily and then listened intently as King Cassidy recalled the various players he had bucked up against through the years.

"Some players play the game primarily on its mathematics: the chances of a certain card coming up, the size of the pot versus the size of the bet that may win it, and so on. Others rely on people-reading: how a player acts in a certain situation, whether it's possible to confuse him or to bluff him out with an outlandish bet."

Nevada, nodding eagerly, said, "Go on. Go on."

"In cards, as in life, the instinct type of gambler is the most fearsome because he's likely to bet you all his money with nothing. Or he might call you with all his money with ace-high. He's like a lion—everybody's afraid of him."

"Which kind of player are you, King?" Nevada asked with interest.

"I'm of the people-reading category," he said.

Nevada laid aside the menu, shook out her napkin. "And Johnny?"

King Cassidy's blue eyes crinkled at the corners. "The boy's definitely a lion. Dexterous and dangerous, that's John Roulette. A big, fearless cat." He shook his silver head and laughed heartily.

Nevada laughed with him. And when the laughter had subsided, Nevada asked, "Will you and Johnny play again tonight?"

"I can't speak for Johnny. We've been invited to sit in on

a big game." He leaned back in his chair. "The competition will be quite stiff. It will be a game that offers the kind of opposition Johnny needs to sharpen his teeth as a world-class poker player."

Nevada felt herself becoming hopeful and excited. Impulsively she placed her hand on King's forearm and asked, "These . . . gentlemen, would they . . . ah . . . object to having a lady present during the game?"

King Cassidy covered her hand with his. His silver eyebrows lifting inquiringly, he teased gently, "Any lady we know?"

"Not a real lady. Me. Could I come to the game with Johnny?"

"My dear," he said with calm authority, "if John Roulette brings enough money, he can have an entire harem, so long as they remain quiet and don't go looking over any shoulder but his."

She was the only female present.

She sat quietly atop a velvet stool just right of Johnny's chair, her left hand possessively riding his right shoulder. The private salon with its dark mahogany paneling and wine-red carpet and private bar and bartender was definitely a man's domain, but Nevada felt right at home.

She was unbothered by the whiskey drinking and the cigar smoking and the occasional muttered oath of a player with a second-best hand. Raised in an all-male environment, Nevada was at ease and completely happy spending the night with Johnny and King and four other skilled and serious poker players.

The reaction to her presence had been mixed, at first. King Cassidy and the rich New York furriers, the Nolan brothers, had no objection. But the Philadelphia steel magnate was incensed, saying he refused to play with Nevada present. Johnny had smiled and coolly replied, "If the lady goes, I go." The wealthy Pennsylvanian, anxious to have a go at the dark Mississippi gambler, promptly reconsidered and acquiesced.

Lastly, there was the handsome and rich blond scion of an Ohio carriage-building family, who was on his way to England to marry a distant young cousin of Queen Victoria's. The blond man smilingly welcomed Nevada's feminine presence. And foolishly spent more time studying her than his cards.

Johnny, unreadable as he always was when playing high-stakes poker, unwittingly thrilled Nevada, by intermittently taking the small hand she placed atop his shoulder and holding it warmly in his or pressing it to his lips, allowing the silkiness of his mustache to brush back and forth over her sensitive palm.

It meant nothing to the stone-faced poker player beyond a desire to draw on the luck she brought him. Not for a second did he consider that the idle gesture made Nevada's heart pound. When, on a folded hand, Johnny leaned back to relax, he nonchalantly draped his long arm across Nevada's lap. His cool black eyes never leaving the baize, he thoughtlessly patted and squeezed her leg through the silk gown, his long, dark fingers sliding around to stroke the sensitive back of her knee.

Nevada thought she would expire with joy.

Later, after Johnny had cast off his jacket, loosened his collar and rolled up his sleeves, Nevada had grown so attuned to the slightest movement of his shoulder, the faintest pull of the muscle and sinew, she could almost have told what kind of hand he held without even looking. That too thrilled her. She alone knew when Johnny was tense.

The competitors seated around the table saw only a

player who, with the passing of the long evening and the growing of his dark whiskers and the sleepy drooping of his heavily lashed lids, looked even more formidable and cool and unreadable.

His expression remained the same, no matter the cards he drew. But the warm hard muscles beneath Nevada's fingers bunched and tightened and shared with her his secrets. It was a wonderful heady experience, strangely intimate. And Nevada, her eyes riveted to his dark rigid face, felt as close to Johnny as if they were making love.

Her gaze slowly lowered to the white shirt half open down his dark chest and she felt her breath grow short. What, she wondered anxiously, would Johnny do if she unobtrusively slid her hand up over his shoulder and down. Carefully gauging what his reaction might be, she wisely waited for an opportune moment.

It was Johnny's turn to deal.

He fanned the deck faceup on the slick baize, his brown hands as deft and sure as a surgeon's. His face obscured behind a cloud of rich blue cigar smoke, he dealt the well-shuffled cards out to the players, then placed the deck facedown before him.

He picked up his own cards. With the quick, sure movement of his thumb, he spread them barely enough to read what they were before once again pushing them together. It was done so quickly, Nevada never saw what he was holding.

The cigar still stuck between his even white teeth, his black eyes devoid of expression, he waited for the first bet to be made. Nevada, her palm pressed to his shoulder, knew before Johnny's turn came, that he was going to call and raise.

"To you, Roulette," said one of the New York Nolans.

"Call your hundred," said Johnny. "And raise you five hundred." He slid his chips over the green baize.

The betting was spirited and heavy. Not one of the six players dropped out. The pile of chips at the table's center grew higher. And higher.

On the last round of betting, King Cassidy, the blond Ohioan, and one of the Nolan furriers dropped out. Johnny, the remaining Nolan brother, and the Philadelphia steel magnate called.

Nevada's hand gently moved over Johnny's back to his left shoulder. Then up and over. Pausing, she waited to see if she was a bother to him. So intense was he, his attention so snared by the game, he never noticed when she slipped her fingers into the open collar of his white shirt.

For a moment she let her hand lay atop his prominent collarbone. Then drawing a shallow breath, she rose from her stool to stand directly behind Johnny. She moved her hand slowly but steadily down, down until it rested directly over Johnny's heart.

There her hand stayed, pressed firmly to the warmth beneath which Johnny's heartbeat drummed heavily against her open palm. Nevada was not quite sure what excited her most, the tickle of his crisp chest hair or the heat of his flesh or the beating of his heart. It was the same fierce beating that she had felt that night on the *Gambler* when they had made love. And now, as then, it seemed to become her own as it pulsed through her fingertips just the way it had pulsed through her naked breasts then.

If the muscles of his back had revealed a measure of Johnny's tenseness, the rapid pounding of his heartbeat told her so much more. Her own heart in her throat, Nevada stood leaning for support against the back of his chair, knowing beyond a doubt that her dangerous lion was intent on taking the large sum of money resting on the table.

With nothing in his hand.

Nevada's heart raced with Johnny's as the betting grew fierce, the stack of chips taller, the tension in the room almost palpable. It seemed to her it would never end, that none of the three would ever drop out. And, if they did not, then Johnny would be the loser.

The blond Ohioan finally shook his head and tossed in his cards, saying, "Gentlemen, it's getting a little too steep for me."

The Philadelphia steel magnate grinned. Johnny Roulette's deadpan expression remained the same. The magnate said, "What about you, Roulette?"

His heart thumping against Nevada's hand, Johnny called the smiling Philadelphian. And raised yet again. The smile left his opponent's face. The man straightened nervously in his chair and studied his cards.

There was total silence in the room. No one said a word or made a move.

"Goddammit!" The bested Philadelphian finally exploded and angrily threw in his cards. Then said almost immediately, "I don't suppose you'd be willing to show me what you have?"

Johnny gave no answer. Just fixed him with a cool stare. Then purposely fanned out his cards so that Nevada, and no one else, could see what he was holding. A pair of deuces. The seven of diamonds. The king of clubs. And the ace of hearts.

Nevada didn't smile, gasp, or register any emotion. But her fingers reflexively tightened over Johnny's drumming heart.

The lion had bluffed.

And won.

20

∾∾∾∾∾∾

The trouble began in London.

The day of their arrival had started as one of exciting promise. A brilliant sun, the likes of which was rarely seen in the British Isles, shone brightly down in greeting on the gleaming white hull of the SS *Starlight* as it berthed at Southampton.

Nevada, her cheeks aglow and her eyes sparkling, stood at the crowded railing, clinging to Johnny's arm with one hand, waving with the other. The crossing had been wonderful. Johnny had spent nearly all his time with her. He had been fun and charming and Nevada was sure it was only a matter of time before his heart belonged entirely to her.

On the dock Johnny hurried them aboard the boat train for the long ride into London. The train was very crowded; not enough room for them all to sit together. Johnny found a couple of seats together and insisted King Cassidy and Miss Annabelle take them.

Then he grabbed Nevada's hand and, running interference for her, pulled her along behind him, searching for a place to sit. The car was full. They went forward into the next one. And the next.

Just as the train was pulling out of the station, Johnny spotted one vacant seat at the very front of the car, beside a dozing elderly man. He quickly guided Nevada to it. She sat down and Johnny, assuring her he would be fine, stood in the narrow aisle with a shoulder propped against the forward wall as the locomotive picked up speed. Tired from a long night of poker, Johnny's dark head was soon sagging on his chest, his drowsy eyes closed.

Nevada shot up from her seat and pulled on his sleeve. His eyes came open. "What is it?"

"You," she said, smiling up at him. "You're dead tired. Take the seat and I'll stand. I'm not the least bit sleepy."

Johnny shook his weary head and closed his eyes. "Sit down, Nevada."

She didn't. She said, "I know—you take the seat and I'll sit on your lap. I'm not very heavy."

Drowsy dark eyes came open again. Johnny grinned. "I am a bit fatigued."

So Johnny carefully crawled over the old sleeping gentleman, slid into the seat, and pulled Nevada down on his lap, wrapping his long arms around her waist and lacing his fingers together.

"You comfortable?" she asked.

Leaning his dark head back against the tall padded seat, he grinned at her. "Wake me in London."

"I will," she said, and smiled fondly as his thick lashes restlessly fluttered, then swept down to rest on the high brown cheekbones.

Johnny was sound asleep. He slept all the way to London and Nevada, far too excited to sleep, enjoyed every lovely mile of the trip. After leaving the industrial area of Southampton behind, the train wound its way across the lush green countryside of England and Nevada Marie Hamilton thought she had surely never seen anything more pleasing to the eye.

Unless it was the dark handsome face in repose only

inches from her own. She spent as much time admiring Johnny as she did England. It was wonderful fun to sit there on his knees and to leisurely study the dear face that looked almost boyish in slumber. She examined him with an intensity he would never have tolerated had he been awake.

Nevada noticed, for the first time, that there was a tiny white scar an inch below Johnny's right ear. And still another just beneath his strong chin. Instinctively puckering her lips, Nevada conquered the temptation to kiss the tiny white scars. Other than those small imperfections, he was without blemish.

Jet-black hair, an errant shock adrift over his forehead, his smooth olive complexion, his well-shaped nose, his beautifully sculpted lips beneath the sleek mustache, Johnny Roulette was nothing short of beautiful to the adoring young woman wrapped carelessly his strong, sleeping arms.

Johnny never roused until the train pulled into the London station and Nevada had to firmly speak his name.

"Johnny, we're here. Wake up."

His eyes still closed, Johnny automatically hunched his wide shoulders and slid lower down onto his spine, hugging Nevada closer to him and licking his lips. Her own mouth was now no more than a couple of inches from his. Nevada trembled.

"Johnny," she said again more loudly.

"Hm?" he murmured, and slowly started coming awake. Blinking to focus, he said, "Where are we?"

She smiled and, gently pushing on his broad chest, levered herself back a little. "Johnny Roulette, you must be the soundest sleeper in the world!" Her fingers itched to push back the rebellious black hair from his forehead.

"So I've been told," was his response as he straightened,

loosened his hold on her, and raised a hand to run it through his dark, disheveled hair. "We here?"

"Yes, we're in London."

Yawning, he said, "Did you enjoy the ride through England?"

"More than you can imagine."

At the station King Cassidy said good-bye but promised he'd come to call within the week and Nevada, noticing how Miss Annabelle colored when King kissed her hand, wondered if she too had enjoyed the train ride.

Johnny swept her and Miss Annabelle into a cab and Nevada, smiling happily, rode through the London streets with the now rested Johnny pointing out famous landmarks.

Her smile widened when the carriage rolled to a stop before the imposing hotel on Brook Street and Johnny lifted her down to the sidewalk. A liveried footman stepped forth to greet them and welcome them to Claridge's, bowing and hurrying to hold the hotel's heavy doors open wide.

Inside, they were warmly welcomed by the hotel's suave manager and Nevada, her sweeping gaze examining her lavish surroundings, felt certain she was going to like London.

But then she stepped into Claridge's perfumed lift and came face-to-face with a tall, strikingly beautiful woman with hair the color of summer wheat and eyes like emeralds. Nevada's heart sank when she whirled about to catch Johnny looking over her head, smiling engagingly at the pretty blonde.

By the time they reached their apartments on the hotel's third floor, the joy as well as the sun had gone out of Nevada's world. Intuitively she sensed great danger. She glanced again at the well-dressed woman whose flashing green eyes were staring with frank admiration at Johnny Roulette.

"Dear me," said Miss Annabelle, when the short, smiling bellman showed them into a high-ceilinged suite with walls of ivory and gleaming furniture and tall front windows, "it's begun to rain. I didn't see a cloud in the sky on our ride into the city."

"Only a short summer shower," assured Johnny pleasantly. "It won't last." He peeled some bills off for the bellboy.

"You're wrong," said Nevada, moving dispiritedly to a window. Sporadic drops of rain hit the polished glass and trickled down, streaking the panes. Nevada, lifting a forefinger to follow the path of one slow-moving droplet, said prophetically, "It will rain all afternoon."

Miss Annabelle, removing her hat and gloves, said, "Well, it will make little difference to me. I want nothing more than a warm bath and a nice long nap."

Nevada turned around. Hopefully she said, "Johnny, why don't we find a game? With the rain, there's nothing else we can do."

"No," he replied, without explanation. But then he didn't have to explain. Nevada knew. Sadly, she knew.

When, half an hour later, Johnny stepped from his adjoining room, freshly shaved and bathed and changed, Nevada prayed he would ask her to go with him, wherever it was he meant to go, and knew he would not. He didn't.

Nevada jumped up, hurried to him, and asked, "Will we be having dinner in the hotel this evening?"

"Why don't you and Miss Annabelle have supper sent up."

She swallowed hard. "What about you?"

He smiled. "Don't worry about me. I'll manage." And he was gone.

The afternoon was never-ending for Nevada. She restlessly paced the large sitting room, anxiously listening for the sound of his footsteps in the corridor. The rain continued to fall slowly, steadily. Nevada never knew when sunset came, because there was no sun to set. Just bleak gloomy skies and a big dreary room and a lonely young girl sitting in the window seat, hugging her knees and wondering where Johnny was.

And what he was doing in the rain.

"I simply adore making love in the rain," said Lady Ashley. She stood at the tall windows in the well-appointed sitting room of the suite directly above Nevada. The elegant blond beauty turned about and smiled at the tall dark man. "Don't you, Roulette?"

"Rain or shine, Lady Ashley, so long as it's with you," Johnny replied gallantly. Yawning, he lolled lazily in an easy chair of rich plum velvet, his dark eyes half closed. Adam-naked, he stretched his long, bare legs out before him, unashamed, gladly going along with Lady Ashley's charade, whatever it might be.

No sooner had he knocked on her door than she led him into the parlor, introduced herself, and asked, "Did you have difficulty finding me?"

"Not really," said Johnny, seeing no need to say more.

She smiled. "I'm glad. I wanted you in the elevator. I want you now."

"I'm here."

She stepped closer, swept her well-manicured hands over the breadth of his shirtfront. Her eyes met his. "I want to undress you. May I Mr—"

"Roulette. John Roulette."

"Ooooh! A Frenchman. Do you make love like—"

"Half French, on my father's side," Johnny cut in. "My mother was Irish."

"I see. May I undress you, my handsome half Frenchman?"

"If you like."

She said no more. With a swift dexterity that amazed him, Lady Ashley Wellington stripped him bare, then slowly walked around him, openly admiring his dark male nudity.

"Would you like a drink, Roulette?" she said, laying his folded clothes over the sofa's back. She inclined her golden head toward a well-stocked drinks trolley.

"I'll join you in a small brandy. Nothing stronger," said Johnny. "Then perhaps you'd like to get undressed."

Lady Ashley smiled, gave his mouth a playfully biting kiss, and said, "Not just yet."

Now, half an hour later, the beautiful blond noblewoman standing before the tall, rain-splattered windows still had on the expensive beige silk afternoon dress she was wearing when she had let him in. She had not removed so much as the long rope of pearls from her throat or the handmade kid slippers from her feet.

Never a man to rush or to question a woman's unique desires or tastes in lovemaking, Johnny lounged there in the chair, comfortably naked in the shadowy room, neither embarrassed nor nervous. Obviously the lovely Lady Ashley was playing her own special kind of love games, and that suited him fine.

She was, even fully clothed, a very provocative woman. She exuded a sexuality so strong he had picked up on it in their brief encounter in the elevator earlier. That sophisticated seductiveness was even more pronounced now and Johnny looked forward to a long, rainy afternoon of enjoyable sex.

Lady Ashley, her emerald eyes transmitting a potent heat, slowly advanced on Johnny. When she stood directly before his chair she said huskily, "Do you know what I want to do, Roulette?"

"Tell me, dear." He smiled and reached for her hand.

Her fair face flushed and she said, "I could never actually say it aloud."

His thumb gently stroking the back of her hand, he pulled her down onto his lap and encouraged her. "Then whisper it to me, Lady Ashley."

Smiling, she cupped his smoothly shaven jaw in her hand, leaned close, and whispered into his ear. Told him exactly what she wanted to do to him, and in the most graphic of terms. Johnny felt the half arousal he'd worn for the past half hour become painfully complete.

Before he could speak Lady Ashley pulled away, looked at him hungrily, and slid off his lap to kneel between his spread legs.

She wrapped delicate fingers around him and smiled like a pleased cat about to take its first taste of rich cream. "You're so much a man, Roulette. So beautiful." Her green eyes glazed with passion. "Soooo big!"

She bent her perfectly coiffed blond head to him and Johnny's hands gripped the chair arms.

In minutes Lady Ashley was rising to stand before him once more. Smiling down at the limp, sated man, her soft laughter competed with the sound of the raindrops peppering the tall windows.

Lady Ashley reached behind her head and unhooked her cultured pearls. Dangling them down to tickle Johnny's bare belly, she said, "I'm going into the bedroom to get undressed." She released the pearls; they fell and lay there on Johnny's lower stomach. She looked pointedly at his flaccid groin and said, "Stay here until you can wear the pearls on it. Then bring them to me." She licked her lips suggestively. "And join me in bed."

Lady Ashley, lying naked against the satin-cased pillow, clapped her hands with glee when Johnny walked into her bedroom minutes later. He slowly advanced, the pearls draped around his rigid erection.

Lady Ashley happily crawled across the soft bed, reached out to reclaim her pearls. Johnny stood statue-still while she leisurely eased the long luminous rope from him. Then he pulled her up into a kneeling position, kissed her hotly, and lowered her to the bed, following her down.

The pearls, soon forgotten, slipped from Lady Ashley's opened hand and she sighed breathlessly. "I do so enjoy making love in the rain."

21

─────◍◍◍◍◍◍◍─────

"There are times," said Miss Annabelle, "when elbows can go on the table. Which is when?"

"When no one's looking?" Nevada said, grinning from ear to ear.

Miss Annabelle glanced at her sharply. "The gesture is strictly taboo at formal dinners," she said. "It is, however, acceptable at formal gatherings between courses or while resting."

Dauntlessly guiding her extremely bright but annoyingly cavalier charge through the confusing how-to's and social graces she needed to master in order to become a true lady, Miss Annabelle sat across a pink damask-draped table from Nevada. The table, on wheels, had been rolled into their Claridge's suite by a white-jacketed steward. He stood, his gloved hands folded before him, waiting to serve lunch.

On this surprisingly sunny September noon in London the day's lesson centered around table manners. Nevada, in the role of a visiting luncheon guest, had entered the sitting room with its ivory walls and Chippendale furniture and deep rust-hued carpet, smiled at Miss Annabelle, and said, "Hello. My name is Nevada Marie Hamilton. It is nice to meet you."

"Well done!" Miss Annabelle praised her. "Except I

think we must drop Nevada and become simply Miss Marie Hamilton."

"Why the hell would I want to do that?" Nevada's hands went immediately to her hips.

Miss Annabelle's fine brows lifted. "I notice, dear, that when you become upset you still swear. You must learn to control your temper. Swearing, at any time, is out of the question."

"I'm sorry, but good Lord . . . ah . . . why would I want to drop my name?"

"*Nevada* sounds flamboyant and untamed and, frankly, rather *déclassé*."

"It does?"

"I'm afraid so, dear."

Nevada sighed with frustration. "This becoming a lady is really a big pain in the—" She caught herself. "Fine, in public I'll be Marie. Here I'm still Nevada. All right?"

"Very well. Now, Miss Hamilton, won't you have an appetizer?" offered Miss Annabelle.

The white-jacketed steward stepped forward, held out a tray to Nevada. She stared at a silver canapé tray and made a face. Lifting her disapproving eyes from the oysters and clams within miniature tartlike pastries, she said, "Ugh. That's disgusting!"

Miss Annabelle scolded, "If the hors d'oeuvres tray is passed to you, simply say, I don't care for any, thank you."

Nevada nodded.

When they sat down to the meal Miss Annabelle gently reminded, "Nibble, don't wolf. Sip, don't slurp." The waiter had placed a bowl of lentil soup and a hard roll before Nevada. "Get the arms up over the soup," Miss Annabelle went on. "Break the roll into bite-size pieces. Leave no crumbs on the tablecloth."

"Uh-oh, my thumb's stuck," said Nevada, attempting to break the roll. "This thing's like a rock!"

Ignoring her complaint, Miss Annabelle said, "Dip the spoon into the soup. Bring it to the lips and gently tip the contents into the mouth. Do not slurp."

The meal and the lesson lasted for more than an hour. And when it was finished and the patient steward wheeled the dishes from the suite, Miss Annabelle drew a loud groan from Nevada when she said, "Let's work on your posture now. You're still not walking . . ."

And so it went, and so it had gone for the past eight weeks. Ever since their arrival in London. It seemed to Nevada that almost every waking hour was spent on tiresome exercises that bored her to tears. She had never realized that she didn't know how to walk, speak, eat, sit, stand, dress, or laugh properly until the monotonous, never-ending instructions had begun.

A thousand silly rules of etiquette swimming around in her aching head, Nevada went to bed each night more frustrated and discouraged and downright listless than she'd ever been in her life.

But Miss Annabelle's relentless tutoring was not the only reason for her gloom. Since their arrival in London she had hardly seen Johnny. Save for a few evenings when he had requested that she accompany him to a gaming hall, they were never together. And even then, when they were together, they were not alone.

The fine British ladies were as much if not more enamored of the sleekly handsome Johnny Roulette as were their American counterparts. From the moment he had stepped into Claridge's elevator and caught the discerning eye of Lady Ashley, he had hardly had time for his other love. Gambling.

The lavish Claridge's apartments he shared with Nevada

and Miss Annabelle were used by Johnny for little more than sleeping and changing his clothes. And often as not, he didn't even sleep there, a fact that greatly disturbed Nevada's sleep.

An unending parade of voluptuous redheads and stunning brunettes and elegant blondes were breathlessly squired about town by Johnny. Cultivated ladies all, but Nevada noted with jealous fury that for all their fine manners and high-toned ways and aristocratic names, they were not too well-bred to stay out all night with Johnny!

Especially the regal, sophisticated, snobbish Lady Ashley.

The only thing that made the London stay bearable was King Cassidy and his frequent visits. Nevada was fond of the likable silver-haired man who told interesting stories of his youth in the wild, exciting West.

When King dropped by Claridge's, he always carried a bouquet of fresh-cut flowers and as often as not, thoughtful little gifts for her and Miss Annabelle.

And when King was in the suite, seated on the long English Chippendale sofa, stroking his silver goatee as he spoke, Miss Annabelle seemed to change before Nevada's very eyes into a shy, slightly nervous, more youthful woman.

After his first few visits Nevada cunningly turned Miss Annabelle's quiet fascination with the silver king to her own advantage. Eager to forgo her boring studies, if only for an hour or two, she was quick to suggest that King take them out for a stroll or a ride, complaining that they had been "cooped up" forever.

The dapper silver king had gallantly agreed. And then made short work of persuading the hesitant Miss Annabelle that a respite from the four walls at Claridge's would be good for her, would make the roses bloom in her fair cheeks.

In a gleaming navy-blue landau pulled by a pair of high-stepping, perfectly matched bays, the trio made excursions around the old city. It was King who drove them through Mayfair, casually pointing out the great residences behind whose heavy doors dwelled, or had dwelled, the likes of Lord Dover and Lady Berkeley of Stratton and the Earl of Scarborough and Lord Burlington and Sir Nathaniel Curzon.

Nevada was impressed that a western silver king would know who lived in London's fine houses. And Miss Annabelle was surprised and delighted when they visited Agnew's on Albemarle and the silver king—escorting them through the vast art gallery, where the walls were hung with crimson damask and the staircases were of polished oak—readily identified the works of the great English and French and German masters.

And King was the one responsible for showing them the Tower of London and the adjacent Tower Bridge. He took them for a stroll one fine sunny morning through St. James Park. He pointed out the exclusive shops around Oxford and Bond streets. He showed them the Royal Opera House. St. James Church. St. Paul's.

Even Buckingham Palace.

"Lord, wouldn't I like to go in there!" said Nevada, staring, transfixed at the huge palace. "Wouldn't that just be a hoot?" She turned to look at the middle-aged couple across from her in the carriage. Miss Annabelle was wearing that expression of reproof that made Nevada aware of her slip-up. King was smiling warmly, his blue eyes twinkling with merriment, as though he found nothing wrong with what she'd said.

Addressing Miss Annabelle, she said, "If I sounded

common, forgive me, but I would love to go inside Buckingham Palace."

Softening, Miss Annabelle said, "I know, dear. But I'm afraid it's out of the question."

Nevada looked from Miss Annabelle to King. He said, "I'm sorry, child. I'm afraid it would take better credentials than mine to secure for you an invitation from the Queen."

He looked truly remorseful. It touched Nevada. She flashed him a lovely smile and said, "Who cares? Let's go to Piccadilly Circus!"

On a chilly, foggy evening in late September, King Cassidy, a gilt-covered box of fine Belgian chocolates in one hand, his varnished malacca cane in the other, impulsively stopped by Claridge's for an unannounced visit with his two favorite ladies. Miss Annabelle was alone in the suite. She was quick to explain that Nevada had accompanied Johnny and Lady Ashley out for an evening of gambling.

King, realizing they were alone for the first time, suddenly felt almost as timid as the quiet genteel lady facing him. He was becoming very fond of Miss Annabelle, felt almost like a bashful young suitor as he stood smiling down at her.

Miss Annabelle, her splendid manners forgotten in the face of her nervousness at being alone with the dapper dynamic man to whom she was absurdly attracted, did not invite King Cassidy to sit down.

"I—I'll tell . . . ah . . . Nevada you came by," she heard herself stammering. "She'll be sorry she missed you."

It sounded like a dismissal to the dashing but sensitive silver king. He had been about to suggest that the two of them go out to dinner or to the theater, but obviously the patrician southern lady was not interested in spending an evening alone with an old western ruffian who talked too much and laughed too loudly and drank whiskey straight.

"You do that, Miss Annabelle." He backed away bowing, and Miss Annabelle was puzzled by the expression that had come into his vivid blue eyes. For a second the vibrant King Cassidy looked almost hurt.

When she closed the door after him Miss Annabelle sighed and wandered aimlessly across the room. She laid the heavy box of chocolates on a marble-topped table and went to stand before the tall front windows, feeling decidedly melancholy. Drawing a weary breath, she gently pulled the peach silk drapery aside and looked down at the street.

King Cassidy was on the sidewalk below, preparing to step out of the cold night up into the waiting blue landau. His hand on the carriage door, he turned suddenly and looked up. Straight at her. Hidden in shadow, Miss Annabelle glimpsed a side of King Cassidy she had never seen before. The man who was always smiling appeared cheerless on this bleak, foggy night. A gust of wind picked up tendrils of his gleaming silver hair, blew them into his strangely unhappy face. He shivered, hunched his shoulders, and hurriedly ducked into the landau.

Miss Annabelle stood at the window long after King's carriage had driven away. She wondered where he would spend his evening, and with whom. And then silently chided herself for being a foolish old maid. Rich, attractive, spirited gentlemen like King Cassidy never lacked for company.

Feeling a sudden chill in both body and soul, the lonely spinster turned from the window. Hugging her arms to her sides, she crossed to the brightly-blazing bronze marble fireplace, dropped down onto the padded footstool where

Nevada often sat, and stared forlornly into the warmth-giving flames.

Spectacular in a daring gown of eggshell satin, Lady Ashley was more than a little irritated. Her noble jaw was set, her teeth clamped firmly together, her large emerald eyes snapping with displeasure.

Johnny Roulette, his dark evening jacket carelessly open, the scarlet silk lining showing, was in a fine mood. Leaning lazily back against the plush velvet of the leased landau's wide backseat, he wore a pleased smile and his dark eyes flashed with excitement.

Nevada, the billowing skirts of her midnight-blue taffeta gown spilling over onto Johnny's bent left knee, was smiling, her blue eyes gleaming with mischief. Her mood was buoyant, despite the obvious indignation of Lady Ashley.

Nevada was well pleased with herself. She had managed all evening long to place herself firmly between Lady Ashley and Johnny, which was no easy feat. In the posh clubs Nevada had caught the daggered looks the titled blonde kept casting at her. Johnny never noticed. He was too engrossed in gambling. And winning.

Relying on Nevada's ability to bring him luck, he thought nothing of holding her hand or squeezing her bare shoulder or grinning indulgently when she possessively draped herself against his broad shoulder.

Lady Ashley noticed and was not amused. And that amused Nevada no end.

When, thousands up, they left the first club to try their luck at another, Johnny's spirits were soaring. He didn't mind when they climbed into the carriage and Nevada somehow situated herself in the middle, directly between him and Lady Ashley. The other woman minded.

It went that way all evening but Lady Ashley, determined to maintain her cool dignity, said nothing. She didn't dare let Roulette get the idea she was a clinging, jealous female. She knew Roulette's kind. Crowd him just once and she'd lose him for sure.

So she quietly seethed and hoped that Roulette wouldn't often insist that they take the beautiful little brat along. It was apparent the bitchy child was mad for Roulette, though he swore that Nevada was only his charge, his unwanted responsibility, the young daughter of an old and dear friend who had passed away, leaving Nevada in his care.

Lady Ashley was very astute. She would have bet all the thousands Johnny had won at London's gaming tables that the ill-mannered girl had been in his bed. No woman looked at a man the way Nevada looked at Roulette if he'd never made love to her.

The knowledge both repelled and titillated the jaded Lady Ashley. Roulette had been entrusted with the innocence of the young daughter of a dear dying friend and what had the callous cad done? He had promised to protect the helpless girl and instead had used her to satisfy his base sexual hungers.

Outrageous. Disgusting. Unforgivable.

Just what kind of man was this unprincipled Roulette who seduced children? He was, Lady Ashley admitted to herself, the most exciting man she'd met in years. And she wasn't about to lose him to some starry-eyed twit who was foolish enough to think she could compete with a wise and worldly woman who knew all sorts of ways to excite and pleasure the sensuous Frenchman.

"This is it." Johnny's deep voice broke into the reveries of both women as the carriage came to a stop beneath a streetlamp. "Home. Claridge's."

" 'Night now, Lady Ashley," Nevada said sweetly, turning to the simmering blonde, then smiled wickedly when Johnny, stepping down, leaned back inside, put his hands to Nevada's small waist, and lifted her out. "Johnny and I will see you soon," Nevada said pointedly, still smiling.

But her smile quickly turned to a frown when Johnny, setting her on her feet, again leaned inside the carriage and said, "I'll see her upstairs and be right back."

"I'll be waiting, darling," Nevada heard her adversary say in tones dripping with honey.

Not nearly as adept at maintaining her composure as Lady Ashley, Nevada immediately began lecturing as Johnny, taking her arm, guided her into Claridge's vast lobby.

"Johnny, it is past two in the morning. You should send Lady Ashley home and go to—"

"Thanks for tonight," Johnny cut her off. "We won several thousand. You were just what I needed tonight." They stepped into the elevator. The doors closed after them.

"I am exactly what you need every night," she said, swaying to him.

"Don't start that, Nevada." He gently pushed her away.

"Are you going home with her?" she demanded hotly.

"I'm going anywhere I please," he replied coolly.

"God, you're so damned blind!" she told him.

"My vision is perfect," he informed her.

"No. No, it's not. If it were, you could see that Lady Ashley has got her claws into you, but good."

He chuckled derisively. "You think that only because you're a naive child. Lady Ashley is a beautiful worldly woman who enjoys my company, just as I enjoy hers."

The elevator stopped. The doors opened. Nevada didn't move. Johnny took her arm and forced her out into the silent corridor. They reached the suite's carved door.

Nevada turned to face Johnny.

She said, "You think I'm naive, but it's you who are really naive."

"Good night," said Johnny, and he turned and walked away.

She watched until he disappeared inside the elevator. Then tiredly went inside, crossed the drawing room, and went straight to the front windows. Anxiously jerking the peach silk drapery aside, she peered down at the gleaming black landau, waiting in a pool of light from the street-lamp.

In minutes Johnny stepped out of the dense fog and into the light, opened the coach door, and climbed inside. Before the carriage could pull back out into the street, Nevada saw Johnny's dark head bend to Lady Ashley.

She stood there a long time after the carriage had disappeared, feeling cold and lonely. She allowed the drapery to fall back into place, crossed to the bronze marble fireplace where a fire still burned. She dropped wearily down onto the padded footstool and stared forlornly into the low-burning flames.

22

⬡⬡⬡⬡⬡⬡

The rains came.

The official beginning of autumn brought with it unremitting rains to the British Isles. The weak autumn sun could no longer manage to shine its way through the heavy, cloaking clouds, and each day ended just as it had dawned—cold, dismal, and rainy.

The dreary weather added to Nevada's growing gloom. She wished more than once that they had never come to this huge faraway city with its depressing climate. Fall had always been her favorite time of year back home. Crisp cool mornings. Warm sunny afternoons. And chilly brisk nights.

Not here.

Here, autumn was cold and dark and rainy. And the rain was not the strong torrential kind that lashed the lower Mississippi on hot afternoons. There, great thunderheads suddenly boiled up in the cloudless skies and great rumbles of thunder shook the earth and soon huge raindrops pummeled the region with the ferocity of an angered beast.

Then as quickly as it had come the storm was over, the sun came back out, and everything glistened, clean and new and beautiful.

In London the rains were never violent and sudden.

They were slow, drizzly, and constant. They chilled a person right down to his bones and Nevada blamed Miss Annabelle's steadily worsening cough on London's continual pervasive dampness.

On a drizzly October afternoon Miss Annabelle, looking paler than usual and tired, came into the sitting room carrying her gloves and the ever-present umbrella. She smiled at Nevada and said, "Lady Holland is calling this afternoon's gathering a garden party, but I would hope we shan't really be out in the garden."

"I would hope you wouldn't be out at all," said Nevada, finding it strange to be the one scolding, rather than being scolded. She looked at the tall slender woman who had become very dear to her. "Miss Annabelle, let me call a bellman; have him send Lady Holland regrets."

"No, child. Cap'n Roulette, dear, dear man, was so pleased when his Lady Ashley arranged my invitation to Holland House. I'd not want to disappoint him. Besides," she said truthfully, "I'm most anxious to meet Lady Holland, Mary Augusta."

Nevada rolled her eyes heavenward. "Put all those snobby lords and ladies in a tow sack, shake them up, pour them out, and you couldn't tell which one is which. They're all alike, if you ask me."

Miss Annabelle said, "The weather has you out of sorts. Perhaps after you and King Cassidy drop me off at Holland House, he'll think of somewhere new to take you. Cheer you up a bit."

"The only thing that would cheer me up is for us all to get a boat back to the blessed United States of America!"

"The third Marquess of Londonderry built Londonderry House," said King Cassidy as he pointed, directing

Nevada's attention to the imposing dwelling on their left. "Said to be one of the most splendid homes in London."

The silver king and Nevada were driving through Park Lane in the rain, after having deposited an excited but pallid Miss Annabelle at Holland House at precisely three o'clock. King Cassidy was doing his best to entertain the moody homesick Nevada—and failing, if her uninterested slouch was any indication. Still, he pressed on manfully, calling her attention to Dorchester House, hoping she'd be charmed with its understated elegance.

He drew only a groan from the bored Nevada.

"What is it, child?" he said patiently. "Tell me. Tell old King and I'll try to fix it."

That brought a quick smile to Nevada's mobile face. "King, it's just that I'm bored with London and this constant misting rain. And I'm tired of all these stiff British hoity-toity folks with their big mansions and their butlers and maids and footmen and nannies. Lord Almighty, I'll bet the *dogs* are all pedigreed around these parts."

King Cassidy chuckled and nodded. "You have a point. Perhaps Park Lane and its inhabitants are a trifle stuffy. What would you like to do this afternoon? Name it and we'll do it."

"You mean it, King?"

"Would I lie to a young lady who proudly bears the name of my beloved home state?"

"Oh, I forgot to tell you. Miss Annabelle thinks I should drop Nevada, just go by Marie Hamilton." She made a face. "What do you think?"

"Miss Annabelle is probably right." He stroked his silver goatee and added, "With the bluebloods you can be Marie. With me you'll always be Nevada."

"It's a bargain. Now, what I would really like to do is to see some of the exciting things in London."

"Exciting things?"

Laughing, she jammed an elbow into his side. "You know, the wicked places. Like Kate Hamilton's!"

"Saints preserve us! Where did you learn about Kate's place?"

"I overheard a couple of sports at the roulette wheel the other night. They were discussing a red-haired woman there who is a contortionist. I'm not sure I know exactly what that means but they said—"

"Never mind that. I really don't think we should—"

"Oh, please, King. All I want to do is drive by. That's all—I promise."

Thinking that the fair Miss Annabelle would surely have his head should she find out, the permissive King Cassidy allowed himself to be talked into showing his enchanting young friend some of the seamier sides of old London town.

When the carriage rolled to a stop across the street from Kate Hamilton's house off Leicester Square, Nevada, anxiously peering out through the drizzle, said, "Do you suppose Kate Hamilton is kin to me?"

King Cassidy laughed. "I rather doubt it. Kate's fat and swarthy and officious. I see no resemblance."

Nevada whirled about to face him. "How do you know what she looks like?"

King cleared his throat and did not answer.

She pressed on. "A couple of our hotel maids say that the Shah of Persia visited there when he came to London. They say Kate's place is one of the most recherché brothels in the world." She fixed King with her wide blue eyes. "What does *recherché* mean?"

"Rare. Choice." He paused. "Uncommon."

Her eyes as big as saucers, Nevada said excitedly, "Really? Tell me about it. Is the house itself uncommon or do you mean the women who live there?"

Shaking his silver head, King tapped on the coach's ceiling, signaling his driver to move on. "Were I you, I'd keep to myself all you've heard about Kate's."

Nevada laughed easily. "You mean don't tell Miss Annabelle. I wouldn't, she'd be shocked right down to her corset stays if she knew such places existed! Why, I mentioned the other night that I'd like to see a bare-knuckle prize fight and I thought she was going to faint." Nevada sighed and settled back against the tall seat. "Let's face it, King, Miss Annabelle is not like us. She truly is a cut above."

"Ah, that she is," agreed King Cassidy, smiling wistfully.

The sad facts were brought home to him once more. Any senseless attraction he felt for the prim southern lady would be best kept as secret as their ride past Kate Hamilton's brothel. Either would be equally offensive to the sweet refined Miss Annabelle.

Miss Annabelle's afternoon at Holland House had been enjoyable. It had also been tiring. By bedtime she was feeling uncommonly weak and running a slight fever. By the next morning she agreed to let Nevada call the hotel's doctor. By late the next afternoon the hotel's balding physician suspected pneumonia.

Johnny and Lady Ashley walked into the Claridge's suite as the doctor was leaving. When he first saw the short balding man with his worn black leather bag, Johnny was sure something had happened to Nevada.

"What is it? What's she done?" said Johnny, reaching out to grab the shorter man's lapels.

Half afraid of the big, fierce man towering over him, the

meek doctor said, "Sh-she's done nothing, sir, but I'm afraid she has contracted pneumonia, all the same. She should be taken round to the hospital if she's not feeling better by nightfall."

"A healthy young girl like her . . . she couldn't possibly . . ." Johnny, his dark face set in lines of anguish, released the shaken man and hurried to the large bedroom Nevada shared with Miss Annabelle. Not bothering to knock, he pushed open the door and hurried inside.

He stopped short when he saw the ashen-faced Miss Annabelle lying in bed, Nevada on her knees beside her. Johnny came directly to the bed, knelt down beside Nevada, and after giving Nevada a quick, reassuring glance, said, "Miss Annabelle? Dear, can you hear me? It's Johnny." He reached for her pale hand.

Her eyes opening tiredly, Miss Annabelle gave him a weak smile. "Cap'n Roulette, I'm so glad you're home."

"Miss Annabelle, I want to take you to St. Ann's Hospital," Johnny said. "Will you allow me?"

Her eyelids slipped closed. She nodded feebly. "Yes. Now that you're back, I'll go." She struggled to open her eyes once more. "We couldn't leave Nevada alone, you see."

"Yes, I see," Johnny said softly. "Don't you worry, Miss Annabelle. I'll look after Nevada."

The ambulance came within thirty minutes. Johnny rode in it with Miss Annabelle. Nevada and Lady Ashley followed in the black landau. Nevada, worried about her dear friend, was silent on the ride. Lady Ashley, quietly studying Nevada, felt her dislike of the dark-haired beauty grow with each passing mile.

Disgruntled that Miss Annabelle's sudden sickness was going to make them miss the debut of Gilbert and Sullivan's new opera at the Savoy Theater, Lady Ashley wondered miserably if it would also mean that Johnny would feel it his duty to play protective nanny to his spoiled ward. A resourceful woman, Lady Ashley silently began making plans.

King Cassidy showed up at the hospital, kissed Nevada's cheek, and whispered against her ear, "Thanks, child, for sending me word. You know how fond I am of Miss Annabelle."

"I knew you'd want to call," she murmured.

"Indeed," replied the silver-haired man. Then, attempting to mask his deep concern, he said, "Don't worry, child. They'll take good care of her here."

The quartet remained at the hospital well past dark. Finally the bespectacled physician, Dr. Theodore Hatcher, exiting Miss Annabelle's room, told them there was no need for them to remain. They should all go home and get a good night's rest.

"He's absolutely right." Lady Ashley was quick to agree. "There's nothing we can do. Let's go."

"I'd like to stay here with her," said Nevada. "What if she needs us? What if she wakes up and no one's here?"

"Shh," said Johnny, putting a comforting arm around her. "Dr. Hatcher said she's sleeping peacefully. You need rest too. I'll bring you over bright and early in the morning. All right?"

Nevada finally nodded and agreed, reluctantly, to leave.

King Cassidy said, "I think I'll just stay for a few more minutes." He smiled and explained. "I've nothing planned and I'm not tired."

Johnny, walking between the two woman, ushered them out of the antiseptic-smelling hospital and into the chill, rainy night. No sooner were they inside the roomy landau than Lady Ashley realized Nevada had once again managed to sit between her and Johnny.

Leaning out a little, Lady Ashley said to Johnny, "I suppose it's too late for the theater. We're not dressed and—"

"I'm sorry," said Johnny. "It is too late."

She gave him a sweet smile. "No matter, really. There's still time for the wine supper afterward at the—"

"I don't think so," said Johnny. "Not tonight."

"Very well," Lady Ashley said evenly, "If you'd rather not." She looked from Johnny to Nevada. Nevada, arms folded, was staring straight ahead. Lady Ashley said, "Nevada, Johnny and I are aware you don't wish to be alone tonight."

Nevada's head snapped around. She wondered what the woman had in mind.

"I've a lovely idea," Lady Ashley continued, smiling at Nevada. "You've not been to my home yet, have you? I've a lovely secluded manor house in Mayfair. Lots of space for guests. We'll go directly there, have cook fix us a meal, then you may choose any room you wish and get a good night's sleep. How does that sound to you?"

Nevada looked at Lady Ashley as though she had suggested some unspeakable perversion. "I am not about to spend the night with you and Johnny!"

"Nevada!" Johnny reprimanded.

"You misunderstand," said Lady Ashley quickly. "You'll have your own room." She smiled at Johnny. "Johnny and I will occupy ours." She looked at Nevada and added smugly, "Just as always."

Nevada glared at her. Then turned to Johnny and said, "I am not going anywhere but to Claridge's. If you won't take me there, I'll jump out of this carriage right now and walk there." She lunged for the door.

Johnny caught her, pulled her back with strong fingers encircling her arm. Then with an apologetic shrug for

Lady Ashley, he said, "She's upset over Miss Annabelle. You better drop us off at Claridge's." His black eyes met Lady Ashley's and he added, "I promised Miss Annabelle."

"Certainly, darling." Lady Ashley was agreeable. And when the carriage stopped at the Brook Street entrance and Nevada jumped out into the rain, Lady Ashley caught Johnny's arm, gave his sensual mouth a kiss, and murmured, "I'll miss you, darling."

"I'll see you tomorrow," he replied, and slid across the seat.

She anxiously caught his arm. "Please be careful, Roulette."

Johnny grinned, touched her cheek. "It'll be just for one night." He kissed her quickly and added carelessly, "What could possibly happen in one night?"

As midnight approached, a solitary figure sat alone in the shadowed hallway of St. Ann's Hospital. A nurse in starched white uniform and cap came out of Miss Annabelle Delaney's room.

King Cassidy came to his feet and looked anxiously at the nurse. A stocky woman with a ruddy complexion and kind eyes, she addressed him with a smile, "You Yanks are all alike. Emotional. Excitable." She gently shook her finger in his face. "Worry too much. There's no change in the patient's condition. Miss Delaney is quite sick. Still, I do not believe she's in great danger."

"If that's the case, why can't I go in to see her?"

"The patient is in a deep, exhausted sleep. She'll never know you're there."

"Nor will the doctor, unless you tell him."

Nurse Harvey sighed. "You Yanks are also quite persuasive. Go on then, if you must, but let doctor catch you and I'll deny—"

"I'll accept full blame," said King. He flashed her a winning grin and added, "Nurse Harvey, you truly are an angel of mercy."

Inside Miss Annabelle's room King Cassidy's smile quickly died. Tiptoeing to the bed, he looked down at the pale still face and felt his heart kick against his ribs. For a long, silent time he stood staring down at her, hardly daring to breathe. Unmoving, unblinking.

Then the air exploded from his tight lungs and the worried man leaned over the bed, reached out and tenderly smoothed a limp lock of hair back off her damp temple. His fingers lingered to caress her pale face.

"Miss Annabelle? Can you hear me?" His voice was a raspy whisper in the night-silent room. Not an eyelash flickered in response. "Miss Annabelle?" He waited, his eyes locked on her face.

He pulled the chair up closer to the bed and sat down. Smiling fondly down at the sleeping woman, he gently took her cool fragile hand in both of his and said softly, "Annie, dearest, dearest girl. My sweet Annie."

King Cassidy stayed at Miss Annabelle's bedside through the long, rainy night until a nurse wearing a nun's cowl came on duty a little after four in the morning and ordered him to leave.

Miss Annabelle, struggling against the bonds of drug- and fever-induced sleep, labored to open her eyes, strained to hear the deep raspy voice more clearly, and murmured softly, "King? King?"

Her head tossed on the pillow and she patted frantically at the mattress, searching for the warm male hand that had lovingly held hers. "King, King? Where are you? Don't go. Don't leave me!"

Her voice no more than a strangled whisper, she continued to call his name as her eyes came open. Then she looked hopefully around the empty room. And quickly realized it had only been a dream.

A sweet, impossible dream.

23

∽∽∽∽∽∽

She awoke with a start.

Her heart drumming loudly in her ears, Nevada bolted straight up in bed, the horror of the nightmare filling her with dread and panic. Swallowing convulsively, she tried to speak, couldn't. Trembling like a leaf, she threw back the covers and finally managed to choke out, "Miss Annabelle? Miss Annabelle, I had this terrible dream and I— I . . ."

Her eyes fell on Miss Annabelle's empty bed and the truth dawned. Miss Annabelle was not here with her. Miss Annabelle was sick and in the hospital. She was alone, all alone in the big, dark bedroom.

Her teeth chattering with fear and with cold, Nevada put her hands to her cheeks and told herself she must stay calm. It was just a nightmare, a ghastly, gruesome nightmare. It hadn't actually happened, wasn't going to happen. Running her hands up and down her chilled, stiff arms, she recalled with frightening clarity the macabre dream that had awakened her.

Johnny was on a Mississippi riverboat, playing cards below decks. A fire in the paddlewheeler's galley had quickly spread to the dining room and on to the cabins. It was a dark cold night and terrified passengers jumped overboard and swam for their lives.

But Johnny was trapped!

Her hand at her mouth to choke back the sobs threatening to erupt, Nevada, shaking so violently she could hardly function, anxiously lunged from her bed and dashed across the carpeted room. She yanked open the door and rushed through the spacious sitting room to Johnny's closed door.

Her hand on the polished brass knob, she waited, trying desperately to get a grip on her tensed nerves, delaying until the furious pounding of her heart could slow a little. Silently telling herself everything was all right, that Johnny was sleeping just inside, that he was safe and here with her, Nevada quietly pushed the door open and stepped inside.

The silken drapes at the bedroom's tall windows had not been closed against the night. A steadily falling rain pelted the uncovered glass. It was cold, much colder than in her own room. The gloaming from London's streetlamps and the buildings' gaslights bathed the bedroom with a pale ambient light.

Directly across from the door, in an oversized custom bed hung with rich brown velvet, Johnny Roulette slumbered peacefully, the white silk sheet riding his bare waist, a long muscular leg stuck outside the covers.

Staring at him, Nevada took a long deep breath of happy relief and turned to leave. She paused, glanced back at the sleeping man. Should she cover him? He wore no pajamas; what if he should catch pneumonia like Miss Annabelle?

Nevada tiptoed to the bed, looked down on Johnny, and felt her just-slowed heartbeat race once more.

He lay in the very middle of the huge bed, on his back. His head was turned to the side, the midnight-black hair tumbling over his forehead and onto the silk-cased pillow. His beautiful black eyes were closed, but his lips were slightly parted to reveal the gleam of wet teeth.

His smooth brown shoulders were very dark in the half

light and the appealing fanlike pattern of hair on his broad, bare chest narrowed to a heavy black line going down his stomach and disappearing beneath the covering sheet. One side of the sheet, caught and clutched in Johnny's left fist, was pulled and stretched below a prominent hipbone, almost exposing that most male part of his long lean body.

That he was naked was evident. That he was warm, despite his nakedness and the damp chill of the room, was just as evident. That he was so devastatingly male and desirable in his warm naked slumber that Nevada longed to explore his powerful nude body, was a fact of her life.

Her eyes caressing what her hands longed to touch, she softly, impulsively said his name.

"Johnny." It was an awed breathless whisper in the quiet room. He didn't stir and all Nevada could hear was the sound of the rain drumming against the windows. And her own heartbeat. "Johnny, Johnny," she repeated a little louder.

She needed him to tell her that everything was going to be all right. Needed to hear that deep, sure, drawling voice murmur words of comfort that would drive away any lingering fear and doubt. If only he would waken and assure her that Miss Annabelle was going to be fine and that he would not be playing cards on some burning riverboat, then she could go back to her own room and rest.

"Johnny, wake up, please. Wake up. I'm afraid and I need to talk to you. Johnny?"

He did not respond. He drew a deep, slow breath, released his death grip on the sheet, and flung his long, bare arm up over his head.

Nevada frowned in frustration and started to say his name again. But she stopped, and a smile touched her lips as she recalled the day on the boat train when she had sat on his lap. He had slept all the way to London, undisturbed by the commotion around him, and it had been difficult to rouse him even when they pulled into the noisy station.

Johnny Roulette was undoubtedly a very sound sleeper. Short of leaning down and shouting into his ear, there was little hope, or danger, of awakening him.

And he looked so warm and peaceful, while she felt so cold and upset. If she dared lie down beside him for just a few minutes, he would never know the difference. She need not even touch him, just stretch out atop the sheet near him until the terror of the dream had completely vanished.

The idea of crawling into bed with Johnny Roulette made Nevada's pulse race with excitement and apprehension. All too vividly she could recall how it felt to share a bed with this gorgeous, virile man. Remembered so well the sweet joy of sleeping in his arms, of being snuggled warmly to his hard body, of them both being as bare as Johnny was now.

A need to feel close and comforted began to change to physical desire and Nevada was tempted to pull her long lace-ruffled nightgown up over her head and toss it aside. To lift the silky sheet and climb nude into bed with the sleeping, naked man. To press her bare, eager curves to the length of his hard-muscled body until he awakened and became so aroused he could not resist making love to her.

She didn't do it.

Instead Nevada very gingerly put a nightgowned knee on the bed and held her breath. When Johnny didn't stir she cautiously, carefully climbed up onto the high soft bed and lay down on its edge, facing him. Folding her hands beneath her cheek she lay quietly on her side, staring trans-fixed at the dark handsome profile half shadowed in the soft night light.

Her eyes traveled down from his face to the broad, bare

chest, rising and falling evenly. And finally farther down to where the thin silkiness of the white sheet did little to hide the jet-black growth of dense crisp hair covering his groin. It reminded Nevada of the way Johnny's fine white silk shirts could not entirely conceal the dense black hair covering his chest. She had always thought the effect terribly sexy.

This was even sexier.

Instinctively Nevada moved just a bit closer to Johnny. Just enough, she told herself, to avoid the risk of falling off the high bed's edge. Close enough to hear his slow, steady breathing. Close enough to pretend, if only for a sweet moment, that he was hers and she his, that they slept in the same bed every night. That they would be sleeping together for all the rest of their nights.

Her glowing eyes on his face, Nevada smiled. His countenance, like his physique, bespoke strength, masculine and unashamed. Her gaze ran affectionately over the rugged figure beside her and her skin tingled. How small she seemed against such muscled power. And how cold she was in her long nightgown, while Johnny was warm in his nakedness.

Dreamily Nevada sighed. Her eyelids began to grow heavy and she told herself she should get up. Return to the warmth of her own bedroom and get some sleep. Sighing again, she slid her cold, bare feet beneath the covers and stretched lazily.

And fell asleep.

In slumber Nevada turned onto her back and automatically reached for the sheet, pulling it up over her chilled body. She burrowed down into the softness of the bed. And still she was cold. She turned onto her side, facing away from Johnny and drew her knees up.

The drizzling rain stopped in the wee hours of the morn-

ing and with the clearing of the dark winter skies, the
temperature dropped dramatically. The frigid cold of the
London air invaded the interior of homes and hotels all
over the city. At Claridge's, the big, dim bedroom where
two people unknowingly slept in the same bed had grown
uncomfortably cold. Covered with only a slick silk sheet,
the sleeping pair sought heat where they could find it.

Nevada never roused when Johnny, sound asleep, put a
long arm around her and drew her to him. Her eyes barely
fluttered, but she moaned in her slumber and snuggled
gratefully to his warmth.

Instinctively she backed up against Johnny; he curved
his big, naked frame warmly around her. They slept peacefully on, cuddled together, his body around hers, her slender, gown-clad back and bottom pressing his bare hair-
covered chest and belly.

A hint of gun-metal gray was just beginning to lighten
the dark skies when Nevada, licking her lips and inhaling
deeply, came half awake. Her sleepy eyes flickered open
just in time to see a gently groping brown hand find the
ribbon-laced opening of her nightgown. In the half slumber
still claiming her, it seemed like the most natural thing in
the world.

So Nevada simply lay there and luxuriated in the warm
pleasure of the moment. From under heavily-lashed,
sleepy, drooping lids, she watched in sweet, lazy wonder,
waiting without urgency to see what that hand meant to
do.

With the same swift, sure dexterity of the wide-awake,
card-dealing Johnny, long lean fingers found their way
down inside the batiste nightie to quickly cover a soft
rounded breast.

Nevada's eyes slid closed and a smile of mild elation

curved her lips. For a long, pleasant time, Johnny's hand didn't move at all. Merely closed warmly, protectively over her right breast, gently shielding it from the cold. It was wonderful, marvelous, the best. Her sleeping lover possessively covering her breast.

The best soon got better.

Nevada's breathing changed when those long dark fingers began to stir ever so subtly. At first it was only a slight, elusive caress, almost a reflexive action. A gentle squeezing, a pressing of his warm palm against the soft nipple.

She bit her bottom lip when his fingers lifted while his palm remained and began to move in slow, seductive circles over the aching crest that was rapidly growing taut from his touch. It was while that talented palm rubbed the highly sensitive center of her breast that Nevada became heartstoppingly aware of Johnny's rock-hard erection against her buttocks through the thin batiste of her gown.

Eyes closed again, she instinctively pressed closer to his intense heat and hardness, squirming with spiraling erotic pleasure and heightening expectation. As if this movement of her body had been the silent invitation his was awaiting, Johnny's slim hips began a slow, surging motion. A lazy rhythmic thrusting of his naked throbbing tumesence against her barely covered bottom.

Nevada gloried in the sleepy, languid prelude to lovemaking. Her aroused body bemoaned the loss when Johnny's warm palm deserted the nipple he'd coaxed into hardness. But then it trembled with ecstasy when, with all five fingers, he gently began to pluck at the desire-darkened bud.

Nevada lay there in the warm, sleepy darkness and thrilled to the exquisite touch of the only lover she'd ever had. Wrapped in his strong arms, pressed to his naked strength, she felt as if she were a fine instrument being expertly played by a talented virtuoso. His beautiful long-fingered brown hands stirred in her a divine symphony of passion. A sweet yearning that would soon grow so intense, she would turn in his arms and offer her very soul to him.

As if her master had read her thoughts, Johnny's hand left her breast and Nevada felt herself being gently turned onto her back. Eyes dazed with ecstasy, she got only a glimpse of Johnny's dark face as it lowered to hers.

Not even bothering to open his sleepy eyes, Johnny's warm lips covered hers and his tongue made lazy circles around the interior of her mouth.

The slow hot kiss continued as he took a handful of her nightgown and began bunching the fabric in his fist.

Nevada sucked at Johnny's thrusting tongue and felt the soft batiste rising steadily up her tensed legs. Slowly, surely he worked the gown up until it lay in wispy folds around her hips. Deepening his sultry kiss, Johnny's hand moved up under the raised gown and came to rest on her stomach.

As he'd done with her breast he caressed her flat, bare belly with the tips of his fingers and his palm, stroking languidly, awakening sensitive, quivering flesh. On fire, Nevada writhed and squirmed and undulated. Her legs eagerly parted to him, anxious to receive his hand, longing for those magic fingers to touch her where the heat was fiercest.

Johnny's caressing hand began its expected descent. It closed over her, cupped her gently for an instant. Then as he swept his fingers through the dense black curls between her thighs, his mouth left hers, moved to the side of her throat.

Breathless with excitement, Nevada murmured his name. "Johnny . . . Johnny—"

"Nevada?" Johnny's shocked eyes finally opened and he came completely awake. "Nevada!"

24

━━━━━━━━━━━━━━━━━ ∿∿∿∿∿∿ ━━━━━━━━━━━━━━━━━

The Master of the Spinning Wheel glanced at Nevada as the tiny white ball came to rest on number eleven. Her number. And the uniformed croupier announced in crisp Oxford tones, "A repeater, ladies and gentlemen. Number eleven has come up once more." Smiling at Nevada, he said more softly, "The lovely lady from the Colonies has won again."

The dealer pushed four stacks of square red checks her way and one of the two men standing directly behind her chair said in a low, rich baritone voice, "What did I tell you, Ben?" Then Johnny's dark hand touched her bare shoulder and he spoke to her. "Tip the boys and let's get out of here, Nevada."

"You are amazing, my dear," Ben Robin told her as Johnny stayed behind to cash in their winnings.

He looked at the lovely young woman smiling up at him, thinking that she bore little resemblance to the heavily painted, cheaply gowned strumpet Johnny had taken off the *Moonlight Gambler*. Still, he mused thoughtfully, she's the daughter of a drunken river rat and the apple never falls far from the tree. It would be unlikely that the dark-haired beauty could actually fool Britain's aristocracy.

Ben Robin guided Nevada away from the green felt roulette table. They crossed the large gray-carpeted gaming room with its floor-to-ceiling murals and lighting elements trimmed with gold leaf and cut glass. In the mirror-lined main lobby Ben draped the warm cape around Nevada's bare shoulders and he said, "You're responsible for making my arrival in London a very pleasant one indeed and I'm most grateful." He grinned and added, "I thank you very kindly, Miss Hamilton."

Nevada was about to make a proper reply when Johnny joined them, swirled his black cloak around his wide shoulders and said, "What are we waiting for? Let's go to Crockford's and challenge their baccarat dealer."

Nevada said little on the ride through the rainy London streets, wedged between Johnny and Ben. The two men laughed and talked and made foolish wagers on anything and everything. They would, she thought idly, bet on the time of day. Since Ben Robin's arrival the two gamblers had made wagers on when the rain would stop, whether King Cassidy would come by the Claridge's suite, even on what color gown Nevada would choose for the evening.

Smiling, Nevada was more than content to listen quietly as the pair talked of the upcoming poker game. *The* game. The big one that had brought them to London and would soon draw master players from around the world. The game scheduled for the night after Guy Fawkes Day, November 5th.

Nevada was more than a little grateful that Ben Robin, the wealthy hotel owner from Memphis, Tennessee, and a sporting friend to Johnny, had shown up early for the action.

Robin's weekend arrival had miraculously sprung her from a kind of prison far worse than those with bars on the windows. Since that dreadful night two weeks ago when she had fallen asleep in Johnny's bed, Johnny had been so distant to her that she had wondered if he would ever forgive and forget.

The sight of him looming naked and dangerous before her, his voice as hard as his predatory eyes, was still vivid enough to make her cringe. Never had she seen a man as angry as Johnny had been that cold morning.

Flint-faced, his black eyes were deadly mean when he had snatched the covers off her and forcefully jerked her from the bed and set her on her bare feet. Trembling, she had stood before him, frightened, unsure what he might do next.

He had reached out, clutched the ribbon-laced opening of her gown, and twisting the filmy bodice in one tight fist, jerked her up onto her toes even as his dark, enraged face bent to hers. Blinking with fear, she had clutched at his wrist and hoped he didn't mean to choke the life from her.

His voice as cruel as his face, he said, "If I had wanted you in my bed, you'd have been there." The tendons in his powerful neck stood out in high relief and his strong hand wrenched the batiste bodice so fiercely, she heard the fabric tear. "And if you really wanted to become a lady, you'd keep your damned legs crossed!"

He hauled her up into his arms and marched out of the room. She knew better than to try and defend herself. He was far too angry to listen. Through thinned lips he continued to lecture her as he crossed the sitting room, the heart in his naked chest hammering forcefully against her trembling breasts.

"Do all our plans for you mean nothing? Do you want to be a child of the river all your life, looked down on by the gentry? Do you have so little pride and self-respect you'd be happier as one of the *Gambler* girls? Do you?" He strode into her room, went straight to the bed, and dumped her onto it. "Answer me!"

Struggling up onto her elbows, Nevada looked up at his face and saw the cold intensity, the determination. His black eyes were so murderous that she nervously lowered her own. And found herself looking straight at Johnny's still rigid masculinity, pulsating with power and passion.

Struck by the fascinating fact that a man could be as angry as Johnny was with her and yet still obviously desire her, Nevada said honestly, her own blood still high, her need for this dark, dangerous man as potent as ever, "I am a child of the river. And so are you. For all your mysterious past, you're just a river rat like me. We're two of a kind. Why deny it?" Her eyes crawled back up to his face. "Why deny ourselves?"

"Damn you!" Johnny shouted. "I'm going to make a lady of you if it kills you." He jerked the counterpane from Miss Annabelle's empty bed and swirled it around his nakedness. "If it kills me!" And he turned and stormed from the room.

Since that morning his cold demeanor had frightened her far more than his dark, fiery anger had. He was coolly polite when, later that same day, he had escorted her to the hospital to visit Miss Annabelle. And with Miss Annabelle's recovery and return to the Claridge's suite three days later, Johnny couldn't wait to take his leave.

She had seen him only once in the following week and then he had ignored her as pointedly as if she were no more important than a piece of the furniture. The neglect would most surely have continued if not for the arrival of his old friend and boon gambling companion.

Out of the blue three days ago Johnny and Ben had come by the suite in the late evening and Johnny, as though he and Nevada had never had a cross word, suggested that perhaps she might like to join them for dinner and the opera.

Nevada had been mystified. And pleased. And she wasted no time slipping into one of her most elegant gowns. Radiant, she'd hugged Miss Annabelle, then happily joined the two men in the sitting room, expectant, eager.

And soon found that an even more pleasant surprise was awaiting her. Lady Ashley would not be joining them. It would be just the three of them.

They had gone to a small, charming restaurant on the south bank of the Thames and Nevada, catered to by Johnny and Ben as well as the capable staff, felt for all the world like the regal lady Johnny insisted she become.

Now, driving toward Crockford's on this cold rainy night, Nevada felt almost indebted to the light-haired, easygoing Ben Robin. Thanks to him, Johnny's cold neglect had totally disappeared. She was sure Ben Robin's presence was responsible.

In fact, Ben Robin's presence in London did have something to do with Johnny's sudden change of heart. But if Nevada had known exactly what that something was, it would have broken *her* heart.

Court Circular for November 9:
Our sovereign lady, Queen Victoria, will honor the Scottish-born scientist Alexander Graham Bell at a formal reception and dinner at Buckingham Palace.

Johnny's dark eyes lifted from the newspaper. He lowered *The London Times* and took his first drink of morning coffee. He set the cup down and smiled. Nevada, looking very sleepy, had come into the drawing room. Her rose silk robe was haphazardly tied, the tousled dark hair spilled around her shoulders, and she was barefoot.

" 'Morning," she mumbled, sliding into the chair across from him.

" 'Morning, yourself," Johnny said warmly, and grinning, held up the folded *Times* between thumb and forefinger. "Know what this says?"

Frowning and yawning at the same time, Nevada shook her head.

Johnny returned to the announcement he'd just read and read it again to her.

"So?"

"So it happens I've come by invitations to the Queen's reception for Mr. Bell."

Her sleep-droopy lids opened wide. "Invitations to Buckingham Palace? I don't believe you. How? Where? Why would the Queen invite—"

"King Cassidy says you'd like to see the palace," Johnny cut in.

She stared at him, astonished.

Carelessly he said, "Would you like to go to the reception for Alexander Bell?"

Silence.

"Nevada?"

Speechless, she watched his full lips stretch into a grin.

Looking straight into her widened eyes, he repeated the invitation.

"I want to take you to Queen Victoria's dinner at the palace."

Still she said nothing.

Johnny continued in a warm, level voice, "You don't have to say yes now. The occasion—three weeks from Wednesday—is formal, of course, and it might be a bit stuffy."

"And Lady Ashley?" Nevada finally spoke, still staring at him.

"What about her?"

"She resents my tagging along."

Johnny gently shook his dark head. "She won't be coming." He smiled. And did not mention that Lady Ashley was responsible for producing the Queen's invitation. Lady Ashley was on the Continent and would not return to London until after the Bell reception. "Only be the two of us. Just you and me."

"No Lady Ashley? No Ben Robin? Not even Miss Annabelle?"

"Just you," he drawled lazily, "me, and the Queen."

The three weeks leading up to the big event were wonderful for Nevada. Johnny took a renewed, flattering interest in every thing that she said and did. He was waiting each morning to share breakfast with Miss Annabelle and her and stayed for her daily lessons.

He complimented her on her table manners, he nodded his approval when she read to him in French, he grinned and followed her gently swaying hips with his dark eyes when she practiced walking about the carpeted suite with a book atop her head.

He huddled with Miss Annabelle to discuss the gown they should choose for the upcoming palace affair and he promptly accepted when Miss Annabelle asked if he'd like to accompany Nevada and her when they shopped for the dress.

Discerning, extremely hard to please, his taste impeccable, Johnny accompanied them to London's West End. There he ushered them from one Regent Street couturière to another, determined to find the extraordinary fabric, the right hue, the exquisite design to best drape Nevada's small, youthfully curvaceous body.

Dozens of bolts of satins and brocades and folice and

sultane were spread on his bent knee, examined by his lean brown fingers, examined with his keen black eyes. And discarded. Numerous designs and sketches were poured over, discussed, considered. And turned down.

"*Monsieur,* you have seen all there is in zee shop!" The short, plump little French couturière at Rassac's threw up her hands in dismay. "*Mon Dieu,* I have such a headache!" She slammed the heel of her hand to her forehead.

Unbothered, Johnny asked, "Have you velvet the exact color of the mademoiselle's eyes?"

Frowning, the dressmaker took Nevada's arm, looked into her eyes, then hurried into the back room, muttering in French. But when she returned, she was smiling and she carried a huge bolt of sky-blue velvet, the exact hue of Nevada's large, lovely eyes. She walked straight to Johnny and dumped it onto his lap.

Hands going to her wide hips, the little woman said, "I suppose you wish to design zee gown as well?"

His palm gently running over the supple velvet, he said, "I'll trust you to do that, Madame de Kerlerec. Something extraordinary, *s'il vous plaît.*" He rose and smiled at her. "And, the mademoiselle will need a cape. Perhaps the same blue velvet lined with ermine, what do you think?"

And so it went.

Johnny couldn't have paid more attention to Nevada during those golden days if she had been his adored intended. And she couldn't help but hope that soon that's just what she would be. Johnny's sweetheart. Johnny's fiancée. Johnny's wife.

Even Miss Annabelle began to think that maybe the worldly Cap'n Roulette had actually begun to care for the dark-haired young beauty. He'd hardly spent any time with Lady Ashley lately. And it was Nevada, not Lady Ashley, he was taking to the Queen's formal dinner.

The prospect made Miss Annabelle smile. Nevada, so young, so romantic, desperately needed to be loved. And Cap'n Roulette, though he didn't yet realize it, surely needed love as well.

The older woman sighed wistfully.

Everyone needed love.

25

〰〰〰〰〰

They all waited.

Miss Annabelle was seated primly on the English Chippendale sofa, her pale eyes lifting every few seconds to the walnut-cased clock on the mantle, her hands twisting a lace handkerchief in her lap. King Cassidy sat stiffly on a blue-and-rust patterned wing chair, nervously stroking his silver goatee as he stared into the flames blazing in the marble fireplace.

And Johnny, smiling, relaxed, and sure of himself, looked strikingly handsome in black swallowtail coat and matching trousers, white shirt, white vest, white tie.

With easy, catlike grace he moved to the tall front windows and looked out at the London night. Over his shoulder he said, "The rain has stopped. The stars are out. It promises to be a clear, perfect night."

"It will be perfect," he heard a pleasing feminine voice declare softly. Johnny slowly turned and his smile broadened.

Nevada stood across the room, a dazzling vision in sky-blue velvet. The new gown was magnificent. Fashioned in the latest style, it tastefully accentuated her charms and revealed her figure. Long, snug sleeves hugged her slender arms, coming to a point atop her small hands, and the gown's tight bodice dipped appealingly low over her pale, exquisite bosom.

Her waist appeared unbelievably tiny, the curve of womanly hips and firm little bottom only hinted at by the gown's clever ruffles and draperies. The flowing velvet skirt spread out into a long, supple train of yards and yards of soft blue velvet pooling around her small feet.

Her gleaming black hair was dressed in elaborate puffs and braids, and one long, shiny curl fell attractively onto a bare creamy shoulder. The shimmering sapphire-and-diamond necklace rested on her white, perfect bosom. Glittering with blue fire, the necklace's large center teardrop sapphire nestled and winked appealingly from the shadowed valley between her high, full breasts.

Nevada stood, poised, serene, her sparkling blue eyes aglow, her heart beating a slow, regular rhythm beneath the soft blue velvet bodice. She smiled sweetly when Miss Annabelle, the first of the awed admirers to speak, said breathlessly, "You'll be the most beautiful woman at the palace tonight."

"The nobility will claim you for their own," exclaimed a proud King Cassidy, coming to his feet, his eyes crinkling with pleasure. More softly he said, "My dear child, you are truly a regal lady, through and through."

Pleased, Nevada never noticed the quick, self-satisfied expression that flashed across Johnny's dark face. Johnny crossed to her, came to stand directly before her.

Grinning down at her, he reached out with thumb and forefinger to pluck the huge, fiery teardrop sapphire from between her perfumed breasts. He held it in his palm.

"The exact color of your eyes," he said and the back of his lean hand gently brushed her bare flesh. Nevada felt a sweet warmth spread through her body. The heart beneath Johnny's hand doubled its beating when he looked into her eyes and said, "My dear Miss Hamilton, I'm extremely honored to be your escort on this memorable evening. I daresay no more beautiful young lady has ever been presented at the Court of St. James. You will dazzle them all, just as you dazzle me."

He smiled lazily at her. Then his hand released the heavy blue sapphire and his low-lidded eyes watched it fall back into place on her creamy, flawless flesh. Nevada saw him swallow anxiously and she suddenly felt giddy with an unfamiliar female power.

A premonition struck her, its force amazing. This was to be the night of nights! And being presented at court was only a small part of the whole. Before the lovely evening ended, her life, she knew, would be forever changed.

Ready for the glorious adventure to unfold, Nevada said, "Johnny, we really should be going. We'd not want to keep Her Majesty waiting."

A closed landau plus four waited downstairs at the curb. Nevada's happy laughter carried on the clear night air when Johnny, helping her up into the roomy carriage, lifted the flowing train of her skirt and carefully arranged it around her feet.

Once seated beside her, Johnny took off his silk top hat and white gloves, dropped them on the seat between them, and put a gentle hand to the back of her velvet cape's high collar.

"Will you be warm enough?" he asked, turning to her, his black cashmere cloak falling open over his bent knees.

Cuddled snugly within the folds of lush white ermine that lined her long velvet cape, Nevada smiled. "Yes, thank you, Johnny."

And so the handsome pair fell into their roles for the evening. Nevada, the beautiful genteel lady, her voice soft and modulated, her back erect, her deportment tranquil.

Johnny, the good-looking gentleman, his manners quite polished, his conversation cultivated.

Yet underneath the composed exterior of the lovely lady and handsome gentleman, each experienced a growing measure of excitement. A building exhilaration that had little to do with Queen Victoria's reception.

Giant bonfires lit up the cold London skies as the landau traveled across the giant city. Shouts of joy and jubilation came from happy revelers dancing in the cobblestone streets. Nevada turned questioning eyes to Johnny.

"They're celebrating Guy Fawkes Day."

"Who is Mr. Fawkes?"

Johnny grinned. "An unbalanced Englishman caught setting explosives beneath the House of Lords."

"My heavens, I hope he's locked up!" said Nevada.

Johnny chuckled good-naturedly and took her hand in his. Twining his long dark fingers through her satin-gloved ones, he said, "Fawkes was arrested and hanged back in the early sixteen hundreds." He absently pressed her hand to his trousered thigh. "They burn him in effigy every November 5th."

Mortified by her display of ignorance, Nevada felt her self-assurance suddenly slip alarmingly. "Oh, Johnny, what if I embarrass you before the—"

"You won't," he cut in smoothly and squeezed her hand. "Ask no questions and pretend you have the answers. They'll never know the difference." He grinned and added, "We're almost there, Nevada."

"Marie," she reminded him. "Miss Marie Hamilton."

"I stand corrected."

The landau rolled along the Embankment and through the Queen's Horse Guards. The Beefeaters, in full dress, were in their places. Lights blazed from every window of the huge yellow palace and Nevada took a long, deep breath and smiled nervously at Johnny when the carriage came to a stop before the royal dwelling.

Footman in scarlet and gold sallied forth—and then it was all like a lovely dream for Nevada.

She was swept up into the majestic palace where the fur-lined cape was whisked from her shoulders. Her hand on Johnny's arm, she climbed the grand staircase decorated with flowers and lined with Yeoman of the Guard.

She was ushered into the reception room, where the great officers of state as well as the ladies and gentleman of the court were assembled, including the inventor, Alexander Bell. Everyone in *gala*.

Mr. Bell was speaking enthusiastically of his latest invention, one he intended to demonstrate for the Queen. Something he called the telephone.

Before Nevada had time to catch her breath, they were all moving into a magnificent hall. The Supper room. There she and Johnny sat down to dinner at a huge round table with dukes and duchesses, foreign royalty, special ambassadors and envoys. A seven-course meal was served on plates of gleaming gold, while a string quartet played in the background. Nevada, drinking champagne from crystal bearing the royal crest, made easy table conversation with the Duke of Connaught on her right and with the Prince of Naples to her left.

The dreamlike quality of the glamorous evening and the freely flowing wines helped put her at ease. That, and the warmth and approval she saw shining in Johnny's dark eyes each time she looked at him.

And so from the *crème d'orge* to the *baba au curaçao,* Nevada handled the long sumptuous meal and her aristocratic table companions with effortless sophistication and charm.

When dinner ended, the guests went into the Queen's

vast marble-floored ballroom where Nevada and Johnny joined the presentation line. At the head of the line was the honored guest, Mr. Alexander Graham Bell. Then the colonial premiers and their wives were presented. Then the special envoys. An Indian prince and the officers of the Indian escort, who held out their gleaming swords to be touched by Her Majesty.

Then suddenly there she was, standing before Britain's reigning monarch. She, Nevada Marie Hamilton, child of the Mississippi River, was being presented to Her Majesty, the Queen. Curtsying deliberately slowly, just as Miss Annabelle had demonstrated over and over, Nevada knelt before Her Royal Highness, Victoria, the Queen of England.

When she rose, Nevada smiled at the middle-aged woman with the round childish face who did not look the least bit noble or elegant, although she wore a gown the whole front of which was embroidered in gold. There were huge glittering diamonds in her cap and a wide diamond necklace hugged her fleshy throat.

Despite all the royal trappings, the Queen was tiny and dumpy. Her mouth was pursed and her eyes were slightly bugged. But those unattractively bulging eyes held a warm, friendly expression that made Nevada feel welcome and completely comfortable in this historic palace.

And when the pudgy little sovereign said, "Miss Hamilton, you and I are the same height. You must tell me the name of your couturier," Nevada felt faint with triumph.

"Your Majesty, I shall be most happy to do so." So the short dumpy Queen and the tiny beautiful American discussed gowns and dressmakers while the procession of guests waited for their turn to be presented.

The Queen's band was playing as Johnny led Nevada onto the dance floor. She had never danced with Johnny before and the experience was such a pleasant one, Nevada never noticed when Queen Victoria, in less than an hour, took her leave.

Johnny did.

Bending, he whispered against Nevada's perfumed curls. "Her Majesty has left. Let's slip away."

Outside, the night had grown much colder. The sky, for a change, was clear. Stars glittered in the inky blackness. And in Nevada's happy blue eyes.

As their landau drove away from the palace, Johnny praised her impeccable behavior. Everyone thought she was a great lady. And if that was not enough to make her glow, he wrapped his long arm around her and pulled her close, saying, "Ah, sweetheart, you're cold. Let me warm you."

Nevada was happy.

She was in the arms of the man she loved, riding in a grand carriage through the cold London streets after a splendid evening at Buckingham Palace. And she still had that feeling that more incredible surprises were in store before the cold winter night was over.

She snuggled close to Johnny's warmth and smiled dreamily. And barely lifted her dark head when Johnny shouted to a street urchin hawking papers on the corner. The dirty-faced boy hurried to the slow-moving carriage, held out the late edition of *The Pall Mall Gazette,* and said, "Why, thank you, governor" when Johnny tipped generously.

When they arrived back at Claridge's, Miss Annabelle had retired for the evening. The fire in the grate had burned low but the sitting room was warm and cozy. Johnny helped Nevada out of her cape, touched her bare shoulder, and said, "Do you suppose Miss Annabelle is asleep?" His dark eyes flashed and his easy smile suggested that he hoped she was.

"I'm sure of it," Nevada said.

"I've ordered champagne sent up." His fingers slid along the sapphire-and-diamond necklace around her throat. "Why don't you get more comfortable? I'll do the same." He grinned engagingly. "Then join me for a nightcap."

In her darkened bedroom Nevada was very careful not to wake Miss Annabelle. She tiptoed straight to the dressing room and closed the door behind her. And then hurrying anxiously, she prayed nothing would go wrong, that Miss Annabelle would sleep the night through, and that she and Johnny could be alone.

Suddenly wondering exactly how comfortable she was supposed to make herself, Nevada stood in the mirrored dressing room undecided. She debated what she should slip into. And quickly made a daring choice.

Nevada stripped down to the skin, save for the diamond-and-sapphire necklace. Smiling mischievously, she drew from the glass-doored armoire a pale blue nightgown she had purchased at Harrods but had never worn because of its seductive sheerness. She slipped the lovely nightie over her head, pulled it down over her breasts and hips, and looked at herself.

She blushed hotly.

She was as naked as if she wore nothing at all; the gauzy gown hid nothing. Absolutely nothing. Nevada bit her lip, considered changing, then smiled and lifted her chin. Feeling wonderfully naughty, she pulled on an ice-blue silk wrapper over the revealing gossamer gown. She tied the robe's sash and then carefully folded back the silk lapels so that the sparkling necklace as well as a generous expanse of bare bosom would show. Slipping her feet into a pair of satin slippers, she brushed the puffs and braids from her hair, allowing the long black tresses to spill loosely down her back.

She blew out the lamp and tiptoed from the mirrored dressing room across the darkened bedroom and, reaching the door, took a deep breath, glanced one last time at Miss Annabelle, and went out to meet Johnny.

With limber grace he came to his feet when she entered. And the thought struck Nevada that all the royals were not back at Buckingham Palace. Johnny looked like some kind of lord in a dark burgundy jacket of soft velvet and open-collared silk shirt all ruffled down the front.

A shiver of excitement skipped up her spine when he said, his voice deep and sensuous, rich as fine brandy, "That palace crowd would really think you beautiful if they could see you now."

She came to him, stood directly before him. "And you?"

His black eyes pierced her, but before he could respond to her question a soft knock on the door caused him to turn his dark head.

"Excuse me," he said and crossed the room.

A hotel steward wheeled in a linen-draped table bearing candelabrum, champagne, caviar, and candies. Johnny winked at her and Nevada laughed softly, thinking to herself that they *were* two of a kind, they most surely belonged together. Johnny, like her, was planning a long, lovely night of self-indulgence and sweet decadence. Just the two of them. Alone together in the privacy of his room. A romantic fire in the fireplace. Chilled wine. Crunchy caviar. Rich chocolates.

And a big soft bed.

When Johnny closed the door behind the departing steward, he turned and said teasingly, "Will my lady join me in a bit of very private celebrating?" He lifted the chilled champagne from its icy depths.

Nevada smiled and softly replied, "My lord, I can think of nothing that would please me more."

She could hardly wait to hear his toast, but just as they raised their stemmed glasses there was another soft knock at the door.

Ben Robin walked past Johnny and into the suite as though he had been expected. Clutching the lapels of her robe together, Nevada looked from Ben to Johnny, puzzled.

"I hope I'm not . . . ah . . . interrupting anything," Ben said, noting Nevada's nightclothes.

"Not a thing," Johnny assured him. "Come on in and have a drink with us."

Johnny poured another glass of champagne, handed it to Ben Robin, and looked around for the newspaper he'd bought from the street boy. Spotting it on a drum table beside Nevada, he asked if she would bring it to him.

Annoyed that Johnny had invited Ben to join them on this night of nights and wondering why the sudden interest in the *Gazette,* she picked up the paper and held it out to him.

Grinning, Johnny took it, turned to an inside article, skimmed it, and folded the paper. Handing it to Ben Robin, he said, "Read it for yourself. Aloud, if you please."

Baffled, Nevada listened to Ben Robin read aloud from *The Pall Mall Gazette.* He read of the night's royal reception at the palace and of them, Johnny Roulette and Miss Marie Hamilton, having been presented to the queen. Her slight irritation fled.

Excitedly she flew across the room. "Let me see that, Ben! Johnny, we're in the paper. Isn't that wonderful? I can't believe it." She snatched the newspaper from Ben's hands and sank down onto the couch, reading and rereading the article, totally engrossed.

When she lowered the paper she realized that Johnny

was laughing. And that Ben Robin was counting out bills into Johnny's palm. Lots of bills. Big bills.

The counting finally stopped.

Ben said, "An even one thousand."

And Johnny, taking the *Gazette* from her, handed it to Ben. "And your receipt." Johnny wadded the bills in his hand and said, "It was so easy, I feel almost guilty taking your money, Benjamin."

Ben Robin was smiling when he replied, "I deserve to lose." He glanced at Nevada. "I've no doubt you were a true lady tonight. My congratulations." He stood up, ready to leave.

The smile left Nevada's flushed face. Warily she rose from the sofa. "Why are you congratulating me, Ben?"

"Why, because, my dear, you—"

"You fooled them at the palace," Johnny laughingly cut in as he stuffed the bills in the breast pocket of his burgundy velvet jacket. "They took you to be one of them, a true blue-blood."

"But of course I am not," said Nevada, her voice flat.

"No," said Johnny evenly, "and neither am I. That's what made it a challenge."

Nevada's blue eyes had lost their sparkle. She stared at Johnny. "You took me to Buckingham Palace on a bet?"

"Ah . . . I'll say good night," Ben Robin said. With the newspaper tucked under his arm, he made his exit.

"Yes. And we won, didn't we, Lady Hamilton," said Johnny carelessly. He offered his hand to Nevada. "One thousand pounds. A year of comfortable living, by most standards."

Ignoring his hand, she said, an icy edge to her voice, "You bet with Ben that you could take me to Buckingham Palace and pass me off as a lady?"

"Yes, indeed, darlin', and you came through with flying

colors. There was not one duke or prince there who suspected your background." He laughed aloud. "The nobility thought you a true lady."

Stunned and deeply hurt, Nevada stared at Johnny, fighting to keep back the tears that were stinging her eyes. She had thought he was beginning to care, when all the time he had been grooming her to win a bet. This night had meant nothing to him. She meant nothing to him.

Her pride swiftly surfacing to cover the hurt, Nevada said, "I'll tell you this much, Johnny Roulette, I am damned sure more of a lady than you are a gentleman."

"Well, sure you are, hon." Johnny's broad smile slipped slightly when he realized she was angry. "I never said—"

"I'll tell you something else," she interrupted, her voice as cold as the London night, "I have had enough of England and of you."

"Now, Nevada, you don't mean that." He remained seated, unbothered by what he took to be an idle threat.

"I never meant anything more in my life."

"Look, sweetheart, you're—"

"I want my money. Including my cut of the thousand pounds you won tonight."

Johnny nodded. "And you'll have it. Tomorrow I'll go to the—"

"Not tomorrow. Tonight. Right now!"

"Nevada, lower your voice. You'll wake Miss Annabelle." Johnny came to his feet.

"I don't give a damn if I wake everybody in the hotel!" she shouted.

Johnny's black eyes narrowed. He took a step toward her. But his tone remained low and well-modulated when he told her, "I said lower your voice, Nevada."

"I heard you the first time but you obviously have not heard me. It's over, Johnny. All over. No more bossing me around. I'm not an obedient child. I'm a woman and I'm leaving."

"You'll leave when I say you can leave." Growing angry now, Johnny swiftly crossed to her and stood towering over her, his demeanor threatening. "You know I need you with me for the big game."

"That's your hard luck, not mine. I'm not staying for the game."

Johnny experienced his first real pang of uneasiness. He immediately tried a different tack. He reached out and gently clasped her upper arms. "Ah, sweetheart, you're upset. You'll feel different tomorrow." He favored her with his most irresistible smile, his white teeth flashing dazzlingly beneath his sleek mustache. "If after the game you still want to leave, I'll permit it."

"Damn you and damn your permission!" She shrugged away. "I don't need either one! I can and will do just as I please."

Johnny's heart was beginning to kick against his ribs. My, God, she really meant it. She was planning to leave him. He couldn't let that happen. He *wouldn't* let it happen. She was his. His good-luck charm and she was staying.

He again pulled her close against him and pressed his tanned cheek to hers. "Baby, baby, I'm sorry. Don't be angry."

"Johnny, let me go." Nevada was unreachable.

Johnny pulled back a little to look at her. She refused to meet his glance. He said, "Nevada, if you really want to leave London, then certainly that is your right."

Her eyes slowly lifted to his. "Thank you. Now if you'll kindly let go of me and—"

"All right. But won't you at least stay until after the game?"

"No, damn you, I won't. You can kiss your good-luck charm good-bye!" She stepped away from him.

Scowling, Johnny said, "I'll do that." He effortlessly caught her and pulled her back to him. His gaze lowered to her lips. He was confident that if he kissed her, she'd be putty in his hands, just as always. But Nevada read his thoughts.

"It won't work, Johnny," she said in a flat, determined voice.

Knowing it would work, Johnny lowered his dark head and covered her mouth with his. His tongue easily parted her lips and he kissed her with a long, slow warmth, determined to melt away the ice and the anger. Nevada neither struggled nor participated. Her small soft body did not mold itself to his, her arms did not come around him. Johnny deepened the kiss, drawing her closer, cradling her head against his shoulder. Slanting his heated lips on hers, he brought his hand up to her face, caressed her delicate jaw, moved his lean fingers down the side of her throat where the shimmering diamond-and-sapphire necklace rested. Then to the satin lapel of her blue robe. Gently he tugged, urging the robe apart. He found the sash at her slender waist and eagerly untied it. His hand sought the rounded softness of her breast.

Still he got no response. Shaken, he finally lifted his head, his breath short, his heart hammering in his chest.

Nevada, her soft lips wet and swollen from his kiss, the open blue robe exposing her luscious body beneath the gossamer gown, looked him squarely in the eye. Defiant and beautiful, she stood there toe-to-toe with Johnny, a highly desirable, totally independent woman, unafraid and unyielding.

She said very softly, "For me you no longer exist. If ever

we meet again, I don't know you. You and I have never met."

Then she whirled around and walked quickly across the room, the blue robe flaring out behind her. At her bedroom door she paused, turned, and looked back at him. "You never wanted me for anything but to bring you luck gambling. Well, from now on, Johnny Roulette, I'm betting on myself!"

Part Two

26

〰〰〰〰

In the rosy, spectral glow of sunrise, General Andrew Jackson easily sat his rearing stallion. At noon when the Louisiana sun was high overhead, the general was still there, his hat lifted in flamboyant salute. At dusk when the warm afternoon gave way to the chill of southern night, the proud warrior and his stallion still dominated the square named for him.

And late at night when the Crescent City slept and a dewy sheen settled over the grassy park surrounding the mounted general, the fiery Jackson remained wide awake, his blazing eyes lifted to the night sky, his back held militarily rigid.

Nevada stood alone at the iron lace–trimmed balcony of her luxuriant Pontalba Building apartment and stared fixedly across St. Ann Street at the gallant general. In the week she had been in New Orleans she had seen hardly anyone but the general. She enjoyed his company because, with Andy, she didn't have to make small talk and smile and be charming and pretend that she was gay.

Located in the very center of the square, across St. Ann Street from her red apartment building, the huge green statue expected nothing from her, wanted nothing of her. She liked it that way. She liked the mute general. If she felt like talking to him, she did. If not, he didn't mind. He was there for her at any hour of the day or night.

It was well past midnight, a chill winter wind caused Nevada to hug her arms to her side and shiver. General Jackson never noticed the cold. Not for the first time, she wished that she could be more like the indomitable statue. How convenient it would be to feel nothing.

Nevada sighed and let her gaze drift from the dauntless monument to St. Louis Cathedral, its tall white spires rising to the dark sky. Next to the church the old Cibaldo was silent. Across the square the usually bustling French markets were empty, the long wooden tables and bins bare.

At last the wistful young woman looked to her right, toward the calm Mississippi, its muddy waters shimmering silver in the winter moonlight. A solitary steamer, far in the distance, blew its whistle and the mournful sound seemed to pierce right through Nevada's lonely heart.

For as long as she could remember, a steamer's whistle had been part of her life, had made her squeal with delight when she was a happy river child, had made her heartbeat quicken as she grew older.

The faraway blast brought back fond memories of a huge sandy-haired man with twinkling blue eyes and thunderous laughter and a heart as big as the river. They'd spent many a happy day together on the winding Mississippi, she and her papa.

But the whistle brought memories of another man as well. A dark, raven-haired man with smoldering black eyes and a devilish grin and no heart at all. She'd spent one passion-filled night with him on the river and her life would never again be the same, while his had changed none at all.

Tears started to spill from Nevada's sad eyes. She let them fall. There was no one to see her cry except old Andrew Jackson and he wouldn't tell. So she stood alone in the night on the cold New Orleans balcony and wept openly for the uncaring man across the ocean who was as much a man of stone as the carefully sculpted general.

She cried for a long time. Cried until her head was aching and her eyes were swollen and puffy. Cried because she missed Johnny so much, loved him so desperately that her days and her nights were filled with an agony of a kind she'd never known existed. Cried because she would have to make it on her own and she wasn't sure she could do it.

And finally, when she was all cried out, Nevada lifted her tired head, looked toward the mounted general and told him, "That's it, Andy. The last time. After tonight, November 20, 1876, there'll be no more tears wasted over Mr. Johnny Roulette!"

Staring out at the rain-dampened city, Johnny Roulette smoked a thin brown cigar in the darkness. It was well past midnight but he wasn't sleepy. It was the day of the game. The big game. The game for which he had traveled to London.

Johnny drew on his cigar, pulled the hot smoke deep down into his lungs, then slowly released it, forming perfect circular smoke rings with his rounded mouth.

His thoughts were on the upcoming game. And Nevada Marie Hamilton. He had counted on her being at his side, had brought her across an ocean as his Lady Luck. He wondered if could win without her.

Johnny blew another smoke ring and leaned his dark head on the deeply cushioned back of the oyster-and-gold brocade chair, one of a matching set that graced the elegant upstairs drawing room of Lady Ashley's Mayfair town house.

The hell with Nevada Hamilton. He'd been gambling

since he turned fourteen and he had won plenty of money since then. Long before he knew there was a Nevada Hamilton. He didn't need her. He didn't need anyone, he never had.

Johnny came agilely to his feet. He crossed to the big bay window. The cigar stuck firmly between his teeth, he stood naked in the night, squinting out at the well-manicured lawns and the rain dripping rhythmically from the mansion's steep roof.

He drew a long, deep breath, crossed his arms over his bare chest, and told himself it was perfectly natural to be edgy and restless the night before the big game. That's all it was. Maybe a glass of brandy and a hot tub would make him sleep.

Johnny continued to stay as he was, standing there looking out at the rain, tired but not sleepy, lonely but glad he was alone. At least he thought he was alone.

"Darling?" Lady Ashley spoke his name from the doorway.

"Mm?" He never turned around.

Lifting the long, whispering skirts of her dressing gown, Lady Ashley hurried to him. Standing just behind him, she laid a hand on his bare back and said, "Darling, is something wrong? I woke up, you were gone. I grew worried."

"Just not sleepy," he said and drew on the cigar.

"It's the rain," said Lady Ashley. "You Yanks tire of our frequent rains."

He didn't answer.

Laughing softly, sure she knew just how to calm his jitters, Lady Ashley quickly took off her gown. She stepped up behind Johnny, put her arms around him, and pressed her naked body to his. "Love," she whispered, her hands sweeping teasingly over his broad chest, "you're chilled."

Johnny made no reply. He just stood there smoking his

cigar, looking out at the rain while his accomplished lover stroked his chest and pressed kisses to his back and murmured endearments in a husky, breathless voice. Her skillful hands moved down to his flat belly and she began to rock her pelvis forward against his hard buttocks.

"Forget your silly old card game, love," she said as her hands slipped lower. "Think about this." And her right hand encircled him and began the gentle sliding caresses, up and down and up again. She smiled when she heard his sharp intake of air. And when he made a move to turn to her, she said, "No. Not yet. Let me touch you this way until neither of us can stand it any longer."

Johnny shrugged negligently. And stood there in the darkened room, his feet apart, arms at his sides, the cigar still clamped between his teeth, while the naughtily determined Lady Ashley touched and stroked and molded his responsive body into a beautifully formed rock-hard erection.

At last her hands dropped away. Johnny turned to face her. She jerked the cigar from his lips, stabbed it out in a crystal ashtray, and beckoned to him with her hands.

"Come to bed, Roulette," said she, and he did.

"Stryker, have the carriage out front at precisely eight-thirty this evening. You'll be driving Miss Annabelle and me to the Wilsons' party in the Garden District."

The big man nodded. "Will you be needing me to run any errands this afternoon?"

Nevada pondered for a moment. "I think not. We did our shopping this morning. We'll likely rest all afternoon so we'll be fresh for the party."

"Good enough, Miss Marie."

"Oh, and Stryker, the party is a buffet supper, so we

won't be having the evening meal here. Think you can manage?"

"Don't worry about a thing. Now, if that's all, I'll be back here this evening at eight-thirty."

"Thanks, Stryker."

The big man left and Nevada smiled at his disappearing back. He was a good man, nothing at all like his physical appearance. His countenance was almost frightening—a nose many times broken, a wide slash of a mouth, and eyes that were often narrowed in defiance. His shoulders were immense, his chest deep and powerful, his hands huge.

But he was truly a gentle giant. At least with her. And Miss Annabelle. And that was all that mattered.

When she and Miss Annabelle had returned from London, Miss Annabelle said that it was neither proper nor safe for the two of them to live in the French Quarter with no man around for protection. Stryker had come immediately to mind. She had sent a message to him on the next steamer upriver, and five days later she answered the bell to see the *Moonlight Gambler*'s big bouncer standing before her.

"You needed me, here I am," was his simple greeting.

She and Miss Annabelle were amazed to learn that Stryker's talents were many and varied. He could cook as well as the best Creole chef, ride like a pony expressman, sing like a baritone opera star, shoot like a marksman, fight like a pugilist, and spin tales with the best of imaginative storytellers.

Stryker also got around.

Within twenty-four hours of his arrival in New Orleans, every river rat on the levee and every moneyed swain in the city knew that the formidable Stryker, his suit jacket concealing a pistol stuck in the waistband of his trousers, was keeping a watchful eye on the beautiful dark-haired Miss

Marie Hamilton and her companion, Miss Annabelle Delaney.

And everyone in New Orleans knew that Miss Annabelle Delaney was of the Old Guard, a respected member of Louisiana's true upper crust.

So invitations to teas and soirees and wine suppers and dances began arriving at the exclusive Pontalba address as soon as the gentry heard that Miss Annabelle Delaney was in New Orleans. And after that first long, lonely week that Nevada spent in sorrowful solitude, the two of them attended galas almost nightly.

Determined she'd keep her vow to old Andy's statue, Nevada hadn't allowed herself to cry since. She was going to do exactly what Johnny told her to do. What he had groomed her for, educated her for.

She was going to find a rich, handsome gentleman who would be kind and thoughtful and loving. And when she found him, when he proposed, she was going to say yes!

And then she'd be so happy there would never be one day, one hour, one minute when she would think about Mr. Johnny Roulette!

Her resolve firm, a radiant, smiling Miss Marie Hamilton swept up the steps of the Darcy Wilson mansion that cold December evening, Miss Annabelle Delaney at her side. Among old and dear comrades, Miss Annabelle smiled and greeted friends and introduced Nevada as Marie Hamilton, one of the Tennessee Hamiltons.

The gay and glittering elite of New Orleans were captivated by Nevada's youthful beauty and natural charm. The Honorable P. T. Beauregard, for whom the party was given, insisted on accompanying her to the buffet table. The revered talkative general, whose attack on Fort Sumter had opened the War between the States, clung tenaciously to her slender arm until a distant cousin, down

from St. Louis, saw Nevada's dilemma and came to her
rescue.

"I'm sorry, Cousin Beauregard," said the pert red-
haired Denise Ledet, looping her arm through Nevada's,
"but I've promised the Cooper twins I'd introduce Miss
Hamilton to them. May I borrow her? I knew you'd understand."

"Well, I . . . she . . . I was about to . . . ah . . .
tell her of . . ." Beauregard hemmed and hawed, then finally admitted, "I suppose Miss Hamilton would rather
have supper with you youngsters."

"Thanks, Cousin," said Denise, and swiftly drew Nevada away, whispering, "You'll have to forgive Cousin
Beauregard. Mama says he's in his second childhood already. But I say he thinks he's still the dashing Confeder-
ate general. Poor thing lives in the glorious past and cannot resist a pretty girl." Denise laughed and it was a warm,
musical sound that Nevada found very pleasing.

"I understand you recently returned from a lengthy trip
abroad. You were in London, presented to the Queen, I
hear. Didn't you just hate London? I did! Rained every day
until I thought I'd go mad and, besides, Mama wouldn't
let me have any fun. I met the handsomest stage actor at a
party, but nothing came of it because I was not allowed to
see him! Is your life as boring as mine, Marie?" Denise's
warm brown eyes bore into Nevada's.

It was instant friendship.

The two young women gossiped and laughed and spent
the rest of the evening together. And when it was time for
Nevada and Miss Annabelle to leave, Denise clasped
Nevada's hands in hers and asked anxiously, "You know
where the statue of Andrew Jackson is, Marie? Will you
meet me there in the morning at precisely ten o'clock? Will
you help me pick a dress for next week's reception at Whit-

ington Hall? You are invited, aren't you? Have you ever
been to St. Louis? Will you—"

"Denise"—Nevada managed to interrupt, laughing and
happily squeezing her new friend's hands—"you don't give
me time to answer."

"I know, I know," admitted Denise. "Mama says I talk
too much. Do you think so? I don't mean to and I know
it's ever so rude, but I—"

"I have to go."

"Meet me?"

"Yes. Oh, yes." Impulsively Nevada hugged the slender
redhead, pressed her cheek to Denise's and murmured,
"Good night. I'll see you in the morning!"

Nevada was still smiling as she settled back in the carriage for the ride to the Pontalba. She had never had a
girlfriend, she realized suddenly. At least not one her own
age. Miss Annabelle was her friend, of course, and the
entertainers on the *Gambler* had been, but that was all. All
her life had been spent among men.

She turned anxiously to Miss Annabelle. "May I meet
Denise Ledet in Jackson Square tomorrow and go shopping with her and her mother?"

Miss Annabelle patted Nevada's hand. "Of course you
may, dear. The Ledets are fine people. Their recent move
to St. Louis was New Orleans's loss, I assure you."

Nevada was so excited that night she could hardly sleep.
Up the next morning with the sun, she dressed with care,
choosing a dress of light blue wool. Studying herself in the
free-standing mirror, she thought how perfectly the sapphire-and-diamond necklace would match her dress. And
what fun it would be to nonchalantly let slip to her new
friend that the expensive necklace was a gift from a lover.
But of course that would be inappropriate. To wear the
glittering jewelry in the daytime. And to admit she'd had a

handsome lover. So she would wait until the Whitingtons'
gala to wear the necklace and then when Denise asked,
she'd simply smile mysteriously and lower her lashes.

With Stryker conspicuously trailing her, a laughing,
lighthearted Nevada dashed across St. Ann Street and into
the square at five minutes to ten. Denise Ledet was waiting. Seated on a step directly below the mounted Jackson,
she bounded up the minute she saw the tiny, dark-haired
girl approaching. They met and embraced as though they
were the dearest of friends. Which they soon would be.

"Are you hungry?" asked Denise and, not giving Nevada time to answer, continued, "Did you know that the
best *café au lait* and *beignets* in all New Orleans are served
in the Café du Monde right here in the Place d'Armes?"
She grabbed Nevada's hand and led her across the es-
panlade, still talking. "It isn't really the Place d'Armes
anymore, I know. Hasn't been for years, but *Grand-mère*
Ledet says she'll never call it Jackson Square. Says Jackson
was nothing but a backwoods loud-mouthed ruffian, and
how dare they rename her beloved Place d'Armes after
such a man!"

Nodding, Nevada prayed Denise's *Grand-mère* Ledet
never learned that she, Miss Marie Hamilton of the Tennessee Hamiltons, was actually Nevada Hamilton, daughter of a whisky-drinking keelboatman. Would Nevada have
been invited to go shopping with the aristocratic Ledets?
Certainly not.

But they didn't know, so she spent the long, lovely day
shopping and gossiping and laughing with Denise and her
mother. In a little shop on Toulouse, Nevada purchased an
antique fan for Miss Annabelle, explaining to Denise that
she wished to cheer up her companion, knowing full well
that the inquisitive Denise would promptly asked what was
wrong.

Enjoying being able to have some small secret to share with her new friend, Nevada took Denise's arm, guided her a few steps away, and whispered, "You won't repeat what I tell you?"

"I'd allow the *garde de ville* to arrest me and cart me off to the calaboose before I'd utter a word!"

"Well . . ."—Nevada glanced around—"as you know, Miss Annabelle and I have been in London. We met a remarkable man on the crossing to England. King Cassidy. Dapper, middle-aged, and so rich that the Queen of England herself is poor by comparison. King is—"

Eyes wide, Denise interrupted, "And Miss Annabelle fell madly in love with him, but he already had a wife back in—"

"No, no, nothing like that. But I believe that she did grow quite fond of him. And he of her. You see, they . . ."

Nevada's perception of the unlikely attraction between King Cassidy and Miss Annabelle was not far off the mark. She rightly guessed, and shared with her friend, that both the silver king and Miss Annabelle had been victims of unrequited love in their youth and were afraid of being hurt again.

"So you're saying that Miss Annabelle rejected King Cassidy before he had the chance to reject her, and vice versa," mused Denise thoughtfully.

"Precisely," answered Nevada.

"Well, I can certainly understand that. If a man stomped on my heart, I'd be afraid to offer it to another. I'd be a spinster just like Miss Annabelle. Wouldn't you?"

Nevada's blue eyes narrowed. "No. No, I wouldn't."

"You'd risk having your heart broken a second time?"

"Never!" Nevada too quickly exclaimed, caught herself, smiled, and repeated more softly, "never."

27

At fifty-five, Quincy Maxwell was still a handsome woman and well aware of it. She had kept her slim figure. Her light chestnut hair was thick and lustrous, with only a few threads of gray. Save for a few wrinkles at the corners of her large green eyes, her face looked much the same as when she was thirty.

If the stately widow had wished, she could have been married any number of times in the past quarter of a century. She did not wish. She enjoyed her life just as it was: Respected mistress of the roomy Lucas Place town house in St. Louis's most fashionable section; revered mother of the one of the town's most eligible and intelligent young bachelors; envied member of St. Louis's governing aristocracy.

Quincy Maxwell was very pleased with her existence, very comfortable. The thought of a man in her life, another husband, made her wrinkle her patrician nose in distaste. Save for that short, disconcerting phase more than twenty-five years ago when she had sacrificed herself for money and then was helplessly swept away by the man's coarse animal passions, she was repelled by the idea of physical love.

Even back then, when she had succumbed to the hungers of the flesh, she had felt dirty and common, ashamed in the cold light of day for the things she'd done in the hot darkness.

That was all behind her now, and she was glad. For twenty-five years there had been no man in her life except her cherished son, and hers was a pleasant, satisfying life.

Quincy Maxwell wanted nothing more than to continue to live out the rest of her days in the Lucas Place town house with the dutiful son she loved so much.

Quincy Maxwell frowned.

She must have another serious talk with her son. How many times did she have to point out that it was now up to him to insure their lovely way of life? There was nothing more she could do. She had done her part years ago. Now it was his turn. He was the one who had to see to it. Their future was in his hands—and time was running short.

Quincy Maxwell rose from the small cherrywood secretaire in her upstairs bedroom. She had spent the past half hour handling her correspondence, mainly answering the RSVPs to the season's many parties. She picked up the stack of envelopes and went downstairs in search of her son.

On that cold Sunday afternoon in December, Malcolm Maxwell was seated in his favorite easy chair before the fire, reading. A tall, slender man with light chestnut hair, green eyes, a straight, narrow nose, and lips so beautifully shaped they were almost femininely pretty, Malcolm was placid, intelligent, and kind.

A professor of literature at Washington University, Malcolm was as content with his life as his mother was with hers. He had his chosen profession, an extensive library of fine books, his poetry club, several stimulating acquaintances, a handful of good friends, and one very dear one. He, like Quincy Maxwell, wanted his life to continue just as it was.

"There you are," Quincy said, entering the warm library where her son sat reading, his long legs stretched out to the fireplace.

Malcolm's green eyes lifted to hers. He smiled. "Mother. I thought you had gone out." He laid the book aside.

"I'm leaving shortly." She walked to the fireplace, picked up the poker, and carelessly jabbed a smoldering log. "I thought before I left we might have a little talk."

Malcolm Maxwell tensed. He knew what was coming. "Certainly, Mother."

She turned to face her son. Crossing her arms over her chest, she smiled and said, "Darling, the social season's in full swing. So many parties, it's impossible to attend them all."

"Such a shame," said Malcolm.

His mother stopped smiling. Her arms came uncrossed. "Malcolm, don't be insolent with me. I'll not have it. There are a number of important parties coming up that I insist you attend." Her jaw hardened slightly.

Malcolm sighed, beaten. "Very well. Choose the ones you wish to go to and I'll be happy to escort you."

Quincy's smile returned. She stepped forward, put a hand to her son's cheek. "You'll enjoy them, dear, if you'll just give yourself a chance. The Taylors are giving an egg-nog party. The Bradfords a tea. A wine supper, as usual, at the Crowleys' and . . . and . . . oh, yes, those Ledets who moved here recently from New Orleans, they're having a big New Year's Eve gala." She moved her fingers fondly to her son's temple, stroked the thick chestnut hair.

"Mother, I've never even met the Ledets." He caught her hand in his.

"I know. They have a daughter, Malcolm. She's nineteen—tall, slender, with lovely red hair. A charming girl."

"And she'd make some lucky man a good wife?" His light eyebrows lifted accusingly.

His mother snatched her hand from his. "Yes, she would."

Nevada, Miss Annabelle, and Stryker arrived in St. Louis, Missouri, on the cold but sunny afternoon of Friday, December 29, 1876. A very excited Denise Ledet and her distinguished father, Davis Ledet, were waiting on the river landing to meet them.

Nevada spotted Denise's bright red hair blazing in the sunshine and began waving furiously. In minutes the two girls were embracing while Davis Ledet greeted Miss Annabelle and shook Stryker's hand.

At the Ledets' big Georgian mansion on Thirteenth, the visitors from New Orleans were warmly welcomed by the beaming Mary Ledet and a staff of cordial servants. Within an hour of their arrival the three had been shown to their respective quarters and Nevada and Denise were closeted in Denise's huge bedroom gossiping and giggling.

". . . and on Sunday night we're having the grandest party this city has ever seen. It's formal, of course, and Daddy's hired a full orchestra and Mama's got the cooks working 'round the clock and she's ordered so many flowers it'll take every florist in town and, oh, Nevada, wait until you see my ball gown. You'll simply die! I mean, it's cut to *here*!" She stuck a forefinger into the middle of her chest. "Mama says I'll scandalize everyone and Daddy'll never allow me to wear it, but I can handle Daddy. We'll have imported champagne and I'll bet I get tipsy and you will too, and we'll have to decide early in the evening who we most want to kiss us at midnight. You do like to kiss, don't you? I do. I've kissed three different gentlemen in my life and—"

"How did you manage?" Nevada laughingly cut in.

"Why, I—what do you mean?" She twisted a fiery curl around her finger.

"I wouldn't think a gentleman could catch you with your mouth shut long enough to kiss you."

Denise screamed with laughter. Then said, "I do go on, don't I? It's just that I'm excited to see you again." She laughed again, then added in a naughty whisper, "Besides, a kiss is better if your mouth is open!"

The snow had stopped at nightfall and shortly before nine on New Year's Eve it was clear and cold and beautiful outside, the pure virgin snow glistening in the glow of the winter moonlight.

And inside the Ledets' Thirteenth Street mansion, gas lights blazed and the orchestra tuned and two excited young women dressed for the party.

The diamond-and-sapphire necklace at Nevada's throat perfectly complemented the shimmering blue ball gown of iridescent taffeta. Denise, lifting the skirts of her pink velvet, hurried excitedly into Nevada's room, saying, "It's time, Marie! The guests are arriving and . . . and . . ." She stopped speaking, stared openmouthed, and reached out to touch the magnificent teardrop sapphire. "Marie Hamilton! Who gave you that stunning necklace?"

Nevada smiled enigmatically and fingered the glittering diamonds caressing her throat.

Astute, inquisitive, Denise whispered excitedly, "You've a rich married lover whose wife is an invalid and he can't divorce her, but he worships you and you meet secretly and make love and he showers you with jewels and—"

"Denise!" Nevada stopped her and changed the subject. "You look beautiful in the pink velvet." Her eyes went to the low-cut bodice her friend had promised would scandalize the crowd. It was not nearly so daring as she'd expected. Denise was a tall, slender girl with only gentle curves.

Denise read Nevada's thoughts. "My bosom may not be as pretty as yours, but I have absolutely gorgeous legs. Only trouble is, I never get to show them." She made a face. Then grabbed Nevada's hand and said, "Come on down to the dance."

Elegantly dressed couples were already turning about on the dance floor when Nevada and Denise swept into the ballroom. Whispering behind her hand, Denise supplied names to the faces gliding past them.

"Oh, look, there's Professor Maxwell," she said, nodding to a tall young man standing across the room, drinking champagne. "Malcolm Maxwell is one of the most eligible bachelors in St. Louis. Isn't he handsome? He's also from a prominent, moneyed family."

"Really?" Nevada said. "How is it no woman has managed to catch him?"

Denise shrugged her shoulders. "I don't know. I understand plenty have tried. That's Malcolm's mother standing beside him, talking with Miss Annabelle."

At that moment Miss Annabelle spotted Nevada and Denise. She smiled and pointed the girls out to Quincy Maxwell, who immediately turned and said something to her son.

Malcolm Maxwell drained his champagne glass, set it aside, and started toward them while Denise squeezed Nevada's hand and whispered, "He's coming over. He's going to ask one of us to dance, I just know it!"

Malcolm Maxwell introduced himself, smiling warmly. He said gallantly, "Would that there were two of me that I might dance with you both." Then he offered his white-gloved hand to Nevada and led her to the dance floor.

In his arms Nevada smiled up at him and said saucily, "I forbid you to dance with any other woman tonight, Mr. Maxwell." Astounded, Malcolm made a misstep.

Nevada threw back her dark head and laughed gaily. She and Malcolm Maxwell danced the night away, and by the time the gala ended, Malcolm had asked permission to call on her the next evening. And every evening.

A month after that lovely New Year's Eve party, Malcolm Maxwell proposed to Nevada.

Her answer was yes.

"Dear, are you sure you're doing the right thing?"

"Absolutely." The carriage, hitting a bump, bucked as though emphasizing Nevada's answer.

Miss Annabelle, gripping the seat, remained skeptical. "You've known Malcolm Maxwell for only six weeks and . . . and . . ."—she lowered her eyes—"and what about Cap'n Roulette?"

Nevada's lovely face remained composed, her blue eyes calm. "What about him?"

Almost apologetically the older woman said, "Well, we both know that you were once in love with him and I'm just afraid—"

"Well, don't be. I'm not. I am going to marry Malcolm Maxwell and I couldn't be happier. Malcolm is all the things Johnny Roulette is not. I'm a very fortunate woman."

"Now, dear, don't misunderstand me. I, too, think Mr. Maxwell is a fine young man, but it's just . . . well, Cap'n Roulette was—"

"A charming gambler who, because he needed my luck, afforded me the opportunity to become a lady. Johnny made it possible for me to move in social circles where I might meet polished, wealthy gentlemen like Malcolm."

She smiled serenely and added, "I'm sure he'd be quite proud of my accomplishment."

"I suppose, still . . ." Miss Annabelle softly sighed.

"What is it?"

"You're very sure you no longer care for the cap'n?"

"Yes," said Nevada. "I'm sure."

Miss Annabelle looked down at her gloved hands in her lap. "I knew a man like Cap'n Roulette once a long time ago." She lifted her eyes to Nevada's. "It changed my life forever."

Shocked at the revealing statement, realizing she knew nothing of Miss Annabelle's early years, Nevada touched the older woman's arm, "Why, Miss Annabelle? Because you married him?"

"Because I did not."

The two women rode in silence the rest of the way to the Maxwells' Lucas Place town house.

As soon as Nevada had accepted Malcolm's marriage proposal, Quincy Maxwell promptly decided on a late summer wedding, stating that mid-August would be acceptable. That would give her six months to plan the festivities. Then she insisted that Nevada and Miss Annabelle move immediately into the Lucas Place town house to prepare for the wedding—no need for them to return to faraway New Orleans.

So now on a bitter cold day in mid-February, exactly six weeks after Nevada and Malcolm had met at the Ledets' New Year's Eve party, the two women were on their way to the Maxwells'.

Malcolm was not at home when they arrived, but Quincy threw open the big front door, cheerfully welcomed them inside, and showed them up to their rooms, saying, "Our home is now your home."

She introduced them to the small staff—a middle-aged

rather sour woman called Lena who did the cooking; Minnie, the maid; and Blake, a stringy fellow who wore a constant expression of disdain, the Maxwells' butler. The aging gray-haired black driver was not introduced but Nevada had previously heard Malcolm address him as Jess.

Stryker had gone back to New Orleans alone, closed down the apartments, and had all their belongings shipped to St. Louis. When he returned he disappointed Nevada by saying that he would live in a residential hotel room near the Maxwells' home.

"But, Stryker," she had said, "you must remain here on staff and—"

"When you're married, then we'll see." He awkwardly patted her slender shoulder. "Rest assured, Nevada, I'll be around, if you need me."

"Very well, but I shall continue your pay."

"No, Nevada. I'll find something. Don't trouble yourself about me."

Nevada and Malcolm were sought after by St. Louis's chic hostesses. Fetes were given in their honor and they graciously attended, but Malcolm confessed to his beautiful bride-to-be that he much preferred the meetings of his poetry-reading club and musical evenings in the town house's spacious paneled library, with its marble fireplace and shelves of leather-bound books and the gleaming concert-grand piano.

Nevada preferred the parties and excitement and gay crowds, but reminding herself that she was a very lucky young woman, she went out of her way to be hospitable to Malcolm's learned academic friends. Especially to Richard Keyes, the young, dark, talented pianist and composer who, at twenty-eight, played with the St. Louis symphony and was Malcolm's dearest friend.

Nevada knew how important a best friend could be. Where would she be without her dear, talkative Denise? She sensed that Malcolm found Denise's constant chatter annoying, but he never complained. She'd certainly not complain about Richard Keyes's occasional brooding presence at the town house.

On a windy day near the end of March, while Malcolm was at the university and Miss Annabelle and Quincy were shopping, Denise came over for the afternoon. Upstairs in Nevada's room, Nevada, listening while Denise filled her in on all the latest gossip, went to stand at the French doors.

The tall doors opened onto a double-tiered gallery that overlooked the winter-brown lawn, and at the far edge of the yard a white summerhouse looked desolate and lonely. Beyond the gazebo, a white *garçonnière,* the curtains all pulled, looked lonelier still.

Her gaze was drawn, as it often was when she was alone in her room, to the silent guesthouse. Nevada frowned, recalling the day she had asked Malcolm about it. He had seemed uncomfortable and immediately changed the subject. Since then she had noticed that Minnie cleaned the unused place twice a week, but no one ever stayed there.

Interrupting her girlfriend's monologue, Nevada said, "I wonder if . . . if anyone ever lived in the *garçonnière.*"

Denise joined her at the French doors. "Doesn't look it. Is it locked?"

"Yes, but I know where they keep the key." She began to smile and looked at Denise.

"Let's hurry," said Denise.

Nevada jerked the French doors open and the young

women, not waiting to don wraps, dashed out onto the balcony, down the back steps, and across the broad yard. When they stood before the guesthouse Nevada told Denise the key was on the ledge above the door. Her tall girlfriend found it, put it into the lock, and turned.

Holding on to each other as though they were in a haunted house, they inched into the dim interior. They felt their way to a window and when Nevada pulled back the drapery, light flooded the large room filled with heavy, masculine furniture. A huge bed dominated the far wall, a fitted counterpane of gray velvet pulled tightly smooth across it, the gleaming mahogany headboard rising to a height of at least three feet on the gray-blue wall.

Dropping Denise's hand, Nevada went to the tall armoire, opened the doors, and gasped. Men's clothes hung in a neat row. They were fine clothes—or had been once. Examining a jacket, she said, "These clothes have been here a long time. They're out of fashion."

"Do you suppose they belong to Malcolm?" Denise asked.

"No. No, they are not to his taste and, besides, they wouldn't fit him. They're too large."

"Look at this," said Denise, standing before a chest of drawers. She held a framed picture in her hand.

Eyes wide, Nevada hurried to her. She stared at the faded daguerreotype. A man and woman were smiling. The woman held a baby in her arms. The child looked to be no older than a year. The man was dark-haired and huge. The woman was fair and pretty.

Nevada took the picture and raised it closer to her face. She studied it with interest and had the strangest feeling that she had seen the man before.

"I know him," she murmured aloud.

"Who is he?"

Nevada slowly placed the image back on the chest and frowned. "I don't know."

"You just said—"

Nevada shook her head and laughed. "How could I know him? Of course I don't. I couldn't. Let's go back to the town house, I'm cold."

28

⦿⦿⦿⦿⦿⦿

A bitter-cold winter at long last turned into warm, welcome springtime in St. Louis, Missouri. By late April it was possible and pleasant for the inhabitants of the old river city to sit on their galleries in the evenings and enjoy the balmy Mississippi breezes.

At the Lucas Place town house on a fine April evening, Nevada stepped out onto the veranda to join her fiancé. Rising, Malcolm came to her, took both her hands in his, lifted them and kissed the warm palms.

"I'm a lucky man," he said, his voice soft.

Nevada smiled at him. Malcolm brushed a kiss to her cheek. He smelled not unpleasantly of peppermint and expensive hair tonic, but while his soft lips moved over her cheek, Nevada's eyes closed. Painfully she recalled the scent and taste of Johnny Roulette, the mastery of his hard, heated lips.

"I'm lucky too, Malcolm," she said, opening her eyes, willing Johnny's image to leave her. She squeezed his hand and nodded yes when he asked if she'd like to sit for a while on the gallery.

Malcolm led her to a padded sofa and they sat listening to the night sounds, holding hands in the shadows while silvery moonlight bathed the well-manicured yard beyond the broad porch.

Nevada sighed and told herself that she *was* lucky. Lucky, even if the slender professor whose tapered fingers laced loosely through hers was not the most exciting and passionate man a woman might imagine. He was certainly one of the most intelligent, considerate, kindest.

And safest.

The sexual danger exuded by the reckless, charming Johnny Roulettes of the world was missing in the gentle, controlled Malcolm Maxwell. Nevada was glad it was so. When she thought back on her unforgivable animalistic behavior with Johnny, she was appalled. Not only by the fact that she had allowed him to make love to her the first night they met but also because thereafter she had brazenly thrown herself at him, her great passion for him clouding her judgment. Such disgraceful conduct seemed strangely foreign to her now.

Malcolm made it easy for Nevada to keep her wits about her. He was ever the refined gentleman, and so she was quite naturally ever the refined lady. Alarming physical attraction, of the kind she had felt for Johnny, was absent in her relationship with Malcolm, and that suited her fine.

She now had exactly what she wanted. An attractive aristocrat with wealth and position who cherished her and wanted to marry her. With Malcolm Maxwell she would have a good home, security, and children. And if blazing ardor continued to be missing, even after they were man and wife, it mattered little. The dizzying sensations of carnal ecstasy quickly paled beside the agonizing pain of shattering rejection.

So Nevada sat in the warm April shadows with her intended, feeling a sense of peace she'd never before known. Early-blooming roses below the front steps sweetened the heavy night air and fireflies came out to dart dizzily atop the trimmed hedges, and as Malcolm spoke in his soft calm voice Nevada gave silent thanks for her good fortune.

"Would you like to stroll in the moonlight?" Malcolm asked, after a comfortable lull in their conversation.

"Mm, not really. It's nice here." She cuddled more closely to him, leaned her dark head on his shoulder. And raised it immediately. "Wait—yes, yes, I would. Why don't we walk out to the *garçonnière* and . . ."

"No. Certainly not." Malcolm's tone of voice bordered on sharpness.

Nevada stared at his unsmiling face. She laughed nervously and said, "Malcolm, why ever not? The guesthouse is the only part of the property you've not shown me and . . . and . . ." Her voice trailed off.

Malcolm's delicate features relaxed. He squeezed her hand. He said, "Nothing there to see. The *garçonnière* hasn't been used in years. I should consider having it torn down, I'm sure we won't be needing it. We've plenty of room for our guests in the main house." He smiled and added, "As you well know."

"Mm, that's true," said Nevada, smiling, knowing she could pursue the subject no farther. Still, she was curious. Ever since she and Denise had sneaked inside the *garçonnière* that windy March afternoon, she'd been fascinated by the mystery and secrets it contained. She'd find Jess, the old black man, alone someday and ask him about it.

As he had done down in New Orleans, Stryker quickly, quietly acquainted himself with the city of St. Louis. From the riverfront docks to the Broadway Street taverns, from the downtown Soulard markets to the tree-lined boulevards of Clayton, the big man got around—he listened, looked, learned.

On a rainy afternoon in early May, Stryker's wanderings

found him across the street from Washington University. It was shortly after two in the afternoon. Stryker looked up, noticed a tall, slender chestnut-haired man descending the steps of the ivy-covered university. Squinting, he recognized Professor Malcolm Maxwell. The professor hurriedly unfurled an umbrella, lifted it above his bare head, and dashed toward a waiting carriage where an aging black man sat atop the box.

Stryker watched as Malcolm spoke to the driver, then climbed quickly inside the covered carriage. A suspicious sort by nature, Stryker considered it strange that Professor Maxwell would be leaving the college so early in the day, especially since Nevada had commented that her fiancé never arrived home before six.

Intrigued, Stryker turned up the collar of his rain slicker, walked to the hitching post, unlooped his mount's reins, and swung up into the saddle. Following at a respectable distance, Stryker trailed the Maxwell carriage as it clip-clopped along rain-slippery Washington Avenue. Mildly curious, he continued to follow when it turned left on Grand, drove to Page, and turned yet again.

Before a rooming house on Page Street the slow-moving carriage pulled over to the curb and stopped. Professor Maxwell alighted, dashed up the walk, and disappeared inside the red brick building while the carriage and driver once again waited. A block away Stryker dismounted, tethered his horse, and walked slowly toward the red four-story building.

In the small foyer Malcolm Maxwell shook out his dripping umbrella and mounted the stairs to the second, then on to the third-floor landing. At the end of a dimly lit hall he rapped lightly on the door. When it swung open he stepped quickly inside.

Stryker drew up even with the rooming house and

glanced warily at the waiting carriage. The driver was already dozing, the rain dripping from the lowered brim of his hat. His narrowed eyes on the building, Stryker stepped through the gate and went up the walk.

Inside, he inquisitively followed the wet footprints left on the uncarpeted wooden floor by the man who had entered just before him. Those footprints led upward and stopped before a door on the third floor at the very end of the corridor.

Frowning, Stryker stood directly before that wooden door. He heard arguing, exasperated male voices growing louder. Then Professor Maxwell's distinctive voice, raised in anger, saying, "Because, I have told you, those are the conditions of Louis's will!"

Stryker's narrowed eyes widened. He leaned closer, but the voices again became muffled. He could not make out what was being said. He finally turned and walked quietly away. He went back outside and to his horse. Shaking his big head, he rode away, baffled and uneasy, feeling as though his niggling suspicions were warranted.

It was uncanny, but from the beginning he hadn't been comfortable with Nevada's choice of a husband. He didn't know exactly why, but he had been strangely uneasy since she had first told him she intended to marry the mannerly college professor.

Now he was downright worried.

Stryker felt helpless. Something was very wrong, but he was not certain what. The only thing he was certain of was that Professor Malcolm Maxwell was not the right man for the young, beautiful Nevada Hamilton. But he didn't dare say as much to her.

Stryker was still troubled when he reached the riverfront. The rain had stopped. The sun had come back out, hot and bright, glinting on the snowy white steamer, *White*

Magnolia. She's early, Stryker thought to himself. The *Magnolia,* up from New Orleans, was not due until sundown.

Hired on as one of the strong backs to unload her cargo, Stryker dismounted, tossed the reins and a coin to a small black boy, and shrugging out of his rain slicker, rushed forward. His strides long and determined, he was hurrying toward the berthed *Magnolia* when all at once he stopped short. He squinted. He stared. He opened his mouth to call out, closed it without saying a word.

Stryker started to grin.

Not thirty yards ahead on the wooden landing a man sat on an overturned cotton bale. Coatless, his wide shoulders slumped in an attitude of easy relaxation, he smoked a long, thin cigar and seemed to be totally unbothered by the rapidly heating afternoon sun beating down on his bare dark head.

The sun was just beginning to set on that same warm May evening when Maxwell, having just arrived home and apologizing profusely for his tardiness, smilingly escorted Nevada into the high-ceilinged dining room where Miss Annabelle and Quincy were already seated, awaiting the young couple.

Quincy Maxwell was at the table's head. Miss Annabelle sat at Quincy's right side, her back to the room's arched doorway. Malcolm hurried Nevada around the long table, drew the chair out for her across from Miss Annabelle, then took his own place opposite his mother.

"Terribly sorry I'm late," he apologized to the two older ladies. "An interminable meeting after regular classes." He shrugged helplessly.

"You must be exhausted, Professor Maxwell," offered Miss Annabelle, unfolding her linen napkin.

"I didn't realize there was a faculty meeting today, dear," said his mother.

"I must have forgotten to mention it." He again smiled at Nevada. "Never mind that now. I'm here and I wish to propose a toast."

He lifted his stemmed glass of port. The others followed suit. He said, "May we always know the happiness and peace we enjoy this evening."

They drank of the wine and the leisurely meal began. The conversation was pleasant and light. Nevada was chewing a succulent bite of rare roast beef when suddenly Quincy Maxwell's heavy sterling fork slipped from her hand and fell to her plate with a loud clatter.

All talk ceased.

Startled, Nevada jerked her head up to see what Quincy was staring at. She swallowed convulsively, almost choking, and her own fork went the way of Quincy's.

There in the arched doorway, a muscular shoulder leaning against the polished jamb, stood Johnny Roulette.

When he'd attracted everyone's attention and all were alarmingly aware of his presence, Johnny languidly pushed away from the door and, smilingly devilishly, strode on into the room, advancing on the shocked group.

Her open mouth rounded into an O of disbelief, Nevada heard Johnny say in that deep, familiar drawl, "Ah, how grand to be back in the bosom of my dear family. It's been too long. Much too long."

29

Nevada stared. Miss Annabelle stared. Quincy Maxwell stared. Malcolm Maxwell stared. The startled diners were totally speechless. Every one of them.

Quincy, her face fiery red with emotion, glared at the presumptuous intruder, gripping the arms of her chair and shaking her head as if in denial of his existence. Malcolm, an expression of extreme contempt on his face, rose from his chair so swiftly, he overturned his wineglass. Nevada, immobile, a hand at her tight throat, gaped at the tall imposing man, thinking she must surely be losing her mind.

Only Miss Annabelle, as silent as the rest, looked pleased to see him. Her delighted gaze followed Johnny when, grinning impishly, he walked directly to the head of the table, leaned down, and pressed his tanned jaw to Quincy Maxwell's scarlet cheek.

"Mother of mine! So glad to see me you're speechless? I'm touched," he said, laughing as he circled the table. He stopped beside Miss Annabelle's chair and looked down at her with true affection. "Miss Annabelle from Louisiana! Wonderful to see you again, my dear."

"Cap'n Roulette," murmured Miss Annabelle, her eyes shining, her hand lifting to his. "I—I had no idea . . ."

She cast a puzzled glance at Quincy Maxwell. "I didn't realize that you—"

"Were a member of this fine old southern family?" Johnny finished for her. He squeezed her hand, released it, and walked around to the still standing, clench-jawed Malcolm. Patting the shorter man's slender shoulder, Johnny said, "Professor, you failed to tell your visitors you had a baby brother? I'm hurt. Truly hurt."

"What are you doing here, John?" said Malcolm coldly, twisting away from the dark, laughing man.

Johnny shrugged. "I was homesick."

"You expect us to believe that?" Malcolm said, a vein throbbing on his high pale forehead.

Quincy Maxwell found her tongue at last. "You've no right to—"

"Never so surprised to see anyone—" exclaimed Miss Annabelle.

"Can't just walk in here and—" Malcolm muttered.

Everyone seemed to be talking at once, but Nevada heard little of it. Her heart was pounding furiously and her brain was spinning with confusion. Johnny Roulette and Malcolm brothers? Quincy Maxwell Johnny's mother? Dear God, no! It couldn't be, it couldn't. But . . . then what was Johnny doing here? Why had he shown up in St. Louis, of all places? What had she ever done to deserve this horrid turn of events?

"Sure I can. This is my home, or had you forgotten?" Johnny said calmly to Malcolm, and his smiling eyes dismissed the irate academician.

Nevada felt all the breath leave her tense body when those black, teasing eyes finally came to rest on her. Would he give her away? Would he recklessly pull her world out from under her? A wave of nausea threatened to overwhelm her. Dear Lord, would Johnny brag to his brother that he had . . . had . . .

Johnny now stood directly beside her chair. In a low, soft voice he asked, "And who, may I respectfully inquire, is this lovely young lady?" Dark eyes flashing, he reached for Nevada's cold, stiff hand. He bent and pressed a kiss to it, managing as he did so to wink almost imperceptibly at her.

"She's Miss Marie Hamilton," Malcolm said irritably. He motioned for Johnny to release Nevada's hand.

Johnny ignored him.

Malcolm went on, "Now that you've greeted everyone, perhaps you'd allow us to finish our meal in peace."

Eyes never leaving Nevada, Johnny replied, "Surely your guests won't mind if I share the meal. Would you, Miss Hamilton?"

Nevada swallowed with difficulty and, trying in vain to free her cold hand from Johnny's large warm one, started to speak.

Before she could utter a word, Johnny addressed the bristling Quincy: "Have Lena set another plate. I'm starving." With one last secret squeeze of Nevada's hand, he released it and drew up a chair beside her.

Quincy Maxwell's regal nose wrinkling with disgust, she said sharply, "We try to preserve a measure of decorum here. Your suit is badly wrinkled and your—"

"Ah, yes, my valet forgot to press it," said Johnny, unruffled. "And I shall have to be very severe with him." His dark eyes twinkled. He sat down, turned to Nevada, and said, "Miss Hamilton, I'm afraid you caught me on a bad day." His long fingers skimmed over a darkly whiskered jawline.

Her own appetite gone, Nevada was forced to sit there

while Johnny began to eat heartily, blithely ignoring the obvious displeasure of the Maxwells.

Clearing his throat, Malcolm looked from Miss Annabelle to Nevada and said, "I know you both must be a bit curious." He inclined his head toward Johnny. "John is not actually my blood brother. You see, when I was three years old Mother married John's father, Louis Roulette. She was a widow, Louis Roulette a widower, and . . ."

Nevada listened distractedly to Malcolm's explanation and learned that Johnny Roulette's father, Louis Roulette, had married the widow, Quincy Maxwell, more than twenty-five years ago. He had moved his bride, and her young son, Malcolm, into the town house with him and his own son, two-year-old John Roulette. Louis Roulette died not a year later.

Dazed, Nevada nodded and smiled and tried to comprehend. It wasn't easy. The news was too new, too shocking; and besides, the big dark man sitting so close to her commanded her attention. Nervous but keenly alert, she too had immediately noticed that the usually meticulous Johnny was frightfully unkempt. Cautiously observing him from beneath lowered lashes, Nevada noted that the rumpled gray suit was not all that was wrong with his appearance.

The French cuffs of his fine silk shirt were slightly frayed. His preferred gold studs had been replaced with inexpensive mother-of-pearl. His handmade Italian shoes were badly in need of a shine. His rich black hair was a trifle too long, touching the collar of his shirt, and the nails of those beautifully tapered gambler's fingers were clean but ragged.

In spite of herself Nevada experienced a fleeting instant of triumph. She *had* been his luck! Without her he was a loser.

"I suppose you've been losing at cards again"—Quincy Maxwell's words were coated with venom—"and that's why you're here."

"Why, Mother," said Johnny, "how can you always be so suspicious of my motives?" He turned his attention immediately back to Nevada. "Miss Hamilton, it's so fortunate that you, for whatever reason, are visiting my dear family. Promise we shall become better acquainted?"

Flushed, Malcolm promptly set Johnny straight. "You shall have every opportunity, John. Miss Hamilton has agreed to become my wife."

Johnny didn't so much as lift a dark eyebrow in surprise. He smiled and said, "How grand. When is the happy day?" His black eyes impaled Nevada.

"More than two months away. I'm sure your profession will have taken you away from St. Louis long before then," said Quincy Maxwell with cool authority.

Johnny grinned at the quietly seething chestnut-haired woman. He leisurely took a drink of water from a gleaming crystal goblet. He patted at his black mustache with a snowy white napkin. He announced, with the same cool authority she had demonstrated, "I wouldn't dream of missing the wedding." He turned to Malcolm, "Congratulations, big brother. Need a best man?"

Nobody got a great deal of rest at the Lucas Place town house that night. Well past midnight Miss Annabelle was still lying awake in her bed, wondering at the coldness of a family who would fail to mention the existence of one of its own members. Wondering as well why Johnny had never spoken of them. Wondering why Quincy had resumed the name Maxwell after the death of Johnny's father.

In Quincy's spacious bedroom suite, she and Malcolm were huddled together, whispering. Quincy was assuring her anxious son that Johnny's unwanted presence would not endanger their well-laid plans.

"You are worrying needlessly, darling," Quincy soothed. "How many times must I assure you that John Roulette doesn't know the terms of his father's will?"

"I realize that, Mother, but you know John's way with females. If he's to stay here for two months, there's the possibility that Marie—"

"Malcolm, Malcolm! Have you so little confidence in yourself? Not to mention in Marie? Darling, you're twice the man John Roulette is, and let me assure you, a high-born, cultured young lady like Marie would never be attracted to a common scoundrel like John Roulette!" She shook her head.

Unconvinced, Malcolm said, "Mother, plenty of well-bred women have been so drawn to him, they've—"

"Very well. I know, I know." She waved her hand for him to be silent. "Marie Hamilton is not some bored wife or lonely widow. She's a very bright, very sweet and innocent young lady and I sense, from her unveiled aversion to him at the dinner table, that she'll not fall under his spell."

Malcolm nodded reluctantly. "Perhaps you are right."

Quincy rose from the velvet chaise lounge, came to him, and standing directly before him, said, "Of course I am." She smiled and added, "You must show Marie plenty of attention, Malcolm. When you aren't at the university, be with her. Don't let her out of your sight." She lowered her eyes, then lifted them. "Be more physical, darling."

"Mother!"

"I mean it. No law says you have to wait until after the ceremony to make love to the girl. Take her to bed."

Again Malcolm exclaimed, "Mother!"

His mother simply smiled, kissed his cheek, and said,

"Remember, my darling son, we want the girl pregnant just as soon as possible."

At the other end of the corridor Nevada, still dressed, paced her room, her heart beating erratically, her thoughts tumbling over one another in a jumble of confusion.

"Damn, damn, damn!" she muttered under her breath, wondering how her luck could be so abominable. So this was Johnny's mysterious past! Of all the families in all the cities in all the world, why did Johnny Roulette have to be a member of this one? Would his sudden appearance keep her from becoming a member of it herself?

Nevada gritted her teeth.

If Malcolm and his mother were to find out she was a fraud—not a blue blood whose innocence was intact but a low-born river child who had been to bed with Johnny—they'd . . . She squeezed her eyes shut and made a face.

She could not let that happen! She couldn't let Johnny ruin everything. She would get him alone as soon as possible, beg him, if necessary, to go away.

Nevada's eyes flew open and suddenly she smiled.

Money!

That was the answer. Johnny Roulette was flat broke! That's why he was so unkempt, why he'd come here. He had no place else to go. His luck had turned sour. He'd lost consistently and had completely run out of money. Tapped out!

Nevada had most of the money they had won in London. She'd give it to Johnny in exchange for his agreeing to leave immediately. Such relief flooded her that she spun around giddily, sure she'd come up with the answer to all her problems.

She hurried to the French doors, peered out across the yard to the *garçonnière* where Johnny had gone directly after dinner. She frowned. There were no lights on inside;

obviously he was in bed asleep. She wished he were awake. Wished she could slip out there right this minute, give him the money, and tell him to be gone by sun-up!

In the white guesthouse, Johnny Roulette was very much awake. Stretched out on his back in the big mahogany bed, he smoked contemplatively in the dark.

He had no idea how the hapless Nevada had come to cross paths with Malcolm Maxwell, but there was little mystery as to who was behind the romance between the mismatched pair.

Quincy Maxwell had been trying to push the reluctant Malcolm into marriage for the past five years and Johnny knew the reason. The bulk of Louis' Roulette's fortune was still intact. The terms of the will stated: "The first male heir to marry and produce an offspring is to be the beneficiary of my estate."

Johnny grinned in the darkness.

Quincy had no idea that Johnny was aware of the conditions of the will. But he was and had been for years. Ever since the old black slave Jess, overhearing a conversation between Quincy and Malcolm, had learned of it and told him.

Johnny chuckled to himself.

Much as she wanted to get her hands on the Roulette fortune, the snobbish Quincy Maxwell would be embarrassed and outraged if she were to learn that Nevada was passing herself off as a southern aristocrat. If the truth surfaced, Nevada would find herself promptly kicked right out on her delectable little derriere.

Johnny stubbed out his smoked-down cigar in a crystal ashtray and closed his eyes. He was, it seemed, the only one in residence who had nothing to hide. The household, and the city, knew him for what he was.

A degenerate gambler. A known rake. A constant embarrassment to the respected Maxwells.

Totally relaxed, Johnny Roulette grinned, sighed, and fell asleep.

30

‒‒‒ ⚬⚬⚬⚬⚬⚬⚬ ‒‒‒

"I want you to leave, Johnny Roulette," Nevada told him hotly the very next morning when she managed to catch him alone for a minute in the foyer of the town house.

"Might I have my morning coffee first?" he teased, reaching out to pluck absently at the lace encircling a puffed sleeve of her pale green summer dress.

Irritably brushing his hand away, Nevada pressed on. "I know why you're here. You're broke!"

Johnny laughed good-naturedly. "After all I spent on your education—all those lessons wasted." He sighed dramatically, "Try expressing it *low on funds* or *temporarily without means. Broke* sounds a bit crass and—"

"I have money, Johnny," she cut in. "Enough to stake you to a game downriver and—"

"Will you go with me?" he interrupted.

"Will I—what are you talking about?" She glanced nervously around, terrified she'd be caught talking to him.

"To find a game. Sit on my right side, rub my shoulder, bring back my luck."

"And risk being seen with you? Certainly not!"

"In that case . . ." He shrugged and started to step around her.

Frantically she grabbed his shirtsleeve, stopping him

cold, her blue eyes flashing fire. "If I agreed to sit in on one game with you, would you clear out then?"

"Then? When exactly is *then*? Define *then*."

"Damn you!"

"Whoa!" He shook his dark head as though shocked. "Dare you talk that way before the learned Professor Maxwell?"

"If I give you all the money I have—and it's thousands —will you clear out? Leave St. Louis for good?"

Johnny tilted his head and scratched his chin thoughtfully. Before he could answer they heard Malcolm's footsteps as he descended the stairs, and Nevada, alarm leaping into her eyes, whirled about, lifted her skirts, and hurried toward the dining room with the sound of Johnny's deep, irritating laughter taunting her.

Johnny was still laughing when he sauntered into the dining room. Nodding good morning to Miss Annabelle and Quincy, he went to the sideboard and began filling a china plate as Malcolm entered and greeted everyone.

Taking his place at the head of the table, Malcolm frowned at Johnny's broad back and commented, "You're up awfully early, John. Does this mean you have a job of some sort?"

A full plate in his hand, Johnny turned slowly about, grinning. "Bite your tongue, Professor." He circled the table, set his plate down near Nevada's left elbow. "I forswore working when I was fifteen." Johnny slid agilely down into the chair, smiled at Nevada, shook out a napkin and draped it over his right knee.

"What then, may I ask, are you doing up so early?" said Quincy. She cast a smirking glance at Johnny and added, "I don't recall you ever rising before the middle of the day."

"That's true," answered Johnny, favoring his step-

mother with a wide grin, "and I do extremely dislike alter-
ing the habit of a lifetime, but the fact is I have a bit of
business to conduct downtown this morning."

Mother and son exchanged anxious looks.

Malcolm, setting his coffee cup back in its saucer, said,
"Oh? May I inquire what kind of business?"

Johnny looked his stepbrother squarely in the eye.
"Sure. Go right ahead," replied Johnny, then said no
more.

Malcolm's green eyes narrowed with annoyance, but he
tried again. "Anything I can help you with?"

"Not unless you'd like to cosign my note. I'm going to
the Planters National Bank to see about a loan. I've run a
little short of money." He cut into a stack of hotcakes
dripping with maple syrup.

"If you get the loan, will you be leaving?" Nevada
blurted out. Then she caught herself and quickly amended
her question. "Ah, I mean, if you aren't planning on seeking local employment, I suppose you—"

Johnny chewed and swallowed. "Seeking employment?
Miss Hamilton, I had assumed that by now your fiancé
had apprised you of the fact that his little brother never
seeks employment. You see, I'm a gambler. That's my profession." He leaned lazily back in his chair and, still looking directly at her, said, "Fortunately, gambling can be
found anywhere." He paused for effect. "Even right here in
my old hometown."

"You've never"—Malcolm directed Johnny's attention
back to him—"remained in St. Louis for very long." Malcolm smiled as an indulgent parent might at a wayward
child. "As I recall, you generally get restless after only a
few days and drift on." He poured cream into his coffee
from a small silver pitcher. "What would make this occasion different?"

Johnny's black eyes cut quickly to the small dark-haired woman seated stiffly beside him. Looking boldly at Nevada, he said, "Nothing." He leaned back up to the table. "Everything." His gaze swung back to his stepbrother. "Call it maturity, if you will. Truth is, I'm tired of roaming. I intend to stay right here for the rest of my days." Smiling, he turned his full attention to the plate of hotcakes before him.

Feeling for all the world as if she were suffocating, Nevada called on all her reserve to show that nothing was amiss. She casually turned the conversation to the upcoming monthly meeting of Malcolm's Shakespeare Society and saw her fiancé's tense face relax a little.

"I'd almost forgotten," said Malcolm, smiling at Nevada. "It is next week, isn't it? A nice group. Father Leonine is back from Italy and Bess Thompson has returned from her country place."

"Good. I'm looking forward to meeting them both. I thought we'd serve some of those little sandwiches that . . . that . . ." Nevada paused, her train of thought momentarily nudged off the track by a hard, heavy knee leaning impertinently against hers. "And . . . we could also have . . . ah—"

"Some of that delicious peach brandy," Miss Annabelle quickly spoke up.

Quincy joined in. "Yes, yes, the peach brandy and perhaps some of those . . ."

Nevada was forced to sit there and smile and nod, while Johnny's sinewy thigh pressed hers familiarly beneath the table. She slid hers away. His determinedly followed. She gave it another try. His foot was on the hem of her skirts. She was trapped. He was taking full advantage of it. She was furious. He was enjoying her fury. She wanted to kill him.

Johnny turned an innocent, questioning look on her. "Is something wrong, Marie?" he asked, interrupting his stepmother's idle chatter.

"Why, not a thing, Mr. Roulette," answered Nevada evenly, quietly seething.

Johnny grinned. "Well, as I said, I must go downtown." He wiped his mouth, tossed his napkin on the table, and laid a hand on the back of her chair. "I was thinking," he said pointedly, "that it would sure be nice to have some company." He paused.

Nevada held her breath.

Johnny felt, through his tight trousers and her full skirts, the tensing of her slender body. He knew she was petrified that he was going to suggest she go with him. "Would you care join me . . ."—he looked across the table—"Miss Annabelle?" He could almost hear the whoosh of air rushing out of Nevada's bursting lungs.

"Why, I . . . yes, Cap'n Roulette, I would like to accompany you downtown," said Miss Annabelle. She looked at Quincy Maxwell. "That is, unless you have plans, Quincy."

"No, not a thing. Ride along if you'd like," Quincy said graciously. Then frowned when Johnny rose and came to pull out Miss Annabelle's chair. To him she said, "Surely you don't mean to go out in public dressed as you are."

Johnny's blousy-sleeved white linen shirt, open at the throat, pulled snugly across his wide shoulders and broad chest, while a pair of fawn-hued trousers stretched almost indecently tight over his lean flanks and long legs.

"I was lucky to rummage up these," said Johnny. "I couldn't find my matching jacket."

His stepmother remembered exactly what had happened to it. Lacing her fingers together beneath her chin, she said, "You got into a fist fight in one of those horrid gambling dens one summer night seven years ago. You were brought home around dawn with your face and your suit jacket bloody and torn."

Johnny smiled, remembering. "Ah, you're right. I was celebrating my twenty-second birthday. Let's see, the Red Garter, I believe it was. Or perhaps Lavender's? What a time I had!"

Quincy was nodding encouragingly, delighted that the crude, crass John Roulette was carelessly confessing to behavior she found abhorrent. Behavior she was certain Miss Annabelle and Marie would also find abhorrent. It wouldn't take them long to understand why she and Malcolm felt as they did about John Roulette. He was, and always had been, disrespectful, rebellious, and frivolous. He was, she found, also arrogant, lazy, and vulgar.

"You don't mind if Miss Annabelle and I ride along with you this morning, do you, Malcolm?" said Johnny.

Malcolm had no choice but to say yes. "Very well, but we'd best be going. I'm due at the university in a quarter of an hour." He turned to Nevada. "Walk me to the carriage, Marie?"

The open black brougham waited in the drive, old Jess standing beside it. Nevada, her arm looped through Malcolm's, strolled down the walk directly behind Johnny and Miss Annabelle.

"Jess, is that you?" Johnny shouted gleefully and started to laugh.

The old man blinked in the bright morning sunshine and stared and finally his wrinkled face broke into a wide grin. "My Lawd, it cain't be . . . I'se seeing things, I sho is!"

"No, you're not, Jess. It's me and I'm home," said Johnny, hurrying eagerly toward him.

"By the saints above if not be Mist' Johnny, as I lives

and breathes!" The gray-haired black man was shaking his head and grinning.

In three long strides Johnny reached the stooped old man and Nevada watched, transfixed, as the pair laughed and hugged and slapped each other on the back.

"You old rascal, you been behaving yourself?" Johnny asked, hooking a long arm around the old man's shoulder.

A work-calloused black hand jerkily lifted to touch and pat Johnny's smiling, handsome face. The old man laughed with tears in his eyes. "I has tried, Mist' Johnny. What 'bout you?"

"Nope. I haven't even tried. You know me, Jess."

"Yassir, I does. I knows my bad boy!" And they both roared with laughter.

Malcolm was not amused. "Jess, I'm going to be late."

"Yassir, Professor Maxwell. Right away, Suh," said Jess, wiping the tears of joy from his eyes.

Malcolm turned to Nevada, "Good-bye, dear. I'll see you late this evening." He kissed her cheek, helped Miss Annabelle into the carriage, and climbed in himself.

Johnny gave Jess's shoulder one last affectionate pat and helped the old man up. Then he turned and approached Nevada. She saw the wicked gleam in his eyes.

Johnny said, "Good-bye, dear. I'll see you this afternoon." And kissing her cheek, just as Malcolm had done, he murmured under his breath, "And we'll find us a card game, Lady Luck."

31

Nevada was on pins and needles.

And had been from the moment she'd looked up to see Johnny Roulette standing in the arched doorway of the Maxwells' dining room. A week of worrying and wondering if he would expose her for the fraud she was. Each time he opened his mouth to speak she cringed.

Now, pacing restlessly back and forth in the drawing room, she jumped when the solid oak mantle clock chimed loudly. Two in the afternoon. Malcolm was at the university. Old Jess had driven Quincy across town to a meeting of her garden club. Miss Annabelle had gone up to her room to rest.

And Johnny? Why, right out there in the white *garçon-nière,* unconcerned about anything, totally relaxed. No doubt enjoying the turmoil his presence had stirred.

Nevada squared her narrow shoulders. She had to know if he meant to ruin everything for her. She'd been dying to get him alone, but there hadn't been an opportunity since the night he arrived. If she hurried, it would be out to the guesthouse and back with no one the wiser.

Her decision made, Nevada fled the silent drawing room, climbed the carpeted stairs, and went directly to Miss Annabelle's closed bedroom door. She stood just outside and softly called Miss Annabelle's name. No answer. Nevada spoke again, a little louder. Still no answer.

She smiled. Miss Annabelle was deep into an afternoon nap, as were the servants. Nevada rushed to her own bedroom, stepped inside, closed the door. Crossing the room, she caught sight of herself in the free-standing mirror and speculatively approached her reflection.

Leaning forward, she pushed her heavy dark hair back over her shoulders, then grabbed up a brush and drew it through her tousled locks. She pinched her cheeks to give them color and wet her lips. She turned to the left, she turned to the right. She placed her hands on her small waist and critically appraised herself from head to toe.

She smiled, pleased.

Then immediately made a face at herself. Ashamed that she would even consider her appearance and its possible effect on Johnny, she promptly quit primping. She shook her head about and sent her long curly hair back into casual disarray. She'd not have him thinking she cared about looking nice for his sake.

Nevada stepped out the open French doors giving onto the balcony. She went to stand for moment at the gallery's white railing. She lifted a hand to shade her eyes and peered across the immaculately manicured yard to the small white guesthouse almost hidden now in a summer-green forest of weeping willows and tall oaks and flowering rosebushes.

She took a deep breath, slowly descended the back stairs, and looking all about, practically flew across the sun-splashed grounds. She stopped a few feet from the *garçonnière,* looked about again, and spotting no one, ducked under the low-hanging limb of a live oak, and stepped up to the door.

It was ajar.

Nevada knocked loudly on the doorjamb and waited for Johnny's tall frame to appear and fill the doorway. It never happened.

A deep, lazy voice, coming from the depths of the room, said uninterestedly, "It's open."

Rolling her eyes heavenward at his rudeness, Nevada gritted her small white teeth, jerked the screen door open and stepped into the *garçonnière*. All the draperies were pulled against the afternoon sun. The room was almost dark. Standing just inside the portal, she blinked in the sudden dimness, searching unsuccessfully for Johnny.

"Over here, honey."

Her head snapped around, her gaze following the sound of his voice until she located him. Flat on his back on the huge mahogany bed. His white shirt was open down to his waist, exposing the crisp black hair on his chest. The out-of-fashion trousers he wore pulled tautly over a flat belly and slim hips. His long, stretched-out legs were crossed at the ankles. His feet were bare.

Long, crossed arms cradling his dark head, he was looking directly at her and his black eyes gleamed in the dim light. Johnny nodded his greeting and his lips stretched into a slow grin of sexual appraisal. Standing there, backlit by the glaring sunshine, she was frightfully alluring. So tiny she appeared to be a mere child, save for the very womanly curves evident beneath the soft fabric of her summery pastel dress. Her wild dark hair was in need of brushing, her delicate jaw was rigid, and her expression one of apprehension mixed with anger. Undeniably appealing.

"What took you so long, darlin'?" he drawled indolently.

Nevada's reply to his tactless question was "Get up from there. I need to talk to you!"

Johnny chuckled, agilely rolled off the big soft bed, and

came to his feet. He raked brown fingers through his coal-black hair, then idly shoved the tails of his rumpled white shirt down into his trousers.

"Won't you have a seat, Miss Hamilton," he said politely, bowing, and sweeping a long arm out toward the pair of leather easy chairs before the cold fireplace.

"I will not. I haven't the time."

"No? I'm disappointed. I thought perhaps you had changed your mind about a game. The card room down at the Majestic Hotel is full every afternoon and we might—"

"I'm not here to talk about gambling."

He looked at her as though puzzled. "What then? Is something bothering you, sweetheart?"

"You know very well what is bothering me. Why did you have to come back here? Was it to torment me? And just when are you going to leave?"

"You're forgetting I had no idea you were here. I've made no secret of the fact that I came here because I had no place else to go." Johnny drew a fresh cigar from a box on the bureau. Searching about for a match, he said, "Surely you realize that tormenting you is the last thing I'd dream of doing."

He stuck the unlighted cigar between his teeth and propped an elbow atop the heavy chest of drawers. Nevada looked at him standing there, his arm resting on the polished wood, right beside the framed daguerreotype she'd seen that cold March day when she and Denise had slipped into the guesthouse.

Momentarily distracted, she crossed to him, curious. Glancing at the picture as though for the first time, she reached out, picked it up, and said casually, "Anybody you know?"

His laughing eyes never lost their teasing light. "My

mother and father," he said. "And the baby—me. Adorable, don't you think?"

"You . . . you look a lot like your father."

"So I've been told."

"Was he . . . a—"

"Gambler? No, a businessman and a very successful one."

"Really? Why didn't you follow in his footsteps? Surely you could have been something more than—"

"Ah, well, my dear, I think I've done rather well for someone who was cut off in his youth without a shilling." He took the framed picture and put it back in its place. "Besides, it's your fault I'm not currently prosperous."

"My fault? Hardly! As you recall, I offered you all the money I have. That offer still stands, if you'll take it and go."

"Tempting," he said and ambled away. He picked up the long gold tassel of the heavy drapery, gave it a tug, and flooded the dim room with afternoon sunlight. "Very tempting. And very curious as well. Why, I wonder, would a young lady offer to pay a gentleman thousands of dollars for nothing." He frowned as though genuinely puzzled.

Fighting down the urge to shout at him, Nevada, leaning back against the tall bureau, said conversationally, "I have what I want." She smiled engagingly. "I'd like you to have what you want as well."

"I see." Johnny nodded and, dropping down into one of the matching leather chairs, hooked a knee over its arm, swinging his bare foot back and forth. "I guess I never knew how much you cared. Never thoroughly appreciated what a selfless, kind person you are, darlin'."

Continuing to smile, Nevada pushed away from the chest, came to Johnny, dropped to her knees beside his chair, the frothy skirts of her dress mushrooming about her. Her expression angelic, her voice warm as honey, she laid a hand on his knee and said, "I do care about you, Johnny. Very much. I'd like you to have—"

Deep masculine laughter interrupted her. Nevada faltered and stopped speaking. Her seraphic face quickly changed. His lean brown hand swiftly covering hers, Johnny said, "I think I liked you better before you became a lady. As I recall, you were delightfully honest back then."

She tried to snatch her hand away, but he refused to release it. She hissed, "Are you suggesting that I'm a liar?"

Forcefully pressing her hand flush against his hard muscular leg, Johnny leaned forward in the chair. "You sneaked out here this afternoon while no one was looking. You offer me bribes to get me to leave town. And you have the nerve to say you're doing it for my sake!" He laughed again, captured her jutting chin, and tilted her face up to his. Leaning close, he said, "Sweetheart, you must be forgetting who you're talking to. It's me, Johnny, remember? You can level with me."

"All right!" she shouted, her blue eyes narrowed. "I'm sorry you came here, sorry you found me. I want you to leave."

"Why?"

"You always know everything! You tell me!"

He grinned and skimmed his thumb over her bottom lip. She angrily turned her head away. He turned it back. "Nevada Marie Hamilton, you came out here to buy my silence. Isn't that it? Well, darlin', you can relax. I wouldn't dream of telling the learned professor and his overly protective mother that Miss Marie Hamilton of the Tennessee Hamiltons once entertained,"—his deep voice added an extra inflection to the word *entertained*—"aboard the *Moon-*

light Gambler, a gambling palace down in Memphis or that I was lucky enough to share a heated night of—"

Furious, she forcefully threw his hands off and shot to her feet, jabbing a finger in the air toward his face as she said, "Tell them any damned thing you please, you bastard! I don't care. Go right now and place it on the front page of tomorrow's *St Louis Post!*"

"Perhaps I would," he said, coming to his feet, "but there's a rather easy three-card monte game waiting for me down on Olive."

She whirled and stormed away.

He laughed and called after her, "Do come again when you can stay longer."

"You go to blazes!" she called over her shoulder, banged out the door, ducked under the live oak, and stormed angrily across the yard.

Sinking back down into the chair, Johnny continued to laugh.

That evening Johnny had been absent from the dinner table and Nevada had given silent thanks for small favors. She was so angry that she wasn't certain she could have been civil had Johnny been present.

Without him dinner was a pleasant, leisurely meal, and afterward when Malcolm had suggested they go outdoors to enjoy the lovely May night, Nevada had contentedly nodded. On the long settee Malcolm spoke of books and music and of their wedding. And before they realized it the hour had grown quite late.

Not sleepy, they remained on the moonlit veranda. When Malcolm's arm went around her shoulders Nevada smiled at him and turned her face to his. Malcolm bent his head and kissed her fully on the lips, a sweet, soft, gentle kiss. Then he kissed her again. And then once more. Several kisses. Warm, tender kisses of affection.

At last he sighed and said teasingly, "All this kissing has made me quite thirsty." He squeezed her shoulder. "Shall I see about some refreshments?"

"I'll go, Malcolm," she offered.

"No, no. Stay just as you are. Won't take me a minute." He kissed her cheek, rose, and was gone.

Nevada sighed, leaned back in the comfortable old settee and dreamily closed her eyes, then opened them. And gasped with shocked dismay when she saw the flare of a match at the far east corner of the porch. Horrified, she watched the orange circle of illumination light the dark, smiling face of Johnny Roulette.

Up off the sofa in a flash, she stormed over to him. He was lolling there in a cane-bottomed chair, tipped back against a porch column, the newly lit cigar stuck between lips that were lifting into a devilish smile.

"How long have you been here?" she demanded. "You've been spying on us, haven't you! Answer me—how long?"

"Long enough to feel a bit sorry for you, my dear."

"I beg your pardon!"

"Those kisses." He shrugged wide shoulders. "Even from here I can tell they left something to be desired."

"That isn't true." She quickly denied it. "Th-they were wonderful kisses. Kisses of deep devotion. You're . . . just . . . jealous."

"Jealous?" He laughed softly. "Surely you jest." He came to his feet and stood towering over her.

"I am not." She tipped her head back, looking up at him. "I actually do believe you're jealous, whether you'll admit it or not." She gave him a smug smile.

"Nope. I'm really not." Johnny took the cigar from his

mouth and sailed it across the lawn. He reached out, put a hand to her shoulder, grinned, and said, "Now if good old Malcolm had kissed you like this . . ." And before Nevada could stop him, he had pulled her up against him and his lips were on hers. He caught her with her mouth wide open and took full advantage of it. While she struggled and whimpered and shoved impotently on his hard, ungiving chest, Johnny kissed her with a power and passion that was so blatantly sexual, Nevada felt the heated blood surge through her veins despite all her efforts to remain unaffected.

With one muscular arm hooked firmly around her, he held her soft curves against his unyielding length and kissed her hungrily, aggressively, his tongue plunging deeply, rhythmically into her warm wet mouth. And when, finally, she had quit struggling and her moans of outrage had changed to soft little sighs of excited bliss, Johnny took his lips from hers, smiled down into her lovely, upturned face, and said, "Now, if Malcolm had kissed you like that, then I might be a tiny bit jealous."

He released her, stepped agilely down off the porch, and walked away without a backward look.

Stunned, shaken, Nevada stood there looking foolishly after him, her heart pounding, her wits scattered.

"Bastard!" she finally muttered bitterly under her breath. "Blackhearted bastard!"

"What, dear? I didn't understand you."

Nevada turned about to see Malcolm, a tray holding two tall, frosty glasses in his hands.

"Nothing, Malcolm." She smiled and came to join him. "I didn't say a thing."

He held up the tray. "Iced lemonade, darling. This should cool us right down."

32

❦❦❦❦❦❦

The Missouri summer kept growing hotter.

The final days of May were more like August. Dry and scorching hot. No rain for more than three weeks had caused old Jess's well-tended lawns to fade and lose their rich emerald-green beauty. The tall, waxy hedges turned yellow, leaves curled up and fell to the parched earth. Beneath the troubled bushes a carpet of brittle dead leaves covered the crusty ground.

Even the mighty Mississippi was suffering the effects of the rainless weeks. The wide waterway was no longer bank-full and riverboat pilots complained that new sandbars were rising up daily out of the murky stream.

At the Lucas Place town house Nevada followed the example of Quincy and Miss Annabelle. She took to the privacy of her bedroom in the hottest part of the afternoons and stripped down to her underthings. Still she was too warm. And in her discomfort she found it extremely exasperating to see Johnny Roulette working outdoors, barechested and bareheaded, beneath the beating rays of the fierce summer sun, a wide grin on his olive face as though he was enjoying himself.

"The big fool," she muttered to herself one blistering afternoon as she stood just inside the open French doors of her bedroom, wearing nothing but her lacy chemise.

Johnny was out there in the yard again, raking dead leaves, carting them away, hauling buckets of water for the thirsty rosebushes. Doing all the hard, heavy work while old Jess, a sweat-stained slouch hat on his graying head, sat in the shade and grinned and pointed and issued orders. He the boss, Johnny the laborer.

Her jaw set in keen annoyance, Nevada lifted her heavy, wilted hair up atop her head and stood there thinking the relentless sun would soon fell Johnny. Surely a man who never did any manual labor, never lifted anything heavier than a deck of cards or a pair of dice—or a woman's skirts —could not hold up to such strenuous, punishing exertion in the intense heat of the day.

Especially not near-naked as he was.

Nevada wrinkled her small nose and her blue eyes narrowed. Johnny had cut the legs off a pair of trousers not directly above the knees but high up on his hard brown thighs. So now to her dismay—to say nothing of Quincy Maxwell's—he worked right out there in plain sight wearing nothing but the indecently truncated pants.

A sheen of sweat covering him from dark head to bare toes, he went about his work with an easy offhand grace in every movement. The lean and rippling muscles, starkly male and powerful, pulled and stretched and glistened. The midnight-black hair, as wet as if he'd just stepped from his bath, fell in damp curls over his forehead and clung to the back of his neck. The modified breeches, offensively tight and sweat-dampened, adhered to his hard belly and lean buttocks.

"Show-off!" she muttered to herself. "No modesty whatsoever. It's downright disgusting." But she continued to stand there and watch the disgusting, immodest show-off, even as a fine sheen of perspiration covered her own hot body and caused the satin-and-lace chemise to stick to her flushed skin.

With thumbs and forefingers, Nevada pulled the chemise's bodice away from her sticky flesh and blew down inside the extracted fabric. The rush of air on the perspiration-soaked skin felt most refreshing, so she continued, deriving what little respite she could from the damnable heat.

The sound of singing, very near, caused her to stop. Her head snapped up. She listened, looked frantically about, and spotted the top of a ladder leaning against the balcony's top railing. Horrified, she saw first Johnny's dark head and then his bare brown chest come into view, a pair of shears in his hand.

Those flashing black eyes looked straight at her as he snipped at a dying morning-glory vine, his deep baritone voice growing louder:

> Frankie and Johnnie were sweethearts,
> Oh Lordy, how they could love . . .

Nevada slammed the French doors closed so violently, the glass shuddered in the panes. Not bothering to find the drapery pull, she yanked the heavy curtains together as though the demons of hell itself were hot after her.

With the closing of the doors and draperies, she'd shut out the sight of his mocking dark face, but she could still hear that deep voice singing a song aimed at reminding her of the one night she wanted to forget.

Clasping her hands to her ears, she fled to her dressing room, but even there she heard the last lines of the refrain:

> He was her man,
> But he was doing her wrong.

It was more than an hour later when Nevada, freshly bathed, her mood lightened, came downstairs. She paused midway down to neatly tie the bow at the center of her low bodice. She had been looking forward to this afternoon for days. Denise Ledet was to return to St. Louis after two weeks in New York City with her folks. And she had promised Nevada that she would come right over and share all the news of her exciting trip.

Nevada was very eager to see her friend, but she began to frown as she reached the bottom of the stairs. A problem she hadn't thought of before suddenly plagued her. What if the sweating, half-naked Johnny was still out there strutting around? Like it or not, women—all women—found him attractive. What if Denise saw him and . . .

Nevada crossed the foyer, slipped out the front door, and walked onto the broad gallery. She listened, she looked, she even called his name. She swept down the porch steps and walked around the house. The ladder was gone. So was Johnny.

Double-checking, making sure, Nevada—wishing she had put on her bonnet—made a thorough search of the grounds and did not encounter her tormentor. She even went so far as to walk out to the *garçonnière* to look for him. She knocked on his door, called out, peered inside, and finally gave a great sigh of relief.

She hurried back to the main house, secure in the knowledge that he was gone. She knew Johnny. He was already downtown at some smoky old card parlor. Obviously his luck had turned. Since the day of the three-card monte game, he had been elegantly turned out once again. New summer suits and expensive tailored shirts and Italian shoes. And the gleaming gold studs.

"It's Denise, she's here!" Nevada exclaimed happily

when the Ledet landau rolled up the driveway at four o'clock.

"I'm as anxious to hear about the trip as you are, Marie," said Quincy Maxwell, seated on a striped silk sofa in the large drawing room.

"I'm glad your dear friend has returned," said Miss Annabelle, and quickly rising, stopped Nevada to retie the bow at her bodice.

The two young women hugged happily. After a half hour Miss Annabelle, knowing the two friends were eager to share secrets, suggested diplomatically, "It's still quite warm this afternoon. You young ladies might find the gazebo a bit cooler. Minnie could serve you some iced tea and—"

"Yes!" It was Denise, dying to get Nevada alone so that she could regale her with tales of a young man she'd met in the big city. She jumped up. "Let's go out, Marie. Right now."

In seconds the two, holding hands and laughing, were crossing the sunny yard to the vine-covered octagon-shaped structure at the far edge of the property.

"Thank God for Miss Annabelle," said Nevada. "Out here we can be alone."

"And have I got lots to tell!" bragged Denise.

"Good. No one can hear us. They can't even see us once we get inside."

"Perfect," said Denise as she stepped inside the vine-enclosed white-latticed gazebo. "Just wait till you . . . you . . . For heaven's sake . . . who . . . ?" The talkative Denise was suddenly silent.

When Nevada stepped in out of the sunlight she saw the reason. There on a long padded chaise lay Johnny Roulette on his back sound asleep. He wore nothing but the skimpy cut-off tan trousers.

"Oh, good Lord!" murmured Nevada. "Come on, let's go."

Denise didn't budge. Just stood there staring, her mouth agape, her eyes wide with interest. "N-no . . ." Denise managed weakly, mesmerized by the sleek dark skin, the massive chest, the long muscled legs of the handsome, half-naked stranger slumbering peacefully there in the afternoon heat.

"Denise!" Nevada scolded. "Let's leave before he wakes up."

Denise remained where she was. "Wh-who is this?" she breathed, and Nevada saw that her girlfriend's scrutinizing gaze was drawn by the sweat-dampened thick curling hair covering Johnny's broad chest. Denise swallowed as though her throat had gone dry; then her eyes slipped down to the long dark fingers laced atop a naked belly. And finally to the damp fabric stretched across slim hips and straining groin.

"I want to go back to the house this minute!" said Nevada, taking Denise's arm, glaring down at the handsome man who looked like a huge sleeping cat—sleek and beautiful and dangerous.

At that minute those great dark eyes, half sleepy, half amused, came open. The wide sensual lips stretched into a quick grin. "Surely," Johnny drawled, his voice low, "you can stay long enough to introduce me to your friend."

Denise gasped with pleasure and Nevada sighed with displeasure as the large, limber man rolled nimbly up from the chaise and stood yawning and stretching unselfconsciously before them. Wishing to high heaven he were gambling downtown where he belonged, Nevada reluctantly made the introductions.

"Denise, this is Johnny Roulette, Malcolm's stepbrother." She shot a look at Johnny's smiling face. "Johnny, this is Denise."

Eyes shamelessly caressing his big, bare frame, Denise's flushed face grew redder still when Johnny took her hand in his, leaned down, and brushed his lips to its back. "Denise, do you have a last name?" he asked, his dark eyes flashing with warmth.

"Ah . . . I . . . yes . . . it's Ledet," said the uncharacteristically tongue-tied, thoroughly enchanted Denise while Nevada ground her teeth.

"Miss Ledet, I do hope you'll forgive my appearance. You see, I've been helping the gardener and I—"

"Oh, Johnny, you look . . . great," trilled Denise.

Releasing her hand, he smiled and said, "Bless your heart, dear. Won't you have a seat? I do so enjoy meeting Marie and Malcolm's friends."

As if Nevada did not exist, Denise dropped down onto the chaise. Johnny sat down beside her. Turning to him, she said, "Do you like dances, Johnny? My parents are planning a big party next month. I do hope you'll come."

"He won't be here, Denise," Nevada said, still standing, her hands on her hips.

Ignoring her remark, never taking his eyes off Denise's glowing face, Johnny said, "Perhaps I can come along with Marie and Malcolm."

Nevada was fit to be tied. Denise sat mesmerized. After half an hour, Nevada insisted to Denise that they return to the house. Reluctantly Denise agreed. But she said to Johnny as they left, "Now you won't forget my party."

"I wouldn't dream of missing it," he replied gallantly.

"Wait here just a minute," said Nevada when she and Denise were several yards away. "Stay right here!"

She turned and hurried back to where Johnny still stood in the entrance to the shadowed gazebo, his long arms lifted, hands clinging to the white beam above his dark head. Nevada stepped up to him and said under her breath, "You'll miss her party, Johnny Roulette! Soon as her parents find out. Everyone knows you're not welcome in the city's best drawing rooms." She gave him a triumphant look.

One of Johnny's raised arms slowly lowered. He grinned, reached out, gave the bow at the center of her bodice a gentle tug. It came undone. He said, "But I'm always welcome in the city's best bedrooms."

"Oh!" She whirled around and stormed away.

33

By six o'clock, when the black Ledet carriage came to collect Denise, Nevada had developed a headache from hearing the excited redhead carry on about Johnny Roulette.

"Never in all my life have I seen a man like that!" Denise had exclaimed as they walked away from the gazebo. "I had no idea such gorgeous male creatures existed—"

"Now, Denise!" Nevada scolded.

"And right here in the house with you . . . wish I lived here . . . I'd slip out to his *garçonnière* and beg him to make a woman of me . . . He's just the kind of man I *must* experience my first taste of passion with . . ."

"Denise, please!" Nevada cautioned again.

"Very important to choose a man who knows what he's about . . . and Johnny is a sexual animal if ever there was one . . . Wonder if he found me attractive . . . ? I'll buy a daring new dress for the party . . . are you aware how his heavenly lips look as if they have kissed dozens—no hundreds—of beautiful women . . . ?"

"Denise, Denise—"

". . . has the blackest eyes and blackest hair I've ever seen in my life . . . so suave and charming and gallant . . . Did you notice how his sleek body is brown all over . . . bet if he took off those short pants, that skin would be just as—"

"Denise June Ledet!" Nevada had finally shouted. "Will you please shut up about Johnny Roulette!"

Denise looked at her, startled. "What is bothering you, Marie? You've been a real crab all afternoon."

"I'm sorry." Nevada sighed. "It's the heat. I think if doesn't rain soon and cool things off, I shall go quite mad."

"Um, well, I think if Johnny Roulette doesn't kiss me at my party—or before—I shall go quite mad." Denise laughed then and pressed her cheek to Nevada's. "Bye, Marie. I'm so glad to be back home. Shall I come over again tomorrow afternoon?" She wore a hopeful expression.

"Ah . . . no, no, Denise, I was planning to go shopping. I still need several things for my trousseau." Denise looked disappointed. Nevada touched her arm. "Come along if you like."

"Yes! I would like. What time? I'll have Edgar drive me over—"

"That isn't necessary. We'll come by and pick you up."

"Oh. All right, then, until tomorrow." She hugged Nevada again, gave one last longing look toward the white lattice gazebo, climbed up into the landau, and was gone.

Heaving great sigh of relief, Nevada turned and went back to the house.

It was still uncomfortably warm when Nevada descended the stairs that evening at a quarter to eight. Malcolm's Shakespeare Society was to meet in the library at eight o'clock and Nevada was guiltily wishing she could plead a headache and remain upstairs. She *did* have a headache and the prospect of spending two hours discussing Shakespeare with a bunch of snobbish scholars sounded dreadful.

Nevada sighed as she reached the bottom of the stairs.

It wasn't that she didn't like Malcolm's learned friends —of course she did—but she wished occasionally Malcolm would take her out for a madcap evening on the town. Alone. Just the two of them.

The thought occurred to her, while she was preparing to endure a boring evening of Shakespeare, that Johnny was right this minute dressing to go out for an exciting night in some plush gaming hall. Hating herself for being a traitor, she suddenly wished desperately that she was going with Johnny. She had suffered through so many dismal dinner parties and ballet performances and poetry readings with Malcolm and his mother.

Preoccupied, Nevada stepped into the dim, silent library where earlier the straight-back striped silk chairs—an even dozen—had been carefully arranged in a large semicircle before a small podium. Stopping, she stood on tiptoe and tried to reach the darkened gold wall sconce just inside the door.

Straining, her arm outstretched, she found to her annoyance that she was too short to reach the gaslight. Already out of sorts, she sighed with disgust, lunged, jumped, and finally muttered, "Damnation!"

Deep masculine laughter froze Nevada in place, but she gasped with shocked outrage when a pair of strong hands gripped her waist and easily lifted her from the floor.

Johnny said against her ear, "Hellfire, honey, I thought you quit cursing." He clucked his tongue. "And after all those elocution lessons!"

"You put me down this minute and I'll thank you to quit spying on me!"

He laughed again, wrapped one long arm around her small waist, the other across her flat stomach. He said, "Darlin', you better light that lamp before old Malcolm comes in here and gets the wrong idea."

Her fingers plucking impotently at the steel band of his imprisoning right arm, Nevada said acidly, "Gets the *right* idea, you mean, don't you?"

"Maybe I'm a little dense. You'll have to explain that statement."

She strained feverishly against her bonds. "Now that you can't have me, you want me."

His reply was a good-natured chuckle and a pressing of his dark cheek to the smooth, undraped flesh of her slender back. "You think so? Switch on the light, Nevada, before the darkness makes me lose control."

With a shaky hand, Nevada turned on the lamp. As honeyed light flooded the spacious library, Johnny lowered her to her feet. Her face red with anger, she immediately whirled about to glare up at him.

"It's getting late, you'd better be on your way."

"I'm not going anywhere," said Johnny and with his little finger brushed back a wispy black curl from her cheek.

"You're not going . . . but you're dressed up. Aren't you going out to gamble?"

"What? And miss the poetry reading?" His heavy black brows lifted incredulously. "Why, I wouldn't think of it!" He grinned and crossed his arms over his chest.

Nevada felt a terrible sinking feeling in the pit of her stomach. "You're teasing me, aren't you? You wouldn't really stay and . . . and . . . You just came by to dole out a bit of misery before you go."

Johnny's handsome face took on a wounded expression. "Dole out misery?" He shook his dark head. "Isn't it amazing how we see ourselves so differently than others see us? I like to think I'm the kind of person who spreads sunshine and happiness wherever I go and—"

"I'm warning you, Johnny. If you stay around here this

evening, you'd better not make one false move!" The fury
in her blue eyes told him she meant what she said.

He said, "Or you'll do what, sweetheart?"

Nevada opened her mouth to give him an earful, but his
black eyes lifting over her head signaled her that they were
no longer alone.

Malcolm came quietly into the room, put an arm around
her waist, and said, looking at Johnny, "If she's angry, I'm
certain it's something you've done. What is it, John? What
have you done to my Marie?"

Johnny simply smiled at his stepbrother, drew a long
thin cigar from the inside breast pocket of his crisp linen
jacket. "Best ask your Marie."

"Darling?" Malcolm's questioning eyes met Nevada's.
"What happened here? What did John say to upset you?"

"Nothing! Not a thing," she snapped, and was immediately contrite. "Oh, Malcolm, forgive me. I've a headache
from the heat and it's made me irritable." She smiled
sweetly at him.

"If that's all, then . . ." He turned his attention back to
the taller man. "But what are you doing here, John? Isn't
it time you go in search of one of your endless card
games?"

Johnny struck a match on his thumbnail and lighted his
cigar. "I think I'll pass on cards tonight. Sit in with your
little group." He grinned with the cigar stuck between his
lips. "Unless you object."

"Object? Why should I?" Malcolm gave Johnny a pa-
tronizing smile. "I suppose even you have heard of Shakespeare. You'd likely be quite stumped were I to mention
Lord Byron."

"Byron? Byron?" Johnny repeated thoughtfully.
"Didn't he deal faro down at Blackie's last season?"

The smile left Malcolm's face. "You are not amusing, John, and if you insist on—"

The ringing of the doorbell interrupted.

"They're here," announced Malcolm, smiling once more and went eagerly to meet his guests.

Johnny and Nevada were left there facing each other, Johnny grinning broadly, Nevada frowning angrily. She took a step closer to him and said, "I mean it. Not so much as the lifting of an eyebrow. You hear me?"

"I'll make you proud, darlin' " was Johnny's smiling reply.

When all the guests had assembled in the library, the group consisted of—in addition to Malcolm and Nevada—Father Leonine, the Catholic priest just returned from the Vatican; Bess Thompson, the plump, pink wife of a bank president; small, dark Richard Keyes, Malcolm's dear friend and concert pianist; Professor Douglas Hammersmith, a nervous little man who taught drama at the university; Jane Williams, a hard-of-hearing eighty-year-old widow; Bonnie Jackson, Katherine Holmes, and Agnes Roberts, a trio of extremely intelligent, extremely shy, extremely thin spinsters.

And Johnny Roulette.

Within moments everyone was seated in the striped silk chairs. Nevada had assiduously avoided taking her place until Johnny had chosen a chair. And when finally everyone had taken a chair, Johnny had—and Nevada was not at all surprised—ended up in the one directly before the podium. There was, not surprisingly, a female on either side of him.

Malcolm stood proudly at the podium.

"Let me warmly welcome you all to what I hope will be a rewarding evening of studying and enjoying the literary genius of William Shakespeare. As you recall, when last we met . . ."

Nevada, from beneath veiled lashes, allowed her gaze to drift from the speaker. She noted the simpering, nervous reaction of the females to Johnny. His strong masculine presence was undeniably potent. He was so big, so dark, he seemed to eclipse everything and everyone around him.

He sat there staring straight ahead, behaving himself for the moment, not even attempting to attract attention, acting as though he was exceedingly interested in what Malcolm was saying. Yet the blackness of his hair and mustache, the width of his shoulders beneath the custom-tailored suit, the twinkling black eyes, the preemptive air of command made it impossible for the ladies to focus fully on Malcolm and William Shakespeare.

That unsettling presence further caused more than one lady taking a turn at the podium to recite her favorite sonnet, to stumble over the words and flush and become flustered. And when midway through the evening Johnny, having asked permission of the ladies, shrugged out of his suit jacket and loosened his tie, the twittering and shifting about and fluttering of fans increased dramatically. They happily overlooked his rudeness when he yawned with boredom as a recitation dragged on too long.

It was Nevada's turn to go to the podium. She had chosen very carefully the passage she would recite. She had rehearsed it over and over again in front of the mirror in her bedroom. She could have recited it backward.

She stepped up to the podium and began, her voice firm and sure:

> Let me not to the marriage of true minds,
> Admit impediments. Love is not love . . .

Johnny slowly slid down in his chair. His knees were wide apart. He lifted his hands and laced them atop his head. He grinned. And winked impudently at her.

Nevada stumbled badly and felt panic overcome her. She couldn't remember the next line! The sonnet she'd spent all week memorizing had gone right out of her head. She stood there, all the color drained from her face, wishing the floor would open up and swallow her. Her eyes on Johnny's dark face, she read his lips as he silently prompted: "Which alters . . ."

Which alters when it alteration finds.

She quoted anxiously, memory returning. And when it was over and she reclaimed her chair, she heard Malcolm say, "John, you've not yet recited." He smiled, expecting Johnny to have to admit he knew no Shakespeare.

Johnny came to his feet.

He walked to the podium, clasped it with both hands, looked out over the group and smiled. Then his deep, sure voice filled the library as he said, his dark gaze fastened boldly on Nevada:

My love is as a fever, longing still
For that which longer nurseth the disease.

The smile slipped and then completely left Malcolm's face. He stared at Johnny, amazed and disappointed. Nevada stared too but she was not astonished. Nothing Johnny Roulette did surprised her. It did, however, make her angry. While she listened to his deep voice adding exactly the right inflection to every line of the beautiful sonnet, she had the overwhelming desire to slap his smug face.

Later refreshments were served to the gathering. Nevada, sipping from a frosted glass, stood at Malcolm's side while he talked with Richard Keyes, Father Leonine, and the drama professor. The subject was still Shakespeare and his works.

A few feet away Johnny was surrounded by tittering females, laughing and nodding and hanging on to every word. When one of the spinsters innocently asked how he got any rest in the scorching hot weather, Nevada heard him reply, without the slightest trace of apology, that he always slept in the nude, winter or summer.

The straitlaced ladies giggled and gasped and gulped from their frosty drinks, envisioning, Nevada suspected, the big dark man naked in his bed.

Nevada loftily decided that the literary ladies were every bit as silly as Denise Ledet!

34

⦚⦚⦚⦚⦚⦚

That night Nevada tossed fitfully in her bed. The hot, humid air was so still and stifling she felt she might suffocate. Not a hint of cooling breezes wafted into her stuffy, too warm room through the tall French doors thrown open to the night.

Her long batiste nightgown clung to her clammy skin and made her miserable. Soft and thin though the filmy fabric was, the gown seemed to weigh her down, making it difficult to turn over. And in her discomfort she felt the need to change positions constantly.

Nevada sighed wearily and punched at the fat pillows. She turned on her side and folded her hands beneath her cheek. She flopped over onto her back and flung her arms up over her head. She lay still for only a second, groaned loudly, and slithered around onto her stomach, irately jerking at the binding tail of her nightgown. Thrusting a bent knee out, she hugged the pillow and closed her tired eyes. They came immediately open. And she turned once more onto her side. She clawed at the choking ribbon tied securely at her throat, irritably pushed the garment's gathered yoke apart.

Feeling as though she might scream to the top of her lungs, she lay there in the heat, suffering in the darkness. And all at once she recalled Johnny calmly telling the learned ladies of the Shakespeare Society that winter or summer he slept in the nude.

She knew it was so.

All too vividly she could recall the cold, rainy night in London when she had gone to his room and gotten into bed with him. He had worn no pajamas that night. If he slept naked on cold British winter nights, she had little doubt he did so on hot Missouri summer nights. And, further, she had no doubt that he was sleeping peacefully, naked, out there in his *garçonnière* while she was wide awake and miserable.

Nevada got out of bed. With swift, eager movements she jerked the hot, shackling nightie up over her head and off. Jaw set, she wadded it up and threw it as forcefully as she could across the room, not caring where it landed.

Naked, she sighed with relief, smiled, and got back into bed. It was, she'd have to hand it to Johnny, much more comfortable to lie on the silky sheets in the buff. Nevada sighed again. She stretched luxuriously. She folded her arms beneath her head and smiled foolishly.

She would, she thought as she dreamily drifted toward blessed slumber, never wear nightclothes again.

The next morning Nevada, rested and fresh, was in Miss Annabelle's room, going over the preparations for the upcoming wedding.

Miss Annabelle, seated at a small Queen Anne desk by the window, was making a list of all that still needed to be done, while Nevada walked about, nodding and making suggestions.

Miss Annabelle said thoughtfully, "Quincy has already ordered the flowers . . . we go for the final fitting of your dress next Thursday. Let's see . . . Mr. Snyder said he'd have the engraved invitations ready no later than mid-July. The bridesmaids and groomsmen will—"

"Know what I wish, Miss Annabelle?" Nevada cut in, coming to stand near the desk.

Miss Annabelle looked up. "What, dear?"

Nevada tilted her head. "I wish that King Cassidy was going to be here to give me away."

Miss Annabelle's light eyes at once grew wistful and she hastily lowered them back to the list. "Ah, yes, that would . . . that would be nice but . . ."

Miss Annabelle felt herself flushing at the mere mention of the man's name. She'd not want anyone—not even Nevada—to know that the handsome silver-haired gentleman was in her thoughts far too often. It was ridiculous and she knew it was, but she sometimes daydreamed about King Cassidy as though she were a young girl. In her foolish fantasies she envisioned the handsome silver king coming for her. And taking her home. Home to the beautiful, beloved Delaney mansion on the banks of the meandering Mississippi above Baton Rouge where she'd grown up.

"Miss Annabelle, are you all right?"

"What? I—I'm sorry, dear . . . I suppose my mind was wandering." She smiled apologetically. "That happens when you get to be my age."

"I said Denise is going shopping with us this afternoon. I hope you don't mind."

"Dear," said Miss Annabelle, reaching for Nevada's hand, "would you mind very much if I stayed behind? It's going to be another warm afternoon and I—"

"You stay right here," said Nevada. "I won't be gone long."

Nevada and Denise were laughing when they came out of the expensive little shop on Locust. The discreetly small

name above the establishment's front door said simply AN-
GELIQUE'S. Nothing more. There was no merchandise displayed to be seen from the street. Rose curtains and pink
shades covered the windows.

Still, everyone knew that the fashionable shop was *the*
place to purchase the finest of ladies' underthings. Frothy,
frilly nightgowns and negligees of antique satins and Chi-
nese silks. Skimpy little chemises trimmed in Belgian lace.
Clinging camisoles and daring drawers and sheer stockings.

Each and every wispy "little bit of nothing" was especially designed to tempt the amorous male. The blushing
brides of St. Louis—if they could afford it—chose their
honeymoon lingerie at Angelique's. No groom, it was
whispered, could resist a bride outfitted at Angelique's. It
was the only way to begin a successful marriage.

Pleased with the beautiful things she had selected, Nevada was smiling when she came out of the shop. Turning
toward the curb, she stopped dead in her tracks.

With his back to the waiting carriage, stood Johnny
Roulette, smiling at Nevada. Elegantly outfitted in an eggshell linen suit, powder-blue shirt, chocolate-hued tie and a
cream-colored broad-brimmed Panama, he was casually
smoking a cigar.

"Johnny!" exclaimed Denise Ledet happily and rushed
forward.

"Ah, Miss Ledet"—he tipped his hat—"how nice to see
you again."

Denise thrust out her hand, hoping he would kiss it. He
did.

His dark gaze came to rest on Nevada. "Choosing something you hope will bring out the beast in my older
brother?" He cut his eyes to the rose-curtained Angelique's

to let her know he was quite familiar with what was sold inside.

Angry, Nevada closed her lips tightly and narrowed her eyes but controlled herself. Speaking coolly, she said, "I would certainly hope that you, Mr. Roulette, are the only beast in the family."

Johnny laughed and said, "Now, Miss Hamilton, just how could you know whether or not I'm a beast?" His dark eyebrows lifted inquiringly.

Nevada lost her temper.

"Get out of the way," she snapped. "I want to go home."

"I thought you might give me a ride," said Johnny, his wide smile still firmly in place.

"You thought wrong," Nevada replied acidly and nudged him aside, anxious to get away.

Smiling, he helped her up into the carriage and turned back to assist Denise. To the awed redhead he said, shaking his dark head, "Miss Ledet, I swear I can't understand it. I've tried ever so hard to become better friends with Miss Hamilton." He flicked a glance at the steaming Nevada. "We are, after all, soon to be brother and sister."

The hardening of Nevada's delicate jaw bespoke just how desperately she longed to shout obscenities at him. Johnny stood there watching as old Jess flicked the whip to the horse's backside. The carriage pulled away and rolled down the avenue with the red-haired, smiling Denise looking over her shoulder, waving madly.

Nevada stared straight ahead.

Denise, sighing, finally turned back around. She said, "I don't know why you don't like Johnny Roulette. As he said, he's to be your brother soon and—"

"Who said I don't like him?" snapped Nevada.

"Well, do you?"

Nevada rolled her eyes. "He's arrogant and rude and I'm not all that fond of—"

Denise wasn't really listening. She said, "When Johnny helped me up into the carriage, he smiled right into my eyes and I'm almost certain that he squeezed my waist more tightly than was necessary. I honestly believe he is interested in me! What do you think?"

Nevada tossed her dark head. "You wear skirts, don't you? That's all it takes."

It was just after they had dropped Denise at her house and were on the final leg home that she saw him. Stryker, mounted atop a big bay stallion, turned a corner and came down the street in her direction.

She recognized him at once and said, "Stop! Jess, stop the carriage, please."

Stryker caught sight of her, pulled up on his mount, and swung down out of the saddle even as Nevada scrambled down from the carriage and ran to meet him. Reaching the powerful giant, she quickly threw her arms around him but Stryker, glancing warily around, set her back.

"Miss Marie, you can't be seen on the streets of St. Louis embracing a man of my class."

Nodding, knowing he was right, Nevada said, "I've missed you, Stryker."

He took her elbow and escorted her back to her carriage. "And I've missed you. Matter of fact, I was on my way out to Lucas Place. We need to talk."

"Good. Follow me on your horse and—"

"No. This is better. I'm leaving and I didn't—"

"You're leaving St. Louis? But, Stryker, you promised that after I was married, you would—"

"And so I will. Until then, I'll be in the employ of a gentleman recently returned from abroad. I'm traveling downriver with him; he's looking to purchase an expensive piece of property near Baton Rouge."

"That's fine, but I want you here when—"

"And here I'll be," said Stryker. He helped her back up into the carriage. "Everything okay?" he asked, his ugly face suddenly stern, protective.

She touched his cuff. "I'm happy." She smiled then and added, "Or I would be, if it would rain. This heat is awful, isn't it?"

"You get on home where it's cooler," said Stryker and waited until she was gone before he remounted. He rode directly to the river and tethered his bay at a hitching post. Then he descended to the to the levee in the hot afternoon sunshine, where he patiently waited in the heat for the Mississippi steamer *Morning Mists* to arrive from New Orleans.

It arrived shortly before sunset.

His narrowed eyes carefully appraising every disembarking passenger, Stryker began to smile when a dapper man sauntered jauntily down the companionway, a varnished malacca cane in his right hand, an orchid in his buttonhole, his silver hair gleaming in the last blood-red rays of the setting sun.

As the sun's last light slowly disappeared, Quincy Maxwell dressed for dinner. And as she dressed she considered the changes that had taken place in her life of late. Quincy wrinkled her patrician nose.

She did not like change.

She would have much preferred that the well-ordered life she had shared with Malcolm remain as it had been. Before Marie Hamilton.

But that was impossible, thanks to the late Louis Roulette! Quincy's jaw tightened as she thought of the big dark

Frenchman who had been John Roulette's father and her
second husband. A wealthy but common man whom she
had married when Johnny was four years old, Malcolm
seven.

No sooner were they married than she had cajoled the
big Frenchman into making a new will. Suspicious, Louis
had refused to leave his wealth to her. Instead he had
drawn up an instrument leaving the bulk of his vast estate
to the son—be it Malcolm or Johnny—who married first
and produced an heir.

Quincy had been less than thrilled with the terms of the
will but had figured that since her son was the elder, the
money was safe; it would go to Malcolm. Looking back
now, it was almost as though the disgustingly lusty, cruelly
vindictive Louis Roulette had known that Malcolm would
never wish to marry!

Well, no matter. Malcolm was going to marry—she'd
seen to that. He would marry Marie Hamilton at summer's
end. And by the time another summer came to a close, a
child of that union would have been born. And Louis Roulette's fortune—and it was vast indeed—would become
Malcolm's. And hers. And she would waste little time ordering the crass, bothersome John Roulette off her property!

After that, well, she didn't really care if the marriage
between Malcolm and Marie survived. Matter of fact, it
might be well worth paying the girl off and sending her on
her way, as well. The prospect of having Miss Annabelle,
Marie, and a squalling, spitting baby underfoot was most
repugnant.

No need worrying about that now though. First things
first. And first, Marie had to get pregnant. Quincy sighed.
And wondered if her absent-minded Professor son had
taken the girl to bed yet. Doubtful. He wasn't like that

rounder, John Roulette. Quincy frowned suddenly. John was a dangerous man, just like his father before him. Coloring at the recollection of the young, virile Louis Roulette and her reaction to him, Quincy worried for Marie's safety. The girl was young and very refined—easy prey for a predator like John Roulette.

It was faint at first. A distant rumble from the south. Nevada turned her head to listen. And heard it again. Rising from the long brocade sofa, she crossed to the window, flung back the curtain, and looked out at the night sky.

She smiled.

A streak of summer lightning flashed across the southern heavens. An echoing roll of thunder followed.

"I do believe it is finally going to rain," she announced, turning to look at Malcolm.

He lowered the book he had been reading all evening. "I —I'm sorry, Marie. What did you say?"

"I said it's almost midnight and I'm growing sleepy." She came back to the sofa. "I think I'll go up to bed."

Malcolm nodded. "I had no idea it was so late." He rose, kissed her cheek, and said, "You go on, dear. I'll see to the open windows." He sniffed at the air. "I do believe you're right. It is going to rain."

In her bedroom Nevada laughed when a clap of thunder was so loud, she automatically jumped. The scent of the rain was sweet, and already, before a single drop had fallen, the muggy air had cooled a bit.

Unhooking her dress, Nevada stepped out onto the balcony and inhaled deeply. The first small, sporadic raindrops began to pepper the white railing. Nevada, looking all about, quickly surmised that the porch's broad overhang would protect her room from the rain; there'd be no need to close the French doors.

Smiling, she went back inside, stripped down to the skin, and climbed atop the turned-down bed as the rain began in earnest, drumming rhythmically on the roof over her head. It was a sound she'd always loved.

She lay contentedly atop the covers in the darkened room, allowing the rain-driven breeze to stroke and cool her bare, heated body. She sighed and stretched and, beginning to grow pleasantly drowsy, finally pulled the top sheet up to her shoulders and turned over onto her stomach.

This is going to be, she thought dreamily as she closed her eyes against the brilliant flashes of lightning, *the best night's sleep I've had in ages.*

35

Flashes of near summer lightning illuminated the dark face of a man lying wide awake on his bed in the midnight blackness. Both hands cradled the back of his head. His elbows angled skyward, the muscles of his bare inner arms pulled tautly beneath smooth bronzed skin. His long legs, stretched out, were crossed at the ankles.

The man turned his head.

There on the pillow beside his face a filmy white batiste nightgown lay. Folded neatly, as though waiting for its owner to step up to the big bed and put it on.

Johnny's hands came out from under his dark head and he slowly reached for the nightgown. For a long moment he held it in one lean hand directly above him. He opened his hand and released it. It fluttered down to settle softly on his naked chest.

Johnny inhaled deeply.

He could still smell the sweet fragrance of the woman who had worn it, despite the fact that the white nightgown had lain on the lawn all night—and atop his bed all day.

Johnny laid a hand on the downy soft gown and instinctively rubbed its perfumed folds down over his belly, back up over his chest, and finally up to his throat. His smile broadened as he draped the intimate garment on his head.

He moved his hands back down to his sides and lay

there for a while, the gown covering his face, the lightning shining through the thin white barrier. Storm-driven gusts of wind swirling through the tall open windows pressed the supple batiste against his nose and his lips, while raindrops drummed rhythmically against the roof of the old *garçonnière*.

The gown was Nevada's. Just why it had been lying on the lawn beneath her windows early that morning was a mystery to Johnny. He could conjure up a scenario, but it was one he did not like. That of his stepbrother sneaking into Nevada's room, hurriedly stripping the gown from her, then making love to her there in her bed while his mother and Miss Annabelle slept just down the hall.

Not quite.

That would be totally out of character for Malcolm Maxwell. More likely it was that Nevada had grown too warm in the middle of the hot June night, had risen, pulled off the gown, and carelessly tossed it away, never realizing that it had sailed right over the balcony.

With thumb and forefinger, Johnny slowly slid the gown down from his face. He grinned wickedly in the darkness as a pleasant memory came flooding back. The memory of being sound asleep on a rainy night in London. Of automatically turning to a soft warmth beside him. Of a pair of baby-soft lips molding themselves, oh, so sweetly to his. Of opening his eyes to find the tempting Nevada in his bed, in his arms.

Clutching the gown to his chest, Johnny rolled to a sitting position, swung his long legs over the bed's edge, and stood up.

His wicked smiled broadened.

Wearing only tight dark trousers and a pair of wine velvet bedroom slippers, Johnny ducked in out of the rain, his

bare shoulders and dark head wet, beads of water running
down his face. Kicking the soggy slippers from his feet, he
stepped just inside Nevada's open bedroom doors. There
he shook himself like a great dog, then spread the damp-
ened white batiste nightgown out on a chair to dry.

Barefoot, he tiptoed quietly to the bed. And felt his chest
tighten. Nevada lay on her side, one knee pulled up and
resting on the mattress, the other pale slender leg stretched
out full-length. The sheet was riding her well-arched right
hip, leaving her torso bare to his perusal.

Several rapid flashes of lightning illuminated the white
bed—and the lovely woman in it—highlighting the pale-
hued breasts and creamy skin and raven hair spilling
around her bare shoulders.

A glorious sleeping beauty. A defenseless naked
nymphet. And he? Good Prince Charming here to awaken
her with a kiss? Or dark, savage satyr come to take her
against her will?

Johnny was not entirely certain which as he anxiously
unbuttoned and shoved his trousers down over his slim
hips, his black, heated eyes never leaving the milky-
skinned perfection awaiting him in the bed. When he was
as bare as she, he very carefully put a brown knee on the
bed and softly spoke her name.

"Nevada."

She didn't stir.

He said it again, a little more loudly, but a boom of
thunder drowned him out. "Nevada."

She remained just as she was.

Johnny didn't lift the sheet, much as he wanted to. He
lay down on his side, close to Nevada but not quite touching her. At least not at first. His breath was so loud in his
ears and his heartbeat thumping so powerfully against his
ribs, he was sure she would waken.

She did not.

So Johnny began to relax. He drew a deep, sighing breath and cautiously put a long arm around Nevada's naked waist. He curved his long body around hers as the thunder and lightning continued. He snuggled to her and with a well-placed, deft big toe, he managed to pull down the sheet lying across her flared hip. In seconds the protective sheet had slipped away, leaving Nevada lying there bare and beautiful.

Johnny cautiously lifted his head from the pillow to admire that which he had undraped. The curve of her bare hip, the firmness of her thigh, the shapely calf of her leg were appealing. But the sweetly feminine part he most longed to see and touch and taste remained alluringly hidden by her bent knee.

Johnny lay back down. And he moved just a little closer, so close the thought struck him, as it had before, that she was so tiny and he so big, he would have to take great care not to crush her with his weight. Guardedly he held the small, naked woman in his arms.

Nevada could actually feel his muscled strength against her back, his powerful arms around her. She sighed softly in her slumber and squirmed more deliciously close to the heat.

Johnny smiled his pleasure and patiently, carefully swept the dark curtain of her tousled hair back away from her sleeping face and nuzzled his nose and mouth against the sensitive spot just below her right ear. Nevada shuddered and licked her lips.

Johnny tenderly nibbled on the side of her throat as his hand cupped a soft, bare breast and Nevada gave a funny little gasp of pleasure. With his warm palm he gently caressed the sleeping crest into a budding point of sweet sensation. He felt the nipple stiffen and seek closer contact as

Nevada instinctively pressed her swelling breasts against his covering palm.

His eyes flashing in the darkness, he led her carefully, slowly, stirring her unconscious sexuality with his conscious stimulation. With feather-light touches and angel-soft kisses Johnny awakened her dormant desire.

And Nevada, sleeping deeply, lay innocently naked in his arms, allowing him to kindle her smoldering passions and coax them nearer to the surface. Immersed in slumber, Nevada enjoyed every second of the sensuous arousal. Keenly alert and watchful, Johnny enjoyed it as well.

She was sweet and warm and heaven to touch. His fingertips worshiped her, gliding and playing with infinite tenderness. Enthralled, he continued the strange sleepy seduction and cringed when a near flash of lightning crashed loudly just beyond the open French doors.

Holding his breath lest the storm waken her, he couldn't believe his good fortune when, turning from her side and onto her back, her thick eyelashes never so much as fluttered. A fragile hand came up to rest against the wall of his chest and Nevada's soft lips parted over her small white teeth, but she remained asleep. And he continued to tenderly stroke the bare female loveliness laid out before him.

When the silky flesh beneath his adoring hand was flush with heat, a slender, thrusting arm came up around Johnny's neck and pulled his dark head down. And never even opening her sleepy eyes, Nevada's soft warm lips sought his and her tongue made lazy circles around the interior of his mouth. The slow hot kiss continued as Nevada's hand slipped down over his shoulder and went between their bare bodies.

Johnny felt the sharpness of her nails raking down his chest and then the flattening of her palm in the hollow beneath his ribs. His breath grew short. She continued to kiss him hotly even as her pelvis made lazy rocking movements against his tight belly.

He thought he might stop breathing altogether when, turning more fully to him, Nevada draped a pale slender leg up over his hip, hooking a bare foot behind his back. Her lips and tongue still pressed to his, Nevada boldly moved her wandering hand way down between their pressing bodies and it quite naturally closed around Johnny's throbbing erection.

Her small warm fingers wrapped tenaciously around him proved his undoing. It was too sweet, too good—he couldn't keep silent one second longer.

Breathless with excitement, he murmured her name in the beginning swell of ecstasy. "Nevada, baby . . . Nevada . . ."

"Johnny?" Nevada's voice was a lazy whisper, her breath hot against his shoulder. "Johnny, Jo—" Her eyes came open and she was awake. Instantly aware that she was naked and Johnny was naked and that they were together in her bed, she was fixing to scream loudly and Johnny knew it.

Swiftly he clasped a hand tightly over her open lips and said against her ear, "Don't, darlin'. You'll bring the entire household down on our heads." Her blue eyes flashed her fury at him and she thrashed and moaned and would gladly have murdered him if she could.

Johnny continued to whisper in low, commanding tones. "I won't move my hand until you promise you'll keep quiet. Will you?"

Her answer was more fierce struggling and whimpering and trying to bite his silencing hand.

"It's up to you, sweetheart. We can stay like this all night, if you like."

More flailing and writhing was the reply, and with each

savage movement, each bucking of her bare curves against his hard length, Nevada succeeded only in keeping her dark subduer sexually aroused. Johnny told her as much, warned her that he would never be able to leave if she didn't keep still.

Finally she gave up. Johnny saw the tired surrender in her eyes. Cautiously he moved his hand from her mouth. For an interminable time they lay there completely still, totally silent, staring at each other—she through cold, furious blue eyes, he through hot, amused black ones.

It was Nevada who broke the strained silence.

"What in the name of God are you doing here?" She scrambled up onto her knees, anxiously jerking the sheet around her.

"It was raining and I was afraid," said Johnny, his sense of humor quickly returning. "Remember when you were afraid that rainy night in London?"

"That was different! I was . . . I . . . if you are not out of here in one minute, I'll wake Malcolm."

"No, you won't." Johnny rose unhurriedly from the bed, stood unceremoniously pulling his discarded trousers up over his slim brown hips.

"I will! You won't get away with this! You've gone too damned far this time!"

Johnny calmly buttoned his pants. Then turned back to face her. "Funny, I was thinking that I didn't go quite far enough. I should have put—"

"Shut your filthy mouth!"

Johnny shrugged. "I brought you something."

"I want nothing from you except your immediate and lasting absence from my life."

Johnny picked up the nightgown from the chair back where he'd draped it. He held it out and said, "Sweetheart, a woman throws her nightgown out on the lawn, a man might think it's an invitation of sorts."

Her eyes narrowed with new anger, Nevada snatched the gown from him and bounded off the bed. Clutching at the covering sheet, she stood glaring up at him. "What I do or don't do with my nightclothes is none of your business, and let me assure you that there are *no* invitations of any kind extended to you. Ever!"

"A shame it is too," said Johnny, thinking she surely had to be the tiniest, the cutest, the most desirable woman who had ever ordered him out of her bedroom on a rainy night.

"Get the hell out of here!"

"I'm going," said Johnny, "and it's just as well. I don't want to make love to you here." He took a step closer to her, stood looming over her. Nevada swallowed and took a step back. Johnny reached out, gently grasped her bare shoulders, and pulled her up on tiptoe. He said, "But I'll be waiting, darlin'. Waiting for you to come to me."

"Stand on your pointed head until I do!"

Johnny grinned as a flash of lightning lit her angry face. Waiting until the booming thunder had dissipated, he said, "And you will come, Nevada. Maybe not tonight. Maybe not tomorrow night. But you'll come. And when you do, I'll make slow, sweet love to you till dawn."

"Get out of here this minute!"

"There are so many ways I want to love you, sweetheart. So much I want to teach you."

"You can teach me nothing!" she snapped. "I've been around!"

He chuckled. "Around what?"

"You're forgetting I am an engaged woman and Malcolm—"

"Has never made love to you."

"That's not so! He . . . we—"

"And he'll never make love to you the way I will. Never."

"That's revolting. You're revolting. Dare you—"

"Don't dare me, darlin'. You do and I won't wait. I'll take you right here, right now." His hands slid up to enclose her raised face. "And that's not the way I want it to be."

She tried to pull free, but he wouldn't let her. He framed her face securely in his brown hands and wouldn't allow her to look away. He made her look straight into his hot dark eyes. In a voice as hot and dark as his eyes, he said, "I don't want to take it from you, sweetheart. I want you to give it to me."

"Never!" she managed weakly.

"Soon," he murmured, kissed her, and was gone.

36

~~~~~~~~

The rain stopped at daybreak.

Its cooling effects lasted for only a couple of days; then the broiling summer weather returned with a vengeance. Another long sweltering week went by with no relief. The mercury climbed up past the hundred-degree mark and lodged there.

It was, however, the perilous and potent heat of another kind that plagued Nevada most. Johnny's arrogant prediction that she would come to him made her furious, but it frightened her as well. She wished that he would grow unbearably restless and leave St. Louis. She wished that her wedding date was not still six long weeks away. She wished that there was no need to wish.

She would not go to him! She wouldn't. She didn't care how many hot nights she lay awake fighting the almost overwhelming desire. It meant nothing. Nothing. If she felt a physical hunger for Johnny instead of Malcolm, it was because she had been intimate with Johnny. Once she was Malcolm's wife and he made sweet, satisfying love to her, she'd never again be tempted by Johnny's brand of base animal passion.

When she was a happily married woman, Mr. Johnny Roulette could live out there in the *garçonnière* forever, for all she cared. His presence would no longer be a threat. She'd be safe at last.

All she had to do was make it through six more weeks. Only six weeks. Nevada began to mark off the days like a prisoner whose sentence was finally growing short.

But, until she was free—married—Johnny's lurking sexuality posed a constant danger. It seemed he was everywhere Nevada turned. Lounging, grinning, waiting. He flirted outrageously and teased her unmercifully. She grew increasingly short tempered and no one—except the devilish Johnny—knew exactly what was bothering her.

Putting it down to understandable bridal jitters, the family, the staff, and her friends were tolerant and went out of their way to be sensitive to her mood swings. Everyone, that is, except Johnny Roulette.

Johnny knew Nevada was on the edge and he wanted it that way. She had held out far longer than he'd expected and he admired her surprisingly strong will. But her commendable resolve made him want her all the more. With each passing day he became more intrigued, more determined. And there were moments when he admitted to himself that he was just a trifle jealous.

Jealous? He jealous? The word and the emotion were foreign to him. But he *was* jealous. Jealous to think that the tempting Nevada would soon be another man's wife. Not that he loved her, certainly not. But dammit, he was the one who had found her on the river. Took her right out of a brothel, dressed her, educated her, launched her. Did he make all those sacrifices to have her end up married to Malcolm Maxwell? Preposterous!

Nevada didn't want to go.

She had told Malcolm as much, but he had simply shaken his head and said, "Dear, we must attend the Ledet party. Why, Denise Ledet is your dearest friend. Her feelings would be terribly hurt if we didn't show."

"But, Malcolm, it's so hot and I—"

"Marie, we've promised the Ledets." He never noticed how Nevada rolled her eyes when he added, "And Mother and Miss Annabelle have promised to go along with us."

So here she was on the night of the party, so listless and lifeless she felt she surely couldn't endure it. And it was all his fault. Johnny's.

She'd had no rest. Every night without fail he waited down there in the heat, in the darkness, prowling, watching, waiting for her. The glow of his cigar in the blackness signaled his constant, dangerous presence. Each night she had stood at the open French doors of her too warm room and watched him lounging about just outside his *garçonnière,* either draped lazily on the white wicker lawn furniture or standing there on his small veranda, leaning a bare shoulder against a white porch column.

Nevada shook her head as if to clear it, looked at herself in the free-standing mirror, and gave her elaborately dressed hair one last pat. Glancing down at the low square neck of her shimmering blue silk gown, she thought that the occasion called for some adornment. The beautiful diamond-and-sapphire necklace Johnny had bought for her in London would be perfect.

She debated for a moment. She rarely wore it because Johnny had given it to her.

Well, the hell with him! It was a stunning necklace and would look just right with her dress. She would wear it to the party.

Taking it from a velvet box placed underneath her lingerie, she draped it around her bare throat and hooked the clasp behind her head.

The gems glittered and winked and took her breath

away. Maybe she shouldn't wear it, after all. Someone was sure to ask where she had gotten it. Well, the hell with them too! she thought, picking up her net gloves. Forcing herself to smile, she went downstairs to meet the others. Praying, as she descended, that Johnny would have the good grace to stay away from her at the Ledets', if he showed. Which was doubtful.

She still couldn't believe that Denise's indulgent parents would allow their foolish daughter to invite Johnny Roulette to a gathering of St. Louis's select. Surely he would not attend, knowing how the gentry viewed him.

Downstairs, they were all ready and waiting: Malcolm, Quincy, and Miss Annabelle. Her hand around Malcolm's bent arm, Nevada went down the walk toward the waiting carriage.

Observing her fiancé's classic profile, she began to feel a bit more content. Malcolm was a tall, attractive man and he looked especially handsome with his face all scrubbed and his light chestnut hair brushed and his custom-cut clothes fitted superbly to his slender frame.

Her hand tightened on his forearm.

Perhaps after the party she could persuade him to take her for a long romantic drive, just the two of them. Ride up to the river bluffs and watch the steamers glide beneath the high Eads bridge with all those twinkling lights strung along its steel double decks.

She was smiling by the time Malcolm, now seated beside her in the carriage, graciously leaned down to arrange the skirts of her pale blue silk gown around her slippered feet. But before he could raise his head, her smile had disappeared.

A lone horseman was coming up the pebbled drive toward them and Nevada knew who it was. Johnny, on a sleek black horse, smoking a cigar, rode directly up to the carriage. He turned his horse around so that he was facing Nevada.

Without taking the cigar from his mouth, he said with quiet sarcasm, "You folks don't mind if I accompany you to tonight's party?"

From that point, Nevada's evening was spoiled. Johnny cantered his horse alongside the landau like a protective outrider. Only there was nothing protective about him. He was a smiling handsome menace and Nevada was relieved when finally the lights and music of the Ledets' Thirteenth Street mansion greeted them.

Malcolm swept Nevada up the steps of the imposing brick residence. In the huge entrance hall with floors of white Italian and black Belgian marble, Mr. and Mrs. Davis Ledet warmly welcomed their guests. After handshakes and cheek kisses, a uniformed butler escorted them straight through the house and outdoors onto the broad back terrace.

The party was elaborate. A pink-and-white striped square tent covered fully one third of the vast yard. Underneath its tall canopy, tables and chairs were set up for dining. Small square tables were set for two, huge circular ones for six or eight, and long rectangular ones for a dozen. All the tables were draped with pink damask cloths. Baby-pink roses in gleaming crystal vases served as the centerpieces. Soft light from pink Japanese lanterns, strung the length of the terrace, cast a lovely pastel glow over everything.

An orchestra, partially concealed behind a dense growth of fuchsia azalea bushes, played music for dancing. A large polished wooden pavilion, constructed specifically for the party at much expense, covered a great expanse of the lawn and offered guests as fine a dance floor as could be found anywhere—and right out in the open under the summer stars.

The lovely party was soon in full swing and Nevada, seated at one of the round pink tables, sipped champagne and sampled the beef Wellington, her wary gaze occasionally sweeping the laughing, milling crowd for the dark face she did not wish to find.

And as she anxiously watched, she nodded and smiled and half listened while Denise, seated beside her, leaned close and whispered excitedly about Johnny. ". . . and if he does ask me to dance, I shall press myself to him closely . . . have looked everywhere and still have not seen him . . . a friend of Mother's heard he was coming and made her husband stay at home so she could . . . if I can persuade him to take a stroll . . . know a private place behind the carriage house . . . hope he'll kiss me passionately and . . ."

Denise was so preoccupied with telling Nevada all her passionate plans that she failed to see Johnny enter the huge pink tent, survey the crowd, smile, and move slowly forward. But Nevada saw him and braced herself. With measured grace he made his way past the pink-draped tables and for a time she was certain he was headed directly toward her. She relaxed a little when she determined that he did not intend to join them.

Malcolm, interrupting Denise's prattling to ask if he might be excused for a moment, drew Nevada's attention away from Johnny.

"You don't mind, do you, dear?" said Malcolm, "I see a couple of old acquaintances I've not seen for—"

"No. No, Malcolm, go on, of course," said Nevada.

Miss Annabelle and Quincy soon drifted away as well. The other diners sharing the round table decided to dance or circulate. Only Nevada and Denise remained. That's when Nevada looked up and saw him. Johnny, seated sardonically apart at a table for two, smoking a cigar. Calmly watching her. Waiting.

His black eyes calmly regarding her, Johnny could hardly keep from smiling. He was amused by Nevada's acting as if she was unaware of him. She was catlike, pretending aloofness when what she craved was a good stroking. And she would get just that from him.

Nevada was in agony. Any minute Johnny would rise and come over. Or Denise would spot him and invite him to join them. It never happened. He stayed where he was. Malcolm returned. Denise left them. And Nevada calmed down.

The party continued and more and more couples took to the smooth dance floor as the sumptuous meal was finished and servants cleared away the dishes. Nevada finally coaxed the reluctant Malcolm onto the floor. He was an adequate if not superb dancer and Nevada, who adored dancing, began to enjoy herself.

Until her bare back bumped into someone else's jacketed back. Apologizing and turning, she saw that it was Johnny. In his arms was an entranced, incredibly silent Denise Ledet.

"All my fault," Johnny said, then added, "What about it, brother Malcolm? Shall we switch partners for the remainder of the dance?"

"I think not," said Malcolm.

"No, Johnneee, please!" Denise came out of her stupor long enough to protest.

Nevada said nothing, just moved closer to her partner. But she couldn't keep from cutting her eyes to Johnny and Denise as they danced away. Denise was doing exactly as she had boasted. She was clinging to Johnny as though she would never let him go and pressing her tall, slender body as closely as possible to his.

Nevada felt her throat constrict. She swallowed and closed her eyes. And told herself she didn't care or that if she did care it was solely because Denise was her dear friend and she hated seeing her get involved with a heartless man like Johnny.

Her eyes came open and she hazarded one more glance in their direction. At that moment she read Denise's lips as she said, "Johnny, would you like to take a stroll in the moonlight?" Malcolm spun Nevada around before Johnny replied, but as the dance continued Nevada looked all about and could not locate the other couple.

The hour grew late, but few of the two hundred invited guests had left the fabulous party. The dancing continued. The champagne drinking continued. The fun continued.

It wasn't all that much fun for Nevada, however. She noted with disgust that the simpering Denise was not the only woman who was drooling over Johnny. Responsible married ladies who should have known better were casting covetous glances at the tall, dark man. Despite all the stories she'd heard about Johnny being unwelcome in the finest homes, none of the interested ladies present seemed to mind that Johnny was nothing more than a handsome river rogue.

Added to Johnny's annoying presence was the annoying heat, from which even the lateness of the hour seemed to offer little relief. Toss in the fact that Malcolm had spent half the night across the broad yard engaged in conversation with a couple of earnest young academic types and it spelled a tedious evening.

It was shortly after midnight when Nevada and Miss Annabelle decided they would try some of the strawberry ice cream everyone was raving about. The two women stood before a long serving table, smiling as a black servant dipped up the frozen delight into crystal pedestal bowls.

"It certainly looks delicious," said Miss Annabelle, as she took the ice cream from the servant.

Nevada dipped a sterling spoon into hers, took a small taste, and nodded her approval. "The best thing I've had all night," she said.

"So far, but the night is young" came a deep voice nearby, followed by low laughter when Nevada's snapping blue eyes met his. Johnny stood beside her.

"Cap'n Roulette," said Miss Annabelle, "you simply must have some of this delicious dessert."

"I intend to have some, Miss Annabelle," he said dryly, immediately cutting his black eyes at Nevada, leaving little doubt the sentence had double meaning. He then said, "Miss Hamilton, may I have this dance?" and bowed extravagantly.

"No," said Nevada, calmly. "Can't you see I'm eating ice cream?"

Johnny unceremoniously reached out, took the pedestal bowl from her hands, and set it back on the table. "You *were* eating ice cream," he told her, drawing her into his arms. "Now you're dancing." And he spun her away and onto the floor.

For a time neither said anything. Furious, Nevada refused to look at him. Johnny, holding her lightly but firmly, grinned when finally she lifted her angry eyes to his. "Isn't it time you left? I should think the master of monte would want to go in search of a game," she said sarcastically.

"Perhaps later. Care to join me?"

"I beg your pardon?"

"Would you like to join me for a game? Doesn't necessarily have to be three-card monte. As I recall, you rather enjoy the spinning wheel."

"Will you keep your voice down!"

"Sorry," he said softly. "Would you like to join me? You've never been down to the Stardust Club. You'd like it —plum silk walls and gold velvet chairs and—"

"Don't be absurd. I'm an engaged woman and I'd thank you to remember that."

"Ah, yes, that's right," Johnny said, lifting her small white hand to study it thoughtfully. He sighed sadly. "Such a pretty little hand and soon it will be rocking the cradle."

She replied evenly, "I can think of nothing better for it to be doing."

His familiar black eyes on fire, he said, "I can. It could toss the dice"—he paused, folded her hand back to his chest, and guided it downward a little—"or bring a man to ecstasy."

She stiffened and tried to pulled her hand away. Johnny wouldn't let her. The arm at her waist tightened and he drew her closer.

Angry, she said, "You're both arrogant and vulgar. You think all women want you—"

"All but you, sweetheart," he cut in smoothly and momentarily stopped dancing. "Why don't you want me?" His fiery black eyes were on her mouth and Nevada nervously wet her lips with the tip of her tongue. "Show me you want me too. Come to my—"

"I don't want you. I don't. I don't." But she did. Oh, God, she did! And Johnny knew it.

"I want you, darlin'," he said. "I want to—"

"I don't want to hear it!" Her heart was pounding and her knees were weak. "If you don't let me go immediately I shall scream my head off!"

Johnny merely smiled and once again picked up the steps of the dance, molding her small, trembling body to his, pressing her pale cheek to the width of his chest and murmuring next to her ear, "See how you're making my heart beat rapidly. Is yours beating fast too, pet?"

"Stop it, damn you," she managed weakly, pulling her cheek away form his chest.

"All right, I'm sorry." Johnny's eyes dropped to the diamond-and-sapphire necklace resting on her smooth ivory flesh. "I'm flattered," he said. Nevada glanced down, then back up questioningly. He explained, "I supposed that since it was I who gave you this necklace you'd never wear it again."

Her haughty spirit returning, Nevada tipped her head back, looked straight into his teasing eyes, and said, "To the contrary, I do wear it. I wear it often. I wear it all the time. I wear it so I'll never forget how much it cost me." She held his gaze and he knew she was not referring to money. "So I'll never be tempted to pay that price again."

37

≋≋≋≋≋

"Wait, Malcolm," Nevada said, when the carriage had pulled up in front of the Lucas Place town house. He had helped his mother and Miss Annabelle out and was reaching for her. "Let's not go in yet. Let's drive down to the riverfront and watch the moon set over the water."

Shaking his head, Malcolm said, "Dear, it's after one in the morning and—"

"And it is Sunday."

"No, it wouldn't be wise," said Malcolm decisively. He put his hands to her waist and lifted her out of the landau.

"You don't know how wise it would be!" she said.

"Why, dear, what is it?" He waved to old Jess, motioning him to take the carriage away.

"I'm sorry. It's nothing, I—" Something caught her eye. She looked up to see a lone horseman cantering up the pebbled drive. Nevada shivered and said almost frantically, "Let's don't go inside just yet, Malcolm. Let's go someplace and—"

"Darling, I told Mother we'd join her in the library for a brandy before bed."

"No, not tonight." Nevada grabbed his arm and drew him toward the front walk, looking nervously over her shoulder at the approaching rider. Inside the big yard she hurriedly guided Malcolm to a sheltering elm and maneuvered him about so that he was standing with his back against its broad trunk.

"What is this, darling?" said Malcolm, puzzled. "You're not yourself this evening."

Nevada put her arms around his neck. "Kiss me, Malcolm. Really kiss me."

Malcolm laughed nervously. Then lowered his face to hers. He kissed her, but it was his usual soft, gentle kiss. No hunger, no fire, no burning passion.

Nevada tried again. She pressed kisses to his throat, his jaw, his ear. "I want you to hold me, touch me." Her lips met his again and she kissed him anxiously, eagerly, kissed him the way she wanted to be kissed. She got only a moderate response. Her eyes tightly closed, she distinctly heard the clatter of horses' hooves striking pebbles. Feeling as though Satan himself were mounted atop that big black stallion, Nevada said frantically, "Malcolm, Malcolm, save me! Darling, please, I want you to make love to me!" And she kissed him again.

Taking his mouth from hers, Malcolm swallowed, set her back, and trying to make light of the situation, said, "I've heard girls say that before."

"And may I ask what you've done about it?" she instantly demanded.

"Why, I did the right thing, dear."

Heart sinking, she said tiredly, "And what was that, Malcolm? A pat on the head and a promise not to mention that they had behaved so abominably?" Sighing, she dropped her arms from him and walked away.

He caught up with her, grabbed her hand, squeezed it, and said, "Don't be upset, Marie. Come morning, you'll be glad we abstained."

"Will I?" she said flatly. "Will you?"

"Yes, yes, we will. Now, smile for me and let's go inside and have a nightcap."

Nevada didn't smile. She said, "No, Malcolm. I don't want to smile. And I don't want a nightcap." They had reached the porch. A rectangle of light from the open front door framed them. Uncaring, Nevada put her fingers beneath her fiancé's lapels, moved them up to his neck. She stared at his mouth and said, locking her hands behind his head, "Last chance."

Malcolm said accusingly, "Dear, you sound like a gambler. That's the way John would express himself."

Her irate gaze met his. "Is it? Then perhaps I'd get farther betting on him." She smiled ruefully.

"Don't speak such nonsense, not even in jest, Marie. John's no good. He has no principles, no morals. He's not fit to be in the same room with a lady like you. A lowborn riverboat ruffian, that's all John is."

While Malcolm and his mother shared brandy and small talk in the library, Nevada, still wearing the blue silk gown, the elaborate coiffure, the diamond-and-sapphire necklace, edgily paced her darkened room upstairs. A caged animal, she prowled and fought the dark temptation waiting just beyond the open French doors.

But not for long.

Not waiting until everyone had gone to bed, Nevada stepped out onto the broad balcony and looked directly toward the white *garçonnière*. He was there, just as she'd known he would be. Johnny, his evening jacket cast off, his white shirt open down his dark chest, restlessly paced in the bright moonlight, a glowing cigar stuck between his teeth.

He paused and stopped, at once aware of her presence. He turned and looked straight at her across the distance of the vast yard. He stood then, still as a statue, his feet apart, hands at his sides. Waiting.

Without another thought or a backward glance Nevada moved toward the back stairs, her eyes never leaving the tall dark figure who was so compelling she was powerless to stay away from him. Hurriedly descending the steep stairs, Nevada was not certain what she'd say. Would she beg him to mercifully leave her alone? Or never to leave her alone?

While the lights from the library made elongated patterns on the lawn and Malcolm Maxwell's soft voice and Quincy Maxwell's light laughter carried on the still night air, Nevada, blind to the light and deaf to the laughter, lifted her blue silk skirts and ran headlong across the moon-splashed lawn toward her waiting destiny.

Johnny didn't come to meet her. He stayed as he was, unmoving, the cigar still planted firmly between his lips, the silvery moonlight glinting on his coal-black hair.

Watching her flying across the vast yard like a small, excited child, he too wondered which it was to be. Would she demand he stay away from her? Or would she fall into his arms?

Suddenly his heart pounded with excitement and he realized that the best memory of his somewhat blasé and checkered love life had been his rather drunken initiation of this enchanting girl, who was both sweetly innocent and amazingly sensual.

Nevada reached Johnny.

Out of breath from the run, she stood looking up at him, a hand at her breasts, her heart hammering with tumult. His handsome face was in shadow, she could not read its expression. But the powerful muscles of his shoulders and arms were flexing and unflexing beneath the white silk shirt. Beads of perspiration dotted the thick dark hair covering his broad chest. He looked so big, so dangerous, so overwhelmingly male.

Johnny lifted a dark hand, took the cigar from his lips, and forcefully tossed it away. He moved closer but did not touch her. Nevada stared up into those dark, flashing eyes and trembled.

She said haltingly, "Johnny . . . I . . . I . . . want you to . . . to—"

Johnny said commandingly, "And I want you too, sweetheart."

He reached out, then curled long dark fingers around the glittering diamonds-and-sapphires and gently pulled her to him, by the necklace. He bent his dark head. His lips hovered just above hers. He said, his voice as humid as the summer night, "I want to undress you, sweetheart. I want you to wear nothing but this necklace I bought for you."

Johnny kissed her then, kissed her the way a highly passionate man kisses the one woman he cannot resist. No awkward, questioning caress. No gentle, building prelude to ardor. No slow, sweet warm-up to desire. Johnny kissed Nevada with such devastating heat and hunger, she melted breathlessly to him and kissed him back with all the fierce craving she had ever felt for him.

With deft steadiness of hard muscles and strong shoulders, Johnny swung Nevada up into his arms and, reluctantly tearing his lips from hers, moved lithely toward his *garçonnière.*

Stepping through the open door, he kicked it closed and crossed the darkened room to his big bed. He lowered Nevada to it, placing her directly atop a trio of tumbled white pillows pushed carelessly up against the bed's tall mahogany headboard.

Leaning over her, Johnny cupped her flushed face in his hands, brushed his lips to hers, nibbled playfully on her soft bottom lip, and said into her mouth, "Nothing but the necklace. All night."

Nevada didn't answer. She couldn't. But if Johnny wanted her to wear only the diamond-and-sapphire necklace, then she could hardly wait to get undressed. She loved this big, dark man with all her heart, all her soul, and she could think of nothing lovelier than to make love to him wearing the beautiful necklace he had bought her.

His hand lightly caressing her upturned cheek, Johnny sat down on the bed facing her, one long leg folded under him, the other foot on the floor. For a long tension-filled moment he stared at her, the moonlight coming through the tall windows by the bed, washing over her. How breathtakingly beautiful she looked there amid his white pillows in her shimmering blue dress. How breathtakingly beautiful she would look there amid his white pillows without the shimmering blue dress.

Johnny leaned forward, touched Nevada's throat with his hand, and kissed the corner of her mouth. "You're beautiful, Nevada. Let me love you, baby. Let me love you till dawn."

"I want you to, Johnny" was all she could manage as his long arms went around her and a murmur of acquiescence escaped her lips as his hands moved eagerly, lovingly down over her back and to her waist.

Nevada made no pretense of wanting him to stop when he began to take her clothes off. Nor did she help him. She lolled there on the pillows while the only man she had ever loved undressed her with a kind of lazy ease that made it wildly exciting.

Johnny took his time.

Starting with her dancing slippers, he leisurely removed first one, then the other, and placed the shoes on the floor. Next came the silky stockings and when they slipped languidly down her legs and off, he kissed her tiny feet until she dissolved into gasps of nervous laughter.

The laughter stopped when he lifted his dark head and looked again into her eyes. Snared by his intense gaze, Nevada felt her breath grow short when his hands moved purposefully up under the folds of her billowing blue gown and effortlessly came away with her lacy petticoat. He draped it carelessly over the foot of the bed.

Idly she thought that Johnny was far too adept at undressing a woman and she'd have to warn him that he was never to undress any other but her. The thought fled when she felt those warm fingers brush her bare flesh and then in seconds he was easing her satin drawers down her hips, past her knees, and off her bare feet.

With infinite care Johnny folded the intimate undergarment and laid it atop the night table. When his heated eyes came back to her, Nevada felt herself flushing. Curling her legs to one side, she pushed the silk skirts down over her feet. It seemed odd that Johnny hadn't taken off her dress first, then the underclothes. He was doing it backward. Or was he? Suddenly it was strangely exciting to be wearing her dress with nothing under it. Naked beneath the soft, sensuous slither of silk, her flesh grew tingly and sensitive.

Then she was back in Johnny's arms and he was kissing her and she closed her eyes, growing warm and pliant. Her lips parted to welcome the thrust of his tongue. His breath was hot against her cheek. It ignited a fever deep within her. Pleasure surged through her when his hands—those dark, deft hands—moved beneath the folds of her skirts.

Her arms twined tightly around Johnny's neck, Nevada arched to him, threw her head back and sighed as he nibbled on her throat and moved his warm, questing fingers up over her bare knees. Those trembling knees instinctively fell apart and she shivered with expectation. Johnny allowed his splayed fingers to move in teasing, tempting circles up the outsides of her pale thighs but withheld the touch for which she most yearned.

Nevada felt as though she might surely burst into flame and she prayed that Johnny would soon—very soon—touch her where the fire burned hottest, touch her where she hurt.

A skillful lover, Johnny continued to kiss and caress the trembling woman in his arms and by the time he lifted the blue silk dress from her, leaving her totally naked—save for the glittering diamond-and-sapphire necklace—Nevada was squirming and thrashing about on the pillows.

She was ready for the kind of lovemaking Johnny intended.

So Johnny only allowed himself a fleeting moment to admire her naked beauty. She was so temptingly lovely he longed to have her lie there on his pillows for a while. His fleeting gaze adored her. So small, so white, so feminine. The lustrous hair dressed atop her well-shaped head, the swanlike throat, the ivory breasts tipped with pale pink, the flat belly, the thick raven curls between her pale thighs, the shapely legs, and cute little toes.

All gloriously bare, save for the glittering necklace, she looked sweet enough to eat.

Johnny gathered the naked Nevada to him and began kissing her again. And the kisses were not confined to her parted lips. He kissed her eyes, her cheeks, her ears. He kissed the sides of her throat. He slid his open teeth along the necklace's twinkling stones. Released it, then bent his head and kissed the flesh it rested on.

Smiling, he said against her dewy skin, "Thank you, sweetheart."

"For what?" she murmured breathlessly.

"For wearing nothing but the necklace I bought you."

"You're . . . welcome," she whispered, as his heated lips climbed the soft mound of her breast and closed around its aching peak. All the air exploded from her lungs as he began to gently suck on the hard nipple. With his lips tugging so sweetly on her, she was hardly aware that Johnny was lifting her farther up on the pillows against the headboard, gently urging her into a kneeling position.

She was only aware of supreme pleasure as his lips moved across her chest to kiss her other nipple. Her hands went into his dark hair and she murmured, "Darling, my darling," as his teeth raked tantalizingly over the sensitive crest and his tongue toyed with her before taking her fully into his warm, wet mouth to suck vigorously.

Nevada watched in breathless fascination that dark handsome face bent to her, the wide, mustachioed mouth enclosing almost the entire swelling white breast as though he would devour her.

Johnny, sensing her deep enjoyment, and enjoying having the hardened nipple in his mouth, continued to kiss and suck her breasts until Nevada was almost beside herself with ecstasy. At last his lips released their sweet treasure and moved down over her delicate ribs.

And while he kissed the bare, flushed flesh he had unclothed, Johnny continued to lift Nevada. Up, up he lifted her, his lips never leaving her flesh. On fire, carried away, Nevada never realized that she was now standing against the pillowed headboard until Johnny said, "Sweetheart, open your eyes and look at me."

Her eyes came open and she looked down at him. Johnny's dark upturned face was on the level of her lower belly. His hands were clasping her hips. Her own hands, though she hadn't realized it before, were anxiously gripping the tall headboard's smooth top edge.

Johnny felt his heart hammering painfully in his chest as

he looked up at the beautiful naked nymph standing before him, the diamond-and-sapphire necklace winking seductively at him, her kiss-pinkened breasts rising and falling with her rapid breaths, her slightly parted legs allowing provocative glimpses of the swollen sweetness protected by the dense raven curls. Nevada automatically bent her trembling knees and attempted to slide back down, but Johnny stopped her.

"No, sweetheart, don't. I want to kiss you," he said hoarsely. "I want to kiss you right here," and moving a slow hand down he placed gentle fingers lightly in the dark triangle of curling hair between her ivory thighs.

Nevada was . . . shocked.

"Johnny, no . . . you—"

He brushed a kiss to her belly. "Let me, let me love you. I want to taste your sweetness, baby."

"Johnny . . ." she whispered in shocked excitement when he urged her legs farther apart with a gentle hand. "No," she softly gasped as he leaned his dark face to her and nuzzled his nose and mouth into the thick raven curls. "No . . ." she whispered breathlessly when he kissed there, his mouth pressing a light, gentle kiss to the ultrasensitive female flesh.

"Yes, baby," he said, never lifting his head. He spoke with his mouth still upon her, his hot breath against her fanning the flames of her desire. "Give this to me," he coaxed in a low, husky voice. "I have your scent and it's so good. I long to taste you. Give it all to me, Nevada."

Beside herself, Nevada wasn't sure which excited her most—his smooth hot lips kissing her in such a forbidden place or his deep, drugging voice saying such intimate things. The highly sexual combination was overpowering. She couldn't possibly resist.

Her own voice no more than a small, frightened whisper

in the hot darkness, she said, "You can have it, Johnny. It's all yours. I'm all yours."

As if that was what he had been waiting to hear, Johnny opened his mouth and touched his tongue to her. Nevada called his name and spasmed from the heightened pleasure. An expert lover, Johnny took it very slowly, for a time doing nothing more than pressing his open mouth and the tip of his tongue lightly to her. Gentle, restrained kisses of intimacy that soon had Nevada bending her shaky knees and eagerly pressing herself to the promise of his masterful mouth.

Attuned to the slightest movement of her hot body, Johnny knew exactly when she was ready to be taken the rest of the way. So he took her. His hands sliding around to grip her bare bottom, he held her to him and sank his face deeply into her. He feasted on her, stroking her with his tongue until she was panting and tossing her head and murmuring his name in wild delirium.

More wildly aroused than she'd ever before been, Nevada, the diamonds and sapphires glittering on her sweat-slick throat, stood there atop his bed, naked in that darkened room, while Johnny, fully clothed, loved her in a way she had never imagined.

She could feel a frightening tension spiraling up and her body growing hotter and hotter, the hottest of all where he was kissing her. So hot it hurt but wonderfully so and she wanted Johnny to kiss her there for eternity. He must never, ever take his marvelous mouth from her; she would surely, surely die if he did.

Just when Nevada thought the pain-pleasure could grow no more intense, it did. Her hands abandoned their tenacious hold on the mahogany headboard and went into the hair of Johnny's moving head.

Frantically gripping the luxuriant dark locks, she

pressed her pelvis to him, and almost in tears, murmuring mindlessly, "Please, Johnny, please, please . . ."

Johnny's supportive hands tightened, cupping the rounded cheeks of her bottom. And he licked and loved and lashed her until he took her over the top. She cried out in her climax, spasming and jerking, her tear-bright eyes frightened, her fingers punishingly pulling Johnny's hair.

He stayed with her while she attained her total ecstasy. Remained just as he was until every tiny tremor had passed and she sagged limply against the headboard. Only then did he take his mouth from her.

His lips wet from her release, Johnny drew her down to him, draping her small, bare body securely to his chest. Her cheek pressed to his shoulder, he gently rocked her, soothing her, murmuring her name tenderly, and pressing kisses to her damp temple.

And when her pulse had slowed and her breathing had returned to normal, Johnny laid her across the bed, leaned down, kissed a bare thigh, and rose. He undressed in the hot darkness, then stretched out beside her, gathering her to him.

The limp, sated girl in his arms felt sure she'd never want to make love again. Apologetically she told him as much. Johnny merely smiled and told her he didn't mind, it was all right, she need only to lie there and relax.

But then he started kissing her, lightly at first, then more passionately, and Nevada changed her mind about never wanting to make love again. Amazed that desire could flare again so quickly, she soon found herself beneath Johnny, her legs eagerly parted to receive him, her head lifting from the pillows to accept his burning kisses.

And then sweet, glorious pleasure as he sank into her and began the slow, steady surging of his slim brown hips. And a moment of surprise that although he did indeed weigh twice what she did, she felt no discomfort. Her pelvis eagerly lifting to meet the downward thrust of his, Nevada looked into his black eyes. Smiling, she said, "It is possible, after all."

"What's that, sweetheart?"

"You on top."

He grinned. "I'm not very heavy when I'm moving."

She laughed and looped her arms around his neck. And then the laughter stopped as they gazed into each other's passion-heated eyes and made slow, erotic love, their perspiring bodies slipping and sliding sensuously in the age-old act.

And so it was all that long, hot, humid summer's night. Just as promised, Johnny made love to Nevada until dawn. On that one lovely night of unbridled passion, Nevada was sure she learned more about lovemaking than most women learn in a lifetime. But, then, they didn't have Johnny Roulette for a teacher.

She pitied them.

At first light Nevada and Johnny lay wide awake in the middle of his big, rumpled bed. Johnny was flat on his back. Nevada, on her stomach beside him, was leaning over Johnny, playfully biting and kissing a wet line down his flat belly.

Johnny put a hand atop her moving head and said, "Honey, let's get out of here, just you and me. Head downriver for New Orleans."

She gave the taut brown flesh one last lick, laid her cheek on his belly, and sighed. "Mm. All right. And get married in New Orleans." She felt him immediately stiffen. She lifted her head to look at him.

"Well, now, honey, I don't know, I thought—"

"Damn you to eternal hell!" she said and shot to her knees.

"Jesus, what's wrong?" He sat up immediately but Nevada was already off the bed and gathering up her discarded clothes.

"Nothing! Not one dammed thing!"

Johnny rose from the bed and went to her. "Now, honey, I didn't say we wouldn't ever—"

"Oh, yes you did!" she hissed, holding her blue dress up before her. "You haven't changed a bit."

Johnny took her arm and pulled her to him. "Will you calm down so we can talk?"

She wrenched away from him. "No! There's nothing to talk about! You told me once you'd never love anybody, but I refused to listen. Well, shame on me for continuing to be a fool!" she jerked her gown over her head.

"You're not a fool, honey. If you'll just wait—"

"No, you wait!" she said, her angry red face poking through the folds of blue silk. "Wait forever! Wait until you're a lonely old man, for all I care. I'm not waiting. I'm marrying Malcolm Maxwell!"

"You can't do that, sweetheart. Not after—"

"Not after tonight? Is that what you were going to say?" She glared hatefully at him as she pulled the dress down over her hips. "Tonight meant nothing. Nothing at all! Not to you, not to me. Not to Malcolm."

"Ah, darlin', stop it." Johnny reached out to touch her but she drew away, baring her teeth at him like an enraged animal.

"The only thing I will stop is *caring* about anybody but myself. I'm slow but finally I've learned. What difference does it make that I don't love Malcolm Maxwell? None. None at all. I'll have a safe, secure life with him and that's all I want!"

"You don't mean that, Nevada."

"Oh, but I do. I've finally decided exactly what I want."

She stepped closer to him and the wild look in her flashing blue eyes raised the hair on the back of Johnny's neck. "And I've decided what I don't want." Johnny flinched when she reached her small hand out to his flaccid groin and wrapped her fingers around him. Coldly she said, "I don't want this. And I don't give a damn where you put it, as long as you never again try to put it in me!"

38

⌇⌇⌇⌇⌇⌇

Nevada felt her throat begin to throb and tears spring to her eyes. But she did not allow the tears to fall. The promise she made to old Andrew Jackson one lonely winter's night was not forgotten.

With the dignity of a queen she stepped back, her head held high. She turned away and left the *garçonnière*— and the big, naked man in it—just as the first pink tinges of the summer dawn streaked across the eastern horizon.

Her first impulse was to run as fast as she could to the safety of her room. She did not do it. She refused to allow any man—be he Johnny Roulette or Malcolm Maxwell— to make of her a frightened, spineless jellyfish. They could both go to blazes for all she cared.

Back erect, chin lifted, Nevada walked leisurely across the dew-beaded lawn as though she were out for a Sunday stroll, not particularly caring if everyone inside the town house was watching her. Let them! Let them ask her where she had been. She would tell them! Might be enjoyable to see the whole stuffy lot of them swallow their tongues in shock!

As it happened, the whole stuffy lot of them did not see the blue-gowned woman leave Johnny's *garçonnière* and cross the vast grounds. Malcolm, Quincy, and Miss Annabelle were all sleeping blissfully in their beds.

However, somebody did see her.

In his small Spartan quarters inside the carriage house old Jess was wide awake. He'd slept fitfully through the night, a feeling of tightness in his chest causing him discomfort. At four in the morning he had given up, risen from his narrow bed, and dressed.

As dawn broke, Jess, coughing and wheezing, sat just inside the open doorway of his small room, shivering despite the warmth of the July morning. He blinked his watery eyes when he saw a flash of shimmering blue silk, and slowly he rose from the cane-bottomed chair.

Scratching his graying head, he stood in the open doorway and watched Nevada walk slowly across the yard. At first Jess's brow wrinkled with worry and his old heart tried to beat its way out of his aching chest. But then slowly he began to smile. The smile grew broader and he bobbed his head up and down, murmuring to himself, "I knowed it! I knowed it all along. Mist' Johnny not aim to let Malcolm and his mama keep that pretty li'l chil' in dey greedy clutches forever! No, suh! Mist' Johnny gwine save her. He gwine have her for hisself. My boy finally has somebody to love."

Wiping the sweat from his glistening forehead, the ailing gardener went back to his chair, chuckling with pleasure.

Nevada first heard about old Jess being sick later that same morning. Meeting Quincy in the drawing room, she realized at once that the older woman was upset about something.

Quincy said, "Marie, dear, I don't know what we are to do!"

Twinges of guilt plaguing her, Nevada replied, "I—I don't understand, Quincy. Has something happened?"

Quincy said with great exasperation, "Jess has taken to his bed. Says he is sick!"

"Oh? I'm sorry to hear that. Is there anything I can do?"

The older woman looked at her sharply. "Have you forgotten? We're to attend Clara Lacy's tea this afternoon. Now who will drive us?"

Nevada frowned. "Surely an afternoon tea can't be as important as a man's health."

Quincy blinked at her. "For heaven's sake, child, we're not speaking of a person. We're talking about a lazy old darkie who is more trouble than he's worth."

Tired from a sleepless night, nerves raw, in no mood to humor this self-centered, unfeeling woman, Nevada said, "Jess is a human being, just like you and me. And I'm going out to see about him right away."

"You wouldn't dare! A young white lady does not go inside the room of an old colored man—why, it simply is not done."

Feeling reckless and ornery, Nevada smiled at the stern-faced older woman. "Then this will be a first. I like old Jess and I'm going out visit him." She turned to leave.

"You come back here, miss! I'll not have you scandalizing this family, do you hear me? I'll tell Malcolm! I will, so help me! Marie, Marie, I'm warning you."

Nevada paid no attention to Quincy's threats. She walked determinedly down the long corridor, out the back door, and onto the gallery. Squinting in the bright morning sunshine, she looked in the direction of the carriage house but could not see it for the trees. She hurriedly descended the steps.

In moments she stood in the open doorway of Jess's modest quarters. Blinking to adjust her vision, Nevada immediately stiffened. There beside old Jess's bed sat Johnny

Roulette. Unaware of her presence, Johnny was patiently bathing the sick man's face and throat with a cool cloth and speaking to him in low, soothing tones of affection.

Nevada ducked back outside before Johnny could catch a glimpse of her. She returned to the town house, her rebellious mission of mercy forgotten. But it was almost impossible to forget that while Quincy Maxwell didn't seem to care whether faithful old Jess lived or died, the heartless Johnny was at the bedside of the old servant.

Jesse was a very sick man. Dr. Timothy Bates, summoned by Johnny, arrived at Lucas Place that afternoon and diagnosed the patient as having a case of summer pneumonia. At Jess's age it could prove fatal. There was really very little that could be done. Just keep him comfortable and see to it he got plenty of fluids.

Two days later, ignoring the reprimands of both Malcolm and his mother, Nevada again went out to visit Jesse. And there ran into Johnny.

"How very thoughtful of you," said Johnny without a trace of cynicism when she ventured inside. Rising from his chair beside the bed, he stood towering over her, his handsome face haggard, his eyes red-rimmed from lack of rest.

Handing Johnny the covered basket she carried over her arm, Nevada said simply, "When did you last sleep?"

Johnny lifted his wide shoulders in a shrug. "I doze here in my chair."

"Go get some rest. I'll stay here with Jess."

Johnny rubbed a darkly whiskered jaw. "Do you think that would be wise?"

Her eyes on the sickly black man, she said, "Since when have I ever behaved wisely?"

"Nevada, I—" Johnny began, but she quickly cut him off.

"I'm here for Jess and for no other reason."

Johnny sighed wearily. "I know, but I wish you'd let me—"

"Well, I won't, so kindly drop it." At last her eyes lifted to meet his. "And don't bring it up again."

Her beautiful blue eyes had lost none of the icy contempt she had shown him the morning she left his *garçonnière*. He had the sad, sinking feeling that those magnificent eyes would retain their killing coldness each time they met his.

"Good afternoon, then, and thanks for coming," Johnny said, and left her there.

She did not respond. But after he had gone, Nevada drew a slow, painful breath and closed her eyes for a moment. Opening them, she sat down in Johnny's chair and scooted it closer to the bed. The chair legs scraping across the wooden floor disturbed the slumbering patient.

Sick dark eyes came open and tried to focus. Confusion showed in their depths, so Nevada, smiling down at Jess, patted his thin chest and said, "Jess, it's Marie. Marie Hamilton, Malcolm's fiancée. I've come to visit you for a while."

"Miz Marie?" His voice was raspy.

"Don't try to talk, Jess. You must get plenty of rest. Are you thirsty?"

Shocked through and through to find a pretty young white woman seated alone beside his bed, Jess struggled to rise. He said, his chin quivering with cold and with fear, "Oh, Miz Marie, you has to git out o' here. Miz Quincy have mah hide, she catch you. Mist' Malcolm too!"

Gently easing him back down, Nevada said, "Nobody is going to have your hide. Nor mine. There is nothing wrong with a concerned friend visiting a sick friend. Lie back. Stop worrying."

Jess shook his graying head back and forth on the pillow. "I ain't nebber had no white ladies fo' friends, Miz Marie."

"Well, I've sure had black men as friends," she calmly stated and told Jess about old Willie and their happy days on her father's keelboat.

He listened and nodded and smiled, and when she fell silent, Jess, raspy though his throat was, began to talk, to tell her of times long past. And when his rambling conversation became focused on Johnny, Nevada was far too caring and considerate to tell him she did *not* care to hear it.

And so she learned, on that hot afternoon at the bedside of the delirious old black man, more than most had ever known about Johnny Roulette. The mysterious past was revealed.

". . . den his papa dies when he's jes' four . . . leave the boy wif Miz Quincy and she nebber did like Johnny . . . nebber treat him de way she treat her precious Mist' Malcolm . . . no, suh . . . shame too, 'cause Johnny was a cute, smart little fellow and needed attention and jes' breaked my heart to see—"

"Jesse, I think you'd better try to rest," said Nevada, gently interrupting.

"Ain't right for no chil' to grow up wif nobody 'cept a black slave what love him. Tol' all de time he not as good, not as smart as dey is. Tol' all de time his papa was no good either. Tol' his own mama was common. Johnny's real mama was a sweet, pretty girl and she love him, but she died with the fever when he jes' two years old . . ."

Jesse continued to talk, to tell of the way the youthful Johnny had been an outsider in his own home, a home that the late Louis Roulette had built, a home Johnny owned, though he had long ago been relegated to the *garçonnière*.

Curious in spite of herself, Nevada leaned close to better hear the raspy words and learned that for years the young, lonely Johnny had tried his best to please his stepmother and stepbrother. He had been bright, well-mannered, industrious. He never drank or swore.

But neglected and ignored, Johnny eventually rebelled. At fifteen he got a job as a faro dealer on the riverfront. By the time he turned sixteen he had quit dealing and was on the other side of the table, winning more often than he lost. At seventeen he was roving the river, money in his pockets, women on his arms.

Nevada didn't miss a word of Jess's long, halting monologue. She was not untouched by the poignant disclosures. The stirring revelations made it easy to understand why the adult Johnny was incapable of love. At a time when he needed love most—as a sensitive, lost little boy—he had been unwanted, unloved.

Feeling a deep sadness pressing down on her chest, Nevada never realized when the old man had finally fallen silent and drifted back to sleep. In his awkward, ineloquent way, Jess had painted a picture in her mind she would have great trouble forgetting.

But forget she would.

She had to. She couldn't go back and change Johnny's childhood, no more than she could change her own. Nor could she change the man that Johnny had become. An irresponsible wanderer, content to spend his life roaming from one town to next, one card game to the next, one woman to the next.

Nevada had spent the first part of her life on the river with a handsome, irresponsible wanderer. She had no intention of spending the rest of it the same way.

39

───────────────❡❡❡❡❡❡───────────────

Sleepy and sinister, his great size filling the small room, his deceptively lazy manner belying the power and passion within him, Johnny's constant presence at Jess's bedside proved to be a continuing distraction to Nevada.

But a deadly danger no longer.

Finally she understood fully what made Johnny tick, what had made him the man he was. And the man he was —reckless and handsome and more fun than anybody she'd ever known—would never fall in love and marry.

Johnny had told her as much the night they met, but she had been far too naive and foolishly in love to listen. She was now no longer the naive, foolish girl he'd taken off the *Moonlight Gambler*. For that matter, she wasn't the same woman who'd slipped out to Johnny's *garçonnière* less than a week ago.

Not that she regretted that last indiscretion. She did not. If she lived to be one hundred years old, she would remember, with embarrassed pleasure, that glorious love-filled night atop Johnny's big bed with the summer moonlight setting the diamond-and-sapphire necklace ablaze.

And she had a gambler's hunch and a woman's keen intuition that that heated night of lovemaking would have to sustain her for a lifetime. She knew instinctively that the man she was going to marry would never, ever do the

things to her, say the things to her, that the highly passionate Johnny Roulette had.

Well, so be it.

Nevada had at long last made peace with herself. She
had put her obsession with Johnny behind her, and along
with it her guilt for betraying Malcolm. Although what she
had done was certainly sinful, it was not as though she and
Malcolm were already married. She would be, she silently
vowed, a good and faithful wife to Malcolm Maxwell.

The peace Nevada had made with herself fairly radiated.
Her newfound air of calm authority pleased the man who
was to marry her. Malcolm was relieved that his sometimes frighteningly volatile and aggressive fiancée had
overnight become a less intimidating, more composed
young lady.

That same serenity had the opposite effect on Johnny.
Highly perceptive, he knew by the look in her eyes, by the
calm dignity she displayed in his presence, that he had
finally lost her. And he didn't like it one bit.

It was on a quiet afternoon when Johnny was seated at
Jess's bedside that the crushing truth finally hit him full
force. He'd been dozing in his chair when a light touch on
his right shoulder awakened him. He opened his eyes to see
Nevada, beautiful and serene, looking calmly down at him.

She said, "I'm here, John. And you may go."

John? Since when did his sweet, fiery little Nevada call
him John? She didn't love him anymore. Jesus God, Nevada didn't love him! She didn't love him, but he loved her.
The tables were completely turned.

"Is something wrong?" Nevada softly inquired.

Smiling at the sad irony of it all, Johnny, rising, said
truthfully, "Yes, sweetheart, something is wrong. Shall I
tell you what it is?"

Tilting her chin up, Nevada looked him squarely in the eye, a self-assured woman, his equal. "If you wish."

"I love you, darlin'. I love you and I want you to love me," Johnny said. His heart was galloping in his broad chest.

Nevada's blue eyes did not flicker with surprise, excitement, or joy. She did not tremble and sway to the tall broad-shouldered man. She simply smiled benevolently but said in a firm, clear voice, "That, John, is your misfortune. I'm sorry, truly I am."

Johnny stood there, reeling from the blow of the words she had delivered with such uncaring ease. He felt as though someone had delivered a mean one-two punch right to his solar plexus. He sucked anxiously for air and fought to keep his balance.

"Are you all right?" she asked evenly, and it sounded to him as though her voice were coming from far away.

"Yes, I'm fine," Johnny replied. He shook his dark head and walked away. He crossed the yard to his *garçonnière* in a daze, threw himself down atop his big bed, ran his hand over his face and through his hair. He shivered in the afternoon heat.

He tossed and turned. He rose and paced. He cursed and ranted. And finally Johnny began to smile, a slow, nervous smile.

Marry Malcolm? How could she?

He still had a month to get her back. And get her back he would. He loved her, really loved her. Loved her deeply, passionately, loved her so much he was totally vulnerable and defenseless. Loved her so much he would be willing, if she'd have him, to marry her and settle down.

From the moment they'd met, Nevada Marie Hamilton was, always had been, always would be, his. She'd be no other man's wife, not as long as there was a breath left in his body.

Nevada did not lose her place in society when word got out among the upper crust that Miss Marie Hamilton had been nursing the Maxwells' old sick servant back to health. On the contrary, she was applauded for her show of selfless compassion and the city's blue bloods murmured that Malcolm Maxwell was indeed a very lucky man to have such a mature and sympathic sweetheart.

Nevada found it amusing and secretly satisfying that she could seemingly do no wrong. She had openly defied the formidable Quincy, and yet the woman who was to be her mother-in-law was going out of her way to be congenial to her. Malcolm, bless him, was making an obvious attempt to be more attentive, more affectionate, after she had flatly told him it was high time he start behaving a bit more like a man soon to marry.

Johnny wanted her—she could see it in his black, brooding eyes anytime they were in the same room—but she was amazingly unmoved and untempted. The prospect of a few stolen hours in his arms no longer held any charm for her.

She wanted respectability and commitment. And the next time she lay naked in a man's arms, it would be in the arms of her husband.

"You know what I think?" asked Denise.

"I've a feeling you're about to tell me," Nevada answered with a smile.

The two young women were lying on their stomachs across Denise's silk-hung bed in the quiet of the lazy summer afternoon.

Denise sat up, hugged her knees to her chin. "I think

that I shall give up attempting to attract Johnny Roulette's attention."

"Mm, might be a good idea," Nevada replied noncommittally.

Denise sighed dramatically. "Know why I'm giving up, even though Johnny is the most charming man that God ever created and I shall never, ever find another who has the . . ."

"Denise—"

"Well, all right, but . . . now don't get angry. Promise?"

Nevada nodded.

Denise stretched her legs out before her, twisted her flaming red hair atop her head, and exclaimed, "Johnny Roulette wants you, Marie Hamilton!"

Idly plucking at the silken fringe bordering the bed's counterpane, Nevada remained totally calm. She yawned and said, "Denise, you really should take up writing romantic stories. I've never known anyone who possessed the talent for making things up the way you—"

"He wants you, Marie," Denise cut in. "He does! I know he does, damn him! So . . . what are you going to do about it?"

Nevada languidly turned over onto her back and folded her arms beneath her head. "I'm marrying Malcolm in less than a month."

Denise crossed her legs beneath her Indian-style and peered down at Nevada. "I know that, but couldn't you make love to Johnny Roulette just once before you marry, so you'll know what it's like? Lord, I would, if he wanted me! I just know it would be the most wonderful experience a woman ever had and I've daydreamed so many times about how it would feel to—"

"Denise"—Nevada rolled to a sitting position—"let's go downstairs and have something cold to drink."

"What do you think? Would you give yourself to Johnny in the name of sweet passion—"

"From what I understand," interrupted Nevada, rising from the bed, "John Roulette's true passion is gambling."

"Mm, could be," mused Denise. "That reminds me, I overheard my daddy's tailor talking about an upcoming high-stakes poker game. Said the biggest gamblers from up and down the river will be in town to board the steamer *John Hammer* when she puts into St. Louis next month. I'll bet Johnny will be dealing, don't you?"

"If there's to be a game, John Roulette will be in it." She sighed. "The last part of him to die will be the hand that throws the dice."

Denise laughed, then shook her head, saying, "I can think of another part that—"

"Denise!"

"Well, can't you? Don't you think Johnny is—"

"John Roulette is reckless. Out for a good time and he usually finds it."

"And that brings me back to you. That absolutely gorgeous man wants you, and I feel you owe it to yourself to just find out—"

"Denise, I'm marrying Malcolm, not John," Nevada smilingly cut her off. "You have the wrong brother."

"No." Her friend corrected her and her face grew serious. "*You* have the wrong brother."

The doctor said Jess's recovery was truly amazing. Less than a week after taking ill he was completely out of danger. The grateful patient credited the two people who had been constantly by his bedside, Johnny and Nevada.

While Miss Annabelle had graciously offered to sit with

Jess and even Malcolm and Quincy had looked in on him once or twice, it was Johnny and Nevada who had pulled him through the crisis.

Johnny was glad the old man was feeling better, but with the return of Jess's health Johnny lost the opportunity to be with Nevada. He tried every trick in the book to get her alone but Nevada was having none of it.

The innocent, adoring woman who had willingly followed him off the *Moonlight Gambler* and across the ocean to England was forever gone. In her place, a self-possessed, don't-trifle-with-me young lady consistently kept him at arm's length.

The days rapidly dwindled away.

Two events loomed just head, events of major importance in the lives of Johnny and Nevada. The first was a high-stakes poker game to be played aboard the palatial steamer *John Hammer*. The second, to take place only forty-eight hours after the poker game, was Nevada's wedding.

The week of both events rolled around. Johnny had finally faced the sad facts. He wasn't going to get Nevada back. She didn't want him, didn't love him, didn't care if he lived or died.

There was only one thing to do. Clear out. Leave St. Louis. Drift on before he was forced to watch *his* woman walk down the aisle to become Malcolm's bride. Leave before his jealous eyes could lift to Malcolm's bedroom windows, knowing that the lovely Nevada was inside, in Malcolm's bed, in his arms.

All through the afternoon excitement kept building in the hotels, bars, and other businesses in St. Louis. It was Thursday. The day of the big poker game down on the levee. The gleaming white paddlewheeler *John Hammer* had steamed into port at dawn, its blasting whistle like a seductive siren's song to the anxious gamblers waiting in the city's finest hotel rooms.

Johnny Roulette, a man who had always felt his heart beat faster when he sat down at a green baize table, was alone in the dimly lit bar of the Southland Hotel. Seated in shadow at a small marble-topped table along the paneled back wall, he shared none of the exhilaration of the laughing, talking gentlemen lining the long polished bar.

"Going to be quite a game," one sport said.

"All the New Orleans and Natchez boys up for it," said another.

"Biggest thing to happen in St. Louis since last year's Democratic convention," someone exclaimed.

Morose, Johnny picked up his glass of brandy, sipped it idly. And looked up when a white-jacketed waiter set a shot glass of whiskey before him with the words that "a fellow gambler insisted on buying you a drink, sir."

Johnny nodded, shrugged, and didn't bother explaining that he did not drink hard liquor. Instead he picked up the shot glass and tossed the whiskey back in one swallow, then held up the glass in salute to whoever was responsible. When another was sent to his table he drank it just as rapidly.

And so it was that a slightly tipsy Johnny Roulette, on returning home, ran into an unsuspecting Nevada later that afternoon in the silent corridor of the town house. Carefully placing a blue porcelain vase of cut flowers on a table beneath a huge gilt-trimmed mirror, Nevada gasped with alarm when she lifted her head and saw in the mirror a towering, grinning Johnny rapidly advancing on her.

She immediately whirled about to make her exit, but Johnny was too quick for her. He took a step forward, his arm shooting out, and he caught her fragile wrist in his long, encircling fingers. Nevada's nervous gaze flew up to his dark face.

His raven hair was disheveled and falling onto his forehead. His tie was askew, his jacket unbuttoned. His black eyes were twinkling and he was grinning foolishly. She knew at once that he had been drinking. And told him as much.

"You are drunk!"

"Who, me?" he said with mock sanctimoniousness. "I think not!"

"I think so," she said, and began clawing at his imprisoning fingers.

"Well, perhaps a wee bit," said he, smiling. "And it's your fault."

"My fault? Really, John, can you never accept the blame for your own actions?"

Johnny shook his dark head in chagrin. "Looks like you're really on to me." He bowed then and said, "I, madam, accept full responsibility for everything. Further, I've finally realized that you do not care for me."

"Good for you!" she said sarcastically. "Keep trying and you'll soon be able to grasp all sorts of obvious truths."

"Now, now," he scolded. "Remember you're a lady. Ladies shouldn't be nasty to anyone." He grinned accusingly, then announced, "To prove I'm a man of some principle, I am going away."

Nevada's eyes flickered. "You are?"

"I am. I know when I'm not wanted and I shall take my leave." He urged her a bit closer. "Just one last request."

Skeptically, "Oh, what is that?"

"Sit in on tonight's game with me aboard the *John Hammer*. Bring me luck. I'll win some money, then clear out and leave you in peace." Nevada was frowning up at him and Johnny mistook her failure to reply immediately as a sign of hope. "What about it, sweetheart?" His voice dropped, softened. "Just a few hours out of the rest of your life." He grinned a little crookedly. "You rubbing my right shoulder and leaning on—"

"Certainly not!"

Johnny blinked. "Why not?"

"You, John Roulette, are unbelievably insensitive. In forty-eight hours I'm marrying your stepbrother. Do you really suppose I'll dash off to gamble the night away with you as though I have no obligations?"

Nevada knew as soon as she had said it that she had chosen the wrong word.

"Obligations?" Johnny swiftly parroted. "Is that how you look on your evenings with old Malcolm?"

"No, of course not." She sighed with annoyance. "I'm going to a special performance of the ballet tonight with Malcolm and Quincy and I'm looking forward to it. While you're at the poker table, I'll be in the Maxwell family box watching—"

"And you'll be bored and wishing you were with me," he stated, daring her to deny it.

She said nothing. Her thick dark lashes lowered over her blue eyes.

Johnny put his free hand beneath her chin, lifted her face. "I'll say it again so there will never be any doubt. I love you, Nevada."

She tried to shake her chin free, but he refused to let her.

"I love you, honey." He fell silent then and stared at her; his eyes, brightened by the whiskey, were filled with love and longing. "If you were to fall in love with me, what would it take?"

"A magician."

Johnny said, "I'll find a magic wand and—"

She interrupted. "Please let me go before someone catches us together."

Johnny nodded, smiling sadly. "Anything you say, sweetheart. I'll leave St. Louis right after the game."

Nevada smiled bravely. "I appreciate that, John."

"Since I'll have to miss your wedding, guess I'd better kiss the bride now."

Nevada stiffened, began to struggle, and found herself easily pulled into Johnny's embrace. Commandingly he took her in his arms, bent her head back across his cradling arm, and lowered his dark face to hers. His lips an inch from hers, so close she could smell the whiskey on his breath, he said, "Stop calling me John. I'm Johnny. Your Johnny." His arms tightened around her, pressed her closer to his hard muscular body, "Kiss me, Nevada. Kiss your Johnny good-bye."

40

At eight-thirty P.M. Thursday, August 9, 1877, Miss Marie Hamilton, stunningly beautiful in a gown of rich white silk painted with bouquets of flowers with a light mixture of gold in the pattern, swept regally up the grand marble staircase of St. Louis's magnificent Theatre Royal on the arm of her tall, chestnut-haired fiancé.

The city's elite, all in their finest, filled the big hall with its enormous crystal-blossomed chandeliers and its gold-leaf Corinthian columns topped by scrollwork. The orchestra, in a pit below center stage, played the overture while elegantly clad patrons of the arts leisurely located their seats.

In the Maxwell family box Nevada settled herself on a gilt-and-satin Louis XVI chair beneath a lighted wall sconce of French hand-blown glass roses. Her slippered feet rested on rich wine-color Savonnerie carpeting. Her bare shoulders were as smooth and white as the alabaster statuary worked in vermeil that graced the private loge jutting from the theater's high curving walls.

From behind her jeweled fan Quincy Maxwell, seated just on the other side of her son, leaned forward and whispered, "Nod to your admiring gallery, my children. Everyone is watching." She smiled at Nevada, then added, "Malcolm dear, why not give Marie a kiss on the cheek."

"Certainly, mother." Malcolm said, quickly putting an arm around Nevada's bare shoulders and brushing his cool soft lips to her cheek in a polite caress. Nevada's lids lowered as the scent of peppermint emanating from the slim pale man brought to mind another man, another kiss. A big dark man who had kissed her with whiskey on his breath and lips as hot as the Missouri August.

The auditorium's massive chandeliers began to dim as the heavy scarlet curtains rose on the Frenchman Delibes's lauded ballet, *Sylvia.*

Three miles away from the Theatre Royal, down on the riverfront, an imposing, well-lighted steamer rode the calm waters of the harbor. Gentlemen as elegantly turned out as those attending the opera climbed the long companionway of the floating vessel *John Hammer,* where the summer's highest-stakes card game was about to be played.

Their hearts drumming with anticipation, their hopes high, the old Mississippi's most skilled gamblers boarded the large paddlewheeler at dusk to try their luck.

The session began promptly at nine o'clock in an opulent below-decks salon where a fully stocked bar and bartender awaited. One large round green baize table with chairs for only six players dominated the richly paneled room.

An even dozen players had shown up for the game. Half would have to wait for a turn at the table. Coins were tossed to determine who got first chairs. Johnny Roulette was one.

As Johnny was taking his seat in the paneled card salon, a temperamental chef in the ship's galley, directly forward of the salon, was angrily slamming pots and pans about, complaining that it was far too hot an evening to be frying shrimp for a "bunch of degenerate gamblers."

Muttering to himself, the little man in the tall white hat and fresh white apron irritably dipped a large serving spoon into a pail of lard and slapped the thick grease into a waiting skillet.

Opera glasses lifted, shoulders held regally straight, her left hand held loosely within Malcolm's, Nevada watched the French ballet and wondered cynically how many others besides herself in the vast auditorium were counting the moments until it was over.

And you'll be bored and wishing you were with me. Johnny's taunting words came back to her. She was bored, damn him, and she did wish she were with him. Could she help it if sitting in on a poker game with Johnny Roulette was ten times as much fun as sitting through a dull ballet with Malcolm and his mother?

Nevada's eyes slid closed behind the shielding opera glasses as the sobering thought flickered through her brain that all this—the ballet, the opera, the Shakespeare Society —was to be her very life for the rest of her life and she didn't enjoy it!

Quickly she lectured herself. She would learn to enjoy it. She'd not been raised to appreciate Malcolm's way of life, but in time she'd grow to love it as much as he. Besides, there'd be other pleasures in her life.

A chill skipped up her spine when she couldn't for the life of her bring to mind what those other pleasures were.

All six players were courtly, impeccably turned out, and bore the unmistakable stamp of the well-to-do. Johnny, in clothes of the smartest cut, languidly smoked a cigar while with his other hand he toyed with a stack of twenty-dollar gold pieces. His black eyes were unreadable, as they always were when he played cards.

Although generally more keenly alert than any of his opponents, Johnny was curiously distracted. His heart was just not in the game. His thoughts kept straying to the dark-haired woman whom he had kissed for the final time that afternoon in the foyer of the Lucas Place town house.

Preoccupied, Johnny made foolish mistakes, costly mistakes: bet when he should have folded, allowed others to take pots that ought to have been his.

Miscalculations and blunders in that kind of fast company spelled rapidly dwindling resources. After less than two hours at the table, Johnny was out of the game. Tapped out. And he didn't particularly care.

Saying his casual good nights to the others, he left the card salon and was making his way topside when he heard a piercing scream coming from the direction of the ship's galley. His pulse quickening, Johnny hurried down the passageway toward the sound, flung open the swinging double doors, and saw, atop the wood stove, flames from a huge cast-iron skillet shooting all the way up to the ceiling.

Finally the ballet ended. Nevada felt like giving a great shout of delight. Instead she graciously stood in the theater's marble-floored lobby to visit with the Maxwells' friends and acquaintances. She nodded and smiled and agreed that the performance was absolutely marvelous. And, oh, yes, how very fortunate they were to have the visiting French troop in St. Louis.

It was well past eleven when the Maxwell carriage was finally heading for home, the fully recovered Jess on the box. Nevada, spotting a bright orange glow in the night sky, pointed and said, "Malcolm, look!"

"Some sort of fire at the riverfront," he said casually.

Nevada felt all the air leave her body. A fire on the

riverfront? Johnny was at the riverfront! "Malcolm, order Jess to go there at once."

Malcolm looked at his fiancée as though she had taken leave of her senses. "Dear, why would you want to go to the river at this hour?"

"Johnny's there!"

Quincy spoke up. "How do you know where John Roulette is this evening?"

Ignoring the question, Nevada, addressing only Malcolm, said, "Please. You must have Jess drive to the levee."

Malcolm began shaking his head. "Marie, even if John is down there, there's no cause for concern. Why, there are often fires on the river and—"

"I know that! I was raised on the river and a fire aboard a riverboat can be a disaster. Tell Jess to turn toward the river!"

Old Jess didn't wait for the command. Already he was turning, changing directions. Lifting the whip from the landau's floorboard, the uneasy old black man flicked it smartly over the backs of the matched team and the steeds nickered loudly and picked up their pace.

The small kitchen fire became a roaring inferno within minutes. The grease-fed flames swiftly began to lick hungrily at the galley's low ceiling. The terrified little chef and his scullery cook fled, leaving only Johnny to fight the blaze.

"Get help!" Johnny shouted over his shoulder. He shrugged out of his jacket and began beating at the flames. It was hopeless. The galley was soon totally engulfed, and flames were leaping toward the paneled salon where the engrossed poker players and a dozen onlookers were unaware of the imminent danger.

Johnny made his way through black choking smoke toward the card room, intent on saving the lives of his fellow gamblers. By the time he reached the salon an entire wall was already in flames. Rushing inside, Johnny reached one bewildered player, quickly tossed the man over his shoulder, and called to another, "This way! Follow me!"

By the time Johnny reached the deck with his burden, the entire steamer was afire. Boilers exploded. Whole buckheads blew out in the blast. Screaming, panicked people were fleeing staterooms in their nightclothes. Late-night diners were scurrying from the endangered dining hall. Desperate pleas for help filled the night air. Men from other craft in the harbor hurried forth, carrying buckets of water and shouting commands to fear-numbed passengers, urging them to jump overboard.

Johnny went back down to the fire-enveloped card salon, bent on saving the trapped players. His eyebrows singed, his face glowing with heat, he lifted an overcome gentleman—still clutching his cards—up in his arms, staggered to the burning door and up the stairs, handing his human cargo to a big, bare-chested stevedore.

Johnny shouted, "He's unconscious but breathing," then turned and went back below. Coughing and blinking the sweat from his eyes, Johnny again entered the burning salon. Looking frantically about, he heard a moan and started toward the sound. His hands out like a sleepwalker's, he moved through the dense black smoke and heat. He didn't hear the groan and creak of wood until it was too late. The burning ceiling collapsed; heavy wooden beams came crashing down, blocking the only path of escape.

Trapping Johnny in the holocaust.

Nevada offered up silent prayers as the landau clattered ever closer to the huge blaze lighting the night sky. Her heart gripped with fear, her palms clammy, she stared with fixed horror at the bright orange flames shooting high into the air.

It was a riverboat, that much was apparent from a mile away. As they drew closer to the conflagration Nevada could see what was—or had been—a huge palatial riverboat with the fire-blistered name *John Hammer* painted in bold black letters above the flaming twin paddlewheels.

John Hammer!

Dear God, the *John Hammer* was the very one! Everyone in St. Louis had heard that the big game was to be played aboard the *John Hammer!*

Nevada was out of the carriage and running by the time Jess pulled up on the reins. Not caring what Malcolm or Quincy or anyone else thought, she lifted the skirts of her silk ballgown and flew madly down the wooden levee toward the roaring blaze.

Knocked flat onto his back by falling, burning debris, Johnny struggled up, crawled on his hands and knees through smoke so black and acrid he could see nothing. Choking and gasping for air, he was disoriented, with no idea where the door was.

His lungs burning, his head reeling, Johnny foolishly rose to his feet and immediately felt the world spin out of control as unconsciousness began its powerful, seductive pull on him.

But just before he blacked out, an eerie apparition appeared in flames and smoke. As Johnny's knees began to buckle, a pair of strong arms reached out to him and, for a fleeting second of complete clarity and grateful understanding, Johnny saw the unmistakably ugly face of Stryker.

* * *

On the landing Nevada made her way through the swarms of stunned, dazed people fleeing the burning riverboat. Despite the screams and shouts of the injured, she hurried headlong toward the blazing boat, ignoring the intense heat.

When a steward, his once immaculate uniform smoldering and torn, staggered onto the pier, Nevada seized his sleeve. "Johnny, Johnny Roulette! Have you seen him? Is he all right?"

The steward's sorrowful eyes locked with hers as he urged her away from the lost vessel. "I'm sorry, Miss. John Roulette was below in the card salon. It went first. I don't believe any of the gentlemen . . ." He shrugged and freed himself from her clutches.

Her teeth chattering, her eyes wide with panic, Nevada stood like a zombie, mesmerized by the flames shooting fifty feet into the air. In stunned disbelief she kept murmuring Johnny's name.

When Malcolm's arms went around her shoulders to draw her away from the inferno, Nevada began to scream and to fight him.

"No! No! Johnny's on that boat! Johnny, Johnny!"

She struggled like a wild woman, beating on Malcolm's chest, sobbing uncontrollably, overcome with grief and with guilt. If only she had been with Johnny, her luck would have saved his life. It was her fault, all her fault!

Inconsolable, Nevada wept and blurted out the truth to Malcolm and his mother. She tearfully told them of her background and of her undying love for Johnny Roulette. She sobbed Johnny's name over and over again, her heart broken. Malcolm, an understanding man, gently comforted Nevada, murmuring words of solace while Quincy remained tight-lipped and speechless. Old Jess was crying like a baby.

Among a large crowd they all stood there on the levee and watched, horrified, while the mighty *John Hammer* burned down to the water line.

All hope gone, Malcolm finally persuaded the distraught Nevada to return to the Lucas Place town house. Once there Nevada sought the comforting arms of Miss Annabelle. The two women clung together and grieved for the man they had both loved.

Miss Annabelle led the weeping Nevada upstairs, leaving Malcolm and Quincy alone in the drawing room.

Quincy spoke first, her tone bitter. "Fitting isn't it? Even in death, John Roulette manages to make fools of us."

"Mother, in all fairness, I don't believe we can blame John—rest his soul—for what has happened here."

"No, I don't suppose. The fault lies with that calculating little impostor upstairs!"

Malcolm lifted the stopper from a cut-crystal decanter. "Mother, you and I are just as much impostors as Nevada." He poured himself a drink of whiskey.

"That's not so," said Quincy, frowning. She sighed wearily, then asked, "Now what will you do?"

Malcolm turned to face her. "I've lost my fiancée but there's always the university. English literature—it's my life's work, my deepest interest."

Quincy glared at him. "That's fine for you but what about me?"

For the first time in his life Malcolm Maxwell stood up to his overbearing mother. "Perhaps you can marry for money. I do not intend to do so."

Before Quincy could give her biting reply, a disturbance in the corridor drew their attention. Nevada and Miss Annabelle, upstairs packing, heard it as well.

The front door burst open and a deep, familiar voice said loudly, "I'm home! Where is everybody?"

Nevada looked at Miss Annabelle, dropped the garment she was holding, and ran from the room. Laughing and crying at once, she flew down the stairs and straight into the welcoming arms of a bedraggled, very-much-alive Johnny Roulette.

Oblivious to those around them, she kissed his soot-streaked face, murmuring, "Johnny, Johnny, Johnny."

Lifting her high in his arms, Johnny laughed happily and said, "Darlin', your good luck saved me. Without you at my side, I was tapped out by ten o'clock!"

"You were topside all along?" she quizzed, her hands sliding over his tattered shirt.

"Not exactly. I went back down to see about the rest of the boys and got trapped. Stryker pulled me out of the fire, saved my life."

"Oh, thank God, and thank Stryker," she said happily and Johnny saw the love shining in her tear-bright eyes.

"Sweetheart," he said, "I love you. I'll give up gambling if you'll marry me."

Deliriously happy, Nevada replied, "Eight to five says you won't be able to do it." She hugged him tighter, kissed a singed eyebrow, and said against his dirty face, "but I don't care."

"You'll marry me?"

"Yes, yes, yes!"

41

⚛⚛⚛⚛⚛⚛

Moon-silvered clouds drifted high above the winding Mississippi River. The mellow lunar light shone down on a slow-moving riverboat of pristine white whose fancy curlicues and gingerbread made the vessel look, appropriately enough, like a giant floating wedding cake.

Wind-swayed white sheer curtains allowed the silvery moonlight to spill into an opulent stateroom and onto a white-and-gold marble topped bedside table. Upon that table, catching and reflecting the light of the moonbeams, lay a carefully placed glittering diamond-and-sapphire necklace. Beside the necklace were a handful of carelessly tossed gleaming gold studs.

On a large, high bed beside the table was a small, pale white, naked woman. Wide awake, she lay carefully on her side, her hands folded beneath her pale cheek, her knees slightly drawn up. Beside her in that soft white bed lay a big, dark, naked man. Sound asleep, he was sprawled carelessly on his back, a muscular arm flung up on the pillow, his bronzed feet apart.

Smiling in the pale moonlight, Nevada looked at her husband's sleeping face and sighed with peace and contentment. Johnny was, she thought naughtily, prettier without his clothes than with them. He had been without them for most of this lovely, lazy trip downriver. And so had she.

Her adoring eyes slid the length of his dark lean body. Lord, he *was* beautiful! He had been a such a handsome groom, standing there in the morning sunlight, smiling down at her.

A shiver of joy surging through her bare body, Nevada dreamily relived the wonderful wedding day, the best day of her life.

The plans had been made swiftly. She and Johnny would marry aboard the riverboat taking them downriver. And they would all go to New Orleans to live. She, Johnny, Miss Annabelle, Stryker, and old Jess. One big happy family.

They had boarded the riverboat *Eastern Princess* at sunup. Immediately the mighty steamer eased away from the levee and headed south. When they passed under the spectacular Eads Bridge, Captain Timothy Bayless, spiffy in his starched summer whites, turned the wheel over to his pilot and appeared on the texas deck.

While the skyline of St. Louis grew smaller and dimmer in the background, Nevada and Johnny stood before Captain Bayless as he performed the wedding ceremony. Crying quietly and holding a lovely bouquet of white roses, Miss Annabelle stood beside Nevada. Grinning as though he knew a big secret, the gentle giant Stryker stood ready to give the bride away. Wiping at his watering eyes with a clean white handkerchief, old Jess, standing beside Johnny, was Johnny's best man.

Captain Bayless cleared his throat, lifted a Bible, and began the ceremony. Johnny and Nevada looked into each other's eyes, then at the captain as he said, "Who gives this bride away?"

They waited. They stared at Stryker. Stryker was sup-

posed to say that he did. Stryker smiled. Said nothing.
Nevada frowned. Johnny gave him a questioning look.

Then a familiar voice from behind said firmly, "I do."

All heads turned to see a smiling silver-haired man with
an orchid in his buttonhole, a malacca cane in his hand,
and a smile as bright as the summer sun on his face. He
came quickly forward.

"King!" Nevada said loudly and impulsively threw her
arms around his neck, hugging him tight.

Shaking hands with Johnny, King Cassidy kissed
Nevada's cheek, then took her hand in his, and placed it on
top of Johnny's. He said to Captain Bayless, "I give this
woman away." And he stepped back, folding his hands
before him as the ceremony continued.

"I now pronounce you man and wife," Captain Bayless
said at last and Johnny swept his bride into his arms and
kissed her soundly while the others laughed and applauded.

When they broke apart, everyone pressed forward to
kiss the bride and shake hands with the groom. Champagne and wedding cake were served right there on the
texas deck, despite the fact it was not yet seven A.M.

While toasts were drunk to the newlyweds and laughter
filled the air, Miss Annabelle, her face flushed, her heart in
her throat, cast a nervous glance at King Cassidy. He was
looking straight at her. And he was smiling. Her knees
began to shake when he approached and took her hand,
leading her to the boat's railing.

"Annabelle," he said quietly, and gently squeezed her
hand.

She looked up at him. "It . . . it is lovely to see you
again, King. I didn't know you had returned from England."

"I've been back for several weeks now."

"Are you . . . will you soon be going home?"

"I'm on my way there now."

A puzzled look came into her eyes. "How can that be, King? Why the state of Nevada is—"

"No longer my home," he said evenly. "I've bought a place just north of Baton Rouge."

Her eyes widened.

King grinned. "A beautiful old place, though it will need a bit of fixing up. The last owners didn't care for it as they should have."

Miss Annabelle was staring at him, her lips parted. "You don't mean . . . you didn't buy—"

"I did, Miss Annabelle. I bought the Delaney family mansion and I mean to live there." King raised her frail hand in both of his, pressed it to his heart, and said, "I'd like very much to have you live there with me. Will you, dear?"

Flustered, happy, nervous, Miss Annabelle said, "I couldn't . . . we couldn't live there together without benefit—"

"Oh, dear woman, I'm obtuse! Forgive me. I'm asking you to marry me. I want you to be my wife. There, I've said it! Turn me down and at least I will have tried." King's eyes narrowed slightly and his hands tightened on hers. "Sweet Annabelle, say yes. Let me take you to your home."

"Yes," she murmured. "Yes. Oh, yes."

King's arm went around her, he kissed her temple, and said, "Shall we have Captain Bayless do double duty this morning, my dear?"

Miss Annabelle, her eyes aglow, said, "No, King. Today's the children's day and, besides, I . . . I always dreamed of being married in the drawing room of my home."

King's blue eyes twinkled. "And so you shall be." He kissed her again and called out to the others. "Miss Annabelle has agreed to be my wife."

More applause and laughter and hugs and kisses. And then Johnny whispered in Nevada's ear, "How long do we have to stay?"

"Why?" she teased. "You aiming to play a morning poker game?"

He replied, "I'm aiming to play this morning but the game's more enjoyable than poker."

"I haven't finished my champagne."

"There's champagne chilling in the stateroom."

Nevada smiled and called to the others, "Thank you all for making this the happiest day of my life!" She looked at Miss Annabelle, winked, and tossed her the bridal bouquet. Then without another word, Johnny picked up his bride and carried her away.

When he reached the door of their stateroom, he bent down so Nevada could turn the knob. Johnny walked inside, closed the door with his back, and stood against it, kissing her.

When their lips separated, he leaned his dark head back against the door and said, "I love you, Mrs. Roulette. More than you will ever know."

Slowly he lowered her to her feet. For a long moment they stood there looking at each other. Nevada, suddenly shy, nervously put her arms around Johnny's waist and buried her face on his chest. He felt her small body tremble against him.

His hand gently cupped the crown of her dark head. He said, "Sweetheart, what is it?"

She tightened her hold on his ribs. "Johnny it's . . . broad daylight."

"I know it is, angel. Does it matter?"

She took a quick breath. "It just seems . . . decadent to make love in—"

"Ah, baby, baby!" He chuckled and pressed her closer. "You'll find that making love in broad daylight is natural and enjoyable."

"Mm?" she murmured, unconvinced. "I don't know."

Johnny kissed the top of her head. "No matter then, sweetheart. We'll simply wait for night."

Nevada lifted her head and smiled at him. "You don't mind?"

"Not at all," he said, his voice low and soothing. "We have the rest of our lives." Johnny kissed her. Then he kissed her again. And once more. His kisses grew hotter, longer, and Nevada clung to him and sighed and felt a lovely warmth spreading through her body.

And while the *Eastern Queen* slowly steamed down the muddy Mississippi in the hot morning sunshine, Johnny lovingly undressed his bride in the privacy of their luxurious stateroom. Nevada never put on the lovely white peignoir. She lay naked in the sunny bed with her husband and sipped champagne and touched and kissed and played and realized that Johnny was right; making love in broad daylight was quite natural and very enjoyable.

And when Johnny rolled onto his back and lifted her astride him, Nevada welcomed the warm, glorious sunlight that filtered in through the sheer white curtains. It allowed her to clearly see the expression on her husband's handsome face as she raised up on her knees, wrapped loving hands around his pulsing erection and guided him into her.

"Ah, sweetheart!" he said as his lean brown hands went to her hips and she sank down onto him. They made sweet, slow, satisfying love while the bright summer sun hid nothing of their close intimacy.

It was glorious!

So glorious that before the hot sun finally set they made love several more times—and not always on the bed. After lunch had been rolled into the suite, they ate a few bites, then made love seated there at the damask-draped table. At midafternoon they wetly mated in the huge marble bathtub. And as the last blood-red rays of the lowering sun bathed their bare, sweat-slippery bodies with a pink warm light, they made love stretched out on the plush carpet at the foot of the bed.

Stretching now and smiling, Nevada thought they must surely be the most decadent couple who ever drifted down-river. And the happiest. They had not been out of their stateroom since their wedding four days ago. Downright shameful!

She yawned sleepily and closed her eyes.

And heard a voice beyond the porthole, declaring they would be passing Memphis in half an hour. Her eyes came open. She smiled. And touched her sleeping husband's chest.

"Johnny." No response. "Johnny, darling, wake up." Nothing. She raised herself up on an elbow. "Johnny." She tickled his chest, leaned over and kissed him, teasing at his lips with her tongue and teeth.

Slowly he came awake. His hand came off the pillow and went into her dark, tousled hair and his mouth opened beneath hers. She raised up, smiled, and said, "If I ask a foolish favor, would you grant it?"

He inhaled, raking his fingers through her long silken hair. "If you want me to make love to you, I'm not sure I'm capable right this minute."

She laughed and kissed him. "Not that. I'd like to go out on deck."

"Like this?"

She gave him a teasing jab. "No, not like this. I want to get dressed and go out for a few minutes. Can we?"

"Mm." He yawned lazily. "Mrs. Roulette, my sweet, I'd be honored to accompany you on a midnight stroll."

They laughed and played as they hurriedly bathed and dressed. Out in the moonlight, at the boat's white gingerbread railing, they watched the lights of Memphis, Tennessee, come up.

Nevada stood clutching the railing, her eager eyes searching expectantly. Johnny stood just behind, his arms around her waist, his chin resting lightly atop her head. Smiling, he knew exactly what his bride was searching for.

They spotted it at the same time.

The old *Moonlight Gambler,* its lights ablaze, music wafting out from its many portholes, moored at its permanent berth on the Memphis levee. Nevada smiled with delight as she looked at the bobbing, blinking craft where first she'd seen her husband.

Were the girls still there? Lilly and Julia and Belle and Betsy. Probably so. Recalling with childish joy that evening aboard the *Moonlight Gambler,* Nevada turned in her husband's arms, looked up at him, and laughingly repeated the girls' excited words.

"Johnny Roulette's back in town!"